BAD ROCK BEAT DOWN

BOOK TWO IN THE MILKY WAY REPO SERIES

MICHAEL PRELEE

EDGE SCIENCE FICTION AND FANTASY PUBLISHING
An Imprint of HADES PUBLICATIONS, INC.
CALGARY

Bad Rock Beat Down
Book Two in The Milky Way Repo Series

Copyright © 2017 by Michael Prelee

EDGE SCIENCE FICTION AND FANTASY PUBLISHING
An Imprint of HADES PUBLICATIONS, INC.
P.O. Box 1714, Calgary, Alberta, T2P 2L7, Canada

The EDGE Team:
Producer: Brian Hades
Acquisitions Michelle Heumann
Editor: Emily Stanford
Proofing by: Mandy Sohrabi-Rad
Cover Design: Brian Hades
Cover Art Elements: outsiderzone
Book Design: Mark Steele
Publicist: Janice Shoults

ISBN: 978-1-770531-152-9

EDGE Science Fiction and Fantasy Publishing and Hades Publications, Inc. acknowledges the ongoing support of the Alberta Foundation for the Arts and the Canada Council for the Arts for our publishing programme.

Library and Archives Canada Cataloguing in Publication
CIP Data on file with the National Library of Canada
ISBN: 978-1-770531-152-9
(e-Book ISBN: 978-1-77053-151-2)

FIRST EDITION
(20170925)
Printed in USA
www.edgewebsite.com

Publisher's Note:

Thank you for purchasing this book. It began as an idea, was shaped by the creativity of its talented author, and was subsequently molded into the book you have before you by a team of editors and designers.

Like all EDGE books, this book is the result of the creative talents of a dedicated team of individuals who all believe that books (whether in print or pixels) have the magical ability to take you on an adventure to new and wondrous places powered by the author's imagination.

As EDGE's publisher, I hope that you enjoy this book. It is a part of our ongoing quest to discover talented authors and to make their creative writing available to you.

We also hope that you will share your discovery and enjoyment of this novel on social media through Facebook, Twitter, Goodreads, Pinterest, etc., and by posting your opinions and/or reviews on Amazon and other review sites and blogs. By doing so, others will be able to share your discovery and passion for this book.

Brian Hades, publisher

Dedication

If I'm ever stranded on a faraway planet and hounded by criminals, there's no one I'd rather have at my back than Wyatt and Jacob. This one is for you guys.

Acknowledgement:

If watching copious amounts of TV during the 1980's taught me anything, it's that when a town has problems caused by scoundrels, it needs a team of reluctant heroes to clean things up. Here's to all the showrunners who made middle school nights so much fun: Stephen J Cannell, Frank Lupo, Glen A Larson and Donald P Bellisario.

Chapter 1

Nathan Teller and two of his crew walked across the tarmac of the Viking 2 Memorial Spaceport at Utopia Planitia. The spaceport's few landing pads and single runway made it stand out as an oasis in the reddish soil and scrub brush of the surrounding plain. A cool breeze blew from the west just enough to move the orange windsock at the edge of the runway.

"What a crap hole," Cole Seger said from behind him.

Nathan smiled and turned. "You say that about everywhere we land."

"Yeah well, we go to some truly crappy places." He spread his arms wide and gestured at the barren plains. "I mean, just look at this place. Earth terraformed this planet two hundred years ago and except for the blue skies and that sickly grass, it looks pretty much like it always has."

"We go where the money is," Nathan said.

Duncan Jax, the second man following him said, "I think what Cole means is that it would be nice if we could repossess a ship on a nice tropical island once in a while."

Nathan spotted the spaceport's administration office. "That's where we need to go."

They continued across the asphalt toward the small administration building. Nathan, the shortest of the three with a ruddy complexion and sandy brown hair wore a pair of jeans, a blue denim work shirt and a light jacket emblazoned with the logo of his company, Milky Way Repossessions. Cole was almost a head taller, with a deep tan that attested to time spent outside. He dressed similarly but with a black leather jacket and shorter hair.Duncan had skin like rich onyx and was almost as tall as Cole. He was stockier with thick arms that showed he worked for a living. Dreadlocks hung down to his shoulders.

A chime sounded when they entered the office and the breeze blew a small bit of red dust across the threshold before they closed the door. "Hey there," a small man with glasses said, walking to the counter. "Can I help you?"

Nathan set a mobi on the counter and reached a hand across to introduce himself.

"Nathan."

"Carl."

Nathan spun the mobi around so Carl could read the screen. "We're here to collect the starship you have sitting over on pad number three. This is the paperwork from the note holder, and a letter of authorization for us to repossess it."

"Didn't pay their bills, eh?" The man said, looking the documentation over. "Well I'm not surprised. Bunch of freaks and weirdos is what they are."

"The note holder says they're some kind of band," Nathan said. "Is that right?"

The clerk nodded. "Yeah, I guess that's what they are. They dress and act like a bunch of damned ghouls. There's a harvest festival this week outside of town about 10 klicks south of here and they're the entertainment." He eyed the document on the mobi again. "So, how does this work? You take their ship and give them a ride home?"

Nathan shook his head. "No, we just take their ship. They're on their own for a ride home."

"Uh-huh," the clerk said. "Well, your paperwork seems to be in order. I imagine you want to take a look at the ship?"

"That's right," Nathan said. "We need to do a pre-trip inspection to make sure she's spaceworthy, then we'll be on our way."

Carl nodded out a window toward the ship in question. "OK, she's all yours. I don't know if anyone is aboard right now."

"If there is, we'll take care of it without making a scene."

They exited the office and followed a sidewalk over to the landing pad. His own ship, the *Blue Moon Bandit*, sat on one of the landing pads behind him with two other crew members aboard; his co-pilot and Duncan's wife, Marla Jax, and Richie Pearson, a machinist's mate.

The men reached the edge of the tarmac and examined the target ship.

"I kept hoping it would get better looking as we got closer," Duncan said, "but it didn't."

The starship was about fifty meters long and wider in the aft section where the main engines were housed. The hull tapered toward the bow where the cockpit perched above a battered nosecone displaying the name of the ship, *Hell's Breath*. The bottom of the hull had charcoal black scorch marks testifying to rough re-entry trips. Angled wings stretched out from the midpoint of the fuselage. The name of the band in white letters stretched along the black upper hull: *Bone Daddy and the Voodoo Choir.* Skeletons and zombies danced among the letters in bright orange and green.

"Nathan, are you sure the bank holding the loan on this heap really wants it back?" Cole asked.

Nathan matched the registration number on the hull to the documents on the mobi. "Yeah," he said. "This is it. Right now I'm more concerned about whether it can fly."

"I'm concerned about what we might catch when we go aboard," Cole said.

"You've had your shots," Duncan said with a grin.

Nathan walked under the ship and ran a hand along the thermal protection system. "Duncan, we really need to look hard at this. I don't want to burn up when we get back to Earth."

"Yeah, I'll check it out."

Nathan walked out from under the ship. "All right, let's do this by the numbers. Duncan, do an external walk around and see if there is anything to worry about. Cole, you and I have the interior."

"I think I'd rather stay out here and do the walk around," Cole said.

Nathan smiled. "Then you should have gone to school to be a starship engineer like Duncan. Come on."

They walked around the side of the ship and Nathan found an entry portal. He flipped down the keypad cover and consulted the mobi, scrolling through the document until he found the code he needed. He punched it in and the door opened. A ramp extended to the ground.

Nathan made a show of waving to the opening. "You're up."

"Yeah," Cole said. "Thanks."

They mounted the ramp with Cole in the lead in case of trouble. Nathan followed him inside the dark cabin. He felt along the walls until he found a row of switches and flicked them. Multi-colored lights came up in the cabin, illuminating it with soft shades of orange, blue and green.

The passenger cabin ran about half the length of the ship. Nathan saw the stock interior seats had been removed in favor of sectional sofas covered in animal print fabrics and low tables bolted to the floor. Clothing, costumes and blankets covered every flat surface. Empty food containers and liquor bottles littered the floor. Brightly colored scarves decorated the ceiling.

"I'm going to be honest, Nathan," Cole said. "This is almost exactly what I pictured the interior looking like."

"This is a complete shit heap," Nathan said. "Do you smell that?"

Cole nodded. "That mixture of sweat, cheap perfume and even cheaper wine? Yeah, I smell that."

Blankets on one of the sectional sofas rustled and a bleary-eyed blonde with a pixie cut sat up. She wore a cropped green t-shirt, sporting the name of the band. "Why are the lights on?" She said. "I'm trying to sleep."

Nathan raised an eyebrow. "What's your name?"

"Tricia," she said. "Who are you?"

"We're here to repossess this ship. Do you know where the owner is?"

Tricia blinked and reached for a bottle of water on the table beside her. She unscrewed the top and took a large swallow before answering. "What do you want with Luscious?"

Nathan consulted his mobi. "Luscious Vonn is the leader of this expedition, right? Goes by the stage name Bone Daddy?" He held up a picture of the man on the mobi.

Tricia nodded. "Yeah, that's him." She stood up and yawned, stretching her arms up toward the cabin roof. "He didn't pay the bills, huh?"

Nathan eyed her taut belly and tight black leggings. "That's right. You should probably gather up your things. We're going to be leaving soon."

Cole moved past her and shot Nathan two thumbs up with a lascivious smile as he moved through the rest of the cabin.

"Where are you going when you leave here?"

"We'll deliver this ship to Go City, New Mexico back on Earth," Nathan said.

"If it will make it that far," Cole said from the back of the cabin near the restrooms. Nathan saw him peek inside and jerk his head back. "Holy Moses. Stay out of there." He pulled the door closed.

"Can I get a ride?" She said. "I've about had it with this traveling circus and if Luscious isn't paying the loan on this ship I get the feeling my pay isn't going to come through."

"You work for this character?" Nathan said. "What do you do?"

"I'm a nurse," Tricia said. "Luscious's manager likes to have one on hand in case the party gets out of control." She started stuffing things in a pink bag.

"I'm sorry but we only take the ship, not passengers," Nathan said.

Cole shot him a puzzled look with both hands up and silently mouthed *"what?"*

She stopped packing and eyed him. "Come on, I just need a ride back to Earth. You're going there anyway, what's the big deal?"

"Yeah, what's the big deal?" Cole said.

Nathan shrugged. "That's just how it works." He turned to Cole. "And you know that."

She dropped her bag. "Well, make it work some other way. I'm tired of this. If I'm not watching to make sure people don't overdose around here, I'm making sure Luscious doesn't grab my ass. I thought this would be a fun gig, but it's really being the only one at the party who isn't allowed to have a good time."

Nathan held up his hands. "I'm sorry about all that but I'm just here for the ship. If you'll excuse me, I have to check on some things." He walked to the cockpit.

Fifteen minutes later, Duncan appeared in the doorway. "Hey, Nathan, we've got company outside."

"What's up?"

"Local law and a line of cars."

Nathan stepped out onto the ramp and saw a Protective Services car at the admin building. An officer spoke to Carl and he pointed at the *Hell's Breath*.

"That doesn't look good," Nathan said. "How are we doing out here?"

"The ship will fly and should survive a re-entry. I checked the fuel tanks and we've got enough to lift off, but we'll have to tank up at an orbital station." He held up his mobi to show Nathan an app with engineering gauges on it. "I've got us synched up with the ship's controls."

"That's good. I'm finished with the pre-trip checklist so I'm going to start it up. I want to be ready to go. Come inside and call Marla and Richie back on the *Bandit* to let them know what's going on."

"Right."

"Oh, and there's at least one passenger inside packing her stuff."

"I saw her. She's cute. You should ask her out."

"I'm busy."

"You haven't been busy for more than a year if my math is correct."

Nathan glanced outside at the line of approaching vehicles. "Well, we're busy now. Let's go."

They moved back inside and Nathan turned left to go into the cockpit. He sat down at the controls, consulted the master codes on his mobi and got the ship running. The officer from Protective Services approached on foot outside. The lawman waved to him and Nathan returned it.

Heavy footsteps on the ramp told him he was boarding the ship.

"Damn it," he said.

Nathan got up and went back to the cabin and saw Duncan sitting on a couch talking to Tricia. The officer stepped through the hatch and nodded. He had gray hair and a drooping mustache. His deeply tanned skin showed a roadmap of lines stretching back years. He stopped just inside the hatch and put his hands on his gun belt.

"You the repo man? I'm Sheriff Jack Talliger."

Nathan nodded and introduced himself. "Here's our authorization," he said and handed over the mobi with the documents. "I imagine Carl in the office called you?"

"He sure did," the sheriff said as he scrolled through the documents, swiping his fingers from side to side. "This looks like it's all in order," he said and handed it back. "You can't have the ship."

Nathan blinked. "What's the problem?"

The lawman tipped his hat back. "Are you familiar with the band, Captain Teller? *Bone Daddy and the Voodoo Choir?*"

"Not really."

"Well, they've been in my county for almost a week so I've become more familiar with them than I ever wanted. They're a bunch of assholes who sing this ear-splitting death rock that sounds like a metal shredder in a salvage yard. They do all sorts of obscene things on stage. The kids seem to like them but I've got farmers out here ready to string them up. It's not just the band either. Take a look." The sheriff pointed outside.

Nathan stepped around him to look out the hatch at the tarmac. A large crowd of people approached the ship from a line of cars at the main gate. Nathan saw dozens of people dressed in leather and rubber with skin dyed orange and green. A young man, with a Mohawk and piercings all over his face, threw something at the ship that bounced off the nosecone. The woman next to him, with a skull tattooed over her bald head, shouted at him. Nathan stepped back inside. "Those are the fans?"

The sheriff took off his hat and rubbed his forehead. "They're awful. They run around half naked, high on whatever the hell they can find, and since they arrived, I've had to deal with an increase in petty theft, assault, public lewdness and drunkenness." He waved his hat toward the outside of the ship. "They've infested the whole town, and I am not an exterminator. I'm simply not equipped to deal with a problem this big. You can't have their ride."

"Look, Sheriff, I appreciate your position here," Nathan said, "but I have a job to do too. I've got to take this ship."

Sheriff Talliger gripped his hat with both hands. "Well, you can take it in the next town. They've got one more show tonight and then they're off to Madlerville. You can pick them up there." He nodded goodbye and started walking down the ramp. The crowd erupted in a chorus of boos and threats as the sheriff exited the ship.

"Did you do this?" Nathan said. "Did you bring them here?"

The sheriff paused. "I need to rest up for tonight, Captain Teller. Good luck."

Nathan watched as the sheriff pushed his way past a woman doing an impression of a unicorn with a plastic horn prosthetic mounted on her forehead. He stepped back inside.

"We need to get out of here," Cole said.

"We can't lift off with the crowd this close," Nathan said. "We'll burn them alive."

"That probably wouldn't be good for business," someone with a thick Southern drawl said from the top of the ramp. Nathan turned and saw a skinny white guy in a costume leaning against the hatch. He had a vest of white bones draped over his scarecrow thin torso. A black cape hung off his shoulders while a matching loin cloth kept him legal. The whole ensemble was finished off with platform boots adorned with silver skulls. Ratty looking brown dreads spilled off his head. He stepped inside and a thin black girl followed. She had a fly away afro standing out at all angles and wore a black dress shredded for an undead effect.

Nathan stepped closer. "You must be Bone Daddy."

The young man spread his hands wide. "We must all be who we are and yes, I am the Bone Daddy. However, you may call me Luscious." He waved a hand at his companion with an exaggerated sweep. "This is the lovely Natasha."

They both sat down on the couch nearest the hatch. Natasha curled into him and wrapped her arms around the singer.

Nathan introduced himself. "Your bank says you haven't made your payments. We're here to collect the ship. If there is anything you'd like to remove, now would be the time. I'm also going to have to ask you to move your fans back. We need to lift off and I don't want to harm anyone."

Luscious grinned and clapped. "That's quite a speech. I bet that works on most people when you show up and try to steal their ship."

"Nobody is stealing anything," Nathan said with exasperation in his voice. "If you don't pay your bills this is what happens."

Luscious motioned to Cole and Duncan. "Get your boys and get off my ship before I have you thrown off."

"You have that backwards," Nathan said. "Get up, get your stuff and get off."

Luscious smirked and winked at Natasha. She opened a small plastic envelope and dumped something into her mouth. She smiled and chewed, making a crunching noise. Luscious leaned over, gave her an open mouthed kiss and Nathan could see his tongue fishing around inside her mouth. He broke it off after a moment and leaned his head over the back of the sectional sofa. After a moment he shook, snapped his head forward and opened his eyes wide.

"Damn, that is amazing!" He threw the envelope to Nathan. "You want some before you go?"

Nathan saw a stamp on the plastic that said "Diamond K". It held some kind of clear crystal inside. He handed it to Cole.

"Look at you old man," Luscious said. 'You come in here with a couple guys and you think you're going to take what belongs to me? I can get a dozen Choir Boys up that ramp and they'll throw you into that field over there before you can blink twice. That's what my fans call themselves, by the way, 'Choir Boys'. Isn't that just delicious?" He licked his lips over yellow teeth. Natasha giggled beside him.

"You do have the numbers on your side," Nathan said.

Luscious's tongue snaked out over his lips again. "I do."

"You mind if I ask how you fit all those people in here?" Nathan said. "I wouldn't think you could fit more than a couple dozen."

"This here is the plane for the band, repo man," Luscious said and stood up. "It's just for me, the Choir and our special guests." He extended a hand to Natasha and she stood up. "Everyone else finds their own way."

"So they bum rides?"

"Whatever, man. Now, it's time for you to get off my ship. Natasha and I need some rest before the gig tonight."

"You sure we can't just take it?" Nathan said.

Luscious stepped up and Nathan saw his bloodshot eyes and the dark pools of his dilated pupils. His platform boots almost made him as tall as Nathan. "Do I need to get some help up here?"

Nathan held up his hands. "Hey, no problem. We're cool. Isn't that right, Duncan? We're cool?"

Duncan nodded and threw him a wink. "Most definitely, Nathan. We are cool."

"Good," Luscious said. "Now go." Natasha smirked and laid a kiss on the singer.

Nathan and Cole moved to the top of the ramp. The crowd jeered them and threw empty cans in their direction. Almost everyone made an obscene gesture of some kind. Nathan spotted the sheriff leaning against the hood of his float car parked against the fence on the far side of the field behind the crowd. The lawman tipped his hat in Nathan's direction.

Luscious stepped close to Nathan's ear. "Nice try, boy, but I learned how to deal with bill collectors and repo men back in Louisiana. You're just lucky Mars doesn't have gators."

Nathan cocked his head toward the singer. "Just remember, I offered you the easy way out." He turned back to Duncan. "Now would be good."

Duncan tapped a control on his mobi and a hissing noise issued from beneath the port side wing. Nathan watched as a cloud of green gas expanded out toward the crowd. They fell back slowly and then started to run, scratching madly as they did so. Screams filled the air and Nathan saw Sheriff Talliger stand up straight next to his ride.

Luscious leaned out to take a look. "What the hell is that?" He said. "What did you do?"

Nathan smiled. "Looks like you have a coolant leak, young man. Don't worry, it's not toxic but it will make them itch something fierce." Nathan turned to Cole. "Would you please show Luscious and his girlfriend off the ship?"

Cole stepped up, grabbed a handful of Luscious's bone costume and shoved him down the ramp. He managed to stay upright all the way down and ran a few steps onto the tarmac before coming to a stop. He turned and opened his mouth. "You don't know who you're messing with! It's not just me!" Then he started to scratch the exposed skin on his chest. He turned and ran away from the ship.

Cole turned to Natasha but she held her hands up. She slipped off her heels and ran down the ramp through the fog at full speed. Nathan slapped the ramp controls and it retracted into the ship. The hatch shut and locked itself.

"We need to move fast," Nathan said. "That won't stop them for long." He turned toward the cockpit and saw Tricia sitting on a couch. She waved to him.

"I guess you're getting your ride back to Earth," he said.

"I guess so."

Nathan couldn't help but notice the nurse had a very nice smile. "Would you like to ride up front? There's a second seat and I'm sure it's less of a bio-hazard than these couches."

She stole a glance at the couch she had been sleeping on before answering. "Sure. Why not?"

The two of them sat down in the cockpit and buckled in. Nathan keyed the intercom. "Guys, are we clear? Is there anyone around us?"

"Good to go back here," Duncan said. "I also got a message from Marla and Richie. They're up in the air waiting for us. They say the sky is clear for takeoff."

"Clear on my side, too," Cole said, "although Bone Daddy and his crowd look very pissed off."

Nathan switched to the radio and called the air traffic control tower. "Viking 2 ATC, this is *Hell's Breath* requesting liftoff clearance."

"Clearance denied, *Hell's Breath*. Sheriff Talliger is requesting you power down and prepare to be boarded."

Nathan smiled. "Copy that, Viking 2 ATC. Please pass along our apologies to Sheriff Talliger and let him know we wish him the best of luck with his pest problem."

Nathan put power to the engines and pulled back on the yoke. The ship lifted off with a jerk and climbed into the sky. The ship responded sluggishly, Nathan noticed, and flew like a wounded duck. He couldn't wait to get back aboard his own ship.

"You must be brave to have flown in this thing for a couple months," Nathan said.

Tricia smiled. "I'm usually too busy to notice the flights."

Nathan returned the smile. "That's probably for the best."

Thirty minutes later Nathan extended the ship's refueling boom at an orbital station and started taking on enough fuel to get them back to Earth. Once he completed the coupling he turned to the communication system and put in a call to his contact at the bank. An Asian man answered and smiled at him from the monitor.

"Hello, Nathan," the man said. "How are you?"

"I'm good, Bao," Nathan said. "I'll keep this short because I know what faster than light communications cost. We got your ship back from the rock band."

"That is excellent news. Job well done."

"Oh, don't congratulate me yet. It looks like they had livestock living in here."

Bao's face wrinkled. "Too bad. We'll inspect it and have it cleaned, of course. That model has quite a resale value as long as it's flying."

"I wish you luck," Nathan said. "Our ETA back to Earth is about four hours as long as we don't run into any problems with the short-range light speed jump."

"That's about six o'clock local time," Bao said. "Will you join me for dinner at The Lantern? I may have another job for you."

Nathan raised an eyebrow. "Yeah? Something good?"

"Let's just say it's a substantial opportunity if you're up for something a little more risky than a flight to Mars."

"Okay," Nathan said. "I'll see you there."

After refueling Nathan programmed in the course for home and stood up. Tricia played a game on her mobi. "I'm going to do a walkthrough of the ship, make sure everything is all right."

Tricia nodded. "Should I just stay here? What if something happens?"

Nathan shrugged. "The ship pretty much flies itself from this point on. Just don't touch anything and you'll be fine. Duncan and Cole are sitting right outside, so if you need anything just let them know."

"Okay."

Nathan wandered back through the cabin. Cole slept on one of the reclining couches. Duncan studied a readout on his mobi. Nathan nodded to him. "How are we doing?"

"The ship's fine. Green lights across the board and there's no problem with the engines."

Nathan nodded. "Good. Let me know if anything changes. I'm going to go below decks and do a look around."

Nathan made his way down the stairs to the lower deck. The lights in the ceiling activated when motion sensors detected his presence. He shook his head at what he saw.

The cargo hold appeared as messy as the upper deck. Suitcases, trunks and crates holding gear lay strewn about the area. Nathan took a few minutes and secured the larger pieces with tie down straps. They didn't need anything heavy shifting around down here during their flight. The smaller items went into bins anchored to the deck.

Nathan came to a pallet covered by a blue tarp. He lifted it to take a look underneath.

"Whoa."

Plastic wrapped bundles were taped up and stacked on the pallet. He took out a pocket knife and slit the shrink wrap while holding the bundles in place to grab one. It weighed about a kilogram. He held it up to the light and examined it. The contents of the bundle resembled broken crystals, exactly like the drugs Luscious and Natasha had used back on Mars.

Nathan counted the rows of bundles and did a quick calculation, coming up with five hundred bundles, each with packets inside stamped "Diamond K". He licked his lips and thought about what he should do. Legally, he had a requirement to turn in any contraband he discovered but he rarely found anything and when he did, it could be a hassle to deal with customs. He didn't know anything about this crystal but odds are it was worth a lot of credits and, quite frankly, he needed a lot of credits.

He searched among the piles of luggage and saw a black duffel bag in one of the bins. He unzipped it, pulled out the few articles of clothing inside and stuffed them into another bag. With a quick glance over his shoulder to ensure he was alone, he reached through the plastic wrap and pulled out some of the bundles. He could get twelve in the duffel without making it bulge. For a moment he reconsidered, but then thought about the pile of bills he had to pay and zipped it closed.

He hefted the duffel bag and found he could carry it without a problem. The tarp went back over the pallet and he tied it down with a few elastic cords. When he got back to the upper deck Duncan had nodded off and Cole snored lightly. He walked past them into the cockpit and dropped the bag on the side of the pilot's seat away from Tricia. She continued playing her game and never noticed. He sat down and took a look at the controls.

"Everything okay down below?" She asked.

"Other than it being a pigsty? Yeah, everything is okay. I had to secure a bunch of loose stuff. Is everything all right up here?"

"I guess so," she said. "No alarms went off."

"That's good," he said, as his left hand fingered the duffel bag. "It looks like we're all set."

Chapter 2

Almost four hours later Nathan slotted the *Hell's Breath* for descent orbit insertion and completed the deceleration process he'd started an hour ago. The blue and white curvature of Earth's sky stretched out in front of them.

"That is beautiful," Tricia said.

"Yes it is," Nathan said. "Views like this are one of the perks of the job."

Tricia pointed toward the ground. "Is that Europe? Usually I'm sitting in the back and don't get to see anything like this. Oh, it is. There's Italy."

Nathan smiled. He hadn't been this comfortable near an attractive woman in a while. A year and a half ago, he had broken up with his last girlfriend because of his obsession with his ex-wife, Celeste. He had even paid a software developer to recreate their honeymoon. His girlfriend wasn't too happy when she caught him. Then Celeste's starship had been hijacked by a religious cult, bringing her back into his life when he delivered the ransom. He scrunched his nose. This was not the time to think about those days. He pushed the thoughts out of his head and focused on Tricia.

"We'll be crossing over Asia in a few minutes and then you'll get to see the Pacific Ocean," he said. "It's amazing from up here. If we get lucky and there isn't any cloud cover you'll be able to see all the different island chains."

The ship jolted and she gripped the arms of her seat. "Is something wrong?"

"Braking thrusters," Nathan said. "We're just slowing down for our reentry. You'll see a light show then. The plasma envelope that forms around the ship is bright red, orange and yellow. It looks like liquid fire."

She grinned. "That sounds exciting. I've never been in a position to see it before."

"It's really something."

As the braking thrusters cut off and Nathan trimmed the attitude of the ship, Duncan and Cole crowded into the cockpit doorway. "Are we coming up on reentry?" Duncan asked.

Nathan nodded. "Yeah, the thrusters worked as expected and we're green across the board. Maybe they took better care of this heap than we thought."

Cole looked at Duncan. "Are you sure about the hull? You did your inspection pretty quickly back on Mars."

Duncan shrugged. "We'll make it. Today isn't the day we explode in a fireball."

"No," Nathan said. "Not today." He smiled and saw a smile form at the corners of Tricia's mouth.

"We better not explode," she said. "I owe a ton on my credit accounts and you know the bank is greedy enough to collect from my mom. No exploding."

A small smile appeared on Nathan's face. Tricia clearly wasn't going to put up with anything from the guys. He nodded at Duncan. "Where's your wife?"

"I spoke to her a little while ago. Marla has the *Blue Moon Bandit* about three thousand klicks behind us."

"Good. Maybe you guys should strap in. We'll start reentry in a few minutes."

"Yeah," Duncan said. "Come on Cole."

Nathan's hired muscle grunted. "I'm just saying, you walked around pretty fast back there. What if you missed something? I don't want to end up as a smear of ash in the upper atmosphere."

Their voices faded as they moved back into the cabin. Nathan shook his head. "You know there's nothing to worry about, right? If we had the slightest doubt about anything we would dock at an orbital station."

"I'm okay," she said with a shrug of her shoulders. "You seem to know what you're doing."

A few minutes later the ship jolted and bounced. Everything started to vibrate and Tricia raised an eyebrow. "I can assume you expected that?"

"We're hitting some air now and slowing down. It's perfectly normal."

"Hey Nathan," Cole called from the cabin. "What are you doing up there? I've never felt anything like that before."

Nathan smiled. "Don't listen to him. He can be kind of a pain in the ass to fly with. I'm going to check things out."

Nathan turned his attention to the readouts and made a small adjustment. The ride smoothed out. "That's better." He glanced up at the cockpit window. "Oh look, there's the plasma."

Orange and yellow fire licked all around the cockpit as the ship plummeted through the atmosphere. Tricia's eyes grew wide. "That's amazing!"

"Sure is," he said. "It's just friction but sometimes it's my favorite part of a flight."

She reached out and took his hand. "It really is quite lovely," she said.

"Yeah," he said, with a suddenly dry mouth. "You just have to have a healthy respect for it."

They rode like that for a few moments, in silence, holding hands. Ten minutes later, Nathan dropped them onto a landing pad in Go City, New Mexico. They deplaned and he stood on the tarmac with the duffel full of Diamond K at his feet.

"Wow," she said. "That was smooth, like we dropped on a cushion. The airlines never land like that."

"Thanks," Nathan said. "Hey, sorry about being so gruff back on Mars. It's just that when we repo a ship we never know who we're running into so it's easier just to get everyone off the ship and fly with our crew. I didn't mean to be a jerk."

She hefted her bag. "It's no problem, really. I'm just glad to be away from that guy."

"Are you going to be all right? You mentioned he owed you some money."

"I think so. He paid me a signing bonus so I still have that in the bank. Don't worry, I'll find something. Good nurses are always in demand."

Nathan blinked against the afternoon sun and cleared his throat. "So are you local? I live around here."

She nodded. "Yeah, my mom has a place outside the city, and I imagine I'll be staying with her for a while. Right now I need to grab a shower and sleep for about a week." She held up her mobi and gestured for him to do the same. They bumped them, and the communication devices chirped as their contact information passed. "Okay, well, thanks for the ride. I had fun. Maybe I'll see you around."

"Maybe."

He watched her walk toward the terminal and let out a breath he'd been holding since they left Mars. Cole walked over.

"Are you having dinner with her tonight?"

Nathan shook his head. "No, dinner tonight is with Bao. He says he may have another job for us. A big one." He checked the time on his mobi and picked up the duffel bag. "I need to hustle home to shower and change. Can you and Duncan finish up here?"

"Sure. Have fun."

—— 《》 ——

Nathan enjoyed eating at the The Lantern for dinner. He generally didn't go to nice places like this unless he was dating someone, and as Duncan had been nice enough to point out, it had been quite a while since he had been out with anyone. He had changed into a lightweight black suit and white shirt with a small banded collar for the meeting.

The downtown shadows spread across the streets, as Nathan pulled up to the restaurant on his float bike. The tinted blue glass of The Lantern glowed like iridescent candy as the sun started to dip below the horizon.

He entered the sliding doors, and the hostess led him to the back of the restaurant. Bao stood as he approached the table. He was shorter than Nathan and wearing a conservative dark blue suit. Nathan shook his outstretched hand and they sat down. A waiter appeared to take his drink order and then left to get it.

"How are you Nathan?" Bao came from Taiwan but spoke flawless English with a slight Southwestern accent.

"I'm good. Mars got a little exciting but nothing we couldn't handle. And you?"

Bao smiled. "You know me, Nathan. I'm always good."

The waiter arrived with Nathan's bourbon and they ordered. They made small talk over dinner, catching up on local politics and business deals being managed by Bao's bank. They leaned back after the plates had been cleared and Nathan nursed his second drink.

"So what's this other opportunity you have for us?" Nathan asked.

Bao held up a vapor stick. "Do you mind?" Nathan waved him off and he put it in his mouth. "I don't normally smoke but after a good meal I enjoy one. Are you familiar with the *Athena Star*?"

Nathan's brow furrowed. "That sounds familiar but I can't remember why."

"It was a passenger liner operated by Great Star Lines. You know, they jump out to places like Alpha Centauri or Sirius and give the passengers the thrill of being in a different star system."

Recognition flashed across Nathan's face. "Is that the one that crashed last year?"

Bao nodded. "Yes, that's it."

"I'm sorry. I remember the crash but not the details."

"The *Athena Star* was on a cruise to the Epsilon Eridani star system. Unfortunately their light speed jump ended with them in the gravity well of the third planet. Before they could correct their course they started encountering atmospheric drag."

"That is one hell of a mistake," Nathan said.

"Indeed. Luckily they followed proper jump procedures and had the passengers secured. They managed to evacuate the ship before it crashed."

"That's right. It went all the way down didn't it? It hit the ground?"

Bao nodded. "Automated systems kept it together and steered it away from populated areas but yes, it crashed and it can't be flown again."

Nathan grunted. "Those things are huge. If you crash something six hundred meters long into the ground you generally get a big hole and a lot of scrap."

"There's a hole, to be sure, but the ship itself is in one piece, more or less. That's why it needs to be salvaged and removed."

"So what does this have to do with us? We're repo agents, not a salvage company."

"You are always so impatient, Nathan. I wanted you to understand the situation. Anyway, there is a salvage company at Epsilon Eridani III picking up the pieces of the *Athena Star*." Bao pulled out a mobi. "They're called Crater Salvage and they are local to Go City. They got the contract to salvage the starliner and started operations three months ago."

"What's your interest here?"

"The bank backed Crater Salvage. The owner is a man named Eldridge Tanner." Bao swiped through the files on his mobi and brought up a picture of a black man in his twenties with close cropped hair and a beard. "He's young and idealistic but he's very smart. He came up with a new method for running the salvage operation and convinced Great Star Lines to hire him. Once he had the contract I liked him as a good risk so I made the decision to loan him several million credits to finance the operation."

"That sounds solid," Nathan said. "What's the problem?"

"Crater's main expense is an ore refining ship used to strip mine asteroids. Tanner refitted the ship to recycle metal and anything else found inside a starship. He also bought and programmed a virtual army of 'bots to do the actual work to cut down on expenses. We were very pleased with his work and had no problems when we followed up with him here on Earth before he left."

"So what happened?"

"During their time here on Earth performing their prep work they met all their key performance indicators and made their payments as expected. As soon as they left Earth and started operations we stopped hearing from them."

"Did they arrive safely? Epsilon Eridani is about ten light years away so communication can be spotty."

Bao shook his head. "I had contact one time with authorities at the nearest settlement. Crater Salvage showed up and started operations as expected. They just aren't talking to us or making payments. So far they've missed three."

"What about the office here in Go City?"

"We've been speaking to a man named Lewis Mairn. He is polite and says the office is in contact with Tanner but they are at a loss for why things are not going as expected."

"So what do you want Milky Way Repo to do?"

Bao took a drag on his vapor stick and exhaled. "I would like to hire you to go out to Epsilon Eridani III and retrieve the *Corkscrew*. That's the recycling ship Tanner is using and it is an asset securing the loan."

Nathan nodded and picked up his mobi after it beeped. "We can do that. I assume the specifications and master control codes for the ship are in the files?"

"Yes," Bao said. "It's large but automated. It's meant to be operated by a small crew, but I'll leave operational decisions up to you."

"Epsilon Eridani is pretty far out. I don't think I've ever been there."

"You'll need to be careful. The system only has one habitable planet and that's the one where the *Athena Star* went down. You shouldn't have to worry about landing, though. The *Corkscrew* is a space bound ship and never makes landfall on a planet. The idea is to dock with it in space and seize the ship."

"Is there anything else we need to know? Is this guy known to be violent?"

Bao shook his head. "No, he's highly energetic and excited about his work but I never saw any indication of abnormal behavior. If I had, I wouldn't have loaned him several million credits." Nathan looked at the picture of the young man on his mobi and thought Bao was probably correct but you could never really tell how someone would act from a photo. That's why he kept Cole on the payroll.

Bao spoke up again. "There is one thing you'll need to be careful about, because I know you run a lean crew."

"What's that?"

"The system isn't well settled. Epsilon Eridani III is a cold planet. It's not like the Arctic but it isn't Hawaii either, so people aren't in a big hurry to run out there and set up home. There is one large settlement and it's close to where the *Athena Star* crashed. It's called Bad Rock."

Nathan shook his head. "I've never heard of it."

"You would have no reason to. There are less than ten thousand people living there and nothing much happens. I did some research on the settlement while preparing the deal. Their main industries are iron mining and steel production. Neither one brings in a lot of credits. Here's what you need to know, though. They don't have much in the way of Protective Services or other societal infrastructure. Their economy is not strong, so there aren't a lot of credits available to pay for things like law enforcement and hospitals. You'll be pretty much on your own out there so you may want to make some changes to your normal operations. I recommend you keep that in mind when you put your bid together for the job."

Nathan sat back and thought about the offer. It sounded good, almost like a slam dunk for a good pay day. This kind of opportunity could pay well, especially given the size and value of the *Corkscrew*. "We're definitely interested. Let me put together a package for you."

The waiter brought the bill over and Bao took care of it. They stood up and shook hands. "I'll be in touch tomorrow," Nathan said. "Will that work for you?"

"Yes, but I have to tell you, Nathan, there is a time element here. I'm responsible for loaning Tanner the credits so if he's done something stupid like run off or embezzled it, I'm going to lose my job. Management at the bank has given me the opportunity to fix this problem so I need to make this count."

Nathan smiled. "Don't worry. We'll get your ship back." They walked outside and Nathan saw the sun had set. The azure light from The Lantern's exterior lit up everything in the parking lot with an electric blue hue.

"I do have one question, Bao. What if we get out there and find out this is all some misunderstanding? Do you still want us to go through with seizing the ship and dragging it all the way back here?"

Bao exhaled and his gaze drifted up to the sky. "Take control of the *Corkscrew* immediately upon arrival. If you think there is a legitimate reason for Tanner to have missed his payments and performance metrics, try to contact me before departing so I can provide instruction. Just make sure you have control of the ship. I want this young man to understand the consequences of failing to meet his obligations. He has put me in a very vulnerable position, and I don't like it." Bao's voice got an edge to it, and Nathan felt like there was a struggle going on inside him to maintain his professional composure as he continued. "Tanner needs to understand that I will sell that ship out from under him and bankrupt his operation."

Nathan held out his hand and they shook. "I'll be in touch tomorrow."

—— «» ——

Across the city, Duncan and Marla relaxed on the sofa in their new condo, looking at financial graphs on a large wall screen. They had moved in a few months ago, after deciding they wanted to live in a more upscale neighborhood.

Duncan pointed to a figure. "You see that? That's a fifty percent loss. That's almost as much as we'll both earn getting that rock band's ship back from Mars."

Marla shrugged and patted his leg. "Investments carry risks. Besides, we both still have our jobs."

Duncan sighed and sat back. "I know, I just don't want to turn wrenches forever, you know? Do you want to spend the next decade sitting next to Nathan co-piloting the *Blue Moon Bandit*?

"No, but it is what it is. I know you think we can invest our way to an early retirement and we've done pretty well, but we're not going to hit a homerun every time we step up to the plate."

"I know, but I just thought this one would pay off." He put his feet up on the table and leaned back.

"What's really bothering you?"

"I think we're getting stuck in a rut," he said. "I think we're static when we should be moving forward. We were doing really well for a while and now things have kind of ground to a halt." He stood up and moved to the French doors leading to their balcony. "I don't mind what I do but I've done it for a while now. I'd like a new challenge."

Marla stood up and opened the doors. The olive skin from her Italian heritage glowed in the morning sunlight. They moved out onto the balcony and leaned against the black iron railing. She waved her hand toward the city. "We must be doing something right. We've got a hell of a view."

"No doubt about that."

Their building was one of the tallest residential towers in Go City. They could see the spaceport a few kilometers outside of the city, and sometimes they would sit out here and watch shuttles race up the launch rails and bang off into the sky.

A black glass tower, rising from the middle of the downtown business district belonging to Saji Vy, stood taller than theirs. Milky Way Repossessions had done a job for Saji a little over a year ago and Duncan had been impressed with what Saji had built after getting to know him a little.

He turned back to Marla, returning her infectious smile and brushing a stray lock of hair over her ear. "Yeah, we've had success, you're right. I just don't want to skin my knuckles anymore, and I don't want you to grind out more time in the co-pilot's seat."

She moved in close and he wrapped his arms around her. They kissed, softly at first and then with more passion. After a moment they broke apart.

"I know you want more," she said. "I know you have this vision of what our life is supposed to be like, and there's nothing wrong with that. Just don't get so wrapped up in chasing your goals that you forget to enjoy what we have right now."

He held her close. "Yeah? You think things are good now?"

"I do."

"Well, why don't you come in here and let me show you how they could be better?"

She reached a hand up and toyed with a couple of his dreadlocks. "I think I'd like a demonstration."

He smiled and hefted her over his shoulder in one smooth motion with his powerful arms. She squealed with delight and he gave her a playful smack on her bottom with his free hand. "Well let's get to it."

Chapter 3

"Fire! Hey, we've got a fire over here!"

Eldridge Tanner raised his head in the direction of the voice and saw Ariadna Macias running from a flaming pile of scrap. His brunette crew chief scrambled for a fire extinguisher ten meters away. Two 'bots continued working within the flames, cutting and sorting the scrap as if everything was normal.

"Damn it," Tanner said and got up from the wooden bench where he had been repairing another 'bot. He grabbed the extinguisher sitting on the ground beside his bench and ran to the near side of the burning pile of scrap. Ariadna and her extinguisher ran for the far side. One of the 'bots standing in the flames, a two-legged model with chipped blue and gray paint stopped working to address him.

"Sir, I'm detecting increased heat levels."

"No kidding. Really?"

"Indeed. It may not be safe for you."

Eldridge squeezed the lever on the extinguisher and hosed down the area with chemical powder. He played the nozzle back and forth across the base of the flames and advanced as they died down. A great cloud of the powder went up in the air as Ariadna moved forward from the opposite direction. Eldridge couldn't see any more flames and released his grip on the extinguisher's lever.

The pile of metal, plastics and various synthetic materials smoldered and a haze of fire retardant chemicals settled across everything like powdery snow. Eldridge coughed and waved his hand to try and get some fresh air. Charcoal black scorch marks on the ground surrounded the scrap pile. He used the toe of his boot to nudge a steel plate out of the way and saw a burned cylinder underneath. A green band wrapped around the top. He pulled on a pair of gloves from his back pocket and lifted up the cylinder. He examined it carefully and saw a thin slice in the side. He held it up to the 'bots.

"Did one of you cut this?"

The one with the chipped blue and gray paint raised an arm. "Yes, sir."

"It's an oxygen tank. If you see any more cylinders similar to this assume they contain gas under pressure and do not cut them. Doing so can cause a fire. Sort them in a pile thirty meters away from the work area."

"Yes, sir."

"Please upload those instructions to the local intranet and code as mandatory."

The 'bot paused its movements for a moment. "Instructions acknowledged. Task completed."

"Thank you."

Eldridge handed the cylinder to the 'bot. It immediately started walking away from the scrap pile it had been processing. He watched as the machine walked out thirty meters and set the cylinder down. Ariadna walked over to him with a smile and slipped an arm around his waist.

"Better late than never," she said.

His face fell to a woeful, dejected expression. "I think I may have made a mistake using my own code to manage these things."

They walked back to the large canopy that provided shelter to his work bench and the other work stations. A 'bot's head lay open on the bench and stared at them with blank eyes. The decapitated body stood nearby, silently awaiting the reattachment of its head. They both took a stool and sat down.

"I thought your code instructed them to drop everything and perform firefighting duties if someone yelled 'fire'," Ariadna said.

Eldridge pulled a mobi out of his back pocket and started tapping. "Well that one did warn me that things were getting hot." He smiled and sighed. "They are supposed to do that. I wrote a sub function specifically for that action and it passed testing. Now it's number one hundred twenty two on my priority list."

"Fighting fires ranks one-hundred twenty-two?"

"Prioritizing the list is item number one. I suspect firefighting will move up in importance once that's accomplished." He leaned back on his stool and stretched. "Just look at that mess."

From their vantage point under the canopy they could see the *Athena Star* stretched out across the red dirt of Epsilon Eridani III. What had once been a glorious six-hundred-meter starliner lay under the dim sun in a twisted, mangled wreck. The bow had plowed deep into the ground and collapsed under the force of the impact from the crash. The forward section of the upper decks had pancaked on top of one another and now the forward half of the vessel appeared like it had been made of clay and squashed by a child's hands. The middle section of the ship had gaps blown in the hull where air pressure from the collapsing forward decks had escaped. The back third of the ship stuck up in the air at about a thirty-degree angle. The main engines had been largely disassembled and dozens of 'bots crawled over the hull like ants on an animal carcass.

The robotic workers came in a multitude of shapes and sizes but most had the humanoid look of domestic 'bots found in people's homes and restaurants. They were a motley looking bunch with varying paint jobs.

Ariadna leaned over and held his hand. "That mess is going to make us a lot of money."

"I know, but we've been working on it for three months and we've just hit our six-week goal. At this rate we'll be broke by the time we finish. How much of the work force is on the job today?"

"Well, the good news is that of the half-dozen human workers you managed to sign up for this effort, one-hundred percent of them showed up. The bad news is, only seventy percent of the 'bots have managed to drag their lazy asses out of bed."

Eldridge rubbed his eyes. "That's not good."

"It's not all bad," she said. "Most of them will be out of the shop today. A lot of the problem is wear and tear on cutting tools and lifting apparatus. The shop 'bots are helping Scooter get them repaired and she says most of them will be back on the job this afternoon. There are about eight that need to have their operating system reloaded." She patted his hand. "Hang in there. No one said running a startup company would be easy."

He grunted. "I have to admit, I thought I really had a better mousetrap here."

"You do but it's going to take time to work the kinks out."

"I suppose. It's just a big risk is all. I'm substituting all these 'bots for human workers and it may end up biting us in the rump."

Ari's eyes narrowed. "Can I ask you a question, honey?"

"Sure."

"What do you suppose that 'bot is doing?" She said, and pointed toward the wreck. "The one that is standing horizontally on the side of the ship, just forward of the port side engine. He's dancing or something."

Eldridge squinted and followed her finger until he saw a 'bot sticking out at a ninety-degree angle from the ship's hull with its magnetized feet. Its torso turned at the waist toward the sky and then snapped back toward the ground. "I'm guessing he just volunteered to become problem number one-hundred twenty-three."

Ari stood up. "It's my shift so I'll go check him out." She gave him a peck on the cheek and walked over to one of the four wheeled carts kitted out as a service vehicle with toolboxes and a small crane.

"Hey, be careful if it catches fire," he said. "None of those others will help you put him out." She smiled and he watched as she drove off. Her brown pony tail bobbed up and down as the service buggy bounced over some ruts.

Eldridge pulled up the metrics dashboard on his mobi. The management software collected hundreds of thousands of data elements and sliced and diced them into reports he could check on the dashboard. He grimaced when he got to the sorting and processing graphs. "What the hell?"

The 'bots crawling on the *Athena Star* like ants cut her into manageable chunks. Others took those chunks to the sorting piles, where another group of 'bots reduced them further and sorted them according to the type of material. Once sorted, 'bots loaded the material into shuttles, or trucks, for transport up to the *Corkscrew* for final processing and recycling. What Eldridge saw on the graphs worried him.

He rose and stuck the mobi in his back pocket. He mounted a float bike and skimmed around the rear of the *Athena Star*. A minute later he dismounted and approached an older man with a gray pony tail sticking out from under a dirty red cap wearing denim overalls and a stained t-shirt. "Hey Fred," he called.

The older man waved to him and stepped away from the 'bots he had been speaking with. "Hey yourself, Eldridge. What's up?"

Eldridge held up his mobi. "What's going on with the numbers? We're about fifty tons shy for processing. Did we have some kind of problem last night? Are the 'bots giving you problems?"

The older man tipped his cap back on his head. "Oh, we've had problems but it's got nothing to do with the 'bots. They're running just fine. It's those damn locals you got sorting piles two and three." He pointed down range. "Them assholes are slowing everything down."

Eldridge grimaced and squinted at the other sorting piles. Fred's pile had a large placard identifying it as 'Pile 1' in bright red letters and it contained less material than the piles labeled two and three that stood fifty and one hundred meters away. The fire had been at pile four and it had less scrap than two and three.

"Now look, Eldridge, I know we had to bring on some locals to get this contract. But the two guys you have running those sorts don't know what the hell they're doing. I went over and spoke to the guy on two and he's got crap in little piles everywhere. He's got the 'bots so screwed up with his bad instructions, they're running half as fast as mine."

Eldridge grimaced. Bringing on the locals had been a concession he'd had to make to the local government and now he regretted it. "Okay, Fred, I'll go see what I can do about getting them straightened out."

"Hell, Eldridge, just fire their ass and get Bobby and Charlie down here off the *Corkscrew*. That's why you brought them out here, isn't it?"

Eldridge walked back to his float bike and mounted up. "I'll take care of it, Fred. See what you can do about getting us back up to quota."

It only took a minute to get to Pile Two and another few seconds after that for his temper to rise. Two men, both scruffy locals with gang tattoos and long hair, sat on folding chairs with a deck of cards on a table between them. Both wore ripped jeans and shirts sporting the Crater Salvage logo. The big one on the left had his sleeves cut off revealing large arms. They gave him a sideways glance when he dismounted the bike and then went back to their game. Eldridge took a deep breath before walking over to them.

As he got closer Eldridge noticed another restriction on his worksite, a couple beers sitting on the table. He took a look at the 'bots and saw Fred had been right. They sorted the main dump pile into progressively smaller piles. Eldridge walked around and saw little hills composed of electronic components and precious metals. The planetside sort should have been rough. The fine sorting took place up on the *Corkscrew* where the automated machines could do it more quickly. Eldridge noticed Truck 4 and Truck 6 sitting mostly empty behind the piles. These shuttles hauled the sorted material up to the *Corkscrew*. The work plan called for them to be loaded and flying up or unloaded and coming down for more material. They should never be sitting empty on the ground. Eldridge turned back to the card game and addressed the guy sitting to his left.

"Turtle, what's going on over here? Your numbers are way too low."

Turtle answered Eldridge with a southern drawl. "Is that so?"

"Yeah, you are tons behind and we have a quota to make."

Turtle turned to his card playing companion. "Daryl, remind me again who we work for. I'm having a hell of a time remembering."

The man called Daryl set his cards down and rubbed his chin. "Well, Eldridge here pays us."

"Yes."

"But we do what Dodger says. So, I guess we work for Dodger."

"I'll be damned if you haven't sized up the situation correctly, Daryl. So, are we doing what Dodger told us to do?"

Daryl picked up his cards. "That we are."

Turtle turned back to Eldridge and stood up. Taller and stockier, he had an air of menace about him. Eldridge took a step back.

"See, Eldridge, we don't have any problems here but if you have some kind of quota issue maybe you should go back the way you came and talk to that old bastard, Fred. He spends a lot time poking around on our piles when he should be tending to his own business."

"Fred's concerned about the numbers," Eldridge said. "I just need things to speed up is all."

"Well, maybe Fred can speed up his production? Oh, or maybe Ariadna can." He turned and threw a knowing smile at Daryl. "Hey, you know what? Maybe Daryl and I should go see her later this evening. See if we can help her figure out a way to get things moving a little faster." He leaned closer. "That okay with you, Eldridge?"

Eldridge stood his ground and a hard look set in his eyes. "You stay here on your own patches. That's the agreement. I just need the pace to pick up."

Turtle put a meaty hand on his shoulder and grinned at Daryl again. "Eldridge, if our work isn't up to your high standards maybe you should speak with Dodger. I could call him if you want and set it up."

Eldridge swallowed and shook the hand off his shoulder. "If I want to speak with Dodger I'll call him myself."

Turtle nodded and held his hands out. "Guess we're all done here, then. Thanks for checking on us." He flopped back into his folding chair and picked up his cards. Eldridge stood there another moment and turned back to the float bike. He gunned the motor and tore off for Pile 4.

— ‹›› —

Later that night Eldridge and Ari sat down to dinner at a table beneath the same canopy that housed his work bench. The tent they shared stood behind them. Ari spooned some baked beans onto her plate and he sliced into a grilled pork chop. A 'bot stood at the camp stove tending to corn bread.

"I'll give you credit, babe, repurposing domestic 'bots does have some perks," Ari said. "I've never eaten this well on a job site."

Eldridge nodded. "I'm glad you like it. Having these things cook for us is a lot easier than running into town for meals. As for repurposing the 'bots for salvage, I'm starting to think that may not have been such a good idea. We're still having a lot of problems. What happened with the one you found stuck on the side of the *Athena Star* this afternoon?"

She groaned. "Oh, yeah, about that. I had to have two other 'bots get him and carry him down. He worked on a cutting team slicing up that section of the hull. The work order specified where he should start. When he got to the correct spot his accelerometer indicated his orientation as horizontal and he expected to fall. His safety subroutines kicked in and he turned to try and climb back up. When he didn't get the expected input of actually falling, his work routines kicked in, and he would try to start cutting. Once he turned back toward the ground, the whole sequence would start over again."

"Even though he stood there magnetized to the hull?"

"Logic loop. The poor baby wound up confused and dancing to a beat only he could hear."

Eldridge sighed and took out his mobi. "I'll update the code so the 'bots don't anticipate falling and only react if input from the accelerometer indicates they really are." He tapped a few lines into the mobi. "There, it's on the list."

The 'bot serving dinner brought a plate of cornbread to the table and set it down. Eldridge took a piece and dipped into his beans. "You're right, though," he said. "They can cook."

"Anything else happen today?"

"I had a little talk with Turtle and Daryl."

Ari put her cornbread down. "Oh yeah? What about?"

Eldridge filled her in on the details of his confrontation and she shook her head when he finished. "Those guys are going to bleed us dry."

He leaned back from the table. "I know, but what can I do?"

"Against Dodger? I don't know. The deal we made with him is the only thing keeping the Bad Rock unions off our back so we can use the 'bots instead of human labor. We pay him for ten positions and Turtle and Daryl are the only two who show up for work. Those two *ladrones* also get to cherry pick a ton of salvage every day for their boss."

"*Ladrones*?"

She smiled. "Thieves."

"Ah," he said, "that's exactly right. The problem for us is that while they have their 'bots sorting for precious metals and rare earth elements they're slowing down the whole operation. We're already weeks behind and it's getting worse every day. Any ideas?"

She gave him a vicious smile. "My dad would have shot them. He didn't put up with *gángsteres*."

Eldridge didn't need a translation for that one. He stared at the *Athena Star*. Ari's dad, Roberto Macias, ran a salvage operation back in Go City where he recycled starships and industrial machinery. Eldridge had worked for him for almost ten years before deciding to go into business for himself. Cleaning up the starliner should be the job that let him and Ari start their business and be independent. Tanner had no problem imagining Ari's fireplug of a father hefting a shotgun almost as tall as he was, and running off the thugs who were shaking them down.

"Your dad operates on Earth and can call Protective Services if he runs into problems. We're out here at the ass end of nowhere. Dodger may be a gangster but he's also got the most men and guns. The nearest town is 10 klicks away and I don't think I trust the police chief."

She took a sip of her drink. "Do you really think he's corrupt? He seemed helpful enough every time we've met him."

"I don't know, maybe he's honest, maybe not." Tanner thought back to the meeting he and Ari had attended with Bad Rock city leaders when they arrived. The police chief, Don Bell, a burly black man in his late fifties had been there with the mayor and city council.

The *Athena Star* crashing outside their city had been the most exciting thing that had ever happened near Bad Rock. The mayor, a small woman named Carol Engster, seemed just as slick and opportunistic as every other politician Tanner had seen. After touring the crash site, she had explained to him and Ari in detail how the residents of Bad Rock had rushed to the scene with every intention of aiding survivors and saving the ship. Imagine their surprise when they got there and found that despite the fire and bluster of reentry, the *Athena Star* had landed relatively intact, with the survivors safely in lifeboats waiting to be rescued. Why, the good Lord must have been watching over all of them that day. Oh, and how many Bad Rock residents did Eldridge plan on hiring for the salvage operation?

Bad Rock had been founded seventy years prior, after the discovery of iron rich ore in the valley near the local river. It grew up quickly to a settlement of about eighty thousand. Steel mills opened to produce the construction materials needed to settle the whole planet. Earth governments predicted that Epsilon Eridani III would be settled fairly quickly because it didn't require expensive terraforming. The only problem ended up being that settlers preferred other locations.

Planets like Olympus in the Alpha Centauri system had been terraformed to include large tropical zones for comfortable living. Beating out an existence on hard scrabble worlds like Epsilon Eridani III didn't make sense unless you wanted to be there. Bad Rock had about ten thousand people remaining and it was the last official settlement on the planet. Tanner had no doubt humanity would eventually experience another wave of expansion but it would probably be a century before it pushed out this far again.

The isolation Bad Rock experienced meant no neighbors to trade with and left the settlers at the mercy of the spacers who made their way out here to take advantage of the lonely settlement. The mayor explained the one steel mill still open produced good quality product but just about all of the economy in the city centered on that one mill.

Eldridge had felt sorry telling her that he would probably need few locals because the majority of the work would be done by 'bots. The gray-haired woman had changed from kindly grandmother to stone faced hard ass in a fast minute. Eldridge promised to hire whoever he could and to utilize as many businesses as possible but the diminutive woman had walked away without shaking his hand and he hadn't seen her since.

The police chief, Don Bell, had just smiled. As the mayor and her entourage walked away Bell turned to him and spoke to him with a deep and gravelly voice. "Is this your first time dealing with politicians, son?"

Tanner had nodded.

"Well, then you've learned your first lesson. Never come empty handed."

Tanner didn't know if that meant the chief had his hand out for a payoff or if he had been letting him know that greasing the wheels at city hall with jobs and opportunity would make things go smoother.

Snapping back to the present, he said, "Here's the thing, Dodger isn't going to care that his goons are slowing down production. We pay him weekly, he takes his salvage daily and if we miss our schedule and go broke out here Great Star Line will just hire someone else to clean up this mess. That bastard will just shake down the next outfit that comes out here and keep making his money. We have to find a way to succeed."

Ari got up and walked around the picnic table. The setting sun had cooled the air and she hugged herself. The cooking 'bot cleared the dishes from the table and took them to be cleaned. Ari returned from their tent wearing a jacket and handed one to Eldridge. He stood up and pulled it on. They moved to a fire pit just past the edge of the canopy. Eldridge squatted and built a small fire. They fell into two of the chairs at the edge of the fire pit. Eldridge put his hands deep into his pockets and let the fire warm him.

"You're right," Ari said. "We need to speed up production. Any ideas?"

Eldridge nodded in the flickering light. "Yeah." He pointed to his left. "Tomorrow I'm opening Pile 5 over there and bringing Bob down from the *Corkscrew* to run it. We're going to redirect the salvage streams to your pile, Fred's pile and Bob's. We're going to restrict the flow to Piles 2 & 3. There's no sense dropping good material in those piles if it's just going to sit there."

"Can you open two more piles? Charlie is still up there. He could come down and supervise another one."

"I thought about that but we don't have enough 'bots running to cut and carry pieces off *Athena Star* to feed two more streams. That would be ideal, though. Let me see what I can do about getting more of them on the job."

They sat and watched the fire for a moment. Eldridge stared up at the stars, growing used to seeing unfamiliar constellations.

"You think they'll catch on? Turtle and Daryl?"

Eldridge shrugged. "I don't care. We have a job to do and I mean to see it finished. Dodger doesn't get a say in how we do that. Turtle and Daryl can always work faster."

Ari checked her mobi, and the bright light from the screen lit up the smooth cheekbones that framed her pretty face. Eldridge wondered how he had gotten so lucky.

"Why don't we go to bed?" she said and stood up. "I'm exhausted."

He slipped an arm around her waist as they walked back toward the tent. "That's too bad. I think I still have some energy."

She leaned up and kissed him. "Well, I might have a little energy left. What about the fire?"

Eldridge smiled and thought about what had happened earlier in the day. The 'bot that had cooked dinner busied itself with packing up the kitchen. "Yeah, maybe I'd better take care of that. I didn't get the coding done for the firefighting so the whole place could go up, and he would make pancakes."

"See you in a few," she said.

Eldridge kicked the fire apart with his boots and poured water on the glowing embers. As the light died down and darkness claimed the worksite, he heard something howl in the distance. Epsilon Eridani III had predators, he knew. Chief Bell had warned him about the local version of bobcats. They had deep purple fur which hid them well in the dark. He turned to the 'bot doing clean up to give it an order but a moving light in the direction of the *Athena Star* caught his attention.

He watched as it played over the wreckage near the dissected engines. The white light moved along the base of the wreck and stopped near a ground level hatch before disappearing inside. Eldridge watched as the interior lit up and the light faded as it moved away from the entry point.

"Goddamn thieves." He grabbed a shotgun from one of the storage lockers and rushed over to the float bike. Then he stopped and turned to the cooking 'bot.

"Tell Ari I saw someone messing around on the wreck and I went to investigate. You're on guard duty."

"Affirmative," it said. "I will deliver the message."

Eldridge put on a helmet and the night vision engaged by default. He gunned the motor and tore off like a rocket across the distance between his site and the wreck. A plume of loose dust blew up behind him.

He got to the *Athena Star* and weaved between piles of salvaged material. Coming to a stop, he dismounted the bike and took off the helmet. He grabbed a flashlight and the shotgun and made his way to the broken hatch where he had seen someone enter.

Eldridge didn't hear anything. The intruder in the *Athena Star* may have heard him approach on the bike but he didn't care. He just wanted to be rid of them. Shining his light on the ground around the hatch, he moved inside.

A large cargo hold was located just inside the hatch but it had been emptied days ago. Anyone hunting for valuables would be sorely disappointed. He saw a light move toward the rear of the large space.

"I saw you come in here," he said loudly and his voice echoed off the metal walls and bounced around the open space. "Step out where I can see you."

No one answered. Eldridge shined the light along the walls. He adjusted his stance to keep his balance on the metal decking because it was tilted due to the wreck. He heard a scrape behind him, like a boot on metal and he turned.

Something hit him across the back and drove the air from his lungs. His light skittered away and pointed toward a corner of the hold. He collapsed on the metal decking and grunted as another blow landed on his back. Someone grabbed his shotgun from him and he heard the action being worked. Shells fell around him on the decking and then he heard a grunt. A few seconds later he heard something that sounded like his gun land with an angry clatter against one of the walls. He curled up in a ball, anticipating another strike but it didn't come. Instead, something jabbed him in the back and his body went rigid as a shock passed through it. He inhaled sharply as pain raced through him and lost consciousness.

Chapter 4

Someone banged on the door of Nathan's apartment. He muted the entertainment system and set down his drink. It might have been early for whiskey but his feelings didn't leave him a lot of reasons not to have a few. Waiting for word about whether he would be working or not made him cranky.

He answered the door and saw his landlord, an Armenian immigrant, standing in the hallway. The burly man sported a stained white tank top that showed off beefy arms slowly going flabby. Dark curly chest hair sprouted from beneath it like weeds.

"Hello, Mr. Baliozian. What can I do for you today?"

"You pay rent, Mr. Teller," he said in broken English. "You are two months behind so you pay today."

"No problem," Nathan said with a smile. "I'll have it in your account by the end of business today."

"You have ship, no? Big ship? Why are you here drinking instead of working? You should be working."

Nathan gritted his teeth and turned to see the whiskey bottle on the coffee table clearly visible from the landlord's vantage point. He shifted his stance. "I just got back from a job on Mars. I should get paid today and the first thing I'll do is pay you."

Mr. Baliozian waved a dismissive hand at him. "Mars? You no go to Mars. You sit right here all the time. You need job. I been in this country three years and I own two apartment buildings." He held up two fingers to emphasize the point. "Real estate my father told me, 'own real estate.'" The landlord laughed and his gut bounced up and down. "Mars. You putting me on."

"I'm really not. We just got back a couple days ago."

Mr. Baliozian's face hardened. "I no care what you do a couple days ago. You pay me two month rent today or tomorrow you living somewhere else. You understand?"

Nathan nodded. "I understand. Now, if you'll excuse me I need to see about my next job."

The landlord threw his hands up and walked off down the hall. He yelled over his shoulder, "Next job? You need 'a' job. Stop being so lazy." Nathan closed the door but he could still hear the landlord when he said, "And stop drinking in day time."

Nathan collapsed back onto the couch and rested a foot on the coffee table in front of him. His mobi chimed with an incoming message. He picked up the communication device and scrolled to the new message. Bao had accepted his proposal for the *Athena Star* job. The message also had a note stating that the invoice for the *Hell's Breath* job had been paid. He breathed a sigh of relief and sent out a group message to the crew, instructing them that they would be leaving tomorrow morning and to prep the *Blue Moon Bandit*.

"Told you we had a job," he said to the empty apartment.

Nathan expanded the display and virtual keyboard of the mobi to make it more like a traditional workstation and easier to use. He logged into his bank's site and checked the balance in the business account. It might be positive now but he sighed, knowing it wouldn't stay that way.

He pulled up a list of the bills incurred during the last job. The price of solid hydrogen fuel had risen again and he had an insurance payment due on the *Bandit*. Big Bulk Mart had also sent him an invoice for the provisions they had stocked the ship with. He paid all three and regarded the remaining balance.

He ran the numbers to figure out what the shares for each crew member would be for the most recent job. The program split the balance according to the default settings, two shares for him and one each for the remainder of the crew: Cole, Duncan, Marla and Richie. The split seemed smaller than he liked.

He had an excellent crew and he knew they could all find work with other ships doing other jobs. Higher pay rates kept them on the *Blue Moon Bandit,* that and the freedom that came with repossessing starships. If he wanted to stay in business he needed them. He could always find other pilots, engineers or muscle but anyone he found would be inferior to the crew he had now, and he would have to go to the trouble of training them. In this line of work, he wanted people working for him that he could count on. Keeping them meant paying them a decent amount of credits even if it meant he earned less.

A quick look around his apartment proved that things could be better. He'd downgraded to an efficiency one-bedroom place in a neighborhood that was either ripe for gentrification or demolition.

Nathan needed better cash flow but Milky Way Repossessions had competitors now eating into their business. He knew of three other firms engaged in starship repo work at least part-time and their competition had driven rates down. When he'd started the business, it had been easy to carve out a niche for himself. Those days were long gone now that other people had discovered you could earn decent credits snatching starships from folks behind on their loans.

Turning back to the display he reduced his shares from two to one and saw the split rise incrementally among the rest of the crew. Hopefully it would keep them satisfied until the next job came along. He considered his decision for a moment, then, like the last half dozen times he'd faced this same dilemma, he pressed the enter key and paid his crew. The business account balance dropped to almost zero.

Next, he checked his personal account and saw he had enough to catch up on the rent so he transferred credits to Mr. Baliozian. At the very least he had a place to live for the next month. If worst came to worst he could move onto the *Bandit.*

—— «» ——

"What are we doing here?" Cole asked with a yawn. "It's early."

He and Nathan sat in a float car outside the offices of Crater Salvage in Go City. The office itself appeared to be a cheap chrome and glass store front in a strip mall. From where they sat, Nathan could see two people inside, a woman sitting at a desk on the right and a man sitting at a desk across the room from her. A small sign hung above the door. Nathan considered that it was similar to the office he kept for Milky Way Repossessions.

"When I spoke to Bao I got the feeling this whole thing could be a misunderstanding over some outstanding bills," Nathan said. "I'm just wondering if it's worth flying all the way out to Epsilon Eridani. Why not stop here first and ask some questions?"

"You think Bao hasn't done that?"

Nathan shrugged. "He said they've called over here and spoken to someone. Sometimes you have to look a person in the eye."

"So we're going in?"

"Yep, but before we do, I wanted to ask you about something. Back on Mars, did you see Bone Daddy and his lady using that stuff?"

"Yeah."

"What was it?"

"It's called 'Diamond K'. It's the latest version of synthetic amphetamines. My buddies in the marshal's office say it's really hit big in the last few years."

"Huh," Nathan said. "That explains Luscious being so skinny."

"Yeah, the physical effects of using it are similar to what you see with other drugs; broken teeth from chewing the crystal, dehydration, loss of appetite and a general feeling of not giving a shit about anything but scoring. This stuff is wicked, though."

"Why?"

"It's cheap, it's easy to manufacture and users don't develop a tolerance. It drives law enforcement and drug counselors crazy. If you get a good cook who really understands how to properly make the stuff, they produce a product that feels like the first high every time. The users chew it and the Dopamine rush in their brain hits them hard, over and over again. It's some deadly stuff. I'm not surprised to see someone like Luscious using it. As soon as I saw him I knew he was on something."

"Yeah, he didn't look healthy."

Cole grunted. "That stuff will kill you. It's hard on your system, especially your heart. Kids in their twenties who use it a lot drop dead from heart attacks or cirrhosis of the liver or kidney failure. Their body heat rises and starts to bake their brain. It will also drive you bat-shit insane and paranoid. You start thinking everyone is out to get you."

Nathan stared at him. "That sounds pretty bad."

"Well, it's made from industrial chemicals like reactor coolant, potassium and ammonia hydroxide."

"And people eat it?"

"Yes they do. I understand the high is potent enough that it's difficult to describe. I mean, it makes you impotent so imagine how good this stuff makes you feel that you're willing to give up sex."

Nathan considered that for a moment. "Nope, I'm not doing that."

Cole smiled. "Yeah, you gave it up the old-fashioned way, by not being able to get any."

Nathan ignored him. "You said it didn't cost much. How cheap is it?"

"Ten credits a gram or so. That's what makes it so prevalent." He studied Nathan for moment. "What's with all the questions? Are we getting into the drug business?"

Nathan grunted. "No, business isn't that bad yet. Let's go inside and talk to these folks."

They got out of the car and approached the office. A young woman greeted them as they entered. A small placard on her desk had the name Molly Stern on it. She had red hair and a nice smile. "Good morning gentlemen. Welcome to Crater Salvage. What can we do for you?"

Nathan nodded and smiled as he introduced himself and Cole. "I'm here to speak with Lewis Mairn."

"That's me," the man behind them said. Nathan turned toward him. Lewis Mairn had a comb over and a generous belly. He wore a mustard yellow short sleeved shirt and glasses. He stood up and offered his hand. Nathan shook it. He pointed to a couple chairs in front of his desk and they sat down.

"Mr. Mairn, I represent Federal Trust and Loan." Nathan watched as the man's smile faltered. "They have engaged our services to repossess the salvage vessel *Corkscrew* for non-payment on the loan. I understand Crater Salvage is currently using the vessel in the recovery of the starliner *Athena Star*."

Mairn nodded. "That's correct."

"Mr. Mairn, we will be leaving shortly. Before we go to the trouble of flying ten light years and shutting down your operation, are you certain this trouble isn't due to some misunderstanding that could be cleared up today with a payment to the bank?"

Lewis Mairn rocked back in his chair and picked up a pen. He twirled it between his fingers. He considered them for a moment, staring from Nathan to Cole and back again. He finally smiled.

"Captain Teller, it's my understanding that all payments required by the contract have been made. I think what we have here is a miscommunication."

Nathan raised an eyebrow. "You think the bank who loaned you money doesn't understand the repayment schedule?"

Marin held his hands palms up. "That appears to be the case. You see, we invoice Great Star Lines, they pay us and then we pay the bank. We haven't received payment from Great Star Lines so there's no way we could make a payment to the bank. They don't get paid unless we do." He sat up a little straighter and smiled, obviously pleased with himself.

"So the whole thing is just a misunderstanding with Great Star Lines?"

"That's right," Mairn said. "Frankly, I'm surprised the bank has gone to so much trouble. I think I'll contact Bao Zhang and put this whole thing to rest. I'm sorry he's gotten you mixed up in this."

Nathan leaned forward and rested an arm on the man's desk. "Lewis, I'm leaving soon to go get that ship unless I hear from Bao. Coming here and speaking with you is just a courtesy and not one I usually extend. Whatever you have going on, I suggest you get it straightened out before I break orbit. Once that happens things get a lot more expensive." He stood up and Cole rose with him. He turned and nodded to Molly. "Nice to meet you, ma'am."

They walked through the parking lot and got back in the float car. Nathan saw Lewis Mairn clocking them from inside the office. "He's sweating. Did you catch that?"

"That's because he's lying," Cole said.

"Yeah, and he's really not good at it. What do you think is going on?"

Cole shrugged. "I don't know. It could be embezzlement. It could be shoddy bookkeeping and the guy is worried about losing his job." He glanced back over his shoulder. "Or he may be banging the receptionist. Do we care? I mean, Epsilon Eridani is a ways out but the pay day on this one is really good. Whatever is going on between Crater Salvage and the bank is their problem. I say we go earn a good paycheck."

Nathan considered it for a moment. It seemed like a straight up deal and the visit really had been a courtesy. Cole had the right idea. Let Bao and Eldridge work out their own problems.

"You're right," he said. "Let's get paid."

He started the float car and it lifted a few centimeters off the ground, joining the traffic outside the parking lot.

Chapter 5

Eldridge rolled his head toward a light shining in his eyes. He raised his arms defensively, afraid whoever had attacked him in the *Athena Star* had come back. Something gripped his arm tightly and the light moved. When the spots cleared from his vision he realized it was a medic 'bot.

He shook his arm loose and sat up straight, realizing he was on a stretcher on the ground outside the wreck. The 'bot took hold of his arm again. "Please stay still, sir, until the diagnostic scan is complete. It will only take a few seconds."

"Ari?"

He heard the creak of springs on the utility cart and Ari appeared. "I'm right here."

"How am I?"

"You're a hell of a lot better than you have a right to be. What were you thinking, running off in the night like that?"

Eldridge opened his mouth to explain but the 'bot interrupted him. "Mr. Tanner is recovering nicely from the electrical shock. There is no permanent damage and his vital signs have returned to normal."

He stood up and hugged Ari. "I'm sorry; it was stupid to run off like that."

She resisted him for a moment and then returned the hug. "Yes it was. Now tell me what happened and make it good. One minute I'm in the tent getting all ready for sexy time with you and the next I have a 'bot looking at me in the altogether telling me about you heading off to the wreck."

He grimaced. "I'm sorry about that but someone was out here. I figured they were scavenging the wreck. I thought I could scare them off."

"So why didn't you take me with you? I could have literally ridden shotgun and saved you from getting knocked out."

"I didn't take you because I didn't want you to get hurt."

"How did that work out for you?"

"Not so good. How did you find me?"

"I took the service cart after you with the cooking 'bot. We found you unconscious on the deck of the cargo bay."

He nodded slowly. "So you didn't see anyone?"

"No, just you, lying on the deck. You've been out ever since."

Eldridge moved back inside the cargo bay and Ari followed. He powered up a set of work lamps and the area flooded with light. Just as he remembered, the bay was empty. The 'bots salvaging the wreck had cleared out every crate, pallet and shipping container. He turned back to the hatchway.

"I came in through there and saw the light over there," he said, pointing toward the rear of the cargo bay. "Then someone hit me and shocked me."

Ari put a hand on his shoulder. "The 'bot and I found you right here," she said, indicating an area to their right. "I called Fred out here and we treated you as best we could. Once we determined your injuries weren't life threatening, Fred took a few 'bots and checked the area but they didn't find anything except your shotgun and flashlight. Are you still thinking scavengers?"

He shrugged. "Maybe. We've had people from Bad Rock sniffing around out here before but no one has ever been violent."

"I'm not sure they wanted to be violent. You were shocked, not shot and they emptied the shells from your gun. They didn't even steal that."

"So they wanted something else." He looked around and turned in a slow circle, taking in the large, empty area. "There's really nothing else to be interested in here." He wandered off in the direction he'd seen the light last night. There was an interior hatch and he opened it. The metal door squealed on hinges that were straining against the angle of the wreck. Eldridge and Ari stepped into the next compartment.

"What's that?" She said, pointing to a large tank.

Eldridge pointed to a metal label near a gauge. It was marked NaK. "This is a reactor coolant storage tank full of sodium-potassium alloy. The label says it holds five thousand liters and," he moved to the side and checked the pressure gauge, "it's full. I think there's another one in the compartment across the bay. This stuff is hazardous so we'll need to be careful with it."

They crossed the bay and Eldridge noticed the door was already open and hanging at an odd angle. They stepped into the compartment. As he suspected, it had an identical tank. Eldridge checked the pressure gauge and saw it was full as well. He took a minute and looked around the space. Nothing appeared to have been tampered with. He pointed to the floor and they could see fresh footprints in the dust.

"What were they doing in here, babe?" He said. "What were they looking for?"

Ari shook her head. "Probably just scavengers, right? A couple of guys looking for precious metals in the wreckage. The ship is full of it. Maybe we should post more 'bots as guards."

Eldridge nodded. "Yeah, that may be a good idea. They got past the ones working last night. I'll assign an additional six or so tonight."

She put a hand on his shoulder. "Come on, let's get you back to camp. You need to talk to the local police."

He had a puzzled look on his face. "Why?"

"They want you to make a statement. Do you really think I let someone knock you out on our jobsite and didn't call Protective Services?"

He gritted his teeth. "The local cops are hardly Protective Services and I don't need Don Bell sniffing around out here. You should have asked me first." He walked away from her. She reached out and grabbed his hand, stopping him before he could get far.

"Now you listen to me, Eldridge," she said in the voice that was reserved for their most volatile disagreements.

"Someone assaulted you. This isn't just paying protection credits to some Syndicate clown. This is someone shocking you into unconsciousness. We don't have to put up with that. If Dodger and his thugs want to escalate from nice quiet extortion to hurting us, that's where I draw the line. I love you and no one gets to hurt you."

He put his arms around her and pulled her close. "I'm sorry. I shouldn't have snapped at you."

"No, you shouldn't have. I'm just trying to protect you."

"I know and you're right. For all we know it wasn't even Dodger or his boys. It may have been someone from town."

"Maybe, but either way it's a good idea to report it."

He considered her for a moment and relented. "Okay, I'll go see him."

She smiled and hugged him. "Thank you."

—— «» ——

Turtle pulled into the parking lot of Dodge Em's, a strip club on the south side of Bad Rock, and the rusty float car settled to the ground. He got out and Daryl followed him into the black building decorated with a red stripe that wrapped around the building with an arrow pointing at the entrance. Rusted out vehicles filled up about a third of the parking lot. Aside from the strip club, the rest of the block edged toward urban blight.

"Did Dodger say why he wanted to see us?" Daryl said.

Turtle shook his head. "No, but he's pissed about something."

"Why do you say that?"

"The only time he talks to us is to give us an assignment or chew us out. He's got us working out at the wreck site already so he must be pissed about something."

Daryl considered this for a moment. "Did you do anything?"

Turtle gave him a sideways glance. "What makes you think it's me?"

"Because I haven't done anything for the last couple months except sit in that dust and watch 'bots sort garbage."

"Yeah and I've been right there beside you."

They grew quiet again and Turtle surveyed the abandoned buildings. He took a deep breath.

"Okay, let's go see what's got him upset."

Daryl followed him. "You know he's going to be high."

No doubt about that, Turtle knew. Dodger definitely used his own product. "If he is, don't mention it. We don't need to make him any angrier." They reached the entrance door and Turtle pulled it open.

The bouncer sitting on a stool inside the door nodded and waved them inside. A heavy bass beat pounded through the dimly lit club. A pair of holographic dancers, rather than real ones, gyrated on brass poles in the middle stage of three. Turtle could tell because the faster the images moved, the blurrier they became. He watched as a pretty brunette smiled in their direction, her face becoming a jittery smear half a second behind her movements.

Turtle and Daryl walked through the maze of tables toward an office in the rear of the club. A second bouncer stood outside the door. This one didn't sit on a stool and he eyed them as they approached. He nodded to his right.

A set of lockers stood next to the door. Daryl opened one of them, removed a gun and holster from the rear of his belt and placed it inside. He closed the locker door and removed the key. Turtle didn't carry.

"He's on a call," the bouncer said. "Wait here."

A couple minutes went by and Turtle scanned the inside of the club. Unemployed men or those working the night shift populated the place. No one looked sober. Turtle knew they might not have credits for the rent but they could always find enough for booze and bare titties.

He watched as the girls winked out of existence when their time expired. A hefty guy swiped his finger across a reader on the edge of the stage in front of him and a menu displayed in the air in front of him. Turtle watched him select a program and it started.

The guard held a finger to his ear and then opened the door to let them in. They walked into the office and a light over the door turned green. He knew a scanner built into the doorframe checked them for weapons.

Turtle made it three steps into the office and then a pool cue caught him across the back of his thighs. He sprawled out on the floor as his legs burned with pain. He grimaced and saw Daryl get thrown into a chair by a large man.

"What the hell, Dodger? What are you doing?" He turned and saw the fat end of a pool cue swinging through the air. He had just enough time to curl into the fetal position before it crashed down on his left arm.

The mobster breathed hard, sucking air through his mouth. He was shorter than both Turtle and Daryl but powerfully built. He appeared to be in his mid-fifties with long dark hair that had been dyed black. He had thick arms that attested to the hours spent working out in the gym he owned a couple blocks over. Thick curls of dark sweaty hair hung in his face as he glared at Turtle with watery red eyes.

"You screwed up, asshole."

Turtle lowered his arms. "What did I do? I don't even know what you're talking about."

He gestured with the pool cue to the chairs in front of the office desk. "Sit down."

Turtle winced and got to his feet. His eyes never left Dodger as he slumped into the chair next to Daryl. He heard someone clear their throat and he turned to see Dodger's right-hand man, Morris, standing behind Daryl with a gun in his hand.

So, not a pleasant meeting.

Dodger walked around behind his desk and spun the pool cue. Turtle noticed his hands shook and his eyes watered like he was having an allergic reaction. Turtle knew it really meant he'd been chewing Diamond K again. And *that* meant he would be high and unpredictable as hell.

"Dodger, I don't know what happened or why you're upset but if you me give a chance I'm sure I can figure it out and solve the problem." His legs ached where they'd been hit and he stretched them out as much as he could. The boss set the pool cue down on the desk in front of him and dropped into his chair.

He had a plastic pouch in one hand and fished out a crystal with one thick finger. He popped it in his mouth and Turtle heard it crunch under his teeth. "We've had a problem with the Diamond K distribution. Your boy Bone Daddy screwed up and got his ship repossessed." Dodger's red eyes bored into him.

"Luscious got his ship repo'd?"

"He did," Dodger said. "I thought you told me this clown could be trusted?"

Turtle put his hands in front of him. "We grew up together in Louisiana, Dodger. He's solid."

"Then explain his ship being seized with half a shipment of Diamond K on board? Instead of being delivered to a city on Mars a whole pallet is sitting on the wrong planet. That's five million credits, Turtle."

"Are you sure, Dodger? It just sounds weird that his ship would be repossessed. He makes good money on tour and we pay him loads of credits. I don't understand why he would get behind on loan payments." He considered that for a moment. "Should he even have a loan?"

Dodger raised an eyebrow. "I don't care about his finances unless they interfere with my interests, and now they have. In addition to the Diamond K not being delivered, I have your idiot friend asking me what we're going to do about it. Let me ask you, why is this my problem?"

Turtle understood quickly. "It's not. It's mine. I'll take care of this. I have some guys on Earth I'm friends with. Maybe they can get the shipment back from whoever has it."

Dodger leaned forward. "My concern is that whoever has the ship is going to find my product and when they do, Protective Services is going to want to talk to with Bone Daddy. If that happens, what are the odds your friend will keep his mouth shut?"

Turtle nodded and thought a moment before answering. He had no illusions about Luscious taking the fall for having illegal contraband like Diamond K on his ship. Then his legs stung involuntarily where they had been hit and he thought about what Dodger would do to him for recommending Luscious in the first place.

"Don't you worry about him, Dodger. He may seem a little flaky but that's just his stage act. Down deep he is a standup guy who won't crack no matter how hard the cops come at him. You have my word."

Dodger eyed him. "He's an asshole and a weak one at that. You brought him in, Turtle, so you're responsible for him. If he spills his guts and we get a bunch of Protective Services agents out here snooping around, I'm holding you responsible. Do you understand me?"

Turtle nodded. "Yes, I do. Just leave it to me. I'll take care of it." He thought for a moment. What he wanted, what he needed, was to get the heat off him and off Luscious. Then it came to him. "Are you sure the repo agency is legitimate?"

"What do you mean?"

"Well, is it possible someone knew about the shipment on Luscious's ship? Maybe they took the ship to get the stuff? Could this have been a trick?"

Dodger picked up a mobi from the desk. "Your idiot friend said the outfit that grabbed it is called 'Milky Way Repossessions'. Follow up on them and see if they're for real. If they are, we know your friend is an idiot. If they aren't, let me know and I'll take care of them. You're not the only one with friends back on Earth."

Turtle nodded. "Consider it done."

The room got quiet and Dodger helped himself to another crystal before speaking. "So what did you find out about that other thing?"

It took Turtle a moment to switch gears and catch up with the change in topic but he got there after a moment. "The coolant tanks on the *Athena Star* are full," Turtle said, "five thousand liters in each. The impact of the crash didn't hurt them at all."

"Ten thousand liters," Dodger said, "just sitting there. Does Tanner know what he has?"

Turtle shook his head. "I don't think so. He's been giving priority to the precious metals in the equipment and the exotic alloys that make up the hull. He hasn't said anything about recovering chemicals except to leave them alone. I think he sees them as a nuisance and only wants to deal with them when he must."

"We did have to get a little rough with him," Daryl said.

Dodger considered Turtle with eyes desperately in need of rest. "What happened?"

Turtle brushed his greasy hair from his eyes and hesitated before speaking. He wanted to get his words just right. "Tanner saw us sneaking around the wreck last night and came out to investigate. I was inside checking the tanks and Daryl had to stun him to keep him from discovering us. He should be okay."

Dodger shifted his gaze to Daryl. "Does he know you did it?"

"I don't see how he could," Daryl said. "I came up behind him. Serves him right anyway. He's kind of a mouthy sonuvabitch."

Dodger turned back to Turtle. "What's he talking about?"

Daryl looked like he might say something stupid, maybe give Dodger a little lip about talking to Turtle instead of him. Turtle knew that wouldn't be in anyone's best interest so he cleared his throat to get control of the conversation. "Tanner came out to our pile yesterday complaining about the way we're sorting. He thinks we're going too slowly and holding him up."

Dodger leaned back in his chair. "How far behind is he?"

"A month, maybe a little more. I heard him complaining to his girl about it."

"Are we getting our ton of salvage every day?"

Turtle nodded. "We sure are and he's paid up current on the ten positions."

"I don't want him out of business," Dodger said. "You can't keep milking the cow if you make steaks out of it. Speed up the sorting if you can but make sure we get a good ton of salvage every day."

"Sure, thing. We can do that. What about the coolant?"

Dodger smiled, wicked and greedy. "We claim that right away, all ten thousand liters. We can process tons of Diamond K using that as a base. I'm going to send a tanker truck out to the *Athena Star*. You are going to inform Mr. Tanner that we'll be taking it and recycling it for him. I'll have paperwork drawn up showing us as a legitimate vendor so he'll have something to show Great Star Line. They'll want proof of proper disposal. If he gives you any grief tell him we're saving him what he would have paid a real company. Take care of that today."

"Consider it done," Turtle said. "Is that all?"

"You have five million credits worth of product to recover. Do you need anything else to do?"

"No, I think that's it."

"Then we're done."

They left the office and didn't talk until they got to the parking lot. Daryl stopped to retrieve his gun from the locker and clipped the holster into place at the small of his back. Turtle leaned against their float car and held his hands to his legs.

"That sonuvabitch. Who does he think he is, beating on me like that?"

Daryl nodded toward the club. "Don't bitch out here. Do it in the car."

They climbed in and Daryl slipped behind the wheel. Turtle waited until they were up the block before he opened his mouth again.

"That is not the way you treat a man. You don't just beat on him when there's a problem. You figure out a solution and get back to making credits. He's chickenshit."

Daryl nodded his assent. "No doubt."

"I've done nothing but earn for him and this is how he treats me." Turtle lashed out and punched the float car's window several times. Silence fell while he got himself under control.

"It's that crap he chews all day," Turtle said. "You know that, right? He's addicted."

"Of course I know. He was just doing it in front of me. You're right, he's not stable."

Turtle turned, sensing a kindred spirit. "He's putting us all in danger by using that shit, you know that, right? It makes him paranoid and violent. He's going to screw up and make a mistake."

"No doubt."

"Can you imagine if he caught one of us using like that? Walking into a meeting with bloodshot eyes and hands shaking? He'd have Morris dust us right on the spot."

"Yep."

"So what are we going to do about it?"

Daryl kept his eyes on the street. "You shouldn't talk like that."

"Knocking him off wouldn't be the worst thing. We could run things. We're a hell of a lot smarter than Dodger and we don't use."

Daryl shook his head. "I don't think so."

"Why not?"

"It would just start a war to be in charge. The crew would split because everyone would see it as an opportunity and just look at this place," he said and waved his hand in the air. "It's dead. People are leaving and the city is mostly abandoned. Why do you think the Syndicate manufactures Diamond K out here? There's no one around. That's why an asshole like Dodger is running things. Do you really just want to be the next Dodger?"

"No."

"Of course not. Just hang tight. Dodger will self-destruct."

Turtle grunted. "What if he takes us with him when he goes?"

"We're smart. We'll make sure that doesn't happen.

"If I get a shot I might still take it."

Daryl shrugged. "If you do, make sure you pick your time carefully because if you screw it up you're dead."

"Yeah."

Daryl changed the subject. "This Bone Daddy isn't a standup guy, is he?"

"Luscious is a weasel. He'll say whatever he has to in order to stay out of trouble." He bent down and put his head between his knees.

Daryl lit a cigarette and shook the hair out of his eyes. "Why did you bring him into this if you can't trust him?"

Turtle straightened up. "I saw an opportunity to advance so I took it. Dodger needed a way to get Diamond K off planet, and I knew Luscious had his own ship and visited all kinds of places while he toured. It seemed like a natural fit. Besides, we loaded and hid the stuff on his ship and our guys at the stops took it off. We took care of everything. All he had to do was play his gigs."

"You know this guy is going to get you killed."

Turtle considered that. Despite what they'd just talked about, he had no doubt his partner would shoot him if Dodger told him to. Daryl wouldn't rat him out to Dodger for plotting against him but he would do whatever meant keeping his position on the crew. He needed to buy time to formulate a plan. "Okay, let's go check on this repo company. Maybe there's something sketchy about them."

"And if there isn't?"

"There's something sketchy about everyone. Take us back to my place and we'll start digging."

The drive to Turtle's place took fifteen minutes, and they stopped for take out on the way. It was a single-family prefab house in a mostly abandoned residential neighborhood. At one time, it had been full of families and workers for the steel mills but as they closed and people emigrated to other worlds the homes stayed empty. As far as Turtle knew, no one else lived on the block where he squatted. If the house had an owner Turtle had never met them. He had just moved in one day and stayed.

Turtle grabbed one of the take-out containers and started chowing down on shrimp dumplings as he flopped down on a beat up couch with dirty gold fabric. Daryl took his container and a beer to a chair covered in worn red plastic. Turtle logged into his computer, and a large holographic display lit up the living room. He found a search engine and queried the net for information about Milky Way Repossessions. The results consisted of a few advertisements, contact information and a couple small news stories about particular ships being recovered.

"That's not good news," Daryl said. "They look like a legitimate company which means your friend is probably a deadbeat."

Turtle squinted sideways at his friend. "You think a straight businessman wouldn't get his beak wet if he knew about the Diamond K? Let me ask you something; when you fly into a planet, don't you usually go through customs? Why didn't they find anything?"

"Maybe they haven't done the inspection yet. It could be when these repo jobs land, they give them a pass or take care of it whenever they have time."

Turtle considered that. "Maybe. There's nothing here, though. Everything about them looks legit. That's just the net though. I've got other sources." He called up a communications program and entered a payment code using access to a stolen credit account. They ate as the computer designed a circuit that would allow them to have a conversation with someone on Earth. The communication system used quantum entanglement and the warpgate to allow faster than light conversations between Earth's solar system and Epsilon Eridani's. Turtle made sure he always had access to someone else's funds for a call like this. Ten minutes later the newly holographic display lit up.

Turtle set his dumpling container down and tried to make out the person on the other end of the fuzzy display. It appeared to be a middle-aged guy with dark, close cropped hair. He squinted into the camera.

"This is the Wheelhouse." Liquor bottles lined the shelf behind him.

"Uncle Donny?" Turtle said. "Is that you?"

The man made an adjustment on his controls and the picture became clearer. "Yeah, this is Donald Kinty. Who is this?"

"It's Turtle. Can you see me?" This time he made an adjustment and Kinty smiled.

"Oh, hey, Turtle. How's my favorite nephew?"

"I'm doing good. We have to talk fast, Uncle Donny. I'm calling from Bad Rock and I don't know how long the connection will stay up."

"All right, what do you need?"

"Have you ever heard of an outfit called Milky Way Repossessions?"

Kinty's face fell. "Yeah, I know them. Are they giving you a problem?"

Turtle smiled at Daryl. "They grabbed one of our ships from Mars and hauled it back to Earth and we aren't very happy about it. It had some items that we need to retrieve."

Kinty nodded knowingly. "I understand."

"Are they a legitimate operation?"

The older man said, "They are but we had a run in with them about a year, year-and-a-half ago. It left a bad taste in everybody's mouth. Remember that story I told you about somebody ripping us off for twenty-three million credits?"

"Yeah."

"They were mixed up in that. Jack let them go because they identified the real thief," he chewed his lower lip for a moment, "but I'm not as forgiving. One of them broke my wrist and they made us look bad in front of the boss. I'd like to have a reason for getting another shot at them. What's this about your ship? Where is it?"

"It's impounded in Go City. We'd like to get our stuff back or have it eliminated, if that's possible." The picture shifted sideways and threatened to cutoff.

Kinty nodded through the static. "We might be able to work something out. Send me a message with the details."

"Will do." Turtle reached out and killed the connection.

"Your uncle seems like a real hard ass," Daryl said.

Turtle nodded. "The hardest. He runs with a crew out of Go City. His boss is a guy named Atomic Jack. Ever heard of him?"

Daryl had a fearful look on his face. "The guy in the pressure suit? He can set things on fire just buy touching them, right?"

"That's the guy. If these repo guys pissed off my uncle he'll carry a grudge forever." Turtle started composing a message with the details of Luscious's ship and what they needed removed. "Uncle Donny will either get our shipment back or get rid of the evidence."

Daryl nodded. "Good work, Turtle. This may even make Dodger happy."

Turtle grunted. "No, all this is going to do is keep me alive. That dumbass Luscious still lost a distribution route that will have to be replaced." He finished the message and sent it to his uncle. "Let's head back over to the salvage site and make sure everything is all right. The last thing I need is something else going wrong today."

Chapter 6

Nathan arrived at the berth where he kept the *Blue Moon Bandit* and stopped his float bike at the entrance to the launch pad. The ship rested on the tarmac looking like a predator hunched and ready to strike. The gunmetal gray hull was accentuated by blue trimmed, square engine cowlings on either side of the cockpit that ran the length of the ship.

The converted hazardous waste hauler was tough and over-engineered to maintain structural integrity in case of a crash. Most freighters and shuttles depended on an external boost because of the cost involved in lifting hundreds of tons into space but the *Bandit* could launch from anywhere on the strength of its massive engines.

He parked the bike near the ship and walked around to the rear. The aft loading ramp extended between the engine housings and a tool box lay open to the left of it. He ran a hand over the housing of the port side engine and pulled himself up with a grunt to look inside at the thrust vectoring nozzle.

"It's all good, Captain," a voice called from the bottom of the loading ramp. "I fixed the broken gimbal linkage on the directional nozzle yesterday. You have full range of motion."

Nathan dropped down to the tarmac and waved. "Thanks, Richie. Looks good."

Richie Pearson was a machinist's mate on the crew but Duncan had made a project out of teaching him about engines and the ship's systems. Together they managed to keep Nathan and his ship flying on a shoestring budget.

He'd had his doubts about whether Richie would pan out when he'd brought him on the crew just over a year ago but the young man seemed to be doing well with his gambling addiction.

"You're here early," Richie said.

Nathan nodded. "I just wanted to check out the ship and our supplies."

Richie smiled. "Don't sweat it, boss. I made a run into town last night and got everything we need from Big Bulk Mart over on Livingston. It's all on the company's account."

"Good. Thanks, Richie. Since you have everything under control here, I'm going to start the pre-flight checklist." He moved past the younger man and started up the ramp but then he stopped. "Oh, and could you prep the guest quarters? We're going to have a mission specialist with us on this trip."

"Yeah? What kind of specialist?"

"A nurse." He swallowed hard. "We're going to be pretty far out so I thought it would be a good idea to take precautions."

"Yeah, sure. I'll take care of it after I stow these tools."

Nathan continued into the ship. One of the corridors coming off the ramp emptied out into the galley. They used this space as the common area but it could be a little tight. When the ship had been built all of the large space had been allocated below decks in the cargo holds. Duncan and Nathan had converted most of that to hold ship's stores, spare parts, tools and small vehicles like a couple float bikes and tractors. Duncan could fix almost anything on the ship with what they carried, which helped keep costs down.

He moved forward to the cramped cockpit he shared with Marla. Taking the seat to the left, he called up the flight controls to perform the pre-flight checklist.

An hour later he walked over the upper hull of the ship. The *Bandit* might have a few years on her but the solid airframe would perform well for decades to come with the right maintenance. He searched the length of the engine housings for cracks or stress fractures but couldn't find any. In fact, nothing needed immediate attention.

He paused and carefully examined the thrust vectoring nozzles. The ship used these to help keep itself aloft and maneuvering in a planetary atmosphere. Without thrust it flew as well as a rock. The ship had few a control surfaces like ailerons and flaps that could be extended from housings within the hull but no rudder or large stabilizer. The ship needed thrust to fly. He heard a float car pull up at the gate.

An automated cab dipped and settled to the ground to release its passenger. Nathan smiled as he saw Tricia step out, looking lovely in blue jeans, tan boots and a hooded sweatshirt. She grabbed a couple bags and walked toward the ship. Seeing Nathan on the hull, she waved. He returned it and started toward the ladder. Thirty seconds later he walked across the tarmac to meet her and took one of her bags.

"Is this all you brought?" He asked.

"I like to travel light," she said, "less to carry and lose track of. This one," she said, hoisting the second bag, "are the medical supplies you asked me to get."

"Right," he said. "Well, come on inside. Everyone else is aboard so we're ready to go."

"Ok."

Nathan showed Tricia her quarters so she could drop her stuff and then introduced her to Marla and Richie, whom she hadn't met on Mars. Duncan and Cole said hello.

"You can strap in here for liftoff," Nathan said, pointing to one of the seats in the galley near the table. "Taking off or landing you need to be in a seat wearing a vest so you'll be as protected as possible in the event something goes wrong."

She raised an eyebrow as she sat down and adjusted the harness. "Does something go wrong often?"

"No," he smiled, "but I'm glad we have a nurse on board." He straightened up and addressed everyone. He heard buckles click as Cole, Duncan and Richie strapped in.

"Our flight time to the Neptune warpgate will be around four hours and then we'll jump straight to Epsilon Eridani. Flight time to Epsilon Eridani III from the warpgate is about three hours. Once we've cleared Earth orbit and made the light speed jump to the warpgate feel free to move about the ship. Any questions?"

Tricia raised a hand to get his attention. "This may sound stupid but why are we using a warpgate? Wouldn't it be easier to do a light speed jump all the way there?"

Nathan smiled. "That's not stupid at all, and please ask all the questions you want." He paused, wishing Tricia could join him in the cockpit again. "We could jump all the way out there but solid hydrogen fuel is expensive and a lot of it gets eaten up if we make long jumps. That's why we generally do faster than light jumps in system and use the warpgates to travel the greater distances between stars. The toll we pay for using them is much cheaper."

She nodded and smiled. "Thanks. I didn't know that."

— ❬❭ —

"Mister Tanner, I'm getting the idea you don't want to be here," the police chief said from behind the desk. Eldridge sat across from him, holding Ari's hand in Don Bell's office in the Bad Rock police station. Chief Bell appeared to be about fifty, black and a little on the thick side but definitely not fat. He wore a neatly trimmed beard and close-cropped hair that grayed at the temples.

Eldridge shrugged his shoulders, fidgeting with the water bottle in his left hand. "Chief, it's not that I don't want to be here, it's just that I don't have much to tell you and I have a lot of work to do. And please, call me Eldridge."

The chief leaned back in his chair. "Okay, well you know, Eldridge, I just don't buy it. Someone broke into your site and stunned you. It was so bad that the shock knocked you out. Anyone else would be so eager to make a report I'd have to help them calm down, yet you're giving me the impression that talking to the police is the last thing you want to do. Why is that?"

Eldridge shifted in his chair. "Look, it's not like that," he said. "I just have a lot to do and really, what can you do? I have no idea who it was, and that's on me. I should have had the 'bots apprehend them and called you to arrest them. I screwed up."

Bell unscrewed the cap of his own bottle of water and took a sip. He had a case of the stuff in the mini-fridge behind his desk. "Now you see, making bad decisions like that is what really concerns me. You got the contract to clean up the mess Great Star Lines dropped on our settlement and you programmed all those 'bots to do the work for you. To my way of thinking, you're a smart guy. So I have to ask myself why someone like that would go out alone in the dark. I mean, you didn't even have to risk this pretty lady. You could have taken a 'bot with you."

Tanner licked his lips and shrugged. This was like being in the principal's office at school. "No one makes good decisions one hundred percent of the time, Chief."

"That's true, Eldridge, but I'm wondering if you knew who was out there and you just wanted to chase them off. Let me ask you a question; you ever have any dealings with a guy named Dodger since you arrived?"

Eldridge bit the inside of his lip before answering. "No, I don't think I know anyone by that name." He squeezed Ari's hand harder. "Who is that?"

"Oh, he's a local malcontent connected to the Syndicate. I hear he's into things like producing and selling drugs, extortion, protection rackets and the skin trade. You sure you've never met him?"

Eldridge slowly shook his head. "No, that doesn't sound like anyone we've met since we arrived. If he's such a bad guy shouldn't you arrest him?"

Chief Bell leveled his eyes at him. "Oh, I plan to but law enforcement resources here in Bad Rock are limited. We've got a dwindling tax base, you know? It's really just me, six deputies and a few part-timers for the whole city and even though we're a bit of a backwater, we still need evidence of a crime to arrest people. If someone came forward and filed a report about being shaken down for protection and could offer some proof of making payments to Dodger, it would be extremely helpful."

Eldridge's mouth went dry and he took a long pull on the bottle of water. The Chief needed help but he just wanted to finish this job and get away from Bad Rock. "Well, I hope someone like that comes through for you, Chief. Really, but I can't help you." Eldridge stood up and Ari rose beside him. "Now that you have the report let me know if you find anything."

Bell stood and held out his hand. Eldridge and Ari shook it in turn. "We will, Eldridge. You be careful out there. The wreck site is isolated but I'll see if I can't run some patrols your way and keep a better eye on things."

Eldridge held his gaze. "That's all right. I tasked a few more 'bots with guarding things at night. I'm sure we won't have any more trouble."

Bell smiled. "Yeah, probably. Anyway, you kids be safe out there. Even without people stunning you it's dangerous work you're doing."

"Thank you," Eldridge said. Ari waved goodbye and they walked through the station and out into the morning sunshine. They made their way to the float car they had driven into the city and got in.

"He knows," Ari said.

"What, that Dodger is shaking us down? He's probably just guessing."

Tanner punched in the location for their camp and the automatic driver pulled out into traffic. Ari turned to him. "Maybe we should tell him what he wants to know."

Eldridge shook his head and laughed. "I'm not going up against the Syndicate. If I talk to that guy, Dodger would have us buried out in the desert a few hours later."

"They're stealing from us, Eldridge."

He knew her thoughts were of her father and what he would do in this situation.

"Here's the problem, Ari. We're out here at the ass end of nowhere and the only law is Chief Bell and his half dozen deputies. If we file a complaint that the local Syndicate boss is shaking us down for protection money we're pretty much on our own. Do you think Dodger won't have some of those deputies on the payroll? You know those guys don't earn a lot so I bet at least some of them are on the take." He reached out and took her hand. "I want to keep you safe so if that means we let a guy like Dodger get his beak wet, then that's what we do."

She nodded with a sad look in her eyes. "I guess so."

They rode the rest of the way back in silence. When the float car pulled into the worksite Eldridge's eyes narrowed. He pointed to the wreck. "What the hell is that?"

Ari's followed his gesture. "Is that a truck?"

"Yeah," he said. "It's a tanker truck."

Eldridge steered the float car down the trail to the aft section of the *Athena Star* and brought it to a halt beside the silver tanker truck with red stripes. The name on the side of the tank read 'Schem Waste Recycling'.

He got out and approached the driver leaning against the cab. "What's going on here?"

"Who are you?" The man said.

"I'm running the job site and I didn't order any recycling."

The man pulled a mobi from his back pocket and swiped the screen. "Here's the work order. I'm supposed to pull out ten thousand liters of reactor coolant."

"What? Let me see that." Eldridge examined the work order and saw it matched what the driver said. "Have you started yet?"

"Nope. I just ran the hoses inside where those other fellas showed me."

"Well, hold up. There's been some kind of mistake."

Eldridge walked into the hold through the door near where he'd been attacked. He saw Turtle and Daryl lugging a hose toward one of the compartments with the coolant tanks.

"Hey, Turtle, what the hell is going on?"

The tall man with long greasy hair turned to him. "We're pumping the reactor coolant out of these tanks, Eldridge. What's the problem?"

"The problem is I didn't order it and I'm not paying for it."

Turtle nodded. "Well, Eldridge, you're right on both counts. Dodger ordered the recycling and he's paying for it. All you have to do is stand back and let us get this stuff out of your way."

Eldridge pulled up short. "What does Dodger want with reactor coolant?"

Turtle shrugged. "Dodger's business is his own, Eldridge. I just work for him. What do you care anyway? He's saving you the trouble of pumping this sludge out and paying for it. All you have to do is go on about your day."

Eldridge was tempted to do just that and then he turned and saw a disapproving look in Ari's eyes. He thought about her father, Roberto, and what he would do if a couple guys tried to strong arm him on his worksite. Then something else occurred to him. Whoever shocked him last night had been looking in the compartments where the tanks were located. A wave of anger came over him and he turned back to Turtle.

"This stops now. Get these hoses out of here and tell that driver to leave. I make the decisions here, Turtle, not Dodger. The coolant is nothing for you to worry about. Just go back to your pile and sort out your daily salvage."

Turtle stepped in close. "Eldridge, you want to be real careful about making a decision like this. Dodger wants it done."

"I don't," Tanner said. "If Dodger doesn't like it, tell him we had a deal and I'm all paid up. There's a limit to what I'll put up with. Now do as I say." He swallowed hard but held his ground.

"This isn't a good idea. You need to rethink what you're doing."

Eldridge reached down and picked up the large wrench being used to attach the pump hoses to the coolant tanks. He held it out to Turtle with menace in his eyes. "Let me ask you a question, which one of you knocked me out last night? I know it was one of you. No one else cares about what's in these tanks."

"Did something happen, Eldridge? We've been so busy working it's been hard to keep up on news."

Eldridge stepped closer. "You know what I'm talking about. I don't expect you to admit it, though. Guys like you always think you're being clever by playing dumb." He hefted the wrench. "I guess it doesn't really matter. What's done is done but I'll tell you this; if anyone comes after me or mine again, they'll wish they'd just stuck to the deal in place. Do you get me?"

Turtle nodded. "I get you, Eldridge."

"Then get this truck off my worksite. If Dodger has anything to say he knows where I am." Eldridge dropped the wrench and it hit the deck plates with a loud clang. He backed away from Turtle and Ari followed him outside. The truck driver was busy attaching the other end of the hose to his rig.

"There's been a mix up," Eldridge said. "You won't be taking a load out of here today. You need to pack up and leave."

"You sure?"

"Very."

The truck driver studied him for a moment and nodded. He started rolling up the hoses.

Ari slipped an arm around his waist as they walked back to the skimmer. "I'm proud of you," she said. "That took a lot of courage."

He put an arm around her shoulders and they slouched down on the hood of the float car. "Let's sit here a moment and make sure they do what I said. Turtle's the kind of guy who will tell you whatever you need to hear."

They watched as Turtle and Daryl emerged carrying coils of hoses and helped the driver stow them in the undercarriage of the tanker trailer. When they finished, Turtle threw a wave to Eldridge and the truck pulled away. Turtle and Daryl walked away on foot to their pile. Eldridge let out a breath.

"I get the feeling we're going to pay a price for what we just did," he said. "Dodger wants that reactor coolant for something and guys like him are driven by money. If we just cost him some, he'll have something to say about it."

Ari snuggled in. "We'd better figure out why he wants it and be prepared for when he calls."

Eldridge nodded. "Yeah."

Chapter 7

Jennifer "Scooter" McCabe watched as Truck 14 lined up over the bow of the *Corkscrew*. It aligned itself with the wishbone structure that served as the rail system for the automated barges bringing pieces of the *Athena Star* into space to be recycled. The immense recycling ship was comparable in size to the starliner being methodically reduced to tiny pieces. The command deck sat atop the tower structure that housed the engines, living quarters and machine shops. Forward of that structure the main pressure hull housed the grinders, sorters and cargo holds that stored the pieces of the starliner that had been brought up. The wishbone in front of that serviced the trucks from the surface.

The ship had started service half a century ago as a refinery vessel for mining the asteroid belt between Mars and Jupiter. It had only left that duty when the former owners went belly up during a downturn in the precious metals market and put it up for auction. Eldridge had gotten it for a song and retrofitted it to grind and sort starship pieces rather than ore.

Scooter had the watch on the command deck at the moment, so managing the docking procedure fell to her. She angled a camera to get a better view and saw the clamps lining the wishbone close on the barge's accessory mounts. Once locked in, the truck traveled toward the middle of the ship. The recyclable material would be unloaded into a large bay and sorted into different hoppers. She keyed the ship's intercom system.

"Charlie, Truck 14 just docked with a full load."

The speaker emitted static for a moment and then a deep voice answered her from two decks below. "Got it in sight. Thanks, Scooter."

She walked back over to the front of the command deck. A large observation port let her see the length of the empty wishbone and she sighed. The wishbone should be full, with at least five trucks waiting to be unloaded at any time. Eldridge and Ari should be calling up to harass her and ask when trucks would be unloaded and returned to pick up more material. Right now, all they had on board for unloading was Truck 14, and it would be emptied in less than thirty minutes.

The short mechanic adjusted the blue rag holding her blonde hair back. She had her grey jumpsuit rolled down to her waist displaying a green Crater Salvage t-shirt and when she caught a glimpse of herself in the reflection of a monitor she frowned and zipped it up. Being stuck up in orbit wasn't doing anything good for her waistline. Heavy boots thumped the deck as she moved and she still wore her tool belt. Normally, she ran the 'bot shop that kept their automated workforce running. A good effort by her and the other mechanic, Bobby, had gotten most of the machines working and planetside, so she volunteered for a watch on the command deck.

Not for the first time she wondered about the operation planetside. She had access to the same reports Eldridge did and knew they were behind schedule. The customer paid a bonus for finishing early but by her calculations there was no danger of Great Star Lines paying it. The soft feminine voice of the ship's artificial intelligence interrupted her musings.

"Scooter, there is an incoming message."

"From who Genie? The team on the planet?"

"No, from the ship approaching from port."

Scooter snapped her head around to see a gray ship with twin engines trimmed in blue hanging in space to the left of the command deck. Two people sat in the cockpit behind blue tinted glass. One of them, a man, made a movement on his control panel and a spotlight illuminated her through the portal. Scooter turned her head, slightly annoyed, and shaded her eyes.

"Genie, where did that ship come from and why didn't you warn me?"

"My apologies, Scooter. It simply appeared. It may have approached using an oblique angle from a negative attitude respective to the plane of the ecliptic. Our sensors would have difficulty detecting such an approach."

Scooter grimaced. "So they snuck up under us?" She crossed to the intercom and keyed it. "Charlie, Bobby, we've got some company up here. Another ship just dropped in on us. I'm going to see what they want and I'm going to leave this channel open." Both men acknowledged her message.

"Okay, Genie, put them on speaker and let's see what they want. Audio only." With only three of them on the *Corkscrew* she didn't need to advertise the fact she manned the command deck alone.

A smooth voice came out of the speaker. "This is the *Blue Moon Bandit* calling the salvage vessel *Corkscrew*. Do you copy?"

Scooter cleared her throat. "We copy. This is Scooter McCabe representing Crater Salvage. Please state your business."

"Miss McCabe, my name is Nathan Teller and I'm the owner of Milky Way Repossessions. We have authorization to repossess that vessel due to non-payment of the loan on her. I am requesting permission to come aboard to facilitate that repossession."

Scooter muted her microphone to the radio but left her connection to the intercom open. "Oh, what the hell is going on? Do either of you have any idea what he's talking about?"

Charlie and Bobby both responded in the negative.

"Don't let them on board," Charlie added. "Not until we talk to Eldridge."

She took a deep breath and keyed the radio mic again. "Mister Teller, have you spoken with Eldridge Tanner about this? He's the owner of Crater Salvage."

"Not yet, Miss McCabe. Obviously we'll want to speak with him. Is he available?"

"If you hold on a second I'll see if I can reach him." She muted the mic again. "Damn it!" She needed Eldridge. These guys may not be legitimate. This far out they could be pirates posing as repo agents to grab the *Corkscrew*. Eldridge had warned them that they were completely alone out here. Scooter considered her options and made up her mind.

"Charlie, is Truck 14 empty?"

"It will be in a few minutes. Why?"

"I'm going to let them talk to Eldridge."

— «» —

Marla smiled at Nathan. "She sounds scared."

"She looks scared," he said. "Maybe we shouldn't have come up on them like that."

"No, it's better to keep the element of surprise."

The young woman's voice came out of the speaker. "My boss would like to speak with you, Mr. Teller. Can you dock at the airlock aft of the command deck?"

"Affirmative. We'll be over in a few minutes." He closed the channel. "Marla, can you handle the docking? I'll grab Cole and Duncan and we'll get ready to board them."

"Sure. Don't let my husband get hurt."

He smiled. "No problem."

Tricia sat at the engineering station outside the cockpit and rose as he passed. She put a hand on his arm. "Hey, can I speak with you a moment?"

"Sure, what's up?"

"You're going over to the other ship?"

"Yeah, with Duncan and Cole."

"I'd like to go too."

He bit his lower lip and thought about it for a moment. "I don't know, it could be dangerous."

Her hand slid down his arm and gripped his. "All the more reason to bring a nurse along."

Nathan smiled, and his heart skipped a beat. She wanted to come with him, and the thought of things being dangerous didn't bother her. But it bothered him. He intertwined his fingers with hers.

"I'll tell you what. Let us go over and secure the ship and then I'll come get you."

She raised an eyebrow. "I can take care of myself, you know. I wouldn't be out here, with you, otherwise."

"I know," he said, looking into her eyes. "I just need to concentrate when I go over there and if I'm worried about you I can't do that."

"So you think I'm distracting?"

He felt heat rise in his face. "In a good way, yes."

Marla called from the cockpit. "We're just about ready, Nathan."

He squeezed her hand. "Give me a few minutes and I'll come get you, okay?"

She nodded. "All right, but don't get over there and forget me."

"I won't."

He reluctantly let go of her hand and moved aft. Duncan and Cole stood in the galley. Both wore shirts with the Milky Way Repo logo. Cole shrugged into his light leather jacket. Duncan zipped up a dark blue windbreaker with 'Repo Agent' emblazoned on the back in reflective silver letters and picked up a black duffel bag. Nathan felt the ship bump something and they all instinctively put a hand on the nearest bulkhead to steady themselves.

"What's in the bag?" Nathan said.

"A mobi with the command codes for the *Corkscrew* and some tools I might need," Duncan said. "I've also got a change of clothes in case I have to ride back aboard her."

"I don't think you'll need to," Nathan said as they moved to the airlock. "As big as she is, we should be able to fly her by automation." He nodded to Cole. "What about you? No overnight bag?"

"I'm definitely not staying aboard when I've got my own bunk here."

Nathan chuckled and checked the airlock controls. An indicator built into the bulkhead flipped from red to green showing a good seal between the two ships. Marla's voice came over the intercom a moment later and confirmed the reading. "You guys are good to go."

Nathan pushed the intercom button. "We're heading over. See you in a bit."

Duncan spun the airlock wheel and the heavy door opened. Next, the locking lever on the *Corkscrew* slid out of place and the door swung wide. Nathan led them across and held his hand out. "Nathan Teller."

"Scooter McCabe," she said, shaking his hand. "If you'll come with me I'll take you to Eldridge Tanner."

"Thank you," Nathan said and he gave Cole a look that told him to keep an eye out. Duncan closed the airlock door.

"I would have thought Mr. Tanner would meet us in person," Nathan said.

The diminutive young woman led them through tight corridors. "He normally would, sir, but he's tied up with something right now and can't get free. This ship is kind of old so something is always breaking down and we're so busy, Eldridge decided to take care of the problem himself." She glanced over her shoulder. "I saw your ship so you know what I'm talking about, right?"

Nathan took the jab in stride. People could be grouchy when you came to grab their ship.

"Besides," Scooter said, "I'm sure this all a misunderstanding. We're fully funded."

"Miss, we didn't fly ten and a half light years over a misunderstanding. You may want to pack your gear after you take us to your boss. We'll be leaving with your ship." *Chew on that smartass.*

"I see," she said. "Well I'm sure Eldridge will be able to straighten things out." She made a sharp turn and walked them down two flights of stairs. Their footsteps echoed hollowly in the metal stairwell, as they made their way toward a heavy door at the bottom. She punched in a code and the door slid open. "Eldridge is right through here. Watch your step."

Nathan stepped into the compartment and examined it. Long and empty, the space had the number 14 painted on two walls and smelled like a garbage hopper. His gaze turned back to Scooter just in time to see the little blonde sprinting for the door on the other side of the compartment.

He took off after her but Cole ran past him. The door slid open and she tumbled through the hatchway a half second before Cole could grab her. The door slammed shut and he managed to pull his hand back just in time to save it from the crushing force. Nathan pounded on the door and saw her breathing hard through the small portal.

"Scooter, this is very stupid. You need to open this door right now."

She stood on the other side with another man. He had brown hair and he high fived Scooter. She grinned back at Nathan and pushed the intercom button next to the door.

"Sorry about that," she said.

Nathan pushed the button on his side. "Open the door."

"Yeah, I can't do that," she said between deep breaths. "You said you wanted to talk to Eldridge and I've arranged that."

Nathan turned to Duncan. "Can you open this thing?"

Duncan had his bag on the floor and pulled a mobi out. "Of course. We have the command codes. She can have her fun now but I'll have us loose in no time." He tapped the screen on the mobi.

Nathan felt the compartment shift. "Did we just move?"

Duncan nodded. "I think so."

Nathan heard the whine of electric motors from inside the compartment. To his left a row of six jump seats folded down from the wall and he glanced back to the door. It suddenly dawned on him what was happening. He slapped the intercom button. "Don't do this, Scooter."

"You should strap in, sir. It isn't safe to go through re-entry unsecured."

Cole pulled his pistol from his shoulder holster and aimed it at the portal. "Open the door!"

Scooter's eyes grew wide and she moved to the right of the portal. Then her voice came through the intercom. "Don't do that! You're going to want the hull intact."

Nathan grabbed Duncan by the shoulder. "Can you stop her?"

The engineer swiped through the screens on his mobi. "Not before she cuts us loose."

"Damn it," he said. "I can't believe this is happening." He hated that someone had been clever enough to trap them. He noticed Cole standing at the hatch, beating on the pressure door. "Cole, put it away and grab a seat. I think we're going for a ride."

He turned to Nathan. "Are you serious?"

Nathan saw Scooter peeking through the portal again. He didn't see anything in her expression that changed his mind. "I think she's very serious."

Cole scrambled for a seat. Duncan grabbed his bag with the hand not holding the mobi and followed him. Nathan shot one last glance at the portal and felt the compartment jolt.

Scooter and the inner door slid upward and the gravity cut off as they slipped past the artificial gravity field of the *Corkscrew*. Nathan floated off the floor and put his hands up on the ceiling to steady himself. Duncan and Cole busied themselves with straps on the jump seats.

Nathan used the handholds mounted in the ceiling panels to make his way to the seats. Duncan grabbed one of his boots and pulled him down to a seat between himself and Cole. He strapped into the restraint harness.

"I think this is one of the automated barges they're using to haul up scrap from the planet," Duncan said as he clicked the last buckle into place.

Nathan nodded. "Probably the last one we saw come up when we approached." He put his hands in his face. "I can't believe we got caught like this."

"She moved a lot faster than I thought she would," Cole said. "From now on I think we should have a new rule that we go straight to the cockpit and take control of the ship instead of wandering around."

Nathan looked around for a control panel but didn't see one. "Yeah, I can see where that would be a good idea." The barge thrust forward and he felt a force like gravity push him into the seat. "Does anyone see a way to fly this thing?"

Duncan examined the walls across the empty space from their seats and then glanced above them. He reached up and pulled on a handle set into the wall above his seat. It tipped down and a panel opened with a mobi clipped to the door. He pulled it loose and activated it.

A display lit up and gave them telemetry of their movements. Duncan handed it to Nathan and the pilot examined it. "It looks like we're in a descent to the planet," he said with a frustrated edge to his voice. He tapped the screen but the suppressed controls didn't respond. "The controls are locked out."

"I guess we're lucky they remembered to give us air and heat," Duncan said.

"So we just sit back and enjoy the ride?" Cole said. "There's nothing we can do?"

Nathan handed the mobi back to Duncan. "I don't think so. I just hope we're going to some place on the planet that has people and not the middle of nowhere."

Cole had his mobi out but he had a disappointed look on his face. "I can't get a signal."

Duncan pulled his out. "These barges have thick walls because they take a beating. Once we get to the surface we should be able to call Marla for a pickup. Not that I want to make that call." He pointed to Nathan. "I'm going to let you explain how that girl dropped us to the surface."

The barge started to shudder and vibrate.

"If we survive re-entry in this heap I'll be glad to," Nathan said.

— «» —

Eldridge Tanner gaped at Scooter on the screen. "You did what?"

The young woman's face had a frightened look on it and she swallowed hard. "I didn't know what else to do. They came aboard and I got scared they would just take the ship and leave us in a lifeboat or something. The guy said we should pack our stuff. They wanted to talk to you so I dropped them."

"You lured them into a truck and just cut them loose?"

Her look got a little more defiant. "What's the big deal? We use the trucks to go back and forth to the planet all the time. We've all ridden in them."

"The big deal is that we all expect a rocky ride. Did you make sure they strapped in?"

"Oh yeah," she said, then reconsidered. "Well, I told them to buckle in. One of them had a gun so I didn't really go through the whole launch procedure. I just punched the button and let them go. They should be all right, don't you think?"

Tanner sat back in the chair and rubbed his face with both hands. He counted to ten before he said anything because he didn't want to be too harsh. "So worst case scenario I have three guys dropping down to me who may be riding re-entry like canned meat loose in the galley and best case I have three pissed off repo agents, one of whom is armed. Is that right?"

Scooter actually took a second to think about it. "Yes."

"What about their ship? Is it still docked?"

"Yes and their co-pilot is calling us."

Tanner shook his head. This day was screwed. "Okay, secure the ship and don't let anyone else aboard. Don't answer their calls. I'll take care of it."

"Okay."

"Oh, and Scooter?"

"Yes?"

"We're going to talk about this later."

She nodded. "Yeah, I kinda figured."

He closed the channel and stepped out from under the canopy that covered his workspace. A rumble in the sky attracted his attention. He shaded his eyes with a hand and saw a truck dropping down. It angled itself away from him and he groaned. Turtle and Daryl's pile was the only thing in that direction. He raced for his float bike and remembered Ari had it down at the *Athena Star* while she configured a crew of 'bots. The service vehicle sat nearby, though. He mounted up and started moving toward Pile 2.

—— «» ——

Nathan felt the landing thrusters fire and the barge settled roughly to the ground. He swallowed and his ears popped. Cole groaned beside him and retched. Nathan put a hand on his shoulder and squeezed it. "It's okay, we're down now."

Cole had become airsick as they came through the upper atmosphere. Thankfully, there had been gravity when he lost control so the mess landed on the floor and wall beside him and instead of floating around the interior of the barge.

"Remember this the next time you make fun of my flying," Nathan said.

Cole shot him the finger, unable to speak at the moment.

Nathan popped his restraints and stood up. Duncan and Cole followed him to the doors and the engineer found a control panel. Nathan nodded and the large doors at the end of the barge swung open. Morning sunshine flooded the interior of the barge and they exited. Nathan shaded his eyes and saw an enormous pile of scrap metal with several 'bots working on it.

Two guys sitting on chairs playing cards gawked at them in surprise. The taller of the two with long, greasy hair under a cap stood up. "Who the hell are you?"

Cole lurched forward. "If you're Eldridge Tanner I'm the guy that's going to kick your ass."

The guy put his hands up. "Hold on there, bud. I ain't Eldridge."

Nathan put a hand on Cole to restrain him. "Where can we find Tanner?"

"He's up at the main camp. Who are you guys?"

Nathan pulled out a plastic business card and approached the man. "We're repo agents here to secure the *Corkscrew*. I'd love to go through all the introductions but seeing as how we were just dropped to this shit-hole against our will I'm just going to ask you to find me Eldridge Tanner."

The second man stepped up beside his friend and pointed over Nathan's shoulder. "That's him right there."

They turned to look and saw a young black man pulling up in some kind of four wheeled maintenance truck dragging a trailer. He didn't look happy as he parked and dismounted. "Are you Teller?"

Nathan took a few steps toward him. "Yeah. Are you Eldridge Tanner?"

"Yeah, look I'm sorry. Scooter shouldn't have done this." He backed up suddenly as Nathan advanced on him. "Hey, whoa, whoa, she made a mistake, come on."

Nathan stood in front of him, fist clenched. He took a deep breath and let it out slowly as his fist relaxed. "We could have been killed in that thing," he said, pointing to the barge.

"Well, I don't know about killed," Tanner said. "I mean, we use them all the time to go back and forth to the ship." He waved his hands in front of him. "You know what? It doesn't matter. Scooter shouldn't have locked you in there and shot you down here. Believe me, she will be reprimanded. I'm very sorry that happened."

Nathan took another deep breath and stepped back. He reached into his jacket and pulled out a small mobi. He swiped through a couple screens until he found what he wanted and held it out to Tanner.

"We're here for your ship. Failure to pay the loan has resulted in repossession by the note holder. I expect your full cooperation in this matter." Nathan glared at the younger man.

Tanner took the mobi and reviewed the documents. "This can't be right. There's no reason to be behind on our payments. We invoice Great Star Line every month so our cash flow is solid. The bank must have made a mistake."

"Yeah, we keep hearing that. Do you have a guy named Lewis Mairn working for you back on Earth?"

"Yes," Tanner said. "He's our accountant and office manager. He runs the business end of things."

Nathan grunted. "Well, I don't think he's very good at his job."

Tanner opened his mouth to say something but then closed it. Nathan recognized the look. He'd seen it many times before from people who didn't know how the money flowed and were surprised when the roof fell in.

He remembered the two guys standing behind them but Cole had an eye on them. Nathan realized the situation needed to deescalate.

"Do you have some place we can talk in private?"

Tanner nodded and rubbed his hand over his beard. "Yeah, if you'll get on the truck we can go back to base camp."

"All right," Nathan said. "But that's the only place we'd better be going. If I see anything hinky, things could escalate and you don't want that."

Tanner held up a hand. "No, we're all good. Let's just go straighten this out."

They moved to mount up and Cole stooped to pick something up and he stuffed it in his pocket. He climbed onto the back of the maintenance vehicle, taking a rear facing seat next to Duncan. Nathan sat next to Tanner up front.

Nathan twisted around and tapped Duncan on the shoulder. "Why don't you call Marla and tell her where we are."

"Because that's your job."

Nathan smiled. "I changed my mind. Privilege of being the boss."

"I guess," Duncan said. "Must be nice," he got his mobi out. "Do you want her to come get us?"

"Not yet. Just tell her to hold tight and we'll let her know."

Cole turned. "Just so you know, Nathan, I'm not flying in one of those barges again. I'll build a house and live here before that happens."

Nathan smiled. "No worries, Cole. When the time comes to leave we'll be on our own ship."

The vehicle moved slowly up the trail and Nathan noticed Tanner trying to avoid the ruts. The operation was impressive from what he could see. The *Athena Star* appeared more intact than he would have expected after a crash. The automated system had done a decent job of getting it down. Given what he, Duncan and Cole had just experienced, he had a pretty good idea of what that re-entry must have been like.

More 'bots roamed the site than he remembered seeing anywhere else outside of a manufacturing facility. They passed another pile where a gray haired man in overalls directed 'bots that cut and carried pieces of scrap. Tanner had quite an operation.

The utility truck pulled up next to a large canopy that provided cover to a camp stove, tables and a workbench. They got off the maintenance vehicle and Tanner offered them a seat at the largest table. He moved a few things out of the way and offered them something to drink. All three accepted and Tanner pulled a pitcher of something from the small fridge near the camp stove.

"All I've got is powdered orange drink. There's no alcohol allowed in camp. Is that all right?"

"As long as it tastes better than vomit," Cole said. He turned and spit into the dirt.

"Hey, dude, I live here," Tanner said as he poured. "Spit somewhere else."

"I didn't ask to be here," Cole said, throwing him the stink eye as he took a drink.

Tanner nodded and blew out a breath. "Yeah, okay. Again, I'm very sorry about Scooter doing that. She should have contacted me so we could work something out. There's only three of them up there and she said you scared her," he said pointing at Nathan.

"Well, it can be scary when we show up." He shrugged. "Now, I'd like this to go as smoothly as possible but you need to understand, we have a job to do and we're going to do it. If there are problems between you and the bank, you'll have to deal with them yourself."

Disappointment crossed Tanner's face. "That's the way it is, huh?"

Nathan nodded. "Yeah."

Things grew uncomfortably quiet for a moment and Tanner saw him checking out the *Athena Star.* "Would you like to have a look at the wreck? It's really something."

Nathan glanced at Duncan who gave a subtle nod with his head. "Yeah, I suppose a look around wouldn't hurt."

"Okay," Tanner said. "We'll have some lunch and then go on a tour."

Nathan nodded. "Yeah, okay."

Chapter 8

"Are you sure you don't want us to come get you right now?" Marla said as she stared out the cockpit window at the *Corkscrew*. They remained docked at the airlock where Nathan, Cole and Duncan had gone aboard. She turned back to the monitor with Duncan's face.

"No," he said over the comm channel. "Nathan wants to scope things out here on the ground and talk with this Tanner kid. We're not in any danger, so you guys can just sit tight."

Marla's lips curled in a slight smile. "Oh, *Nathan* wants to scope things out? You mean like that wreck? Not you?"

"Well, maybe I wouldn't mind…"

"I can't believe you guys got nabbed and dropped down there."

Duncan shook his head. "Yeah, I'm never going to hear the end of that, am I?"

"Nope."

"Okay, well, it looks like we're sitting down now. I'll check in a little later."

"See you soon, baby. Love you"

He smiled. "Love you, too."

From her vantage point she really couldn't see anything except dull gray hull plates and one small portal of the salvage vessel. She took off her headset, grabbed her coffee mug and walked back into the galley.

Tricia sat at a table. "Is everything okay?"

"More or less," Marla said. She reached over to the intercom mounted on the bulkhead and opened a channel to the ship. "Richie, can you come to the galley?" Marla grabbed some bread and dried tomatoes and searched the fridge for the spread and salami. "They're just idiots." She put the sandwich together and set it on a plate.

Richie walked in. "What's up? The guys never came back."

"There's been a bit of a wrinkle." She filled them in with what Duncan had told her.

Richie grinned. "You see, the tricky part about something like this is knowing where the line is between giving them crap about it and when to stop giving them crap about it," Richie said. "I'm not sure I'll know where to stop."

"Well, if you find Cole stuffing you in an airlock that leads to empty space you'll know you've gone too far." Marla refilled her stainless-steel travel mug with coffee and twisted the lid on. "They want us to stay docked with the *Corkscrew* and wait for their call."

"Just hang out up here with two lovely ladies? I can handle that."

"The only thing you'll be handling is the door, Richie. Stay on the airlock and keep it secured. I don't want anyone getting aboard."

"No problem. It's locked up tight now and I'll plant myself there." The young man grabbed a mug of coffee for himself and made for the airlock.

"Is there anything to worry about?" Tricia said. "Are we in some kind of danger?"

"No," Marla said, shaking her head and she gestured for Tricia to follow her back to the cockpit. Both brought their coffee and food. "This is just an inconvenience. Sometimes the people having their ships repossessed get a little cute. It's really no big deal. Did you get a chance to set up the infirmary?"

"Yeah, we're all set. There's some decent equipment in there already and well organized. Did you do that?"

Marla sat down in the co-pilot's seat and pointed at Nathan's pilot seat for Tricia. The controls at Nathan's station sat dark and inactive. "Yeah, I usually end up handling any injuries. I have a little first aid training and if you let these guys treat themselves it's a disaster. They think you can just walk off any injury that doesn't involve amputation. A few months ago, Duncan sliced a finger down to the bone on a motor head from one of the small tractors we have on board. I caught him back there wrapping it in electrical tape with the plan that he would just get back to work. It took everything I had to make him sit still for the ninety minutes the tissue generator needed to knit it back together. They can be ridiculous."

Tricia laughed. "I know what you mean. When I worked in an emergency room we had a guy come in with a scalp laceration and a huge purple goose egg on his forehead. He asked how long it would take to get him patched up because he had a game to go to that night."

Marla chuckled and took a bite of her sandwich. She chewed slowly and swallowed before asking, "What do you think about Nathan?"

Tricia almost choked on her coffee. "Uh, he's nice." Marla raised an eyebrow. Tricia gave a small smile. "I'm not sure how to answer that question."

"So, does that mean nothing's happened?"

"No, nothing's happened. I've only known him a few days. He does have a way about him, though." Tricia blushed. "I'd like to know him better, if that's what you mean."

"I thought so." Marla grinned.

"But I don't date bosses."

Marla took a sip from her travel mug. "Maybe when you get home, when he's not your boss anymore, you can go out with him then."

"When he called and offered me this job I was expecting an invitation to dinner so he kind of blindsided me. I mean, it seems like he wants to go out, but that would be odd if I'm working for him."

Marla sighed. "He can be kind of lame when it comes to personal relationships. Don't get me wrong, he's a good guy, he really is, but he can just be kind of awkward."

"Well, maybe I'll find out. This is probably a one-off job anyway until I find something more permanent."

Marla nodded and turned her gaze back to the *Corkscrew*. Someone stood watching them from the one small portal she could see. Whoever it was, they had a mobi in their hand and were talking to someone.

—— «»» ——

"That's right," Charlie said to Turtle. The lanky loadmaster watched the *Blue Moon Bandit* from a small portal. "I'm looking right at their ship. They're still docked up here. There's a couple of women in the cockpit having a drink and staring at us. They haven't gone anywhere."

Turtle's voice crackled over the mobi. The connection kind of sucked because Tanner had bought cheap equipment. "Say that again."

Turtle's voice was louder this time, as if sheer volume would help the crappy signal reach him. "I said, let us know if they undock and head our way."

Charlie took advantage of their conversation being audio only and aimed a middle finger planetside in the general direction of where he thought Turtle might be. "Yeah, sure, I'll be in touch if they move." He ended the call and shook his head. These Syndicate guys were kind of a pain in the ass, even if they were paying him five hundred credits a month to be their eyes and ears on the *Corkscrew*.

—— «»» ——

"Are you sure that guy can be trusted?" Dodger said. "He sounds like he doesn't give a shit about anything."

Turtle nodded and hoped he had judged Charlie right. He didn't need someone else he vouched for to turn out to be a failure like Bone Daddy. Dodger wasn't book smart but the sonofabitch could be clever. People underestimated him at their own peril. "When I approached him, he bit right away. I got the feeling that he needed the extra money."

He sat in Dodger's office at the strip club along with Morris, Dodger's operations guy. Turtle had jumped in his float truck and hauled ass over as soon as he and Daryl figured out who had stumbled off Truck 14 when it landed.

Dodger just stared at him and picked up another Diamond K crystal from the small plastic envelope in front of him. His red, watery eyes bore into him. Turtle figured if he kept chewing that stuff like a fat kid eating candy there would soon be room for everyone to advance in the organization. It didn't seem like the boss had much left in the way of molars.

"Three of them came off the truck?" Dodger said.

Turtle nodded. "That's right and a little worse for wear because of their ride down. Do you want me to take a few guys with me when I go back? Right now, it's just me and Daryl."

Dodger considered it for a moment and took the opportunity to grind another crystal into dust and get just a little higher. "No, not yet. I'd like to know a little more about why these repo assholes are here. Just go back and keep your ears open." He turned to the thick little guy sitting in a chair in the corner. "Hey, Morris, do we still have that drone?"

"Sure."

"That kid will fly it for us?"

"My nephew, Cheech? Sure, he'll do it. He used to fly them in the service."

"Okay, give him a call and get it ready. We can see and hear things on the ground with it, right? Without anyone seeing it?"

"No problem, Dodger. We'll be twenty thousand meters up looking down at them and hear every word they say without them seeing us. We don't have any armament, though. That's still on order."

Turtle knew that Cheech had been discharged from the military earlier in the year and had shown up at his uncle's place with the drone, cackling madly about stealing the damn thing. Dodger had been itching to use it ever since. The paranoia from using so much product made him want to spy on everyone.

"That's okay," Dodger said. "If we need to shoot anyone we'll do it on the ground with the guys." He got silent for a moment and picked up another crystal. The stupid bastard made a show out of putting it in his mouth and snapping down loudly on it. "We can take control of those 'bots the kid's got tearing that ship apart, right? Jonesy hacked them is what you said."

Morris' round head bobbed up and down. "He said the security on those things is a joke. We can march them off a cliff if you want."

"No, I just got a little plan rolling around in my head," his hands made swirling motions on either side of his dome, emphasizing the point, "in case these repo guys turn out to be anything other than what they say they are."

Turtle had his own thoughts about some of Dodger's crew. In his opinion, they were mostly cut rate morons in need of a second chance after screwing up somewhere else. Dodger seemed to be slowly fading to a shadow of his former self because he kept chewing the product. Morris, the slob, sat in this club all day watching holographic T&A while he told the other idiots what to do. Jonesy may have hacked into the 'bots Tanner had working the wreck site, but Turtle doubted it was anywhere near as complex as the guy said. Turtle had listened to him brag about it for a week after he'd accomplished it.

They worked a couple hours a day and spent the rest of their time sitting here on bar stools letting their asses get fat while guys like him and Daryl got things done. He figured, he just had to bide his time and wait for his opportunity. He stood up.

"I'm going to get back, okay, Dodger? Keep an eye on things with Daryl." He pulled his dirty cap over his greasy hair.

"Yeah, get out of here, Turtle. Let us know if your contact on that ship calls you."

"Will do." Turtle moved to the door and pulled it open.

"Hey, Turtle."

He turned back to see Dodger holding up the plastic business card Nathan had presented him with. "Good catch."

"Thanks, boss." He walked out and shut the door behind him, letting out the breath he'd been holding.

—— ‹‹ ›› ——

Nathan and Duncan sat near the fire pit watching the flames dance in the cool air. Cole stood behind them. "So this is what we're doing, Nathan?" he said. "We're staying for lunch?"

The captain shrugged "They invited us. Most people would have been slinging wrenches at us by now instead of feeding us."

"They kidnapped us, remember?"

Nathan shrugged. "Again, it's not as bad as it could have been."

Cole sat down beside him. "What's going on here? Why haven't we grabbed the *Corkscrew* and started for home?"

Nathan turned back toward the canopy. Tanner and his girlfriend helped the kitchen 'bot with the meal. He turned back to Cole and waved for Duncan to lean in closer.

"We're staying for lunch for a couple reasons. First, the guy asked to talk with us and treated us well."

"Since when do we care about sob stories, Nathan? Every job we go out on some joker has a reason for not paying his bills. Do we care? I thought we show up, grab the ship and leave."

Nathan nodded. "That is the job but I also wanted to see that," he said, pointing to the wrecked starliner. "I have never seen anything that big survive an impact that intact. Aren't you a little curious to take a look around?"

"I am," Duncan said.

Cole shook his head. "I'm not. Not really. I mean, if you want to see wrecked starships, couldn't we do that back home at any salvage yard?"

Duncan shook his head and pointed to the wreck. "Not like that you can't. I mean, just look at the size of it. By all rights that thing should be nothing more than a few million pieces spread out across a hundred square kilometers."

Cole leaned back. "Nathan, what if this guy has a good story? What if he starts spinning a tale that tugs on your heart strings? Do we go home without the ship?"

"Of course not. We have a job to do and we'll do it."

"Hey guys, lunch is ready," Eldridge called from under the canopy. Nathan stood and saw the table set. He got up and Cole and Duncan followed him. Tanner pointed to the bench on one side of the table and the three of them sat down. The kitchen 'bot loaded up their plates and they passed them down.

"Look, Captain Teller, I appreciate you sticking around. After we eat we can take a look at the wreck. It's really something."

Nathan swallowed some of the beans and rice the 'bot had prepared. "Look, Eldridge, we appreciate lunch and that you feel bad about what your crew did, but you understand we have a job to do. I have to seize your ship and return it to Earth."

"That's bullshit," Ari said. Tanner had introduced her when she returned from working about half an hour ago. "We aren't behind on our payments."

"The bank says you are."

"Then the bank is wrong and you're *un idiota* for believing them."

Tanner reached over and gave her hand a squeeze. "Ari, that's not helping."

"Eldridge, we're sitting here eating with the people who are going to take our livelihood. If that ship goes back to Earth, we have to straighten out some stupid mistake that will cost us weeks and thousands of credits. We don't have enough of either to waste."

Nathan set his fork down. "Maybe this is a mistake." An uncomfortable silence followed. "Duncan, I think you should call Marla and have her come pick us up."

Duncan set down a piece of cornbread. "Too bad."

"Wait a minute," Ari said. She stood up quickly, almost tripping over the bench. "Do you have any idea how much effort has gone into this job? Eldridge had the vision for putting all this together."

Nathan held up a hand. "Miss, we really—"

She slammed a hand down on the table. "No, you listen to me. He worked hard for my father in his scrap yard and he learned his trade. My dad is an incredibly difficult man to work for and this man," she pointed at Eldridge, "never complained and never said a word back to him. All he ever did was bust his ass so he could learn. Then he did all this." She spread her arms wide and circled the table until she stood behind Tanner.

"Do you have any idea how complex an operation like this is? To come up with the idea, make the bid, arrange the financing and get all the pieces to fit? We didn't do all of this just so you could show up and take our ship. Do you have any idea how hard it is to run your own business? Do you have any idea how much effort goes into keeping the creditors at bay, to keep people paid when you don't have enough for yourself?"

Nathan nodded. That point stuck.

Ari sat down on the bench, smoldering eyes burning into Nathan's as she held his gaze. Tanner put an arm around her and she picked up her cup to take a drink.

Silence descended on the table. Duncan and Cole wouldn't say anything, he knew, until he spoke. He rubbed his eyes and considered that all he had at the moment was his ship, this single job at the ass end of nowhere, and a dry bank account. If he didn't get another job lined up immediately after this one he didn't know if he would ever fly again. He looked at Ari and Eldridge and they stared back at him. The earnestness in their eyes became too much for him to take and he dropped his head.

Until he and his crew had shown up they had been utterly convinced that hard work and good planning would be everything they needed to succeed. Despite all that, though, something had gone wrong and now the universe had dropped a wrench in the works. But that's what the universe did, right? As soon as you had things figured out, it found a way to screw everything up.

"Ms. Macias, why don't you show us around the wreck?" He said. "I think we'd like to see it."

Chapter 9

Dodger exited a float car outside a group of abandoned buildings on the south side of Bad Rock. A sign above the entryway of one of them read 'Digman Commons'. Empty warehouses lined the street across the way, silently testifying to a once thriving economy.

His footsteps echoed hollowly on the pavement as he approached the apartment building. One of the two guards with him sprinted up the steps and pulled the door open. He entered the lobby and nodded at the man standing across the room near an inner door. The bodyguard pulled that open and he followed a dimly lit hallway past empty apartments with doors hanging half open. Another door stood at the end of the corridor. A dirty sign mounted to the right of it identified the room beyond as the Digman Commons recreation room. Dodger pulled out his mobi and texted a message. A few seconds later, the sound of a heavy magnetic lock disengaging broke the silence and the thick steel door swung wide.

Once inside the room, Dodger took a mask from a hook next to the entrance and pulled it over his head. The enormous room had been enlarged, leaving only a few structural supports to hold up the ceiling. Dozens of women sat at sturdy tables doing various activities.

Dodger studied everyone in the room to make sure the operation was running as planned. To his right, tanks held the raw chemicals broken down into their needed components for processing. Next, the chemists added necessary ingredients and processed the mixture in large batches. After cooling in large refrigeration units, the resulting product got passed to the women in black gas masks sitting at the tables.

They weighed it and bagged it in packages stamped with the 'Diamond K' label. Finally, burly men took the packages, bundled them and prepared them for shipment.

Right now, everyone in the room stood still.

A group of men gathered around a woman on the floor. She made a horrible, squabbling sound and one hand clawed at her throat. The lead chemist hurried to Dodger's side as soon as he spotted him standing in the doorway.

"What's going on?" Dodger said, his voice muffled by the mask.

"It appears that her mask malfunctioned," the tall, thin chemist in the blue smock said. Sweat shone on his bald head and he rubbed a hand over his head. "She got a lungful of potassium hydroxide."

Dodger stared at him. "How? The masks are just supposed to be a precaution."

"A hose broke on the transfer switch. We locked it down and vented the room but she either didn't have her mask on correctly or it was faulty. She took a breath and collapsed."

"Will she survive?"

The chemist raised his eyebrows. "Maybe. She certainly has burns in her esophagus. The medics are trying to stabilize her."

The strangled cries of the woman drew his gaze to her again. Then he noticed the women sitting idle at the packing tables. "Get her out of here and treat her somewhere else. I don't want production down any longer than necessary." He pointed to the women at the tables. "They're going to be useless if they keep listening to that or see her die. We have orders to get out."

The chemist nodded his head. "Of course. Sorry, sir, I'll take care of it right away." He moved to the men helping the woman and shouted at them. One of the men scooped her up and carried her toward the door. Dodger stepped aside as the man passed and the door shut.

He nodded toward the packing tables. The man got the message and stepped in front of the women. "Okay, the excitement is over. Leeann is being checked by the medics. Keep your masks on and get back to work. We still have to make quota and if that means staying late then that's what we'll do." The women went back to work and the chemist moved back to Dodger.

"We'll have this shipment ready on time, don't worry." The man seemed eager to please, Dodger saw, which didn't surprise him. Six months ago, his predecessor had started using the product and missing quotas. After the third such instance, the man had disappeared and Terrence had been promoted. They hadn't missed a quota or a shipping appointment since.

"I have faith in you. Tell me, have you given any thought to our last conversation?"

"About the additional ten thousand liters of coolant? Yes. You see, large ships like the *Athena Star* use sodium-potassium alloy as a reactor coolant so we can certainly use it to manufacture our product. Will you have it soon?"

"Yes, I expected it already but we had a delay. I think it will be tomorrow."

Terrence nodded. "Good." He paused a moment. "You know, that's highly volatile stuff. As discussed, we will have to use some special precautions when we break it down to the components we need."

Dodger raised an eyebrow. "What kind of precautions?"

"I don't want it in here. It represents a danger to the lab so I've had a few of the men commandeer the warehouse across the street and moved some equipment over there." He stopped, and began sweating. "I thought that would be prudent."

Dodger nodded slowly and put a hand on his shoulder. "Good idea. I knew I made a good choice with you." He squeezed the shoulder and dropped his hand. "I'll have that coolant for you soon."

Terrence nodded and went back to work.

— «» —

The small group dismounted from the pair of maintenance vehicles Eldridge and Ari drove and they led Nathan, Duncan and Cole toward the *Athena Star.* Nathan stood still and stared up at the wrecked vessel in awe. Duncan stood beside him and let out a low whistle.

"This thing should be smoking little bits spread all over the hemisphere," the engineer said. "It has no right to be sitting here like this."

Nathan nodded in agreement. He had never seen anything this large enter an atmosphere in a controlled crash and hang together. "I'm guessing the Great Star Line developed one hell of a crash recovery program. I mean, this never, ever happens but if it does, you don't want to pay out death benefits for thousands of passengers."

Duncan pointed to the metal above the cargo bay door. "Look at those ripples in the hull. You see how they compact?" Nathan saw deformations in the plating. "That's the heat of re-entry and the impact with the ground. I wonder what the hull is made of?"

"They use some exotic alloys, let me tell you," Eldridge said. "We've run into stuff like Boron-carbide and some truly crazy ceramic underlayment. The 'bots needed modified cutting tools like purpose built demolition circular saw blades and plasma torches. We thought we had things planned out pretty well but we've been going through them at a much higher rate than we figured. I'm getting shipments in every two weeks to keep up with consumption."

Duncan nodded and rested a hand on the hull. "Didn't stop the bow from collapsing, though." He stepped aside as a 'bot walked by and entered the cargo bay.

Eldridge gestured to the open door. "Why don't we go inside? It's even more impressive."

"I'll bet," Cole said.

The group walked inside but Nathan caught Cole by the arm. "What's up?"

"I don't understand what we're doing here, Nathan. You guys want to look at this wreck? We should be up in orbit prepping the *Corkscrew* for the journey home."

Nathan shrugged. "This is interesting and it's not something you're likely to see again. What are you in such a hurry for?"

"I have a life back home." He grinned. "I'd like to see Kimiyo. I thought the plan was we were going to jump out here, grab the ship and go home, just like always. Now we're sitting around eating lunch with the targets and listening to their sob stories."

Nathan rubbed a hand over his stubbly chin. It had been a long day. "I don't know what to say, Cole. I'm just playing this by ear. I need you to be cool. Just relax and trust me."

Cole's eyes narrowed. "Whatever is going on with them, I just don't care. They didn't pay and we're here to grab their ship. Why aren't we doing that?"

Nathan stepped closer. "Because I'm the boss and I say so. Get it together and calm down."

Cole backed off and held his hands up. "Maybe we should catch up. Duncan will never come out if him and Eldridge start talking about engineering specs."

"Yeah," Nathan said. "Let's do that."

They walked inside the cargo bay and Nathan saw Eldridge had the place lit up with a couple of construction lights mounted on stands. The noise from the 'bots scampering around the outer hull echoed through the large area. Eldridge, Duncan and Ari stood in the center of the compartment. The salvage man pointed to something near the ceiling. Ari watched him but her eyes locked on Nathan's as soon as he and Cole got close. He got a protective vibe from her.

"What's back there?" Duncan said, pointing to the compartments near the rear of the bay.

Eldridge and Ari stole a look at each other before he answered. "Reactor coolant storage tanks."

The group drifted back toward the compartments and Eldridge opened the door of the one on the left. "Came down intact, as you can see."

"If it hadn't you'd have one hell of a toxic mess to clean up," Duncan said. He ran a hand over the tanks and checked the pressure gauges. "This is classified as hazardous material, you know that right? You have to pump this out and make sure the disposal is documented."

Eldridge threw a sideways glance to Ari before answering, Nathan noticed. "Yeah, that's our understanding. Luckily there are a couple contractors in town who can take care of it for us. Why don't we move outside where it isn't so hot and noisy?" The group moved out of the compartment and walked back through the cargo bay.

"Hey, Duncan can I ask you a question?" Eldridge said. "You obviously know as much about this as I do. Why do we have to go through the trouble and expense of having the recycling documented? Most of this other stuff vanishes without anyone knowing what happens to it."

"Because if you didn't document it there wouldn't be a paper trail," Cole said. "There wouldn't be any way to trace what happened to it."

"Why is that so important?"

Cole answered. "It's important because you can make some pretty serious drugs with it."

"Like what?"

Cole dug into his pocket and extracted a plastic envelope. "Like everyone's favorite speed variant of choice, Diamond K." He held the envelope up for everyone to see the stamp on it. "I found this on your worksite when we first landed and ran into those two guys playing cards."

Nathan took the envelope from him and examined it. "This is the same junk Bone Daddy used back on Mars." His eyes zeroed in on Eldridge. "What's going on? Are you guys in the drug trade?"

Eldridge held his hands up. "We've never seen that before."

"Any idea who is using?" Cole said. "I thought you ran a clean worksite."

"I don't like what you're implying," Ari said, stepping up to Cole. "We work honest. Whatever that stuff is, it's got nothing to do with us."

Cole smiled. "And yet here it is on your site."

"You can leave any time you like," she said. "I'm not going to stand here and be accused of making drugs. We didn't even know you could use reactor coolant for that until you said so."

"Mmm-hmm."

Eldridge stepped up and put a hand on Ari. "Come on, honey. No one is saying that."

"He is," she said. "Just look at him. He's got cop eyes."

"Cole, calm down. We don't know what's going on here," Nathan said.

Cole nodded but didn't take his eyes from Ari. "Sure, Nathan. Sorry, Ari. Could be anyone." He turned to go back to the maintenance vehicles but she put a hand on his shoulder.

"Hold on," she said. "You want to know who did this? There's this local mob boss wannabe shaking us down."

"Ari," Eldridge said. "No, we aren't talking about this. Not now."

"Who cares, Eldridge? We pay up. Dodger's got no beef with us."

"Ari, no."

Nathan turned and took a step toward Ari. "Who is Dodger?"

She turned to Eldridge. He sighed, clearly defeated and took a look around. Confident it was them and the 'bots, he spoke. "Like Ari said, he's just some hood. He's shaking us down for some positions and some salvage. It's just the cost of doing business out here."

"I don't understand," Nathan said. "Shaking you down for positions?"

"We're using 'bots for the demolition and the local unions aren't very happy about it. The steelworkers and construction unions wanted to picket us but Dodger stepped in. We pay him for ten positions on my crew and give him one ton of salvage every day. Those two guys you met when you stepped off the truck work for him. They show up and don't do much except siphon off Dodger's ton of salvage. For all that he keeps the union guys off our backs."

Cole turned to Nathan. "That's some pretty basic organized crime. I think they teach that in goon school on the first day."

"Well, it's working," Eldridge said. "We haven't had any trouble from the unions. As for the drugs, I have no idea but it wouldn't surprise me if Dodger's involved. He's always wired up when we meet with him."

Nathan turned the plastic envelope over in his hands and thought about the thousands of similar ones he had, just like it, back home in his apartment.

"We've seen this before. On our last job we repossessed a starship from a band. These things littered the interior."

Eldridge shrugged his shoulders. "I don't know anything about that but if Dodger is making the stuff he's probably selling it. In fact, he sent a tanker truck out here for free to pump out those storage tanks. We didn't know why at the time, but now I guess we know why he wanted the coolant."

"That's probably why you got knocked out, too," Ari said. "You probably caught Turtle and Daryl out here checking the tanks."

Nathan cocked his head. "They assaulted you?"

"It's nothing, don't worry about it."

Ari threw her hands up and started walking around the group. "Stop saying that," she said, her voice rising. "Those two stunned you for doing your job. I'm sick of you blowing it off. Getting beat up is not the cost of doing business." She put her arms around him. "Don't you understand? You can't let this keep going on. Dodger is still going to want the coolant in those tanks and the next time he won't do anything as nice as send a truck."

Eldridge hugged her back. "Baby, we can't start a war out here. I have to play by their rules and keep the peace so we can do our job and get paid."

"That's a very dangerous path you're going down," Nathan said. "Guys like Dodger are everywhere. This isn't the last time you'll have to deal with a man who wants a piece of your hard work for the privilege of leaving you alone. There is always someone with their hand out. Dodger will just suck you dry until the job is done or until you go broke and leave. Then he'll start over with the next guy who comes out here to finish the job. You have to stand up to them."

Eldridge broke free of Ari's embrace and waved his arms wide, gesturing at the worksite. "Look around, Teller. I'm a month behind on my first job, I can barely keep my equipment running, I'm in debt up to my eyeballs and I've got a repo man in front of me who is going to take my ship. Do you really think I'm in any position to fight off gangsters?" he paused for a moment and took a deep breath. "Even if I do, I'll have to deal with the unions."

Nathan nodded. "Yeah, you've got yourself some problems, no doubt about that. The thing is, being in business for yourself is like that. Just one problem after another. There's no manual for what you're doing here just like there isn't one for what we do. That's why you'll be successful, though. If you find a niche and do something well, the credits will roll in."

The salvager leaned back against a piece of the scrapped hull. "Look, I appreciate what you're saying but I really think we have this under control. I'm not like you. I can't just get in my ship and fly off to the next job. I can't come and go as I please because I'm stuck here until the job is done." He paused and caught his breath. "If Dodger wants the coolant, he can have it. I mean, if he takes it we don't have to pay to have it recycled. It's just easier."

Ari raised an eyebrow. "That's not what you said the other day."

Eldridge rubbed a calloused hand over his head. "That's because you keep chirping in my ear about what your daddy would do. I just don't care anymore. If I can pay the guy off and he leaves us alone, then it's just the cost of doing business. We'll know better next time."

Nathan shrugged at Cole. If the kid didn't understand being eaten alive a piece at a time he couldn't say anything to change his mind.

Ari walked back over to the maintenance vehicles and started one up. "We should probably get back to camp."

— «» —

Dodger sat at his desk, watching drone footage from the wreck site play out on the large monitor in his office. The heavy bass of the music from the dancers out in the club reverberated through the walls. He tapped his fingers on his desk to the rhythm of the beat. His head nodded absently as he watched.

Morris's nephew, Cheech, sat across the office at another desk. The tanned young man with dark hair wore a floral shirt, cut-off cargo pants and black work boots. He piloted the drone, giving them the data, in a slow orbit of the *Athena Star* and kept the camera and microphone trained on the group of salvagers and repo agents. As the group mounted their vehicles for the ride back to camp, Dodger turned off the monitor.

"You hear that shit?" he said to Morris.

The bloated consigliere nodded. "They talk too much," he said. "The boy gets it, but that woman of his is a problem. You hear her pushing him?"

Dodger picked up a crystal from the ever-present plastic envelope on the desk in front of him. He dropped it in his mouth and ground it down while he shook his head. "No, not that. I don't care about the kid and his woman. He'll do exactly as we want. You heard him, he knows he's not in a position to stand up to us, no matter how much we bleed him. She can yap at him all she wants. I mean, have you ever known a happy woman? That's all they do, complain about what they've got and about what they ain't got. The thing is, that's Eldridge's problem, not ours. No, I'm interested in the repo men. Remember what he said? 'They can come and go as they please because they got a ship.'"

Morris frowned for a moment and then got it. "You want to use them to move the stuff? Have them take Bone Daddy's place in the distribution pipeline?"

Dodger's head bobbed up and down, like a ball on a spring. "Yeah. Think about it. Those repo guys can probably get in and out of all kinds of places without going through customs inspections because they got authorization to be there. Freight haulers can get licensed ahead of time and skip all the inspections and crap." He nodded at the dark monitor. "I bet they got something like that."

"That could work," Morris said, "if you could get them to do it. What makes you think they'll be up for it?"

Dodger smiled with yellow teeth. "Credits. We just have to make it worth their while. The reward has to be worth the risk. Why don't you run a background check on them and see what their finances look like. Check all the other stuff too, see if there's anything we can exploit."

Morris nodded and smiled. "It's already done," he said as he pulled up a file. "I started checking them out when Turtle called in this morning." He swiped his hand across the display in front of him and Dodger's workstation beeped and came to life. "There's the file. I think there's some interesting data there."

Dodger opened the file. "Good work. Why don't you go get yourself a lap dance while I go through this. Get one for Cheech, too. We had a hot little redhead in here that got scanned last week. Check her out."

Chapter 10

Donald Kinty steered a hover truck down a two-lane road, bordered with metal fencing, toward the south gate of the starship storage yard, just east of Go City. Kenneth Bonto, another member of his crew sat beside him in the passenger seat and said, "You think Atomic Jack will be okay with this?"

"What? Grabbing the Diamond K?" Kinty said. He put a cigarette in his mouth and lit it. "He's going to be ecstatic. Think of the finder's fee on this job. Besides, he's out of town, right? He left me in charge and I say we go get this stuff."

"You say 'out of town' like he's taking a vacation instead of in a Swiss hospital getting another treatment for the radiation poisoning."

Kinty shrugged. "Well, that's pretty far out of town. Listen, don't worry. We go in, grab this stuff and get out. When he gets back, he'll be glad we earned a little extra."

"I guess."

They came to the gate and he turned in. A guard, with curly red hair in a small shack, slid his window open and waved at them. Kinty lowered his window and a blast of hot air hit him. A little air conditioning unit atop the guard shack rattled to life in a futile attempt to beat back the heat. He raised his voice to talk over it.

"Hey, Murphy."

The guard nodded. "Kinty. What's up?"

"Just need a look at one of your ships," Kinty said. "The *Hell's Breath*?"

The guard consulted a mobi and pointed straight ahead. "Pad sixteen. Go straight ahead and then take the first right. It's down three spots on the right."

"Thanks. Has it been wrapped?"

"I don't think so." He checked the mobi again for confirmation. "The notes on it say it's still waiting for inspection and then it's going through a refit. Looks like a repo job."

"That's what I wanted to hear. Thanks, Murph." He handed him a card and a credit voucher. "Give me a call if anyone comes through."

"Will do." The guard tapped a control and the gate rolled open, then he slid his window closed to let the air conditioner catch up. Kinty pulled through the gate and followed the guard's directions. His crew kept Murphy on the take so they could access the storage yard whenever they needed to. The landing pads spread out across the flat desert. Most held small starships in long-term or short-term storage, just waiting for the day they would be put back into service. The ships all had white polymer shrink wrap to guard against corrosion and blowing sand. Kinty turned the corner and spotted their target. He pulled up next to the landing pad.

"That looks like a huge pile of shit," Bonto said. He lit up a cigarette and smoke curled out of his mouth. "Who does it belong to again?"

"Right now, the bank owns it. Those Milky Way Repo morons grabbed it from some band out on Mars and returned it here." He pointed to the side of the ship with the band name on it. "Before that it belonged to *Bone Daddy and the Voodoo Choir*." He shut the truck down, and it settled to the ground on stubby landing gear.

"Man, it's going to be hotter than hell in there," Bonto said. "I bet they don't have the environmental controls cycling."

"Doesn't look like it. Come on, let's get it done."

They exited the truck and walked toward the rear of the ship. Kinty ducked into the little bit of shade provided by the stabilizer and found the ramp controls. He plugged in a small device and watched the lights on the display swirl as it hammered the lock with a brute force attack. A moment later the ramp dropped slowly to the ground. Bonto walked up the ramp and Kinty followed after retrieving his device from the ramp controls. He found light switches along one wall and lit up the cargo bay.

Bonto kicked a pile of clothes out of the way and shoved a storage container out of the middle of the small bay. "Well this is a mess."

"According to Turtle, we only need one thing. He said our item is a pallet full of dope and it should be wrapped up."

"That's your nephew, right?"

"Yeah, my sister's kid. He's part of a crew out on Bad Rock working for a guy named Dodger."

"Never heard of him."

"Turtle says he's an asshole. Have you heard of Diamond K?" Kinty went through the storage areas, pulling aside tarps and moving containers full of stage gear out of his way.

"Yeah, sure. Speed variant."

Kinty took a long step over an open black case that had foam cut outs in it shaped like large speakers. "That's the stuff. Well, this guy Dodger makes it out on Bad Rock and he had the bright idea to use this Bone Daddy as a distributor because he tours the asteroid belt and other settlements."

Bonto laughed and shook his head. "Really? He gave a rock band access to an almost unlimited amount of drugs? Dumbass."

Kinty spotted a tarp covering something in the corner and he worked his way over to it. He pulled the cord holding the tarp loose and lifted it up. He let out a low whistle. "Found it."

Bonto worked his way over to him. "That is a lot of dope." He ran his hands over the plastic wrap and found a tear. "Looks like someone got into it."

Kinty shrugged. "Like you said, they're a rock band."

"How come this hasn't been found by customs yet?"

"The way I understand it, those repo guys don't stop up in orbit for the inspection. The bank or whoever owns it has two weeks to get the inspection done once it lands." A quick glance at the cargo bay showed him they had a pretty straight shot to the ramp. "Why don't you move some of this crap out of the way and I'll get the loader from the truck? I'd like to get out of here sooner rather than later." He wiped sweat from his forehead with the back of his hand.

"Yeah, sounds like a plan."

Kinty walked back out to the truck and raised the roll up door. He lowered the ramp hidden under the cargo box and walked up inside to grab the anti-gravity lifter. A quick look around when he exited the truck showed them to be alone He went back into the *Hell's Breath*. Bonto had the bay cleaned up enough for him to drag the pallet to the ramp.

"Is this all we need?" Bonto said.

"It's all Turtle mentioned. Why?"

Bonto nodded his head upward. "There might be some other stuff we could grab. Make this little side trip pay off a bit."

Kinty considered it. "Why not?"

They found the stairs and climbed them up to the main deck. Kinty found the light switches and lit up the cabin. His mouth dropped open at the mess.

"Holy shit. Have you ever seen anything like this?"

Bonto nudged some dirty clothing away with the toe of his boot. "Just drug houses like that joint over on Sixth. You know, forget I said anything. I don't want anything out of this mess. I've got better things to do than pick through garbage."

"Yeah," Kinty said, holding up a torn leopard skin thong. "This is repugnant."

They went back down to the cargo bay and Bonto cinched the tarp tight over the pallet before Kinty attached the lifter. The load floated about ten centimeters off the deck. Kinty gave a tug and the pallet moved with him toward the loading ramp.

"You think any of this sound gear could be worth anything?" Bonto said.

Kinty nodded. "We could probably get a few bucks for it. Let's get this loaded and we'll come back."

Kinty used the lifter to spin the pallet around so he could push it down the ramp. Bonto followed, talking about how much he thought they could get for the amps and speakers still in the cargo bay.

"Boy, what the hell do you think you're doing?"

The voice startled Kinty so much he almost let go of the lifter. He saw two Customs officials standing next to a marked vehicle, one white, one Hispanic. Both of them had hands on their guns but no one had drawn yet. The white one came around the passenger side door but kept the front of their vehicle between himself and Kinty.

"You just put that pallet down at the base of the ramp and you," he said pointing at Bonto, "get your hands up."

Kinty watched Bonto raise his hands and he maneuvered the pallet to the base of the ramp. Bonto threw him a wink and Kinty spoke up.

"What can we do for you officers?"

"For starters, you can get them hands up and step away from the pallet. Come on now, do what I tell you."

Kinty raised his hands and stood still. "No problem, officer. Our boss told us to come out here and unload some of this stuff. We don't want any trouble. I got his number right here, if you want to speak with him."

The officer doing all the talking stepped around from behind their vehicle and walked toward Kinty and the pallet. His partner kept an eye on Bonto. "I'm Carlton. That's Gutierrez," he said nodding toward the other officer. "What have you all got in here?"

Kinty shook his head. "I really don't know. Like I said, the boss just said to unload the ship so we came on out here with the truck and started pulling stuff off."

The Customs officer stole a look into the back of the truck. "Must have just got started because I don't see anything else back there."

Kinty nodded. "That's right."

The officer put his hands on his gun belt and eyed him. "Why don't you lift the tarp and we'll all see what your boss wants."

"Don't you need a warrant?"

The officer narrowed his eyes. "We're with Customs. Until that ship gets inspected we don't need a warrant. Now, lift the tarp."

"Oh sure, I got you," Kinty said. "I'll have to bend down here to loosen up this cord."

The officer adjusted his hat. "Well, get to it. The sun isn't getting any cooler."

Kinty bent down behind the pallet and shoved hard. It slid forward and he switched off the power to the lift, dropping the load onto one of Carlton's feet. The officer howled in pain and Gutierrez drew his weapon, as his partner screamed.

Bonto moved sideways, away from the commotion and got to his gun. He pulled and got a shot off at the Hispanic officer, catching him in the chest. The man in the Custom's uniform screamed and dropped to the ground. Bonto turned back to Kinty and the other Custom's officer.

Kinty ducked, trying to keep as much cover between him and the officer as possible. He moved carefully around the pallet, wary of the yowling officer with the crushed foot. The officer had a grip on the tarp with his left hand to hold himself upright. Kinty saw blood seeping into the packed sand from the corner of the plastic pallet. The base of the pallet had caught the officer across the arch of his right foot and had him stuck fast. He noticed the officer's hat lying in the dirt and saw a gun rising in his right hand. The cop snapped off a shot that went wide of Kinty's head and he ducked.

The Custom's officer groaned in pain again and Kinty heard more shots. Several hit the sand next to him but the cop couldn't get the angle right. He heard one final shot and the officer screamed and fell to the desert floor.

Kinty stood up and saw Bonto standing nearby with a smoking pistol. "Thanks." He pointed at the officer lying on the ground. "Did you see that tough sonofabitch shooting at me?"

"Yeah, but you had a good idea trapping him with the pallet."

Kinty could feel the adrenaline surge starting to subside now that the action was over and he let out a deep breath. Then Bonto's head evaporated in a pink and red cloud.

Kinty stepped back in shock and another shot threw him backward onto the concrete pad. His hands went to his lower abdomen and came away stained bright red with blood. He gasped for air and stared into the bright sunlight. A shadow fell across him, and he saw Gutierrez staring down at him.

The officer kicked his gun away and bent down to grab his face in a tight grip.

"You so much as twitch and I'll send you to meet up with your friend. You understand me?"

Kinty nodded and then he screamed as the full force of the pain finally hit him. Gutierrez rifled through his clothes, searching for more weapons, then, mercifully, he passed out.

— «» —

Carlton woke up in the hospital and stared at the ceiling, trying to get his bearings. He rolled his head to the side and saw Sergeant McNamara sitting in a chair reading something on her mobi. She smiled.

"How are you feeling?" She said.

He started to talk and his voice croaked. McNamara held up a finger. "One second, the doctor said your throat may be sore." She poured a cup of water from a pitcher and handed it to him. He sucked it through a straw and it tasted better than anything he'd ever had. He cleared his throat.

"Gutierrez?"

She nodded and smiled. "He's fine. Caught a bullet in his vest and he's got a hell of a bruise but he'll be all right." She glanced down at the foot of his bed. His gaze followed to see his elevated and bandaged right leg. He tried to wiggle his toes but didn't feel anything. He glanced back at McNamara and she held up a hand. "Hold on," she said. "Let me get the doctor in here."

She returned a moment later with a young doctor dressed in a brilliant white coat. He swiped a finger over his mobi as he went over the injuries. The doctor said most of his right foot had been partially amputated due to the injury from the pallet. He shouldn't worry, though. They could grow him a new one, good as new. With a smile and a reassuring pat on the arm, he left the room.

Gutierrez came in next and pulled up a chair next to the bed. He wore a white t-shirt and gray workout pants.

"Tough break, man. Sorry about your foot."

Carlton swallowed. "The doc says I'll be down for three months while they put it back together."

"Would have been worse if we hadn't been wearing our vests."

Carlton let out a deep breath. "I guess so. I didn't even think of that. They shot me too, didn't they?"

"Yeah, you'll feel it later when the pain meds wear off. The same bastard that shot me got you in the left side. You'll want to be careful and not move too much. Your rib cage pretty much looks like this." He slowly lifted his t-shirt and Carlton saw an ugly purple and red bruise on the left side of Gutierrez's chest.

"Holy shit. What were those guys after?"

Gutierrez's face got more somber. "Diamond K. A whole pallet's worth, all bagged up and ready for sale on the street. It's worth millions."

Carlton let out a low whistle. "So they were distributing it with that ship?"

Gutierrez nodded. "That's what we think. Obviously those two guys tried to unload it from the ship prior to the inspection. We'll know more in a day or so after we talk to Bone Daddy, the singer who owned the ship."

"We got him?"

"Yeah, Protective Services on Mars already had him on a vagrancy charge. They're sticking him on a flight back here so we can question him."

Carlton grimaced. "Well, good bust or not, I wish I hadn't lost my damn foot."

Gutierrez gave him a little smile. "I know buddy, but at least it's only your foot being regrown."

"What do you mean?"

"That asshole who dropped the pallet on you? When you went down you took a shot at him and blew his pecker clean off." Gutierrez gave him a wicked smile. "He's on the next floor down recovering."

"No way."

Gutierrez nodded and kept grinning. "Look at it this way. You'll get three months of desk duty and a new foot. He's got to wait for the Department of Corrections to decide if they want to pay for a new johnson."

Carlton nodded. "I guess things could be worse."

Chapter 11

Nathan, Cole and Duncan stood under the canopy that housed Eldridge's work station and the table where they had eaten lunch. Ari supervised some 'bots at a pile, in the distance, while Eldridge repaired a 'bot at his workbench. Cole threw a small rock and it bounced along the ground, scaring a small lizard from its hiding spot behind a boulder.

Nathan heard Eldridge say, "Oh what now?"

All three of them turned and saw a float truck inbound to the camp. Nathan stood up straight. Cole and Duncan joined him.

"Who is that?" He said to Eldridge.

"Those two idiots you met this morning, Turtle and Daryl."

The small truck came to a stop next to Eldridge's float bike and the maintenance vehicle. Both men got out and walked over to the camp, kicking up small puffs of dust with their steps.

The taller one with greasy hair pulled out a bandana from his back pocket and wiped his forehead. "Eldridge, how's things?"

"Just fine Turtle. Your shift's over, right? Shouldn't you be headed back to Bad Rock?"

"Yeah, we're going there now. Just need to speak with your new arrivals first."

Eldridge pointed to them. "Be my guest."

Turtle and the smaller one, who Nathan assumed was Daryl, walked over to where they stood.

"You Teller?"

Nathan nodded. "Yeah, that's me. You the one chewing Diamond K out by your pile?"

"No, sir. I never touch that stuff."

Cole nodded at Daryl. "Must be his buddy then. Yeah, look at those teeth. He chews."

Daryl stopped smiling and closed his lips.

"Let's try and keep things friendly, okay?" Turtle said. "We've got no beef with you folks. I'm just here on an errand for my boss."

"That'd be Dodger?"

"That's right. He'd like to have a talk with you."

Nathan narrowed his eyes. "I think I'll pass. I can't imagine what the two of us would talk about."

"Well, hell, Mr. Teller. He's just trying to be friendly." He flashed a smile full of yellow teeth at Nathan. "Won't take long at all. I don't have the details but it's my understanding that it's a business opportunity and before you say no, you should be aware that people make all kinds of money with Dodger."

"Like you and Daryl?"

"That's right."

Nathan gave a small laugh. "Don't you two sit in the sun all day supervising 'bots? And aren't you behind in your quota? How much can you make doing that?"

Turtle bit his lower lip and held back whatever response had jumped up first. He took a moment, formulated a different response and finally smiled. "Why don't you just get in the truck and ride in with us? If you think we work slow now, you should see what could happen if we really put our minds to it."

Eldridge cleared his throat and Nathan glanced at him. The younger man shook his head almost imperceptibly but Nathan understood. Any further slowing down in work would just make life harder on him. Nathan sighed.

"Yeah, okay. Take us to your boss."

Turtle jerked a thumb over his shoulder. "Right this way."

The ride into town led over a road in serious need of repair. The three of them jammed in the backseat, while Turtle drove and Daryl sat in the passenger seat. The truck bounced despite the fact that it floated half a meter off the ground, a fact that didn't escape Duncan's attention.

"You've got a ground following sensor that is out of calibration. That's why this thing rides like a three-legged donkey."

Turtle turned his head enough to talk over his shoulder. "Sorry about that. This old truck of mine needs some shop time but we've been busy out at the site working."

After that, they rode in silence until they finally entered the city proper. Turtle weaved down some side streets until he finally pulled into the parking lot of the club with a sign out front that said 'Dodge 'Em's'.

Cole leaned in to Nathan and said, "I could have driven all over this city, and I would have known to pull in here as soon as I saw it."

"Yeah," Nathan said, "it's exactly what I expected."

Turtle pulled into a spot near the door and parked. They exited the vehicle and followed him inside. Nathan scoped the joint out. A couple of stages with poles, where holographic dancers performed for customers, sat in the middle of the floor. Duncan nudged him.

"You still like the holographic girls, Nathan?"

"You can be kind of a jerk, Duncan. You know that?"

The big man smiled at his boss. "You've got to loosen up, Nathan. Try and have a sense of humor."

They moved between the tables and walked across the club floor. A large bouncer got off his stool and stood in front of the door to a back office. Daryl moved off to one side and pulled his gun and holster from the small of his back. He opened a locker and slid them inside.

The bouncer approached Nathan's group. "You'll have to leave your guns out here, fellas. Dodger doesn't allow them inside his office."

"Then we won't be meeting Dodger in his office," Nathan said.

The bouncer moved toward Cole with his hand out. "Don't be like that, sir. Just let me help you with that." He made a move with a meaty hand to reach under Cole's coat for the pistol he had in a shoulder rig. Cole grabbed his hand, twisted it up behind his back and forced him to the wall.

Nathan turned to Turtle and Daryl as they rushed to their friend's aid and held up a hand. "Stop right there, guys."

Daryl stepped to go around him and Nathan caught him in the throat, hooked a foot behind his ankle and pushed him to the floor. Duncan and Turtle just stared at each other, neither of them moving.

"Stop fighting," Nathan said as Daryl struggled under him. "Your man shouldn't have laid hands on Cole. He's not giving up his gun and if you'd given us time to explain, I would have told you that. If it's a condition of the meeting then take us back to Eldridge."

The door to the office opened and a man stepped out. Turtle held up a hand. "Morris, I can explain."

"Don't worry about it," Morris said. "Dodger said they can keep their guns and to quit screwing around."

Nathan stood up and tapped Cole on the shoulder. "Let him up."

Cole released the bouncer and the man rolled over, rubbing his shoulder. Turtle offered him a hand and pulled him up. Daryl got up and glared at Nathan.

"All right," Morris said. "If you're all done feeling each other up let's talk. Everyone get inside."

Nathan's group went into the office to see a stocky man with muscular arms standing behind a desk. He walked around and held his hand out. "You Teller?"

They shook. "That's right. You're Dodger?"

"That's me," he said and held his hands up. "Welcome to my club."

Nathan introduced Cole and Duncan. "You already know these two," Dodger said, pointing at Turtle and Daryl. "This is Morris. He kind of runs things around here for me."

The man who had stepped out of the office nodded in their direction and took a seat at a smaller desk in the corner. Dodger offered them all seats and went back behind his desk. They all sat.

"So what can we do for you?" Nathan said. "It's your meeting."

"You like to get right down to it, don't you?" Dodger said. "Well, that's okay. I'm the same way. Can't make any money sitting on your ass, am I right?"

"Something like that." Nathan noticed the man's bloodshot eyes had trouble focusing when he tried to hold eye contact.

Dodger clapped his hands together. "Okay, I assume Eldridge told you that he and I are sort of in business together so when I hear that you want to grab his ship I get a little worried."

"You're shaking him down and keeping the unions off his back."

Dodger shrugged. "Call it what you will. I don't hear any complaints. My question to you is, what can we do to make you leave without Eldridge's ship? If you take it away my interest in his business is put in jeopardy."

"You could always shake down the next guy who comes out here."

Dodger pointed a shaky finger at him. "You see, that's a dangerous assumption. First of all, Bad Rock is kind of back water. The good folks running the Great Star Line may decide to abandon the *Athena Star*. I mean, really, who would care? We're ten and a half light years from Earth. It's not like that thing is sitting on the outskirts of Paris screwing up the view of the Leaning Tower."

Nathan opened his mouth to correct him and then closed it again.

"Besides, if another group comes out maybe Great Star Lines will actually give them a decent contract instead of ripping them off like they did that poor kid out there. They may pay them enough to hire the unions here in Bad Rock and that's not good for anyone."

"Not good for you, anyway," Nathan said. "I'm guessing you have some juice but if you got between the union and a legitimate job you'd get crushed like a bug. That means you have every incentive to keep things just the way they are."

Dodger swallowed and grinned. "I'm glad we understand one another. So, what can we do to have you leave without the ship?"

Nathan held up his hands. "Look, I feel for you and I even kind of like the kid. He's doing a good job, despite a whole host of problems but the thing is, we have a job to do too. We're here to repo that ship. It's probably all a misunderstanding but that's for Eldridge to sort out and your problems are just that. Your problems."

Dodger gave him an oily little smile. "Yeah, my problems are my problems and your problems are your problems."

Nathan slid his eyes sideways. Morris sat at his desk and Turtle and Daryl leaned against the wall to his right. If they planned to throw down, they seemed pretty nonchalant about it. "Okay, I'll play. What are my problems?"

Dodger tapped his desk, drumming out a little beat as he pointed at Nathan. "You have the same problem lots of small businesses have. Cash flow, as in, you don't have any."

Nathan shifted uncomfortably in his chair. "I'm not following you."

Dodger smiled at Morris. "You don't have any money, Teller. You're broke. Flat busted."

"And yet here I am in Bad Rock on a job."

Dodger held up a hand. "No, you're right. You do have this one job. Of course, that's no guarantee there will be another and I imagine that's got you in a bit of a twist. I mean, it's got to be expensive doing what you do. Gassing up your ship, paying your crew," he gestured to Cole and Duncan, "insurance, food, and whatever else I'm missing. To do all that you need to have some credits in the bank and you don't have any. You're busted, chief."

Nathan could feel the stares from Cole and Duncan but he ignored them. He had to deal with one problem at a time. He swallowed hard and said, "You've been doing your homework."

"Well, we may be out here at the ass end of nowhere but that doesn't mean we're stupid or lazy. Yeah, we did some digging. You see, you grabbed a ship from Mars last week that we had an interest in."

Nathan nodded. "The *Hell's Breath*? That idiot Bone Daddy worked for you?"

"He did and when you grabbed his ship you kind of screwed things up for me."

"Diamond K?"

Dodger nodded. "Diamond K."

"So Bone Daddy and his little band of clowns distributed for you?"

Dodger nodded. "When you grabbed the ship you flew a ton of product through Customs and landed it on Earth for me. As helpful as that may seem, it we needed it delivered to other places so now I have a whole mess on my hands. Now I have to find someone there to move it for me and I have to get a new shipment out to the guys who are short."

Nathan closed his eyes and pinched his nose. "And that's where we come in?"

Dodger smiled. "You should be happy. This is quite an opportunity. You bring your ship down, we load it up and you make a few stops on your way home. I don't know exactly what you're making repossessing Eldridge's ship but I'll be paying you more. Much more."

Nathan considered it for a moment. If the pallet he saw on the *Hell's Breath* had been the total shipment it meant that it would be split up between three stops. "Where is it going?" Duncan turned to look at him but didn't say anything.

"Interested?"

"I haven't gotten up yet."

Dodger nodded. "Okay, it's three drops, all in the Sol system; one on Mars, one on Ceres and one of the stations in orbit around Europa. We have agreements with dock masters and Customs officials at all three places that will allow you to get in."

Nathan leaned back in his chair. "I'll need some time to think about it. Can you give me until tomorrow morning?"

Cole shifted in his seat and faced him but didn't say anything.

Dodger smiled and stood up, extending a hand. "That works for me." He noticed the sour faces on Cole and Duncan. "It looks like you may have some convincing to do. Factor that into your cost, that's my advice."

Nathan shook his hand. "Yeah. See you tomorrow."

"Turtle, take them wherever they need to go," Dodger said.

"Will do."

They stepped outside to the majestic orange of the setting sun. Turtle got in the truck and started it. Nathan got in the front seat and Duncan and Cole sat in the back.

"We need a decent hotel that has a restaurant nearby," Nathan said. "You have something like that?"

"Yeah," Turtle said. "I can do that."

An hour later they checked in to a small motel and sat at a booth in a mostly deserted diner as night fell, Nathan on one side, Cole and Duncan squeezed together on the other. A waitress took their orders and left them drinks on the table. Nathan pointed to Cole. "You look angriest so you go first."

"What are we doing here? I don't understand. Why aren't we halfway home by now? And why are we listening to that skell, Dodger? What is going on with you?"

Nathan started to answer but Duncan interrupted. "You're really broke, aren't you? Dodger didn't have that wrong."

He nodded. "Yeah, I didn't want to say anything to you guys but I'm pretty much running paycheck-to-paycheck now. After our last job, I made enough to pay my rent, buy instant noodles and pay you guys."

"Why?" Duncan said. "We've been working steady."

"Yeah, but the paydays are getting lighter. We used to be the only game in town. Now there are at least three outfits repossessing vessels either full time or part time. It's pushing the rates down."

"Well, that I can understand," Duncan said. "I mean, it beats financing holographic fantasies."

"You've got to let that go."

"I haven't noticed a drop in my pay, Nathan," Cole said. "Why is that?"

Nathan exhaled loudly and ran a hand through his hair. "I didn't want you guys to know how rough things had gotten. I didn't want you finding other jobs."

Cole shook his head. "You're a moron sometimes. We're supposed to work on shares, no matter what the job pays. I don't need charity from you."

"It's not charity. It's an investment. Lower rates are one thing but losing crew just makes things more difficult. I know you can both get other jobs. Kimiyo would be just fine with you having a job planetside that kept you nearby."

Cole waved him off. "That's not something you need to worry about."

"Look, the business is basically the ship and the crew. If I lose either one then I'm done. I'm finished." Nathan paused, sipped his coffee, and reached for the sugar on the table. "Duncan, you keep the ship flying and Marla is my co-pilot. If you guys go I have to fill two spots."

"There's always Richie," Duncan said.

"He's coming along but he's not ready."

"No, you're right about that."

"Cole," Nathan shrugged. "I need you because every once in a while we run into guys like Dodger and they can be too much to handle on my own."

Their food came and they dug in. It had been a long time since lunch back at Eldridge's worksite. Nathan chewed his meatloaf and stared out the window.

The street outside had that same run down look he'd seen on so many colonies and settlements. Storefronts, some occupied, some empty, lined the opposite side of the road. It didn't surprise him that the Syndicate had a drug making operation out here. He scooped up some mashed potatoes and noticed Cole eyeing him. "What?"

"I'm trying to figure out why you didn't tell Dodger to screw off when he offered you a job moving his product. We've never hauled anything, let alone drugs. I get that you're having some money issues but you aren't seriously considering this, are you?"

"What do you think?"

Cole appeared uncomfortable. "I'm really not sure. I don't know if you said that to give us a way out of that office or if you're really considering it."

Nathan leaned back and shrugged his shoulders. "What's the big deal?"

"It's illegal, for one thing."

"Drug running? Yeah it is, but only because the drugs themselves are illegal. Otherwise carrying them would be as legal as hauling any other kind of freight. It wouldn't pay nearly as good though."

"Nathan," Duncan said. "Drugs like Diamond K are illegal because they're immoral. Look what they do to people. They make people addicts, they break up families and they fund criminals."

Nathan nodded in agreement. "I can't argue with you there. I mean, Diamond K or any of the hundred other things people put into their bodies are terrible for them but isn't it really their choice?"

Cole's face screwed up. "Who, junkies? Are you insane? They can't make a good decision on their best day. You know how I know that? Because they choose to put that crap in their bodies."

Nathan shook his head. "You're not following me. It's their choice. What right does the government have to tell people what they can do with their bodies? If some dumbass wants to waste his life chewing Diamond K and getting high, it's their choice."

"Libertarian nonsense," Cole said. "Duncan's right. That crap is a plague on society."

"I don't disagree with you. I mean, it's not something I would choose for myself but if some guy wants to, why do we make him a criminal? Hell, all it does is give guys like Dodger a way to profit from their misery."

"I spent time as a marshal, remember?" Cole said. "I can tell you a couple things from personal experience. One, guys like Dodger will always find a way to feed off misery. It's who they are. If he didn't make credits selling Diamond K he'd make it pimping out girls. Hell, we know he's already running a protection racket. He's just a scumbag and would be regardless of whether drugs were legal or not."

"Yeah, the man isn't worthy of the air he breathes. What's your second point?"

"You ever see the effects of that crap on people? I mean, up close and personal?"

Nathan shook his head.

"It's one thing to think people should have the freedom to do whatever they want to themselves but this garbage hurts innocent people, not just the ones who use it."

Nathan waved a hand at him. "I'm not condoning that for Christ's sake."

Cole leaned in, his eyes hard. "Doesn't matter. That's what happens. Like with Johnnie Lee, a two-time loser who worked as a leg breaker for assholes like Dodger. I was chasing him after he trashed this kid who stole some White Rook from a courier. You know what that is?"

Nathan nodded. "Some kind of speed, like Diamond K, right?"

"Close enough. This kid, Robbie something-or-other, likes to party and he sees his buddy has a kilo of this stuff. He steals it, throws a huge party and wakes up the next day at a house off campus to Johnnie Lee Beaufort standing over him, baseball bat in hand."

"What happened?"

"About what you'd expect. Robbie ended up losing an eye, the hearing in one ear and I'm not sure he ever learned to walk right again." Cole watched, maybe trying to read Nathan's reaction, before continuing. "Yeah, what happened to him was a nightmare but that's not it." Cole took a pull from his beer.

"We finally got the kid to talk and went to pick up Johnnie Lee at his house. It was a crappy little stucco place with a red tile roof. Could have been nice but no one seemed to care. Anyway, we knew that in addition to him, a woman and her kids lived there so we tried to be careful. We had a whole task force, about a dozen guys, and after scanning the rooms to see where everyone was, we hit the place hard. I went through the door first and saw him stretched out on the couch. I made a beeline for that sonovabitch and stunned him before he could do more than start to sit up. I cuffed him and then the guys started calling from the bedrooms. I left him with another marshal and stepped in. Mom was so high she hadn't woken up despite us kicking in her front door and sounding like a herd of elephants. I looked in the kids' room and saw them on the floor, playing with their toys."

He paused and took a deep breath.

"Each of them had a cuff on their ankle and they were chained to the bed. They could walk around the room and go as far as the closet but that's it. After a moment, this smell hit me and I opened the closet to see a bucket they were using as a toilet. One of the local deputies backing us up, Eve, picked the little boy up and set him on the bed to get the cuff off his ankle and he said it hurt. She pulled up his pant leg up and you could see the cuff biting into his skin and it was all red and infected."

"Jesus," Nathan said.

Cole nodded. "Yeah. Eve started talking to the kids and the medics were treating them when mom finally woke up. She got all hysterical, wondering what we were doing there and screaming for Johnnie Lee but he was already outside in the back of a cruiser. She was kind of spacey and kept saying it's time to go to work, that we need to leave." He paused. "After she calmed down we talked to her and the kids.

"In addition to being a leg breaker, Johnnie Lee was pimping her out. He didn't like the kids making too much noise when he was getting high so he kept them confined in their room. So, that was their life, chained up in their room most of the day using a bucket for a bathroom while some low life pimped out their mom for drug money. Mom would let them out if Johnnie Lee was out working but she got high too. So, mostly this cute little boy and girl just stayed in that filthy room. That's a hell of a life when you're four and five years old."

Nathan swallowed. "Did he abuse the kids?"

"Sexually?" Cole shrugged. "Not that we could tell but if he would have been allowed a few more years, who knows?"

Nathan glanced down at the table before saying anything but then he shook his head. "Look, that's an awful story and believe me, I know it gets repeated often but my position on this is that if drugs are legal, the criminal element goes away. There's no more smuggling and no more dealers. You just get it from a dispensary."

Cole raised an eyebrow. "And how will junkies afford this stuff? You think their welfare payments will cover the cost? Let me tell you, if you're sitting around your house chewing Diamond K you aren't clocking in for an office job or running your own business."

"Addictive drugs take away choice," Duncan said, chiming in. "If you need a hit so bad that you're willing to sell yourself or rob someone to get the credits to score, you really don't have a choice in the matter."

"Well, that's when it becomes a problem with the law," Nathan said. "Besides, that argument might have held water before we had treatments for addicts but not now. Once they figured out how to re-wire people's brains so they wouldn't be addicted it's just a choice. If you don't want to be an alcoholic or hooked on Diamond K you just get treatment. If you want to use it, you keep using it. Getting clean isn't any harder than going to the doctor for a prescription."

"People don't always like the side-effects of the treatment," Cole said, "and it's not always effective. I'll tell you something, tough; they love feeling high. I mean, something like Diamond K is powerful because it's like the first time, every time. It's not old school meth or heroin. Your body never acclimates to the high. You don't chase that first time with stronger doses and get strung out. You know exactly how much it takes to make you feel good, every time. Besides, you can get clean but all that does is reset your situation."

Nathan's eyes narrowed. "What do you mean?"

"Getting treatment and getting clean just leaves you in the same situation that made you want to escape it by getting high. If you had a crappy life before then getting sober isn't going to change that. If you live alone in some awful little apartment and have a job you hate and you started chewing Diamond K to escape that, being sober doesn't solve the root of your problem. All the treatment allows you to do is swing from periods of sobriety to periods of addiction."

"Hey, if you want your life to be better, go make it better," Nathan said. "Only you are responsible for you. That's a choice too."

"So what are you going to do about Dodger's offer?" Cole said. "Are we getting into the drug running business?"

"I'm not," Duncan said. "No offense, Nathan, and you can do whatever you want, just count me out. Marla and I aren't in a position where we have to make a choice like this."

Nathan sat back and considered what his oldest friend had said. It stung. "Let's get something straight, I'm not being forced into this. I do what I want."

"I don't believe that for a moment," Duncan said. "I think if you were flush with credits you'd flick that little bastard off your shoe like something you stepped in. Your financial situation has you considering options you never would have before. Apparently you don't see that as a problem but don't ask me to sit here and listen to you dress it up in some political philosophy."

"And don't ask you to come along, right?"

Duncan took a deep breath and nodded. "Like I said, we have other options. You're a good friend, Nathan, you really are but this isn't just backing your play in some tough situation. I'm used to those. This is just you being desperate. Count us out."

Nathan turned to look outside at the rundown buildings again. It reminded him of where he'd grown up, in some ways. No matter how hard he worked he was always one bad decision away from being broke. He'd done well for himself, but one glance out the window reminded him that he stood as close to the edge as ever. His home town had been just like this. He turned back to Cole.

"How about you? If I decide to do this, are you in?"

Cole slowly shook his head. "Nah, this isn't for me."

"You know, you don't have a badge anymore. You gave that up a while ago."

Cole gave him a little grin and dipped his head. "It's not the badge, Nathan. I just think it's wrong. I've got a good thing going with Kimiyo. Why would I screw that up?"

"Yeah, I can understand that." He pulled a card from his wallet and swiped it through the reader on the table to settle their bill. "I'm going back to my room to think things over. I'll see you guys in the morning."

Chapter 12

Nathan stripped off his jacket and boots before lying down on the bed. He got his mobi out and checked in with Marla.

"How are things going up there?"

"Everything is fine. There's been no movement from the *Corkscrew* and we're still docked with her. Richie is sitting on the airlock door."

"Good. I don't think you'll have any trouble but that's what I thought when we boarded and look how that turned out."

Marla smiled in the video display. "Yeah, we're going to talk about that later."

"Oh, I'm sure." Nathan had no doubt that it would be a long time before he stopped hearing about them being dropped to Bad Rock against their will.

"When are we getting out of here?"

"Probably in the morning. I decided to spend the night because I didn't want you going through re-entry and attempting a night landing in a strange place."

"I appreciate that but I'm sure I could have handled it."

"I know, but you're tired. Get some rest and we'll do it in the morning. I'll give you a call when we're ready."

"I live to serve."

"Very funny. Is Tricia around? I'd like to speak with her."

"Yeah, she's in her quarters. I think she's still up though. You know, she's all right, funny too. I spent most of the day talking to her."

"Yeah, well, I'm sure you already know, but I like her too."

"Then you should make sure she knows that," Marla said. "I'll put you through."

Before Nathan could say anything else the view flipped over to Tricia. She sat up on the bed in her small quarters. He smiled. "How are you doing?"

She smiled back and relief and excitement rushed through him. "I'm good. How are things down there?"

"Boring and dilapidated. I kind of wish I had let you come over with us."

"You make it sound tempting."

Nathan cursed himself inwardly. What made this so hard? "Yeah, I'm... look, you know what? I'm awful at all this small talk thing. Sorry."

Her smile faltered. "Oh, okay. Thanks for checking in on me. I'll see you tomorrow, right?"

"Yeah, Marla's planning on picking us up in the morning, which is not soon enough." Nathan chuckled.

"Well, goodnight." She leaned forward, likely reaching for the button.

"Wait," said Nathan. "Do you mind staying on the line a bit longer? Keep my mind off the moldy ceiling tile?"

She smiled. "It really *is* bad down there. Okay, so we'll just skip the small talk. Tell me your deepest desires and your strongest fears."

"Um."

She grinned, sweet and mischievous. "I'm kidding. Just tell me everything about yourself."

"You sure you want to hear it? You might fall asleep from boredom."

"Yep."

"Okay, I own my own business but I'm not rich. I'm blessed with good friends, most of whom you've met and just recently I got the opportunity to visit the lovely settlement of Bad Rock in the Epsilon Eridani star system."

She laughed and he felt warmth spread through him. "Wow, that all sounds terrific."

He smiled back, finding it difficult not to. "But you knew all that already."

"True."

"I'm from up north, in the Great Lakes region. Have you ever been there?"

"No."

"I'm not surprised. It's kind of rough up there. Lots of unemployment and bad weather. I lived with my mom after my dad died. She wanted me to get out of there so finding a way to accomplish that became her number one job."

Tricia smiled. "You make it sound like she kept you in line."

"Oh yeah. There was no fooling around. I had to keep my grades up and work hard. She set the example working long shifts as a waitress. I couldn't jerk around getting into trouble when she was working her ass off."

"You're a pilot and have your own business. It sounds like she did a good job."

He smiled at the memory of his mom. "I'd say so. We couldn't afford college but the military wanted me. They put me in officer candidate school and taught me to fly."

"That's impressive. Did you ever see any action?"

"Oh, a little. You know, nothing too bad. They stationed me on Mars when they were having the water troubles. Do you remember those?"

"I remember reading about it."

Nathan smiled, glad she hadn't said she'd read about it in history class. "Well, that was probably the most excitement I saw. That time did help me, though."

"Your mom must be proud."

Nathan's smile faltered. "She was. I lost her a few years ago."

"I'm sorry."

He waved her off. "No, it's all right. Anyway, enough about me. What about you?"

"Well, I'm a nurse who just recently completed a whirlwind tour of Mars with a rock band."

"Now that does sound exciting."

"Oh, for sure. What could be better than treating overdoses and constantly examining people's bits for STDs?"

"Wow, when you put it like that, it sounds less exciting."

"Yeah, and I left a good job in an emergency room for that."

"Why did you do that?"

"Eh, I was bored."

"You were?" Nathan said, "In an emergency room?"

"Well, it was dull compared to the job I had before it."

"What did you do?"

She grinned. "Air ambulance."

"Really?"

"Really. I used to fly out to accident sites and help rescue hikers up in the mountains near Go City."

"Are you a thrill seeker?"

Her smile spread a little. "I don't like to be bored."

"And here I've left you sitting in orbit."

"I *did* tell you to bring me along, remember? Of course, you didn't abandon me on purpose so I'll cut you some slack."

This time he grinned. "I appreciate that."

"Is everything all right down there?" she asked with a note of concern in her voice.

"It's a little odd. We met this guy, Dodger. He's the local Syndicate guy. It turns out that Bone Daddy ran drugs for him."

"I wouldn't have thought Luscious had the brains to do something like that."

"He didn't, at least not long term, or he would have kept up on his vessel's loan payments. Anyway, since we grabbed his ship and we have our own he wants me to take over the route."

Her jaw fell open at the suggestion. "What did he say when you told him no?"

He paused for a moment before answering, afraid of disappointing her. "I told him I'd give him an answer in the morning. I didn't want to deal with him tonight. Are you all right? You look a little tired."

"I'm used to long hours. I mean, all nurses are but flying between stars and witnessing a kidnapping seems to have worn me out."

Nathan decided to take pity on her. "Hey, I'm sorry to keep you up. Why don't you get some rest? Tomorrow's going to be busy too."

"Yeah, that's probably a good idea. Are you sure you can sleep in that place?"

"I've been in worse," he said. "Take it easy, okay? If you need anything let Marla or Richie know. They'll hook you up."

"Yeah, they've been pretty great." She paused a moment and he took the opportunity to just look at her, the one good thing in his life.

"Good night, Tricia."

"Good night, Nathan."

The connection broke and Nathan reclined on the bed. She really was amazing, almost more than he could hope for. She was smart and funny but most importantly talking to her was easy. Ever since that hijacking nonsense a year and a half ago he'd been trying to get his life together and failing. But Tricia, being near her just felt right, like he could let go of the anxiety that drove him crazy all the time. He knew what he felt was probably just the excitement of a new relationship but damn if it didn't feel good.

The day had been long and now it felt like it was catching up to him. As tired as he was though, he couldn't help but dwell on what he'd been telling Tricia, about his time on Mars.

The 66th Air Cavalry Group, also known as the Black Panthers, was deployed near Ares Vallis on Mars to support the local government. Nathan had been here six months. Water levels had dropped due to a drought and a battle was forming up between ranchers and the cities downstream serviced by the reservoir.

Snow melt from the nearby mountains replenished the reservoir but precipitation had been scant for a couple years. No matter how hard humans tried to control the red planet it clearly had ideas of its own. A group of ranchers led by a guy named Reggie Fulton had occupied the reservoir's pumping station. They wanted control of the water and the governor disagreed.

Nathan piloted an AHL-30a "Drangonfly" gunship. It had no wings but flew on four massive thrusters, two in the front and two in the rear, and its various armaments and antennae gave it an insect-like appearance.

He turned his ship around to watch the pumping station from a thousand meters up. His Dragonfly had been orbiting the facility for two hours now, and he grew bored of listening to the governor's negotiator speaking in a calm voice with an increasingly angry Reggie Fulton. Nathan didn't know much about psychology but the situation seemed to be deteriorating.

"Wish we'd just shoot the bastard already," his crew chief Ronny Chuff said. "We got a million damn guns out here. We should just light him up and be done with it."

Nathan shook his head. "As long as they don't blow up the pumping station this can still end with no one getting hurt, Ronny."

"If they didn't want to be hurt, they wouldn't be breaking the law and pointing guns at us. You ask me, once you pick up guns and aim them at the government you're a criminal and if that leads to you getting shot, that's too bad. You have to teach these people a lesson."

No one asked you, dumbass, *Nathan thought, but he conceded the man might have a point. The occupying ranchers had pointed rifles at them but Nathan didn't think they could hit a moving target at this distance. Even if they did, he doubted their rifles would harm the Dragonfly.*

"Stay frosty, Ronny, and keep your eyes open."

Ronny Chuff and a younger man, Dabney, occupied the gunner positions behind the cockpit. Each had responsibility for one side of the aircraft. Nathan reviewed the situation to get his mind off Ronny. The pumping station was situated on the dam at the edge of the reservoir. A valley led away to the grazing lands the ranchers used. The governor had the army situated around the pumping station. Further out, Protective Services had roads blocked and kept the growing crowds of supporters and protestors away from the facility.

"Buckeye Two-Six, Buckeye Actual, urgent!"

Nathan straightened up a little in his seat. The voice belonged to his commanding officer, Colonel Tillson. "Buckeye Actual, Buckeye Two-Six, go ahead."

"Buckeye Two-Six, perimeter breach five klicks east of your position. Initiate intercept protocol."

Nathan adjusted course and started toward the breach. "Buckeye Two-Six, wilco. Moving to intercept. Description? Are they armed?"

"One truck, Two-Six. Armed unknown but assume so."

"Roger."

Nathan switched to the aircraft's intercom. "Chuff, we're moving to intercept a perimeter breach. Confirm weapons safe."

"Weapons safe, affirmative."

Nathan swung wide of their normal patrol route and spotted a cloud of red dust moving across the plain. The targeting system for the cockpit locked on and he zoomed in on the vehicle, a short flatbed float truck with rails on the bed. Two people sat in the cab and four people held onto the rails in the back, all of them armed with rifles.

"Buckeye Actual, Buckeye Two-Six. Target in sight. Looks like a truck with armed occupants."

"Copy, Two-Six."

"Weapons hot," Chuff said over the intercom.

"Belay that, Chief! Weapons hold! Confirm!"

"They're armed, Nathan, and sighting on us. I can see them in the targeting scope."

Don't have time for your nonsense, *Nathan thought.* When they got back to base he wanted Chuff bounced off his aircraft.

"Buckeye Two-Six, Buckeye Actual. Something is up at the pumping station. Stop the truck, deadly force is authorized if they won't turn back."

"Copy."

"Weapons hot!" Chuff called from the rear.

Screw him, *Nathan thought, and he closed on the truck. He put the nose of the gunship on the truck, preventing Chuff and Dabney from getting a bead on it from either side. He hovered in their path and switched to the outside loudspeaker.*

"Stop the truck," his voice boomed across the plain. "You will not be allowed to pass."

The truck raced toward them and didn't show any sign of slowing down. Nathan saw a pair of men on the truck's bed aim their rifles at him. That worried him enough to pull back. The thrusters kicked up red dust and he knew he was flying too low, putting himself and the crew in danger just to see if he could intimidate the ranchers into turning back.

"They're going to shoot at us, Nathan!" Chuff called out, excitement in his voice. A month of flying circles around the reservoir had made him antsy.

"Hold your fire," Nathan said, in a calm voice. If the yahoos in the truck opened fire they would be obliterated. Until then, he kept his powder dry.

The truck kept approaching. Nathan shook his head and dropped the Dragonfly lower, flying backwards to match their speed, making sure he stayed right in their path. It closed in, the driver playing chicken and figuring Nathan would move his multi-million credit gunship out of the way of an old farm truck. He pulled back on the controls and raced for open sky. The aircraft looped around and approached the truck from behind. This time he pulled the Drangonfly alongside, the left side of his aircraft parallel with the right side of the truck.

"They're aiming at us again, Nathan."

He saw two of the men in the bed of the truck tracking him with rifles. This close he could see they held serious weaponry, large caliber rifles capable of damaging them. Now they were drawing closer to the pumping station and he couldn't allow them to reach it. He activated the loudspeaker again.

"Last chance. Stop the truck now and lower those guns."

The woman in the front seat shot him the finger with a smile on her face. He shook his head and juiced the throttle, getting ahead of them. The rifles followed.

"Chuff, take out the engine."

Nathan held the Dragonfly stable and his crew chief fired a short burst into the front of the truck. He felt sick as he watched rounds from the port side gun strike the engine compartment of the truck.

The face of the woman in the cab changed from a mocking smile to horror as she realized the men in the gunship had ruined their plans for the day. The float truck dropped to the hard pack of the access road, dug in on the driver's side and flipped. It rolled in a cloud of red dust and Nathan keyed his mic.

"Buckeye Actual, Buckeye Two-Six. Splash one truck. They're going to need a medic and a tow. Buckeye Two-Six clear."

"Copy that, Two-Six. Resume patrol and watch for incoming. Firefight underway at the pumping station."

Nathan moved back to their patrol route and angled his targeting scope to the pumping station. The doors lay on either side of the entrance. Soldiers stormed in and he could see flashes from inside. If the ranchers were shooting it was going to be a one sided battle. They had to be outnumbered ten-to-one. Smoke started coming from the windows but the water never flowed into the valley.

— «» —

The next day found Nathan on the deck of a bar near the base, drinking a pitcher of Margaritas and talking with Sam, the owner.

Nathan sipped his drink. "You said you knew Reggie, right? I'm sorry about how things went down," Nathan said.

Sam took a deep breath and let it out. "Ah, don't worry about it. Reggie was an asshole."

Nathan held up his glass. "So am I."

"There's going to be more fighting, you know."

Nathan nodded. The root cause of the problem, a shortage of water, hadn't been resolved. The governor of the territory had made a speech earlier in the day about settling the problem without violence and how awfully sorry he felt that so many people had died. Nathan had turned it off. He didn't want to hear a bunch of self-serving nonsense.

"So they're flying in water for the ranchers?"

Nathan nodded. "It's a temporary solution. They've got a squadron of heavy lifters coming. They'll shuttle water tanks down from the polar region until the reservoir is filled. It's all bullshit, though."

"What makes you say that?"

"They could have done that without killing anyone. Why didn't someone go to this effort before some ranchers occupied a pumping station? It's like things have to escalate to the point where someone dies before anyone will pay attention and come up with a solution. Those men didn't have to put themselves in harm's way to keep their cattle alive."

Sam nodded his agreement. "That's all true. How are you feeling?"

"I'm better than the ranchers in that truck we shot up. Three dead, three badly injured."

Sam shrugged at the answer. "In this situation, that may be the best outcome possible. I heard you gave them more chances than you were supposed to."

"Yeah, and I got ripped for it from my Colonel, but I don't care. They should have just stopped." Nathan took a drink. "I'm out."

Sam raised a gray eyebrow. "Yeah?"

"Uh-huh. My hitch is up in less than sixty days and I'm not signing up for another tour. I'm going to go do something where I'm not in a position to keep people under a boot heel."

"What do you have in mind?"

"I've got my service benefits. Maybe I'll get my space certification." He waved his glass toward the sky. "Fly around up there and keep to myself. Do what I want and be my own boss."

"Hell, I'm my own boss. Just look around at how well that's turning out." The bar was empty except for the two of them and a pair of ground crew members sitting at a table inside.

"Well, I'll try to be successful," Nathan said with a smile. "Who knows, maybe I'll have my own ship someday."

Chapter 13

After dinner at the motel, when Nathan left them to go to bed, Cole grabbed his jacket and said. "I'll see you in the morning."

"Where are you going?" Duncan said.

"Check out that strip club Dodger runs."

Duncan raised an eyebrow. "Why?"

"That guy is going to be trouble. I'd like to know a little more about him."

"So you're doing a little recon?"

"That's right."

"I'm coming."

"No."

"Yes."

They walked outside the diner and stood on the sidewalk. Cole put a hand on Duncan's shoulder. "Big man, this is what I do. Why don't you go get some rest? Tomorrow is going to be a busy day."

Duncan brushed his hand off. "Stick that 'big man' stuff where the sun doesn't shine. Most of the time I'm stuck on the ship and you and Nathan get to do the fun stuff. I can do more than just fix things."

"I get that, Duncan. It's just that this part can be a little dangerous. I'd hate for anything to happen to you."

"You think I've never been in a club before? I'm not a child."

Cole considered him and then nodded. "Okay, come on then. The first thing we need is transportation."

Duncan pointed at the motel office. "Let's try in there."

They walked across the lot and the door to the office chimed as they entered. A young guy glanced up from the counter. "Can I help you?"

"We checked in earlier," Cole said.

"I remember. Is there something wrong with your rooms?"

"No they're fine. Actually, we need some transportation."

The clerk got a puzzled look on his face. "Well, I think all the rental places are closed. How about a ride share?"

"How about that little yellow number outside with the rust on the back door? Is that yours?"

"Uh… yeah but I'm not letting you borrow it."

Cole reached into his pocket and pulled out a wad of credit vouchers. "When's the end of your shift?"

The clerk eyed the vouchers. "Six hours from now."

He peeled four off. "Here's two hundred. We'll have it back before you need to go home."

The clerk considered it for a moment. "Three hundred."

Cole looked back at the float car in the parking lot. "We could buy it for three couldn't we?"

"It's three or you can walk."

Cole peeled off two more vouchers and laid them on the desk. "Yeah, all right. Here you go."

The clerk dug in his pocket and pulled out a fob. "Take it easy. I need that heap to get back and forth to work."

"Don't worry," Cole said and pointed at Duncan. "If we break anything he can fix it."

Cole slipped into the driver's seat and started the car. It rose unsteadily at first and then leveled out about fifteen centimeters off the ground. He activated the auto-driver and told it to head to Dodge Ems's.

"So what do we do when we get there?" Duncan asked.

"Scope the place out. See if there's anything worth seeing."

"Do you do this kind of thing on every job?"

Cole nodded in the darkness. "If I need to. It's always better to know too much than too little. So, what do you think of Nathan's problem?"

"Which one?"

Cole laughed. "His financial situation. It sounds like he's not doing too well."

Duncan sighed before answering. "It's his own fault. He earns well enough for being a small business but he could spend it better. Marla and I have been looking for a new investment but I doubt he'd sell us a piece of the company. You know how he is about being in control."

"Hold on," Cole said. "Car, pull over here."

The float car pulled to the curb and settled to the street. Duncan opened his door and started to get out but Cole put a hand on his arm.

"Not so fast, Duncan. We're going to spend some time scoping the outside for a while and see what's going on."

Duncan's eyebrows knitted together. "We're going to watch the parking lot?"

"Yes we are." Cole took his mobi from inside his coat, put it in camera mode and trained it on the club entrance. He synched it to the guidance system in the car and turned down the brightness of the screen. "This is what we do while you're up in the ship. I don't think it's going to be as exciting as you think."

"No, I guess not."

They sat in silence for a while, watching people come and go. After half an hour Duncan spoke up. "What did you think of the salvage outfit?"

"I think we blew a whole day here because you and Nathan wanted to see a crashed ship."

"You're always complaining about the places we end up but this job has been fascinating. Eldridge has some good ideas."

Cole shrugged. "Maybe, but he'll get eaten alive by the Syndicate if he keeps paying them off. These guys never stop until all the meat is off the bone." He pointed at the video display. "Isn't that our friend Turtle?"

"Yeah, that's him. I wonder where he's going?"

They watched as Turtle exited the club and made his way to a rusted float car. He weaved as he walked.

He sat up straight and put the camera away. "Car, manual control, please." Cole took the wheel and the float car rose into the air. He counted to five to give Turtle a head start and pulled out behind him.

"We're following him?"

Cole nodded. "I just want to see where he's going."

"He's probably going home to sleep it off."

"Then we'll see where he lives."

Turtle's car moved through the streets quickly and without swerving. "Good thing he's got auto-drive in that heap," Duncan said.

"Definitely."

Turtle lead them across town to a block full of rundown apartment buildings. His car pulled up in front of one and parked. Cole stopped half a block back and pulled to the opposite side of the street. They watched as he stumbled up the concrete steps in front of the building. Someone opened the door and let him in.

"I wouldn't have expected that building to have a doorman," Cole said.

"No, neither would I. Why are there only lights on the ground floor?"

Cole examined the building and noticed dark windows on all the floors above the first one. He opened the driver's side door and beckoned to Duncan. "Let's go take a look around."

Duncans' eyebrows raised. "What? Over there?"

"Yup."

Duncan hurried out of the car and followed Cole across the street to the sidewalk on the same side as the apartment building. They hunkered down beside some overgrown bushes in front of dark storefront.

Cole took Duncan by the arm. "Just follow me and stay quiet, okay? The streetlights are all out along this block so we should be good."

Duncan nodded in the darkness.

Cole moved back to the sidewalk and hurried along it to the corner of the store. Cole peeked down the alley that ran alongside of it and motioned for Duncan to follow. The engineer breathed through his mouth, he noticed. They moved down the alley and Cole checked the area to his right. He could see the back of the apartment building Turtle had entered. Cole held a hand up and pointed to the back entrance. A man with a small rifle stood near the back door smoking a cigarette, partially hidden by a large garbage recycler.

Cole turned to Duncan. "You have guards like that on your apartment building?"

"Maybe they all live here together?"

"Maybe. Let's get closer. You doing okay? You're breathing hard."

"Thanks for noticing. We don't run a lot while we're working on the engines."

Cole smiled. "We'll get you a treadmill down there. Come on."

They bent down and stuck to the shadows. The guard sat down on the steps and took out a mobi. He stared at the screen and kept his head down. Cole raised a finger to his lips and motioned for Duncan to stay put.

He took another look at the guard and then sprinted across the open space to the opposite side of the garbage recycler. He pulled a small baton from his coat and gave it a flick, expanding it as he crept around the recycler to get closer to the guard. The man was watching a movie on his mobi.

Cole jabbed him in the leg with the baton and the guard stiffened from the resulting electrical shock. He slid down onto the stairs unconscious and Cole tossed his rifle into the bushes as he moved silently up the concrete steps to the back door. The collapsed baton went back into a pocket.

The door opened with a tug and he didn't see anyone inside. Cole padded down the dark hallway past several abandoned rooms. As he approached a set of double doors at the end of the hall, the low hum of machinery filled the air. He paused and listened at the doors. The humming noise didn't sound like it belonged in an apartment building. Something inside thudded to the floor and he heard movement on the other side of the doors. He moved back to the first empty apartment and ducked inside. There was no door to close so he hid in the shadows and watched the double doors.

They slammed open and a woman wearing a gas mask pulled a shrink-wrapped pallet out of the room with the help of an anti-grav lifter. For a brief moment, he saw inside the room. Women in gas masks worked at tables. Behind them, tanks with chemical labels and laboratory equipment lined the walls. Then the double doors closed behind her. He waited until she passed and risked a look into the hallway.

The woman pulled the pallet into another large room at the end of the hall near the exit door. He heard the pallet settle to the floor and then she reappeared and made her way back to the room with the double doors. Cole counted to ten and didn't hear anything else. He slipped out of the dark room and moved quickly to the room where she had taken the pallet.

In the dim light, he could see the pallet she had left there and three others like it. He moved behind one and pulled out a pocket knife. After carefully slitting the plastic wrap he reached inside and pulled out a handful of Diamond K packets. He shoved a few of them in a jacket pocket and moved back toward the exit. He checked over his shoulder to make sure no one followed and opened the door to go outside. He started down the steps before he noticed the guard missing from where he had left him.

Someone grabbed him around the waist and they tumbled down the steps to the concrete below. Cole squirmed, determined not to let the guy get on top of him but his heavy assailant had other ideas. He saw the guard's fist raise and he braced for a blow. Then he heard a smacking sound and the guard collapsed. Duncan stood above him, breathing heavily with a length of pipe in his hand. He held out a hand and pulled Cole to his feet.

"We may not run a lot in the engines but we do turn some wrenches," Duncan said, smiling and flexing a huge bicep.

Cole patted him on the shoulder. "I'm thankful for that. He should have been out longer."

"Maybe he's on something."

"Yeah, like this." He held up a packet of the drugs he found inside.

"So this is a drug house?"

"They're manufacturing it here. There's a big room in there I could see with lots of people at tables and there's pallets of the stuff in a separate storeroom all packed up for shipment."

"What should we do now?" Duncan said.

"Let's head back to the motel and get some rest. In the morning, we can talk to Nathan and see if we can do our job and leave."

— «» —

Nathan woke up in the motel room as orange sunlight broke through the curtains. He sat up on the bed and thought about his situation with Dodger. The dealer's offer enticed him because of the credits. Then he remembered last night and thought about Mars again; how it felt to do things because he was ordered to, how it felt to pull the trigger on some ranchers because of a fight he had no stake in.

He couldn't live like that again. No way.

After showering and putting on the same clothes he'd worn yesterday, he decided they had to leave today just so he could change. He headed toward the motel office and saw Cole and Duncan in the parking lot. Cole filled him on what he and Duncan had done last night.

"That was stupid," Nathan said. "You could have been hurt."

Cole waved him off. "We're big boys, Nathan, and we're fine. Now we know where Dodger is making his stuff."

"For all the good it does us. I'm not really sure I care."

"So have you come to a decision about what you're going to do?" Cole asked. "Are you going to run drugs?"

"I spent a lot of time thinking about it last night. I still think people have a right to do what they want. I've been on the side of authority and forcing people to live in ways they didn't want. That's why I started my own business, so I'll never have to follow orders again."

"The thing is, running for Dodger or some other asshole like him just puts you under his thumb. You have to go where he says, when he says and you're dependent on him for everything. So, while I'm sure the credits would be good and I need them, I won't be running for him. We have a company and we stand on our own. If he doesn't like that I really don't care. We'll deal with it."

Cole smiled. "Nathan Teller is nobody's bitch. Is that it?"

Duncan laughed and Nathan smiled. "You're damn straight."

Chapter 14

Squinting his eyes in the back seat, Dodger held up a hand against the rising sun. "Tint the damn windows, would you?"

The car's auto-driver complied and the windows grew dark. He took another swig of coffee from the large mug he held in his hand. The car bounced over some debris and the hover field didn't compensate quickly enough. Hot coffee spilled into his crotch and he cursed while grabbing for something to wipe it up.

He normally did business in the wee hours of the morning so for him to be up at the crack of dawn meant something or someone had seriously screwed up. The call from Morris waking him up had been vague which meant nothing good.

The car pulled into the club's parking lot and he got out and walked toward the entrance as soon as it came to a stop. He walked past the bouncer standing outside without acknowledging him and stormed into his office where he found Morris and Turtle waiting for him. He fell into his chair and it squealed under the assault.

"What's going on?"

Turtle slouched down in one of the chairs facing his desk.

Morris stood up straight, impossibly awake for this hour of the day. "There have been a couple troubling developments overnight."

Dodger waved a hand at him. "Here or on Earth with the shipment Turtle's friends were supposed to recover?"

"Both."

Turtle sat up. "I can explain."

Dodger stared at him. "I'll bet you can but I want to hear it from Morris."

"The short version is that a couple guys from a Go City crew went out to Bone Daddy's ship to retrieve the goods and got surprised by a couple of Customs officers. They ended up in a shootout; the Go City crew got the worst of it."

"How bad?"

"One dead, and his uncle is in the hospital with his junk shot off."

Dodger raised an eyebrow. "Ouch. What about the product?"

Morris paused a moment before answering. "Confiscated."

"Will the guy in the hospital talk?"

"Uncle Donny will keep his mouth shut, Dodger. You can count on him."

Dodger's eyes flashed with anger. "Shut up. The only reason I'm not beating you with a pool cue again is that I honestly don't know if I could stop."

Morris glanced at Turtle. "I'm inclined to agree with him. The guy runs with Atomic Jack's crew and they've always been solid."

Dodger grunted. "Yeah, except for that time they lost twenty-three million credits." He rubbed his bloodshot eyes and pulled a plastic envelope from his desk drawer. He popped a large crystal in his mouth and chewed. "Any chance we can get the pallet back?"

Morris shook his head. "None. It's evidence in the attempted murder of the two Customs agents so it's locked up tight. At this point they've probably got trackers on it just in case we try."

Dodger glared at Turtle. "I'll bet you can't take a piss without screwing it up."

"However," Morris said, "we may not be as lucky with Bone Daddy."

"What do you mean?"

"Protective Services has him in custody on Mars and they're shipping him to Earth."

"Ah, damn it. Can our people on Mars do anything about him?"

Morris shook his head. "No, our people on Mars is one guy, unless you want to call in help from Syndicate management."

Dodger shook his head. "No, don't do that. Things are already getting out of control. I don't want them thinking we can't manage our problems." He paused for a moment and considered how complicated things had gotten recently. "You mentioned something else happened?"

"Last night someone was creeping around the apartment building."

"Yeah? What happened?"

"Someone assaulted a guard on the rear entrance. His relief went out at the beginning of his shift and found him unconscious. He had been stunned and beaten."

"Damn it. Did they get inside?"

"We think so. The guard says they stunned him first and he jumped whoever it was when they came back out but someone hit him from behind."

"Double the guard on the site."

"It's already done. I've instructed them to have two guards at each entrance. No one is allowed to work alone on the doors."

"Good. I'm glad to see someone around here is using their head for something other than growing hair." He turned to Turtle. "Are you working for someone else?"

"What? No, of course not!"

Dodger crunched down on another crystal. "It's awfully strange, all these things happening at once. Don't you think?"

"What do you mean? I haven't done anything except try to fix this mess."

"Really? Because from where I'm sitting you look like the cause of all my problems. Your friend got his ship repossessed and our shipment impounded on Earth. Then, your uncle couldn't get our product back. Now, we've got those same repo agents out here nosing around the wreck of that ship while we're shaking down the salvage crew."

Dodger stood up and started pacing. "Did this guard get a look at the guy who assaulted him?"

"Yes. He said it was a white, tall guy with short hair wearing a leather jacket."

Dodger spun around. "Sounds like one of the guys with Teller yesterday."

"Could be. I'll pull a picture from the security cameras here in the club and show it to him."

Dodger nodded. "Do that but get Cheech in here. We may want the drone up in the air. Do that first." He punched a wall and the room echoed with a loud, flat smack. He stood silently for a few moments and no one spoke. He turned around. "We still don't have the coolant from the wreck do we?"

"No," Turtle managed to stammer out.

"Get a truck ordered. Now. We're getting it this morning." He walked around the desk and advanced on Turtle who leaned back in his chair with wide eyes. "You screw this up, and I'll make you wish you were as lucky as your uncle, do you understand me?"

Turtle nodded his head vigorously. "Yeah, okay. I'm on it."

"Go."

Turtle got up and ran from the room. Dodger turned back to Morris. "There are too many coincidences going on. It's time to get a grip on things."

Morris nodded and held his mobi up. "Cheech is on his way and I'm waiting to hear back from the guards at the building. We'll know if Teller is our guy shortly."

—— «» ——

"You're serious about this?" Eldridge said. "I mean, you're really going to take my ship?"

Nathan sighed and nodded. "Look kid, I'm sorry. I am, really, but we have a job to do and it's time to get it done." He stood in front of Eldridge at the main camp. The kid leaned against his workbench and Ari sat on the stool.

"You can say that again," Cole said under his breath but loudly enough for Nathan to hear.

"I thought about it and you could have your crew keep working onsite while you come back with us and straighten things out with Bao at the bank. If you're able to do it quickly enough you really won't lose any time. You'll just have to run the trucks up and down when you get back until you're caught up."

Ari huffed. "We don't need you to tell us how to run our business."

Eldridge put a hand on her shoulder. "Honey, don't."

She shook it off. "Don't what? Don't be upset that we're going to be even further behind when this is all straightened out? Why don't we just have the security 'bots boot them out of here? There's only three of them."

"You don't want to do something like that," Nathan said, his tone growing more serious. "This job can go very easy or very hard. I would prefer to do it the easy way."

Ari got off the stool and faced Eldridge. "We don't have to let them take the ship."

"You don't have a choice, miss." Nathan took a mobi from Duncan. "We've already logged into the *Corkscrew* and can take control anytime we want."

"Dirty trick."

Nathan gave them a little smile. "Just like pulling us down here, right? You learn a thing or two about what unhappy people will do in these situations. Please, let's not make this any tougher than it has to be."

Eldridge gripped the workbench and then grabbed a 'bot head and fired it off in the direction of the *Athena Star* as hard as he could. "Damn it!" Ari went to him and put her hands on his shoulders. Nathan could hear them speaking softly, trying to calm each other down. Hopefully, the situation wouldn't get ugly. He turned to Cole.

"If they do anything stupid, try not to hurt them too badly. They're just upset."

"I don't think they'll do anything."

Eldridge walked back under the canopy. "Take the ship and I'll go with you to get this all straightened out." He pointed a finger at Nathan. "You're not riding up in one of my trucks, though. Find your own way."

"No problem. We called for our ship. They'll be down in a little while."

"Great."

"Look, if it means anything, I think you're making the right decision."

Eldridge shook his head. "It really doesn't." He turned to Ari. "I'm going to grab some gear from the tent. Will you be all right if it takes me a week to travel and get this straightened out?"

She stared past him to Nathan. "Don't worry. There's nothing here I can't handle."

He wrapped her up in his arms. "I love you so much."

She hugged him back. "Same here." They broke apart a moment later. "Now go get your stuff."

—— «» ——

The mobi on Morris' desk chirped. He picked it up and said, "Yeah? Hold on, I'm putting you on visual." He walked over to Dodger's desk and set down the communication's device. "It's our guy up on the *Corkscrew*," he said to Dodger.

Morris touched a button and Charlie's head hovered above the communication device. "Say that again."

"I said- that ship you have me watching took off. I think they're heading down to the planet."

"How long ago?" Morris said.

Charlie shrugged. "I'm not sure. Definitely within the last thirty minutes. I had to use the can so I don't know exactly."

"Did anyone board your ship before they left?"

"No. That I'm sure of."

"Ok," Morris said and ended the call. "If Teller's ship is coming to pick him up they're probably leaving the planet."

Dodger considered that for a moment and his attention went to the monitor on the wall showing the drone footage from the wreck site.

"Did you get an answer from the guard at the apartment building?" Dodger asked.

"Let me check." Morris thumbed through his messages. "Yeah, here's something." He took a moment and read the message. Then he held his mobi up so Dodger could see it. The message said 'That's him.'

"Sonuvabitch!" Dodger said and pounded the desk. He picked up a crystal and chewed it. "So, they're out at the apartment building sneaking around and figured out where we make the stuff and the next day they're leaving?" He shook his head. "No, that's too much of a coincidence. I wonder who they're working for."

Morris raised an eyebrow. *Maybe it's too much of the Diamond K making you paranoid,* he thought but he kept it to himself. "What do you want to do?"

"Where's Jonesy?"

Morris nodded toward the club. "I called him when I called Cheech. He's sitting out at the bar eating breakfast."

"I hope he hacked Tanner's 'bots as well as he said. Tell him to get ready to take control."

"Will do."

Dodger reached out and put a hand on his shoulder. "After that, get a couple guys and a couple cars. You and I are taking a ride out there."

— «» —

Eldridge came out of the tent with a duffel bag and dropped it in on the table. "I'm going to head up to my ship in a truck and let Scooter know what's going on."

"I think it would be best if Scooter didn't get any more smart ideas," Nathan said.

Eldridge nodded and grinned. "Don't worry about it. She won't pull anything as long as I'm around." He pointed up the road leading to the wreck site and frowned. "What's that?"

They all turned and Nathan saw a tanker truck heading toward them. It passed the canopy and drove right up to the crashed vessel, stopping near the cargo bay.

Eldridge shook his head and stomped out from under the canopy toward one of the maintenance vehicles. Ari went with him. Nathan ran to catch up with him.

"What are you going to do?" Nathan said.

"Give him a piece of my mind. I don't care if he takes the damn coolant but he could at least let me know what's going on."

Eldridge got onto the maintenance vehicle and Nathan grabbed the seat next to him. "I don't want to tell you how to run your business but you may not want to make these guys angry and then fly out of here."

"I know," Eldridge said as he started the vehicle. "I'm just going to let them know to check with me before they do this kind of stuff. And I don't need you telling me what to do."

Ari, Cole and Duncan climbed into the back and Eldridge took them down to the tanker truck. When they got there,

Turtle jumped out of the cab of the truck and hurried over to them.

"Eldridge, you have to let us do this, okay? Seriously, don't interfere."

They got off the maintenance vehicle and Eldridge held up a hand. "You know what, Turtle? I don't have to let you do anything but I'm not going to stop you. If Dodger wants that coolant to make his junk he can have it. Just make sure I have the disposal paperwork I need."

Relief washed over Turtle's face. "Yeah, no problem. You'll have it."

Eldridge sized him up. "Why are you acting so nice? Normally, you'd give me a lecture about how you and Dodger are in charge. How if I want to complain about something, maybe I should go talk to the man himself. Where's all your lip now?"

Turtle held up a hand. "I've had a rough day, Eldridge. Just back off. I'll take care of this and then I'll go back down to my pile."

Eldridge nodded and saw the truck driver uncoiling his hoses. He stepped closer to Turtle. "What did you do to make him angry, Turtle? Hmm? You get the big man mad at you?"

Turtle stuck a finger in his face. "Don't worry about it. Just go do your thing and let us finish this up."

"Sure, go about your business. I won't stand in your way."

Turtle picked up a coil of hose and a wrench. "Good. We'll be done in an hour." He followed the driver inside the wreck.

'Bots approached the wreck and started climbing to their positions for the morning shift. Nathan and the rest of the group made way for them.

"They just start up on their own and get to work?" Nathan asked.

"Yeah, we restrict work to daylight so we can see what's going on." Nathan saw his attention shift as the salvager's gaze drifted past him. "Now who is that?"

Nathan turned and saw a couple float cars moving toward them at high speed. Two cars, one newer and in better condition than the other, bounced across the rough packed dirt of the service road. They pulled up close to where the two crews stood. Dodger got out of the newer car and stomped toward them, yelling. "Are you two working together? Is that it?"

Nathan shrugged his shoulders. "What are you talking about?"

Half a dozen guys got out of the cars behind Dodger and fanned out around them as he paced in front of them. He watched as Morris took his place by the boss's side. Dodger pointed at them.

"Don't screw with me; you know what I'm talking about."

"I really don't and I've got a job to do so either speed this up or get out of my way."

Dodger blinked rapidly, his eyes watering. He wiped them with his knuckles. "You're not just some repo man. You're with Protective Services back on Earth. Did you think we wouldn't figure it out?" He became more agitated and nearly shouted, "We're not stupid."

Nathan stayed calm. "I don't know what you're talking about."

Dodger ran a hand through his hair. "Oh really? First, you grab the ship on Mars that had a shipment on it and then you show up here in Bad Rock. I suppose that's a coincidence?"

"That's the job. I go where the bank tells me."

Dodger leaned in. "I don't believe in coincidences."

"I'm not sure this is one," Nathan said. He stayed calm, trying to keep a lid on things. "On Mars that idiot Bone Daddy missed his payments. Here it's Eldridge. There's no connection between them."

"There's me!" Dodger screamed. "I'm the connection!" He rocked back and forth now and spittle flew as he spoke. "Someone is on to us and you're going to tell me who. Protective Services doesn't have jurisdiction out here so they sent you to investigate." He pointed again. "They sent you to grab Bone Daddy's ship and that led you here so you made up this story about repossessing his ship," he said pointing at Eldridge, "just to use your cover." He shifted to Eldridge. "Let me guess, you aren't really behind on your payments are you?"

Eldridge stood still. "No, not as far as I know."

Dodger nodded his head maniacally, "See? Look at this operation. Don't you think this guy would know if he had missed some payments? Your cover story sucks."

"You're paranoid," Nathan said. "You've been using your own product for so long you can't tell reality from your own delusions."

Dodger, eyes wide, nodded some more. "Oh sure, I'm paranoid. That's what it is. Oh, except for the fact that you sent this guy," he pointed at Cole, "to figure out where we manufacture our product."

Nathan shot a look at Cole who stood silently.

"Yeah, see that's where your cover story falls apart," Dodger raved. "Why would repo agents be snooping around the apartment building where we make this stuff? Tell me that."

Nathan shrugged. "Cole looks out for us. After you offered us Bone Daddy's route we got curious about you. After all, you had all the background you could want on us."

Dodger grimaced and pointed at Nathan. "See, that's not, you're just trying to confuse the issue. Don't." He shook his head like a thought was stuck in there. "Don't do that. Stick to the issue. Do you understand? You came here to see where the Diamond K came from and now you know so you're flying off to tell your masters. A few days from now, this place will be crawling with uniforms. That's the issue."

Nathan leaned forward. "When we got here you initiated contact with us. You called the meeting in your office. I didn't even know you at that point. If you had just left us alone we wouldn't know anything about you. This is all on you."

"No, it's all on you." Dodger paced in a tight circle. Nathan noticed his man Morris giving him lots of room.

"I don't want to haul for you; I just want to do my job."

Dodger waved a finger at him. "Oh you can forget about that offer. I wouldn't let you touch my product now that I know who you are and what you're up to."

Nathan's exasperation slipped into his voice. "Get this through your head. I don't care what you're doing here. That's between you and the law. I don't need any other problems, so leave us out of it."

"No, you're in it now." Dodger paused and the only sound came from the 'bots on the wreck. "You're going to tell us everything you know about us and who you are reporting to."

"Well, that will be easy because we don't know anything and we aren't reporting to anyone."

Dodger fidgeted, picking at a nail. "What do you know about the *Hell's Breath* right now?"

"Bone Daddy's shitheap? It's on Earth in Go City waiting for the bank to clean it up for sale."

"And you don't know anything about a couple of Syndicate guys getting shot while trying to retrieve some product?"

Nathan's eyes narrowed as he thought about the pallet of Diamond K he saw during his inspection of the cargo hold. "What? No. I don't know what you're talking about."

"We sent a couple guys out to the ship to get our stuff and Customs caught them. They jumped them as soon as they came out with the stuff. Now, you expect me to believe you don't know anything about that?"

"You're paranoid."

"I'm not! You think you can talk your way out of this and you can't."

A roar came from above them and all eyes went up. Nathan spotted the *Blue Moon Bandit* approaching Eldridge's camp high up in the sky. Marla bled off excess re-entry speed with a series of 'S' curve maneuvers.

Nathan stepped forward, causing Dodger to take a step back. "As soon as my ship gets down here, we're leaving. You can make your dope and sell it or chew it or shove it up your ass for all I care but it's got nothing to do with us."

Dodger recovered and stood up straight. "Nobody does anything until I'm satisfied." He walked over to Morris and got right in his face. "You tell Jonesy to do what we talked about. Do it now."

Morris took a step back with his mobi to his ear. Nathan shook his head slightly at Cole. Dodger had eight Syndicate guys, counting Morris. He knew they couldn't take them without someone getting hurt.

Five 'bots working nearby in the cargo bay exited the ship and moved around the crowd. Nathan only noticed them when they didn't continue walking past. One of them seized his upper arms in an iron grip and lifted him off the ground. He tried to break loose but couldn't. Cole, Duncan, Eldridge and Ari struggled as well. No one could break free.

He overheard Dodger tell Morris, "Move them into the ship and hold them there. Is Cheech still in the office?"

"This is stupid," Nathan said. "Let us go, right now. There's no reason for anyone to get hurt."

Dodger dismissed him with a wave of his hand. "We're past that now."

The *Bandit* approached overhead with a roar. Morris spoke to Dodger, holding his mobi. "I've got Cheech."

Dodger pointed to the sky. "Tell him to bring that ship down."

Chapter 15

Marla let out a low whistle as the wreck of the *Athena Star* came into view. "Wow, I have never seen anything like that before."

Tricia saw the wreck through the canopy. "And everyone got off?"

"That's the story," Richie said. He stood in the doorway of the cramped cockpit with an arm braced on either side. His green rescue vest had a smiley face drawn on it with a black marker.

"Go strap in, Richie," she said with a sharp edge to her voice. "You know you aren't supposed to be moving around during re-entry."

"Okay. It's just kind of lonely back there."

"You're sitting directly behind the bulkhead. I can hear you talk without the headset."

"Yeah, yeah."

Marla watched as he moved back to the station behind the cockpit. She called Bad Rock air traffic control at the spaceport to let them know she had completed re-entry then adjusted and trimmed the ship for approach. Hidden stabilizers and ailerons slid free of their housings and gave her a little more atmospheric control.

She examined the area for a good spot to land, making sure there weren't any wires or debris in the area. Nathan had sent coordinates but she wanted a good view of the area before setting down.

An alarm sounded, barking directives at her in a clipped computer voice. "Collision! Go Right! Collision! Go Right!"

Her training took over and she jerked the ship to the right as she yelled. "Brace! Brace! Brace!"

"What's wrong?" Tricia said. "What is that?"

Marla had just enough time to glimpse a dark object barreling at them from the left and then the ship shook with a bone jarring impact. Alarms sounded and Tricia screamed. Marla saw her put her arms over her head just like Nathan had instructed during their departure lecture.

"Richie! We took a hit."

"From what?"

"I don't know. I think it hit the port engine cowling. I'm losing control up here."

Another alarm sounded as the orientation of the ship changed and the computer voice gave her another directive. "Pull up! Pull up!"

Marla yanked back on the yoke and saw a lot of ground fill the canopy instead of the sky.

"Pull up! Pull up!" The computer reminded her.

"I'm trying!" Marla yelled back. "Richie, I'm having trouble getting us level. The port side thrusters aren't giving me anything." The ship began to yaw and roll simultaneously to the left.

"I don't think there's anything to give." She heard him say in her headset. He spoke calmly but his voice had an edge to it. "I've got fire alarms all along the port side. I think we're venting thruster plasma. I'm going to have to shut it off."

"Don't! I need it to fly!"

"We'll burn up, Marla! It's venting internally! It's only the port side. You'll still have starboard."

Marla's mind raced. The *Blue Moon Bandit* flew like a brick without thrusters. It had no wings to keep them aloft and just few a control surfaces to help maneuver the ship. She stole a glance at the artificial horizon and saw it tipping.

She started running through what she had left working. The flight computer worked with her, trying to keep them level. That's all she really needed, just to get level and stable until they figured out a solution.

She jerked the yoke again and the ship responded incorrectly. Every move she made seemed thwarted by a lack of control. The starboard engine and the starboard thrusters still worked but the thrust from them actually de-stabilized the ship, pushing them to the left without the counter-balance of the port side thrusters.

The sky spun past the canopy as the ship rotated. They were going to crash, she realized, unless she came up with something.

Panic began to set in but she pushed it back, thinking through the problem. Tricia sat frozen with fear, hanging on to the arms of her chair with her eyes closed tight.

"Tricia, is your vest on properly?"

She opened one eye. "What?"

"Your vest. Is it on properly?"

The nurse tugged on her orange vest. "Yes, I think so."

"Okay, if it ends up activating don't worry, okay? It will help protect you."

Through clenched teeth Tricia asked, "Is it going to go off?"

"Maybe."

Marla examined her controls again. "Richie, are you strapped in tight?"

"Yes. Why?" He sounded scared but held it together.

She didn't answer him. She gripped the thruster control for the remaining engine and pushed it to max. The ship responded with a roar and rocketed through the blue sky.

—— ⟨⟩ ——

"No!" Nathan shouted as he watched his pride and joy shoot away from them trailing thick black smoke. "What did you do?" He struggled harder in the 'bot's grip. "You're a goddamn maniac! My crew is on that ship!"

Duncan managed to get a foot up on the side of the door leading into the cargo bay and kicked off. He rocked but the 'bot held him steady. "Let me go! That's my wife up there!" He kicked again.

Dodger walked over to Nathan and grabbed him by the jaw, getting right up in his face. Nathan could see his eyes darting around crazily and smelled his horrible breath as he spoke. "You brought this on all of us, not me. You stay here for now."

The gangster turned to Morris. "Tell Jonesy I want them secured in the cargo hold until we have the coolant."

His number two nodded and relayed the message.

Dodger turned back to Nathan. "Whoever sent you had a supremely bad idea."

Nathan's breath labored hard from the effort to break free. "We're here to repo a ship you asshole. The bank holding the note sent us."

Dodger gave him a light slap on the cheek. "We'll see. I'm going to be asking you some questions after we pump the coolant." He turned to Morris and nodded toward the wreck. "Get them secured."

The 'bots carried them into the cargo bay. Nathan saw the hoses to the tanker truck snaking off to the right. The 'bots turned left and carried them through another, larger door into a smaller bay. A small work lamp hung from the ceiling in the otherwise empty space. The doors to the bay slammed close and Nathan heard them being secured.

"Eldridge, get us free."

"This is crazy," Eldridge said. "How did things get this crazy?"

"Eldridge," Nathan said more sharply. "Get us free. We have to see what's happening to our ship. Duncan's wife is aboard." *And Tricia.*

The other 'bots continued working on the wreck, oblivious to the plight of their master. Nathan saw Eldridge look at Ari and she nodded to him. He closed his eyes and concentrated.

Duncan turned to the salvager. "Look kid, one of Dodger's goons must have hacked into your software. How can we get control back?"

Eldridge chewed his lower lip. "Give me a second, let me think."

—— ⟨⟩ ——

"Are we stable?" Richie said. "It looks like we've evened out."

Marla ignored him and brushed sweat from her eyes with one hand while gripping the controls tightly with the other. The ship shook violently under the strain of flying on one engine. *In thrust we trust,* she thought. She switched to the air traffic control channel.

Taking a deep breath, she spoke calmly but purposefully. "Mayday, mayday, mayday, Bad Rock ATC, this is the commercial vessel *Blue Moon Bandit* declaring an emergency."

A long period of silence followed and she opened her mouth to repeat her message when a calm voice answered.

"Aircraft in distress, this is Bad Rock ATC, we have you on sensors. What is the nature of the emergency and how many personnel do you have on board?"

"Bad Rock, *Bandit,* we took a strike of some kind in our port engine and have limited control over the spacecraft. There are three people on board."

"Copy that, *Bandit.* Are you stable now?"

"Affirmative, flying level now, but we have limited control.

"What are your intentions?"

To land without drilling a hole in the ground. "Bad Rock ATC, we need a runway cleared for a conventional landing."

"Roger that, *Bandit.* Runway Two-Five Left is clear for you. There is no traffic right now. You have the whole sky."

"Copy that. Runway length?"

"Runway Two –Five Left is two-thousand meters."

"Copy that. Thank you."

She wished she could be as calm as she sounded. Her heart beat so fast and so hard she had to grit her teeth to maintain control of herself. The smell of something burning caught her attention and she turned her head to yell through the open cockpit door. "Richie, are we on fire?"

"I think the fire suppression system has it out," he called back. "You're probably smelling residue from the plasma venting. I'm trying to get the air scrubbers to clean it up. Can you breathe all right? I can close the cockpit door."

Tricia gave her a thumb's up but the fear crept around the nurse's eyes. "No, leave it open. We're good."

"Marla, how are we flying?" Richie said.

She made an adjustment to their heading and the ship turned sluggishly, shaking as she changed course but finally came about. Her heads-up display directed her toward the spaceport and finally glowed green when she had the ship lined up for a straight shot to the runway. She triggered the intercom.

"Richie, Tricia, I'm going to give you an update. First, stay strapped in, don't move around for any reason. My control over the ship is limited." She swallowed hard.

"Richie, to answer your question, I put full thrust to the starboard engine and gained some control. I think the hull of the ship is acting like a lifting body but we have to maintain speed to maintain control. Getting down is going to be tricky."

She paused and Richie said, "We're not landing vertically are we?"

"No, it's going to be a conventional landing."

Tricia had a puzzled expression on her face. "What does that mean? Is that bad?"

"Don't worry, it just means we're going to land horizontally on the runway instead of vertically on a pad."

"You've done that before?"

"Every pilot has. It's part of training." *Never in this ship, though.* She kept that to herself. "This is going to be a rough landing. We're getting pushed to the left because we're on one engine but I think I can deal with that." Something occurred to her then. "Hold on." She keyed the radio. "Bad Rock, *Bandit.*"

"Go ahead."

"We're going to be coming in hot. Request trucks."

"Copy, *Bandit.* Trucks on station."

"Thank you. Bad Rock, do you have barriers?"

"Affirmative, *Bandit.* There is an arrestor system, end of the runway."

"Copy. Thank you, Bad Rock."

"Trucks?" Tricia said.

Marla nodded. "Fire trucks and rescue vehicles."

She switched back to the intercom. "The plan is to use control surfaces to lower our altitude and cut thrust as much as possible. We're going to approach the runway hard and fast. Speed is the only thing keeping us in the air but we don't want it when we're landing." She wanted to explain as much as possible to help Tricia understand the situation. So far, the nurse seemed okay.

"Richie, any red lights I don't know about?"

"Negative, Marla. All systems are green except for the port thruster network. No fires, no reactor problems."

She thought about that. "Confirm, Richie. No reactor problems."

"Reactor is one hundred percent, fully contained. Hey Marla, can't we get into space and avoid landing? I may be able to give you thrusters with some time in orbit."

"I appreciate that, Richie, but I have no idea if we're spaceworthy. Getting up to escape velocity on one engine isn't a problem but there could be damage to the hull we don't know about."

She made an adjustment to keep them on course and the ship shuddered enough that she bit the inside of her cheek to keep from cursing at it. The spaceport came into view. She saw two runways, a tower and scattered hangars. Emergency vehicles sat on the tarmac with their lights flashing.

"*Bandit*, Bad Rock. We have a visual on you and see smoke."

"Copy that, Bad Rock."

"Just to let you know as a formality, we're getting a high-speed alarm."

No shit. "Copy that, Bad Rock."

The yoke shook harder as the spacecraft slowed. "It's going to get rough now," Marla said.

She checked her speed and the readout displayed twice the recommended rate for a conventional landing. "Richie, stand by on the drogue chute. When I tell you, get it deployed."

"Affirmative."

The slower their airspeed got the worse the shaking became. Marla jabbed the control for the landing gear with her thumb and got four green indicator lights as they locked into place.

"*Bandit*, Bad Rock. You're good and straight. You've still got some smoke."

"Thank you, Bad Rock. We'll evacuate wherever we stop."

"Copy that."

The runway rushed up faster than she could have imagined. She had just enough time for a deep breath and then she yelled, "Brace, brace, brace!"

The landing gear made hard contact a moment later. She heard loose objects rattle in the living quarters and Richie grunted. Tricia made a low, frightened noise.

The ship bounced back into the air and Marla forced the yoke forward in an effort to get the ship down and keep it down. The second impact jarred the ship again but not quite as hard as the first. She pulled back on the throttle and cut thrust, but momentum carried them down the runway like a bullet. Indicators painted on the runway flashed by and she applied the brakes, trying to bleed off speed. The ship rushed forward, eating up precious space.

She hollered to Richie. "Chute, chute, chute!"

"Got it!"

The ship jerked as the drogue chute inflated behind it and she stole a glance at a monitor that showed the outside rear of the ship. A large bright orange parachute spun in their wake. The ship continued forward and Marla saw the end of the runway speeding at them. Tricia raised her head to look out the canopy.

"Stay down! We're going off the runway!" Marla yelled.

She saw a black and yellow pattern at the end of the runway go under the cockpit and then they rolled over darker concrete.

Here comes the arrestor system, she thought and before she could shout another warning the ship lurched. The yoke jerked hard under her hands as the seat straps dug into her shoulders.

Then everything went black.

— «» —

"Eldridge," Nathan said. "Get us out of this."

"I've got an idea," The young man said. "Command, priority reset."

All at once, the five 'bots stopped and spoke at the same time. "Confirm command, priority reset."

"Confirmed."

The glow in the eyes of the 'bots dulled and went out. Nathan felt the grip of the 'bot holding him loosen and he managed to squirm free. He saw the others getting loose as well.

Duncan nudged Eldridge. "What did you do?"

"That command reloads the operating system from the local network," he said. "Give me a hand here. Each of them has a control panel on their back. Open it and pull the green circuit cluster. It will keep them from communicating over the intranet and disable them." Ari joined the two of them and they worked fast. The 'bots stood still and didn't reactivate.

Nathan inspected the dim compartment. He estimated the square box to be a little less than five meters on each side. The door they entered through appeared to be the only way in or out. He grabbed Cole's arm.

"We need to get out of here before Dodger and his crew come back."

"I think I can help with that," Eldridge said. He pointed to the back wall of the compartment. "Give me a second." He pulled open an access panel.

Duncan moved closer to Nathan. "How do you think Marla and the others are doing? Do you think they're alright?"

Nathan swallowed. Duncan had a look of sheer terror on his face. He put a hand on his friend's shoulder. "Don't worry about her. It seemed like Marla still had control and that's all she'll need to get them down."

"All that smoke, though… it had to be a fire"

"Yeah but the ship has suppression systems and Richie's still aboard. She's not by herself." He squeezed Duncan's shoulder. "If anyone can get them down, it's Marla. She's a great pilot. I have complete faith in her."

"If anything happens to her, to all of them, I'm going to hurt someone."

"One problem at a time, okay? We need to get out of here so we can help them. Why don't you help the kid?"

"Knock off the 'kid' stuff, okay?" Eldridge said. "And yes, I could use a hand."

Duncan nodded. "What do you need me to do?"

Eldridge waved a hand at one of the corners where a length of metal pipe lay. "Hand me that thing, would you? I need some leverage. The door is jammed in the frame."

"I see it." Duncan crossed the small area and grabbed the pipe. Eldridge took it and worked it into the wheel on the door. Duncan grabbed hold with the younger man and they started pulling on it.

"Where does this door go? Back into the cargo bay?" Nathan said.

Eldridge shook his head. "No, it's a hatch that connects up with the maintenance tunnels that run all over the ship. If I can get this damn door open, we can get out of here and avoid those guys."

Cole stood near the larger door, which they had entered through, pistol in hand. Nathan pointed at the cargo bay. "Do you hear anything?"

"I think they're working the pumps but we should move fast. I don't want those mooks coming back in here while we're all bunched up. If we have to fight with them, we need to be in a better place."

"We're working on it," Nathan said.

Just then, the familiar squeal of tight hinges came from the maintenance hatch and it popped open. Duncan and Eldridge shook hands. Both breathed heavily.

"Okay, we're good to go," Eldridge said. He took a flashlight from a pouch on his belt.

Nathan gestured into the tunnel. "It's your ship, you lead the way. Cole, bring up the rear and help me dog this hatch."

They pulled the door shut and secured the wheel with a length of wire pulled from the ceiling. Then they headed off in the dark tunnel with Eldridge leading the way.

Chapter 16

Marla blinked but the darkness wouldn't go away. She could feel her eyelids moving and could breathe but she couldn't move her arms or legs. It took a moment but she realized she sat upright. Muffled sounds came from somewhere nearby but she couldn't hear clearly.

The ship had gone down. She remembered that. Then what happened dawned on her. The rescue vests had activated. She moved her hand more, pressing harder against the smart foam that enveloped her. Sensing her movements, it started to give way.

She flexed her arms and legs more and the foam became friable, cracking and breaking away as she moved. After a few moments, she pulled at the mass covering her face. Sunlight poured in and she blinked as her view of the cockpit improved. More of the bright yellow mass came away and she turned to Tricia. The nurse was wrapped in bright orange foam.

Smoke and the smell of burnt components filled the air. Richie said the fire was out but that had been before she slammed the ship onto a concrete runway going the speed of a missile.

She released her safety harness and stood up, brushing at her flight suit. Yellow flakes fell to the floor of the cockpit. Tricia's orange cocoon rippled and one of her hands broke free. Marla pulled at the foam around her face and the nurse blinked rapidly.

"Did we make it?"

Marla smiled. "We sure did."

"Are you all right?" Tricia said, slipping into work mode. "Did you hit your head or anything else?"

"I think I'm okay," she said, pausing for a moment to consider the question. Had she blacked out when the ship stopped or had it just been the rescue vest deploying? She shook her head and seemed fine. "Nothing hurts. Let's get Richie and get out of here."

It took another moment to free Tricia completely and then they moved out of the cockpit to the engineering station. Richie stood up from his seat, tugging at electric green foam. He rushed to Marla, throwing a hug around her.

"You saved us! I love you!" He planted a quick kiss on her and hugged her tightly. "I will fly with you anywhere. We should be dead."

Marla hugged him back. "Thank you for keeping it together. I couldn't have done it without you." She stepped back, waving her hand at the air. "We should get out of here, though, in case we're on fire."

"I don't think we are," Richie said. "I think the smoke is just left over from the plasma venting." He touched his workstation but it remained dark. "Then again, I wouldn't have any way of knowing, would I?"

"You're okay?" Tricia asked Richie. She put a hand on his face and gently directed him toward an emergency light so she could look at his pupils. "Does it feel like anything hurts?"

"I think I'm okay."

"Come on," Marla said. "We need to go."

Heading toward the exit, the ship grew darker as they moved farther away from the sunlight coming in through the cockpit. The emergency batteries had clicked on and weak light shone through the smoky air.

They made it to the back of the ship and Richie pulled the release for the ramp. It dropped halfway and struck concrete. They could see daylight but nothing else. They could hear sirens though, and firemen hollering instructions to one another.

Marla squatted down. "I think we sank into the arresting barrier. Maybe we can go out through the top hatch-"

A screeching sound interrupted her, as enormous steel jaws bit into the ceiling and floor of the compartment. Richie grabbed her and Tricia, pulling them backward and into the corridor.

"Holy shit!" Marla exclaimed. "What is that?"

They watched as the remains of the compartment holding the loading ramp tore free like paper. Sunlight streamed in and she raised a hand to shade her vision.

More movement caught her eye as metal tentacles snaked in and grasped them firmly, pulling them free of the wreck. Bewildered, Marla took in the single most horrifying machine she had ever seen, a serpent-like 'bot with large jaws. Red and yellow lights mounted on its head above the jaws blinked brightly. The tentacles holding them were mounted to its sides.

It lowered them to the ground and strong hands grabbed Marla, freeing her from the grip of the terrifying rescue 'bot. Two large firemen in turnout gear set her down gently and two more grabbed Tricia. Richie fought them off and waved hands at them.

"Stop destroying the ship!" He said. "The fire is out!"

Another fireman knelt down in front of her. "Just the three of you?"

Marla nodded. "Yes."

"You're sure?"

"Very."

He motioned to a squad of three men standing near the new opening. "Get in there and get me atmospheric scans. I want to know if we have a reactor problem or any toxic issues." The men nodded and used a ladder to climb up into the wide opening.

Water and foam drifted through the air and made the tarmac slippery. She saw black smoke drifting from the rear of the port engine cowling.

A fireman offered Marla a hand and directed her toward an ambulance. "Let's get you out of here," he said.

"The reactor is okay," she said. "Richie kept an eye on it."

"I understand, miss, but then you landed going the speed of sound and embedded your ship in half a meter of frangible concrete. We can discuss everything in more detail once you're safely away from the ship. Now, please get in the ambulance and watch your step."

He hadn't been kidding about the concrete. The *Blue Moon Bandit* stood on all four landing gear but the tires were mired in the thick, crumbling concrete. Charcoal black skid marks led down the runway to where the ship had finally stopped. They'd gone quite a distance into the barrier before stopping.

Five minutes later ambulances delivered them to the spaceport's infirmary. Medics attached scanners and took their vital signs.

"I'm fine," Tricia said from the bed next to Marla. "I'm a nurse, okay? If I wasn't fine, I would know."

A handsome medic smiled at her. "I'm glad you're a nurse. It means that you know I'm just doing my job, and that you should let me do it."

Tricia smiled sarcastically at the young man and let him attach the scanners.

A tall, thin man who appeared to be in his late fifties stepped into the room. He wore gray slacks and a dull yellow shirt. Perspiration dotted his bald head. He didn't look happy. "Who is the pilot?"

Marla raised her hand. "That's me."

He strode over to her and shook her hand. "I'm Collins. I run the spaceport. You okay?"

"I think so. Can you tell me anything about my ship? Some scary ass thing tried to eat us."

He pulled a chair up to her bedside and slumped into it. "Yeah. That's the rescue serpent. It's a 'bot made to crack open ships and pull out passengers."

"It almost killed us."

He shrugged. "Oh, don't worry about that. It scans the vessel before it starts tearing it apart. No danger to the occupants at all. We picked it up a few years ago with a grant and it's been sitting idle ever since. The guys have never had a chance to use it before so they're all pretty excited."

"They aren't going to use it to tear the ship apart are they?"

"Oh no, it's just for passenger extraction. Anyway, the fire is out and the reactor is in safe mode. There doesn't seem to be any damage, no radiation leakage or anything."

"We need to get out there to look at it and I have to call my boss. I lost my mobi in the crash."

"We'll get around to all that but first I need to get a statement."

Marla rolled her eyes at the thought of paperwork.

"Everything okay?"

"It's just that I thought crashing would be the worst thing that happened to me today. I'm not a fan of regulations and reports."

He smiled. "Let's get started."

— «» —

Eldridge led the party down the maintenance tunnel. It went much farther than Nathan would have thought but he had trouble gauging the distance. His legs became sore from compensating for the downhill angle of the crashed ship. They finally stopped at another hatch and Eldridge tried turning the wheel. Nathan joined him because the kid was struggling. Together they spun it and got the hatch open. Nathan pulled his mobi from his jacket pocket and tapped the screen. A light came on and he shined it around the compartment. Large tanks occupied this compartment too; they were about the same size as the ones in the cargo bay which held the coolant that was so damn important to Dodger.

Eldridge rapped his knuckles on the side of it. "Waste water. Be very careful in here. We don't need to try swimming through liquefied crap."

"That would be one hell of a mess," Duncan said, taking in a breadth of it. "Why is it still full?"

"It didn't pop in the crash and our plan was to pump it dry when we got this far into the salvage."

"Why did you stop here?" Nathan said.

Eldridge pointed to another hatch set into the floor. "That is the maintenance port for the discharge chute. We can drop out here and..." His voice trailed off. "What is our next move?"

Nathan took a deep breath. "First things first. We find out what happened to my ship and crew. If Dodger gets in our way we go through him."

"We may do that anyway," Cole said.

"Can you get the hatch open?"

Eldridge nodded. "Sure. We used it during the initial inspection." He and Ari moved to the hatch and got it open. A ladder rested against the hatch, probably from their earlier inspection, Nathan thought. They moved to go through and Cole laid a hand on Eldridge's shoulder.

"Why don't you let me go first, in case Dodger or his boys are out there?"

Eldridge backed away and Cole climbed down. After a moment, he hollered back up.

"We're clear."

They all descended into the bright sunlight and Nathan could see they had come out about halfway down the length of the ship. He noticed something moving up the access road toward Bad Rock and pointed to it.

"There goes Dodger's tanker truck."

The big rig blew up a plume of dust as it left the area. Several cars followed it.

"They may have left some guys behind if they went in and found us missing," Nathan said to Cole.

"We can deal with a couple guys. I'm not worried about it. Besides, we have to find out what happened to the ship."

Nathan patted him on the shoulder. "Yeah, let's hustle."

Ari glared at him.

"Is something bothering you?" Nathan said.

"You mean other than the fact that you've screwed up our whole deal? No, nothing at all."

"This isn't our fault," Nathan said, pointing at his chest. "We were leaving when Dodger and his goons showed up."

"Well, what are we supposed to do now? Packing up and leaving isn't an option. We still have a contract to complete. This stupid job is literally everything we have."

Nathan started to say something and bit it back. Once again, she'd hit a nerve without knowing it. "Let's just go back to your camp and see what's up. We'll play it by ear."

"As opposed to the plan we've been following up to this point?"

Nathan walked off silently, letting her have the last word. They made good time back to the base camp and Nathan saw nothing much had changed. The 'bots were still working and he even saw a truck lift off toward the *Corkscrew*.

"Hey fellas," a voice said from behind them. They all turned and Turtle and Daryl stepped out from the tent Eldridge and Ari called home.

"Stop right there," Cole said, drawing his gun on them. "Don't take another step and get your hands up."

Turtle grinned and raised his arms. "It's all good, m'man. No need for violence."

Nathan moved to them and patted them down. He didn't find anything.

"Satisfied?"

He motioned to the table where they had eaten lunch yesterday. "Sit down."

They moved to the table and sat.

"Where's your boss?"

Turtle answered. "He had to go but he wanted me to give you a message."

"What's that?"

"You're screwed."

"We haven't done anything," Ari said. "We're paid up."

Turtle held up a hand. "Oh not you, honey, or your boyfriend. You two are fine. Dodger knows you're solid. He's not stupid enough to let an operation this lucrative slip away." He paused. "Unless you help these repo boys. You do that and you'll get the same thing they got coming." He turned to Nathan. "Yeah, boss, you're done."

"Where's my ship?"

Turtle shrugged and a smirk crossed his mouth. "You saw the same thing I did. I'm no pilot but being on fire can't be good."

Nathan turned to Duncan. "Find us a ride. We have to go." He turned back to Turtle. "Your boss should know that he's bought more trouble than he can handle. If my crew is harmed, you're all dead."

Turtle lit a cigarette and nodded. "Yeah, chief, I'm shaking all over." He stood up and Daryl followed. "We're going back to work now. Dodger said he'll catch up with you later."

He moved to walk away and Nathan hit him with a punch that he'd brought with him all the way from his crappy little apartment back on Earth. The one that he could barely keep the rent paid on and where the bills stacked up and where his business threatened to go under and...

And then Cole pulled him off Turtle. Somehow, they'd gone down to the ground and Nathan was straddling the guy, landing haymakers left and right. Cole had his hands under his arms and yanked him up. Stunned silence filled the canopy.

Turtle lay unconscious on the ground, his head a bloody mess and Ari knelt beside him, checking him. Nathan shook loose and turned to Daryl who put his hands up.

"Hey, easy, man. Okay? I got it. I know what you're saying."

"Dodger's paranoid right?"

Daryl nodded, "Very."

"Then he should know he's called down the lightning." Then he heard a sound and saw Duncan pulling up in the same truck Turtle had driven last night. He nodded to it and said, "Let's go."

They moved to the passenger side and Eldridge came up to the truck. "What about us? What are we supposed to do?"

Nathan shrugged. "You heard him. Dodger's happy with your arrangement so just keep working. This has nothing to do with you."

Duncan spoke to him through the lowered window. "You better figure out how they got control of your 'bots. If they did it once they'll do it again. Which way to the spaceport? With the ship in trouble, that's where Marla would have went."

Eldridge pointed west. "Turn left off the access road and follow the signs along the main road. I hope your lady is okay."

"Me too."

It took them half an hour to get to the spaceport. They parked the truck and ran to the terminal. No one greeted them in the empty building, no passengers waiting to depart or families waiting for loved ones. Nathan spotted an information kiosk and the hologram of a plump middle-aged woman started up when he walked up to it.

"Can I help you?" She asked, smiling.

"Did a starship crash here?"

"Flight information is available on the monitors above the gates."

Nathan paused in an effort to get the information he needed. "Has there been an emergency landing today?"

The woman's smile grew wider. "Oh my, yes. Just a little while ago."

Nathan took a deep breath. "Are there survivors? If so, where are they?"

The hologram's smile held steady. "Passengers are in the infirmary. Would you like to see them?"

"Yes."

She pointed to the floor. "Follow the path being lit for you."

They ran, following the yellow arrows flashing on the floor. Two minutes later they went through the doors and saw a group of people around three occupied beds. Duncan rushed to Marla, tears streaming down his face. She sat up and met his hug fiercely. Her tears mixed with his.

Nathan spotted Richie and Tricia and he went to her, sitting on the edge of her bed. Fear gripped him as he took her hand.

"Are you okay?"

She nodded and slid forward, hugging him tightly. "Someone tried to kill us."

"I know. I'm sorry."

He saw Cole shaking Richie's hand.

"I'm all you get," Cole said. "So don't expect a hug or a kiss."

Nathan smiled. "You okay, Richie?"

He nodded. "Yeah." His eyes fell to the floor. "I think the ship's in bad shape."

Nathan swallowed and held Tricia tighter. "Yeah, well, we'll deal with that later." For now, being alive and together was enough.

Chapter 17

"Get everyone ready," Dodger said. They sat in the back office of the club, Jonesy in one of the chairs in front of Dodger and Cheech in the one beside him. Morris shook his head.

"You really think they'll come here?"

Dodger held his hands up. "The repo guys? Where else are they going to go? You know how mad they are right now? Cheech took down their ship." He popped a crystal into his mouth and grimaced as he bit down, anticipating the rush. "The intel we got on that Teller guy said he's cool but if you push him he'll push back. Well, we freakin' shoved him today. They'll be here sometime tonight and when they come, we take them out."

Morris kept pacing as he spoke. "Look, that may be true but there's only, like five or six of them."

Dodger shook a finger at him. "Don't underestimate them. You read the message we got from Earth. When they got mixed up in that business in the Alpha system they killed a couple of guys wearing shimmer suits and they even used some kind of modified virus. I'm not taking any chances. Call the guys in and get them spread around the club, out in the parking lot and across the street in those empty buildings."

"I guess it can't hurt to be prepared," Morris said.

"You are damned right it can't." Dodger pointed at Jonesy. "If this moron had done his job and used the 'bots to hold on to them out at the wreck site, we wouldn't have this problem. I should have been able to interrogate them, to find out what they know. Now, we have to wait for them to come to us."

Jonesy held his hands up to defend himself. "Boss, come on. I couldn't help what happened."

Dodger narrowed his eyes. "How the hell is them escaping not your fault? You had one job to do."

"Yeah but Eldridge designed the things and..."

Dodger held his hands up like he wanted more of an answer. "And?"

"And he must have had some backdoor or something."

"Or he's just smarter than you."

Jonesy fumbled. "Well, maybe."

Dodger pointed a thick finger at him. "I told Cheech to crash their goddamn ship and you know what? It crashed." Cheech grinned at Jonesy. "Figure out what went wrong. If I need to grab ahold of those things again, I want to be able to do it."

"Okay." Jonesy stood up. "I'll get started right now."

"Yeah, go do that."

Jonesy turned to go and Dodger fired a shot glass at his head. The hacker stopped and rubbed the back of his head, "What the hell?"

"Screw up again and I'll take a pool cue to your fingers, get me?"

Jonesy nodded with a worried look on his face. "Yeah, I got it."

It grew quiet for a moment and then Cheech spoke up. "You know Dodger, that kamikaze stunt with the drone took away our capability to remotely spy on the salvagers."

"And?"

The expression on Cheech's face changed. "Well, it's just that if we need to see what they're doing out there, I don't have any way to fly over. I mean, I could probably find something local but it's not going to be military grade. It won't have the audio-visual capabilities we had with the other one."

Dodger waved him off. "Just do the best you can. There's a place downtown that sells that shit. Go see what they've got. Maybe you can build your own."

Cheech stood up. "Okay, I'll go now."

"Hey, good job taking them down, okay? It's just that now we've got other issues. In this business you have to be ready to move on to the next problem."

"No, I get it. I'll take care of replacing the drone."

"Yeah, get going."

The kid left the room and Dodger waved Morris over. "Sit down. All that pacing is wearing me out."

Morris flopped into a chair and had his mobi out, thumbs flying over the screen. "I've got a dozen guys coming over. That should be enough. I'll get them organized when they're all here."

"Good. What's going on out at the spaceport."

"Our guy out there, Collins, called me after he spoke with the pilot who landed the ship and got me a copy of the preliminary report. They're treating her like a heroine. Cheech did a good job with the drone, I mean I know it didn't destroy the ship like you wanted, but..."

Dodger waved him off. "It was a drone, not a damned missile. I know."

"Right, well he tore the ship up pretty bad but not enough to knock it out of the sky. The pilot did a great job, according to Collins. He heard the whole thing go down up in the control tower. She had a voice like ice."

"That's great. We go to the trouble of shooting down a starship and it's got an ace flying it. Do we have any other way to do them in?"

Morris thought for a moment and then shook his head. "There aren't any assets onsite that could do something like that. Collins is just a bureaucrat."

"Is there any good news?"

"She won't be flying it again any time soon. Collins says it won't fly out under its own power. It's buried in concrete up to its belly at the end of the runway."

"That's good. Will Collins let us know when they leave?" He picked up another crystal from the open package on his desk. "I'm telling you, they'll want payback and they'll be coming right here."

"Yeah, I told him. He's doing the accident investigation so he's sticking right by them."

"Good. We still need to know what they know and who they've told. Then we get rid of them."

Morris paused for a moment. "Hey, you don't suppose Teller is being truthful, do you? That they really don't know anything?"

Dodger shook his head. "No way. They grab the ship hauling our product, show up here, and then just stumble across our lab? I don't believe that. Oh, and now they want to leave. Why is that? Who are they reporting to? This operation produces millions in revenue and the law has never found it. No, Teller is working for Protective Services. Maybe we should make preparations to move the lab."

Morris let out a low whistle. "That's a week of downtime, minimum."

Dodger considered that and chewed his lower lip. "Let's find out what they know first. Get the guys ready to lock this place down tonight."

"Will do. Oh, hey, there's one other thing."

Dodger frowned. "Yeah? You don't look like it's good news."

"Remember how you left Turtle and Daryl out there to deliver a message?"

"Yeah?"

"Well, Teller beat the hell out of Turtle and then they took off. Daryl is taking him to the clinic to get him checked out."

"How bad?"

Morris shrugged. "He's unconscious."

Dodger shook his head. "That guy. I don't know about him. He tries, you know? He wants to earn but everything he touches turns to crap." He grimaced. "Tell Daryl to dump him at the clinic and get his ass back out to the wreck site. If those repo losers show up back there I want to know about it."

Morris nodded and started working his mobi. "Will do."

"All right, if you don't have anything else, get this place ready for a fight."

"On it."

— «» —

"Oh my God," Nathan said, taking in the wreck of his ship at the end of the runway. They faced the rear of the ship and he could see the gaping hole the rescue 'bot had opened. The smell of fire still hung in the air.

Thick black skid marks lead up the runway to where the *Bandit* sat. The bright orange drogue chute lay deflated on the ground, moving a bit when the breeze caught it. He turned to Marla and put an arm around her shoulders.

"You did good, honey. I am so proud of you."

"Thanks, Nathan, but I have to tell you, I'm still shaking."

"Looks like you'll have time to get over it." He turned to Duncan. "Can we get aboard?"

The engineer nodded and walked toward the ship. "Yeah, we can go right through the giant damned hole they ripped in the aft section." He shook his head. "Anyway, the fire chief says the ship is safe at this point and the runway is out of commission until the ship gets moved. Everything is at a zero-energy state so don't expect too much to work. We'll be on the batteries because the reactor is shut down."

"No problem."

They approached from the rear. The squared off stern and the engine cowlings on either side of the half-dropped ramp canted slightly off angle because of the way the ship sat in the arresting concrete.

"We'll have to get a crane out here to pull her free," Richie said from behind them. He, Cole and Tricia followed them.

"Yeah," Nathan said. "It could be a hell of a lot worse though. Did the rescue vests go off?"

"As soon as we hit this part of the runway the accelerometers built into the vests activated them," Marla said. "One minute, I saw the runway, the next, we were wrapped up like beef at the market."

"Good." They reached the ship and Nathan hoisted himself up into the damaged engine cowling. "This is the side that took the hit?"

She nodded. "Yeah, but from the front."

"Damn it," Richie said. "I just rebuilt that gimbal linkage."

Nathan patted the thrust vectoring nozzle. "Don't worry about it, that all still looks to be intact. Let's go look at the front."

He dropped down to the tarmac and they walked around the ship. Nathan saw that coming to a stop in the arresting material didn't seem to have harmed the undercarriage. He walked around the port side and examined the engine. His breath rushed out of him and his eyes grew wide.

The normally square engine cowling was flayed open in all directions. Nathan put a hand on the ragged piece of metal hanging down and realized he wouldn't be climbing up into the cowling. Razor sharp edges trimmed every piece of metal.

"We'll need to get up inside and look at the damage," Duncan said from behind him, pulling his attention from the mangled ship. "Richie said the pulsed plasma thrusters vented to the interior."

Nathan nodded slowly, trying to take it all in. He turned to Marla. "How the hell did you land her?"

Marla shook her head. "I just did the job, Nathan. The training kicked in and I did everything you're supposed to do."

"And when that didn't work?"

She smiled. "I did everything else I could think of."

"My wife is a goddamned genius, Nathan." Duncan smiled and took her hand.

"No doubt about that." Something near the cockpit window caught his attention and he moved closer to examine it. He ran a hand over it and traced a crack that ran from the port side straight up to the edge of the frame.

"That should not have happened," Duncan said, getting closer. "That's ballistic resistant polycarbonate. It's supposed to be bulletproof."

"I think she got hit by something with a hell of a lot more mass than a bullet," Nathan said. He turned to Marla. "Did you get a collision warning?"

"Yes, but not much. I had just enough time to jerk the ship to the right."

"So they aimed at the cockpit?" He let that sink in. "They tried to put it right into the cockpit between the cowlings, no doubt about that."

"Damn near did it, too," Duncan said and hugged Marla. "But you can't knock my girl out of the sky." He kissed her lightly on the cheek.

Nathan smiled. "No, you can't. Let's go check the interior."

They mounted the maintenance ladder near the starboard engine cowling and walked across the hull. Nathan held Tricia's hand and helped her up.

"Are you okay?"

Her eyes blazed with anger. "They tried to murder us, didn't they? Those guys you told me about last night?"

"Yeah. Look, I'm sorry. Nothing like this has ever happened to us before. I would never have put you in danger if I thought they would do anything like this."

"You don't have anything to apologize for, Nathan. This isn't your fault."

He stopped and took her hand. "I still put you right in the middle of this."

She shook her head. "Nathan, this nightmare isn't something you're responsible for."

"I told Dodger I wouldn't take his job. That's why he did this."

She shrugged and squeezed his hand. "You're only responsible for what you do. Now come on, let's get inside."

They walked over to the hatch and dropped down inside. Duncan had the emergency power on and they walked down a dimly lit corridor. Marla waited for them outside the port side engine compartment. She jerked a thumb inside.

"I couldn't bear to see my husband cry. They're inside."

Nathan took a deep breath and let go of Tricia's hand. The compartment stunk of burnt paint, lubricant and insulation. "Should we be breathing this?"

Duncan held up a portable air meter. "Sniffer says we're good."

Nathan saw the damage and sighed. He ran a hand over the blackened compartment walls and noted the warped deck under his feet from the intense heat. He put a hand on Richie's shoulder.

"Marla told me what you did for her, getting everything shut down and starting the fire suppression system. You did a good job."

"The automatic systems did most of it. Marla did all the hard stuff."

"You helped buy her the time she needed."

Duncan gave a small grunt. "Just say 'thanks' kid so we can move on."

"Yeah, okay, thanks."

Nathan pulled a trouble light from a wall locker and shone it around the engine itself. It was a total loss and he didn't need Duncan to tell him that. The plasma generated by the engine for thrust had filled the compartment and superheated everything.

"It's a good ship, Nathan," Duncan said. "Picking a converted hazardous material hauler probably saved everyone's life." He patted a burned bulkhead. "She's built tough. That's probably the only reason it held together long enough for Marla to land."

"Yeah, well, don't give me too much credit. It was cheap." No matter what direction his gaze wandered the news sucked. Something caught his eye and he reached under the engine housing. He grunted and managed to pull something free from the burnt mass of wiring and melted steel.

"What's that?" Duncan said.

Nathan held it up in the light. "I'm not sure. It doesn't look like it's a part of the engine." He scratched at the burnt metal plate. "See? The curve is all wrong to be part of the housing."

Duncan took the piece of metal and spit on it, scrubbing at the scorch marks with a calloused thumb. He managed to clear a small bit and printing became visible. "This could be part of what they hit us with."

"Can you and Richie see if you can identify it? It may be useful."

"I'll see what we can find out."

He rested a hand on the engine. "She's going to need a tow home."

"Yeah, no doubt about that," Duncan said. He had the same dismal look on his face as Nathan. "The engine is a loss for sure plus the structural damage, the cowling, the cockpit and whatever else we find." He grimaced. "This is going to be expensive, Nathan."

"No doubt." Nathan hung the light back up. "Let's get out of here. I need some fresh air."

They dismounted and started to make their way back to the spaceport administration building. A tall, black man with graying, close-cropped hair walked out as they approached the entrance, and held up a badge.

"Which one of you is Teller?"

Nathan held a hand up. "That's me."

They walked over to him and he held his hand out. "I'm Chief Don Bell." He pointed to the *Bandit* with his other hand. "And I think you and I need to have a talk."

Chapter 18

Bell insisted they ride to his office in Bad Rock so he, Nathan and Cole hovered into town in his cruiser. The chief had arranged for one of his deputies to come with a larger vehicle to pick up the rest of his crew and take them to a motel. That same deputy would keep an eye on them throughout the night.

The police offices occupied the bottom floor of the rundown city administration building. Dark stains ran down the chipped walls from the roof and a faint musty smell permeated the air.

"There's not a lot of money in the city's budget for upkeep and repair on municipal buildings," he said. "You'll have to forgive us. Come on inside."

They walked down a hall that had a marble floor in need of a good polish. Bell used his handprint to swipe his way into a suite of offices. Inside, a woman sat at a desk watching a bank of monitors. Nathan noted they displayed various locations around the city, including the entrance to the building they stood in. Bell held an office door open and invited them to sit down in the chairs facing his desk.

"You've had a pretty bad day," the chief said as he walked around the desk and took a seat.

"We've had better, that's for sure. Did you want to see us because of the crash?"

The chief held a finger up and activated a small box sitting on his desk. A green light flashed on the status display. "Okay, that's better. Yes, I wanted to speak about the crash."

Nathan pointed at the device. "Is that a recorder?"

Bell shook his head. "No, it's making sure no one is listening in."

"Isn't that kind of paranoid?"

"Yes it is, and that's the way we live in Bad Rock."

Nathan's eyes narrowed. "Why's that?"

"It's because the man who crashed your starship has more resources than I do and is good at avoiding prosecution."

"If you know who did it, I would appreciate you arresting him."

Bell smiled. "Well, knowing something and proving it are two different things. Believe, me, nothing would make me happier than arresting Melvin Thornberry."

"Who?"

"You know him as Dodger. He thinks that's a tougher name and Dodger is all about how things look." He leaned back in his chair, making himself comfortable. "Anyway, I really want to arrest Dodger and I'd like you to help me."

Nathan nodded slowly. "How can we do that?"

"Let's start with what you're doing here."

Nathan dug out a business card and handed to him it across the desk. "Eldridge Tanner is behind on his payments. We're here to repossess his ship and take it back to Earth."

"So why did Dodger crash your ship?"

"I thought you knew that already. From what you said, it sounded like you had some kind of lead or proof or something."

Bell held his hands up. "I have suspicions. Someone has been flying a large drone around the city for the past few months and lately it's been doing racetrack patterns over the wreck site of the *Athena Star*. I know Dodger is shaking those kids down out there to keep the union off their back but I can't prove that either. The thing is, nobody else around here has the resources to fly something like that. The smaller, cheap ones, sure, but even my office doesn't have the credits to buy something like that. I got a good look at that thing one day and it's commercial grade at least, maybe military, but I didn't see any weapons on it."

"All right. What does that have to do with us?"

"Your ship collided with something in the sky over the wreck site. I heard as much when I listened to the recordings from the control tower." He sat up straight and leaned across the desk. "Now, Bad Rock gets one or two flights a week and your pilot sure as hell didn't hit a duck, so what did she run into?"

"You think she hit Dodger's drone?"

"What else?"

Nathan sat silently for a moment. "What would you like from us?"

"The first thing I'd like to know is if you're running Diamond K for Dodger. I don't think you are. After all, it seems like it would be stupid for him to crash your ship, but who knows? Maybe you just made him mad in some way. Maybe he didn't like the idea of you taking Eldridge's ship because it would cut into the profits he's getting by shaking down the kid. Why don't you tell me?"

Nathan caught Cole's eye for reassurance. He had no idea if he could trust anyone on this backwater planet, including the only law in ten light years. "Things are hard here, aren't they Chief? You mentioned budget problems."

"Oh, I've got budget problems, all right but Bad Rock isn't such a terrible place to live." He paused and swallowed. "I mean sure, the economy is awful but the people are good. We do okay. What we really need is for Earth to remember we're out here and start colonizing again. There's nothing wrong with this place that a little investment wouldn't cure."

Nathan thought of Earth and all the cities like Bad Rock that littered the landscape. Hundreds of men just like Chief Bell held out hope that salvation would find its way to them. In Nathan's opinion, none of them understood that a place had to be attractive to get people to move there. That's why a terraformed planet like Olympus, with large swaths of tropical areas, never had to worry about its population decreasing.

"Chief, what's the deal with Dodger? Is he just some local thug or is he hooked into the Syndicate?"

"You've had experience with the Syndicate?"

"Some."

"Dodger's connected." The chief let out a breath. "He's got his hands in all the usual crap these guys engage in, like protection rackets, human trafficking, drugs and fencing stolen goods. I've been able to ascertain that his main source of income is producing Diamond K. You know what that is?"

"Yes, we do."

"Well, we're isolated out here and my department is just me and half a dozen deputies for the whole city. I don't have the resources to really investigate properly." He pointed a finger at Nathan. "That's why I need someone to testify. I need someone to give me something that will stick."

Nathan jerked a thumb over his shoulder. "Well, my ship is sitting crashed out at the spaceport. If you think he really crashed it with a drone, go investigate it. You should be able to pull out anything you need."

Bell laughed a hearty chuckle. "Captain Teller, do you really think I'm going to dig around your ship and find a piece of a drone that's connected to Dodger? Maybe I'll find an identification number that is registered to Dope Dealing Enterprises, a subsidiary of Scumbag, Incorporated? Come on, we both know better."

Cole spoke up. "But you have a deputy doing that right now, don't you?"

The chief smiled. "Of course. We're not amateurs, and neither are you, right Mr. Seger? You're an ex-marshal. How would you handle this?"

Cole considered the question. "I'd call in help from Earth. Resources are your problem so get more resources."

"The request has been in for more than a year. I've been told that it is being considered and they understand the gravity of the situation."

"Well, that sounds like the bureaucracy I know."

Bell turned back to Nathan. "How did you run afoul of Dodger? Come on guys, I need something to work with."

Nathan bit a lip and considered the situation. Maybe Bell could help, maybe he couldn't but trusting him seemed like the right thing to do. "He blames us for screwing up his distribution of Diamond K when we repossessed another ship. His solution was for us to start smuggling for him. Obviously, we're not going to do that."

"Will you testify to that?"

"And spend a few months here while you hold a trial? Come on, Chief. I've got a business to run and I need to protect my people. This guy is a killer."

"You can't be afraid of him, Captain Teller." Bell said. "Help me take him down."

Nathan leveled a gaze at him. "Someone tried to kill my crew and as you pointed out, your department is low on resources. That leads me to believe that you can't protect us if we need it."

"That's how it is?"

"That's how it is."

Bell stood up. "I'll drive you to the motel so you can join your crew."

"Thank you. I'd appreciate that."

— «» —

A couple hours later, Nathan and his five crewmembers sat together in a nearby restaurant finishing a delicious dinner. Bell's deputy watched the front door from a cruiser in the parking lot.

He looked over his crew. Despite having a chance to shower and change clothes, they were all exhausted from the events of the day. He felt beat himself.

Duncan and Marla spoke in hushed tones with the engineer doting on his wife. Nathan smiled as he observed them. Cole and Richie had their own conversation going on and Tricia sat beside him.

She leaned over and whispered in his ear, "They look like they're ready to pass out."

"I think you're right," Nathan said. He stood and held up a glass to make a toast. Everyone quieted down.

"To Marla, pilot extraordinaire."

They all raised a glass and took a drink.

"I know everyone is tired so I'm just going to run through a few things."

"Make it short," Cole said.

He crossed his heart. "I promise. First, Tricia, have you had a chance to look everyone over? How are our people?"

She waved a hand around the table. "No major injuries, obviously. The test results from the spaceport medics and my own examinations show everyone is healthy. The three of us are sore but nothing is broken. I recommend another drink and a good night's sleep."

Duncan raised a glass. "Now, that's good medical advice."

Everyone chuckled and the room grew silent. Nathan cleared his throat. "Next I want to address our situation."

"What are we going to do, Nathan?" Duncan said.

"I'd like to do the job we came here to do. You took a look at the *Bandit*?" He sat down as Duncan answered.

"Yeah, she isn't flying anywhere. The port side engine is a total loss and there is fire damage everywhere. I don't think she's spaceworthy at the moment. Besides the cracked cockpit glass I'm pretty sure there are hull fractures from the plasma venting and collision. We'll have to have her lifted back home."

Nathan sighed but he expected that answer. "I don't suppose this planet has a service like that?"

"No but I have an idea."

"Yeah?"

"We could use three of Eldridge's trucks to lift it up to the *Corkscrew* and put her in a cargo hold. We can repo the ship and use it to get us all home."

Nathan considered it. The *Corkscrew* could easily accommodate the *Bandit*, even if they had to dock it to the outside of the hull.

"I like it. Let's get with Eldridge in the morning and start making plans."

Duncan cleared his throat. "He may be hard to convince."

Nathan finished his bourbon and set the glass down. "If that's the case, I'll remind him that things only got out of hand because one of his mechanics dropped us into this dump. Any objections?"

They all shook their heads. It appeared that everyone wanted to finish the job and get home.

"Okay, then let's get back to the motel and get some rest." They all stood up and started filing for the door. Cole hung back with Nathan while he paid the check.

"Back at Eldridge's camp when you beat the hell out of Turtle, you mentioned that Dodger had 'called down the lightning'. This new plan sounds like we're just packing up and leaving. Which is it?"

Nathan took a mint from the bowl near the cashier and popped it in his mouth. "You know, at that moment I just wanted to kill all of them but seeing everyone healthy around the table here, I don't know. Maybe it's better to take the *Corkscrew* and go home. What do you think?"

Cole put a hand on his shoulder. "I think you're the captain, Nathan, and I'll back your play whatever it is. Why don't you think things over, and we'll see how things look in the morning?"

He nodded. "Yeah, good idea."

— «» —

Morris checked the time. It was just past three in the morning and his eyes itched from exhaustion. He'd been up almost a whole day and now Dodger had him and a dozen other guys hunkered down in the strip club waiting for a retaliatory strike from the repo agents. Dodger sat at his desk, jittery and trembling from chewing K. He looked to be on the verge of a heart attack.

Morris took a deep breath. "Boss, I don't think they're coming. Why don't we send the guys home?"

Dodger's head snapped around and he held a finger up. "Oh, they're coming. They're just waiting us out."

Morris yawned and stretched. "You scared the hell out of them, Dodger. They aren't coming here and starting a fight. If they did, how would they get away? Their ship is sitting out at the spaceport."

"Maybe, maybe," Dodger said. He drummed his fingers on the desk. "They're clever, though, aren't they?"

"Sure, that's what the intel from Earth said but after today they're shaken up. What are they going to do? Only two of them are really dangerous, the captain and his security guy. The rest are mechanics and a co-pilot, none of which have any kind of training. Why don't we get some rest, start fresh tomorrow? Hell, I'll take a couple guys and we'll find them if you want. Finish them off."

Dodger considered it for a moment, he saw. The boss' face twitched and he mumbled under his breath. Moments like this made Morris wonder if he should just shoot the silly sonuvabitch and take over. He watched as Dodger plucked another crystal from the mostly empty plastic envelope on his desk and put it in his mouth. He chewed slowly, grinding the crystal into dust and then wagged a finger at Morris.

"You may be right. You really think they won't come?"

"I think they would be here already."

"Okay, get the guys home and rested. The second it gets dark we find them and bring them back here, find out what they know. Can you get eyes on them?"

"I've already told everyone we know to watch out. There's nowhere they can hide."

Dodger smiled. "All right then, get some rest. Tomorrow is going to be a busy day."

Chapter 19

The sun was barely up when Ari exited the tent she shared with Eldridge and made her way toward the camp stove. She started coffee and then the cooking 'bot activated and asked if she wanted breakfast.

"Nothing yet," she said. "I'll let you know later."

The wreck of the *Athena Star* loomed in front of her like an enormous bad luck charm while she waited for the pot to brew. In another hour or so, everyone else would be awake and the 'bots would get to work. Until then she had the place to herself.

Or so she thought.

Daryl stepped out from behind one of the storage tents with an apple in his hand and said, "Good morning, Ari."

She jumped up, startled and said, "What are you doing here?"

He smiled and nodded toward the coffee. "Where's Eldridge? Still sleeping?"

"Yeah."

"Let's keep our voices down so we don't wake him. I'd like to talk to you."

Ari glanced at the tent. "What do you want?"

"I'm looking for the repo men," he said around a mouthful of apple. "Do you know where they are?"

Ari shook her head. "I haven't seen them since yesterday when you attacked us."

"That's a harsh way of putting things. After all, Turtle's the one in the clinic. He probably won't be fixed up until later today. That Teller guy really beat the crap out of him."

"He deserved it. You all do for what you've done."

Daryl glanced at the tent where Eldridge still slept. "You should be careful how you talk to us, Ari. We're your only friends out here." He walked around the table, drawing closer to her.

She took a step back and cursed herself for allowing this *cabrón* to see her intimidated in any way. "You're our friends? You must be joking."

"I'm not, Ari. You see, we're going to make sure the repo men don't bother you or take your ship. That way you can keep working and we can all keep making credits." He took another step closer. "That's friendly, don't you think?"

She swallowed hard. "Why can't you just leave us alone?"

"We are," he said. "I just need to know where the repo guys are. Are you sure you can't help me with that?"

"I don't know where they are," she said, shaking her head. "They're not friends of ours."

Daryl chewed his apple and considered her for a moment. "Okay, I believe you but if you see them you'll let me know, right?"

She involuntarily took another step back. "You know what? I've got work to do. Why don't you just go do whatever it is you do?"

He leaned in close, and his stringy hair fell forward over his face. "This is what I do." He brushed the hair away from his eyes and held her gaze for a moment. "You're a strong woman, Ari, but if you cross us you'll regret it. It's just you and Eldridge out here and a bunch of these things," he kicked the dormant cooking 'bot. "If you want to keep him healthy don't do anything cute like help Teller and his crew. They're our problem. Just keep your head down and do your job. We'll take care of the rest."

Then he backed away and tossed the remains of the apple into the recycler. "We're looking for them, so just let me know if you see them. That's all you have to do to stay safe and keep things running smooth. Do you understand?"

She nodded. "Yeah, I understand."

"Good. I'll be down at my pile if you need me."

She watched him walk down the service road, his form growing smaller and more distant with each step. A few minutes later the tent flap rustled and Eldridge came out, stretching in the morning light.

"Hey, honey," he said, "what do you want for breakfast?"

Ari rushed to him and hugged him, angry with herself for crying.

"What's wrong?" He said, holding her tight. "Did something happen?"

"Yeah," she said and backed away from him, wiping hot tears from her cheeks. "Let me tell you about it."

—— «» ——

Nathan woke up early in the motel on Bad Rock after tossing and turning all night. Sleeping in a strange place always left him frayed around the edges and the events of the previous day wouldn't let his mind rest. The situation was serious, he knew, and damn near out of control. They had never been stuck like this, without their funds or ship. He sighed and stared at the ceiling.

The texture pattern on it bore a resemblance to the one in the bedroom where he had grown up. Some factory somewhere just pumped these things out for cheap housing. He considered that it might have been a better business to get into than starship repossession.

He reached for his mobi and sent a group message to everyone, rousing the troops to get an early start. He grabbed a shower, changed into fresh clothes he'd grabbed from the *Bandit* and brewed two cups of coffee from the machine in the room. It smelled like motel coffee but beggars couldn't be choosers. Then he made his way outside and spotted the deputy in the cruiser hovering a few centimeters above the parking lot. They nodded to each other as Nathan approached with the coffee.

"Thank you for that," the deputy said as he accepted the offered cup. "I ran out a couple hours ago."

"I'm going to wake everyone up and get them moving out to the wreck site. Is there a car service I can call for a van or something?"

The deputy yawned. "Sure, I'll send you a message with the link. What are you doing out there?"

"Hopefully making plans to leave. I'll see you in a few."

Nathan walked into the motel office and settled the bill, silently hoping the charge wouldn't be rejected. He didn't even want to think about covering the deductible for the damage to the ship. At least he had managed to scrape together the insurance payment before leaving Earth.

The crew started to trickle toward the office. Cole prowled the parking lot, keeping an eye out. A bleary-eyed Marla stumbled over the threshold and Duncan took her arm. Richie yawned and held the door for Tricia. She smiled with no sign of fatigue.

"Why do you look so good this morning?" Nathan said.

"What do you mean?"

Nathan waved at the crew. "Everyone else looks like death warmed over, yet somehow, you're as fresh as a daisy."

She smiled and shrugged as she sipped her own cup of coffee. "I got six hours and that's plenty. Nurses work some pretty crazy shifts, so you learn to sleep when you can and make the most of it."

"You're all right? I mean it's not every day you almost crash in a starship."

"I'm good."

"I'm good too, boss," Richie said, "just in case you were wondering."

"Us too," said Duncan, pointing at himself and Marla, "even if we do look like 'death warmed over.'" Marla threw him a wink.

"Ignore them, Tricia. They can't stand it when I give someone else attention."

"Attention is nice. Breakfast is good too. I'm starving."

Nathan saw a van float in from the street. "We'll get takeout on the way. It looks like our ride is here."

They piled into the vehicle and Nathan walked over to the deputy. "Are you going to be following us all day?"

He shook his head. "The chief just said overnight. Do you think you'll be okay? I could call him if you want."

Nathan considered it but figured they would probably be okay if they stayed out of Dodger's way. "No, we're all good. I'll call you later if we need you. Right now, the plan is to leave so maybe this is all over."

"Okay, have a good one."

He drove away as Nathan got into the self-driving van. He gave it instructions to find a restaurant with take-out breakfast and then go on out to the wreck site. After that, he leaned back in the seat and closed his eyes.

Leaving felt wrong but what he could do? Helping Chief Bell would put them in the crosshairs of a Diamond K addict who had no problem killing them. Despite what Cole had said the previous night about backing him up, he couldn't ask his crew to risk their lives to put some criminal in jail. Let Bell worry about it. That's what he was paid for.

His main concern had to be saving the business. This wasn't the first hard time he'd been through but it was the worst. Being broke didn't matter much when he had the ship to earn credits. Now, though, he didn't have either.

After he'd left the military and got his space certification he'd had a safe but boring job, just flying, no risking his life or fending off gangsters. Maybe he should have just played it safe and stayed in orbit around Earth.

—— ⟨⟩ ——

"You're burning too much fuel, numbnuts. Stop adjusting for every little deviation."

Nathan glowered at the man behind him and bit back a response. Quite a few retorts sprang to mind but actually giving voice to any of them would probably lead to unemployment and right now, he needed this job. If Archie Brandhurst, or Captain Archie as he liked to be called, wanted to complain about fuel consumption, then Nathan would just listen. At least, he would until the end of his contract eight months from now.

"Sorry, Captain. We're experiencing more atmospheric drag than the, uh, plan anticipated."

Captain Archie swung his rail thin frame into the co-pilot's chair, exactly where Nathan hated seeing him. The old man chewed tobacco and constantly spit into the stainless-steel coffee cup in his right hand. "Are you saying my flight plan is wrong?"

Careful to avoid calling his boss an idiot and eager to maintain the illusion of civility, Nathan gave the captain an aw shucks grin before he answered. "Not saying that at all, Captain. I'm just saying that maintaining the altitude indicated in the flight plan is consuming thruster fuel at a greater rate than anticipated."

"How long have you been on the King's Ransom now, Teller? A month?"

"Almost two months."

"And, remind me, how many piloting jobs have you had prior to this one?"

"A few."

"How many jobs piloting in space?"

Nathan bit his lower lip. "This would be my first one."

"Right, and I've been up here in orbit for thirty odd years, so when I tell you the rate of fuel consumption is too high, which one of us probably knows what he's talking about?"

"You have a suggestion, sir?"

"You spent all your military exit benefits on that fancy school learning to pilot in space and I have to suggest you increase your acceleration to maintain altitude? You got ripped off, son."

"The flight plan calls for our present speed."

Archie shrugged and spit tobacco juice into his cup. "It's not carved in stone, Teller. You can make adjustments to it."

Nathan nodded and made an adjustment to the speed. He felt slight pressure as the orbital tug sped up. "It feels like the inertial compensators in the artificial gravity modulator are lagging. You want it on the maintenance checklist?"

Archie shook his head and adjusted his ball cap. "Nah, it ain't so bad. Can't drop credits on every little thing or we'll go broke."

"All right."

"You've got a lot to learn about running a ship, Teller. They're just machines. The damn things never run perfectly one hundred percent of the time. You have to learn to live with things being broken sometimes."

Nathan nodded. "Okay."

Captain Archie checked their position on the co-pilot's display. "I've got the stick for a while. Why don't you go back and help the twins with the next deployment? You could use the practice."

"I'm the pilot."

"Sure, but you need to know how things work on a ship if you want to be a captain someday. Getting your hands dirty is the only way to get an understanding of how everything functions. Go on now, they'll get you up to speed."

Nathan unstrapped and got up. Archie had a contract to clean up orbital debris around Earth. Humans had been launching things into space for almost six hundred years and quite a bit of it lingered there. Large pieces of equipment usually deorbited but the most popular altitudes remained littered with junk. Over the centuries small pieces of equipment had become lost during spacewalks and nations had done ridiculous things like shooting down satellites. Clouds of bolts, metal shards and paint chips whizzed around the planet at eighteen thousand miles per hour like a lethal, razor sharp hailstorm.

He moved down the corridor that ran the length of the ship, passing the sleeping quarters, galley and finally coming to the wide cargo bay that served as the workspace for Archie's twin nephews. Nathan dreaded working with them. He took a deep breath and opened the hatch to the cargo bay.

"It's your fault," he heard a loud voice say. "You reeled the line out too quickly and now it's tangled," Tanker said. He was the older of the two by seven minutes. Nathan knew that because Tanker made a point of telling everyone he met.

His brother Jaimie stood on the other side of the bay digging through a toolbox. They both wore denim coveralls and red t-shirts with the company logo on the back.

"The line came pre-spooled, dumbass." He waved at the large reels of line stacked all over the bay. "I didn't have anything to do with it."

"You fed the reel into the spooler, didn't you?" Tanker worked under the access panel of a large piece of machinery. "Just give me the twelve millimeter so I can untangle this mess."

"Head's up," Jaimie said and Nathan snatched a wrench out of the air. He handed it to Tanker.

"Archie said you guys might need some help," Nathan said.

Jaimie smirked. "We don't need anything. The old man just wanted the cockpit to himself so he could use the comm line to talk to Earline. He's afraid if he doesn't talk to her a couple times a day that waitress will run off with some long-haul driver that comes through the diner."

Nathan shrugged and leaned up against the other side of the spooler. "Well, I'm back here. Is there anything I can do?"

"You could get the hell out of my light," Tanker said, pointing to the floating trouble light. "If I can't see what I'm doing, I can't fix his mistake."

Nathan stood up and walked toward the back of the cargo bay. A porthole there let him see the curvature of Earth outside. Riding over the day side he could see white clouds in the upper atmosphere passing lazily below them. He smiled at the view, never growing tired of it. Reluctantly he turned back to the twins. "Okay, come on. What do we need to do to lay out this string?"

Jaimie nodded toward an apparatus bolted to the floor of the cargo bay near the outer door. "The Goose could use charging. Can you handle that?"

"I think so." Nathan moved over to the device. It had two parts: a sphere dotted with plugs and holes attached to a second, more rectangular piece. He knew it was more properly known as a graviton generator and modulator but the crew of the King's Ransom *just called it the Goose.*

As Nathan activated the device he thought about that. People had struggled with a solution for cleaning up the junk in space for centuries. Big pieces could just be grabbed or pushed into the atmosphere. The small pieces whizzing around numbered in the millions and each posed a danger to the traffic that arrived at and left Earth each day. Archie had come up with a plan that might make him rich. He had been struck by a streak of clever and the Goose lived at the heart of it.

Nathan watched as indicator lights on the device started switching from red and amber to green. He didn't know what they all meant but green usually meant good. "Looks like it's… coming up." He hated sounding unsure of himself. Archie might have had a point about knowing how things worked. "So, how's the spooler coming along?"

Tanker closed the access panel. "I think it will work, at least it will if I can keep him away from it," he said, pointing at his brother. Tanker gestured at the Goose. "You know what that does, right?"

"It creates gravitons?"

"Right. You can't go faster than light speed without mucking around with gravity. I don't understand it myself but—"

"That's because you flunked out of FTL school, numbnuts," his brother said.

"And you didn't? Of course, I don't need to understand it because the heap we're flying in will never go faster than light speed. What we came up with is recycling these—"

"You mean, Uncle Archie came up with it?" Jaimie said.

"Right, that's what I meant."

Jaimie came over and leaned against a reel of line. "What Tanker means to say is that the generator and modulator is used in faster than light flight to generate gravitons, which are the particles responsible for attraction, and align them in a single direction, which is necessary for faster than light flight."

"Yeah, that's what I said. Anyway, the units get too weak for faster than light flight but they're just fine for what we want to do, which is clean up garbage. Do you get how that works yet?"

Nathan shrugged. "It... uses gravity?"

Tanker rolled his eyes at Jaimie and the two of them shook their heads. "Maybe you should just stay up front, man. You know, just fly the ship and let us take care of this stuff."

"Archie wants me to get up to speed."

Tanker wiped his hands on a rag and shoved it in his back pocket. "Okay, look, this isn't complicated. If it was, Jaimie couldn't do it."

Jaimie threw him the finger behind his back.

A red light over the cargo bay door turned amber. Nathan pointed at it. "What's that?"

"That's what we see when we're coming up on a zone," Tanker said. He picked up a pair of gloves from the tool cart and tossed them to Nathan. "Here put these on. You can help."

"I should probably get back up to the cockpit."

Jaimie laughed. "Hell, if Uncle Archie wanted you up there you'd be there. Grab the end of that line and drag it over here."

Nathan slid the gloves on and walked over to a half-used reel behind the spooler. "Right here?"

"Yeah. Now grab the end of that line and give it here. We don't have long."

Nathan tugged on the line but it seemed stuck. He tugged harder but it refused to budge. "What's wrong with this?"

Tanker shook his head. "What are you, a frickin' girl? Give it a hard yank. If we get into position without having that line spooled up we'll miss the mark and Archie will chew our asses."

Nathan gripped the line with both hands and yanked. This time something clicked and the line broke free. Nathan fell on his butt and the reel spun freely, covering him in a wad of monofilament line. He heard Tanker and Jaimie laughing as he got to his feet. He opened his mouth to say something and the spooler started up with a screech and a roar. He whipped around and saw a spinning wheel sucking in line from a different, second reel. Tanker and Jaimie laughed at him so loudly he could hear them over the sound of the machine.

Tanker put out a hand and helped him up, his face red from laughter. "You a little scared?"

"Really? A little fun with the new guy?"

The deckhand shrugged. "It gets boring back here, you know?" He waved him to the porthole set into the cargo bay doors. "Come here."

Nathan went to the porthole, leery of further pranks but Tanker pointed aft "Check it out." A small drone flew away from the ship with the mono filament line attached.

"The drone goes out ten klicks, keeps enough thrust going to make the line taught and then we hit the button."

Jaimie had his hand on a switch. "We send a burst of gravitons down it that lasts for a fraction of a second, creating a field. Anything caught in the field, like screws, paint chips or pieces of old rockets get attracted to the line. All that crap builds up and sticks to the line because the line stays charged with gravitons."

"Get ready," Tanker said. "It goes by pretty fast."

"Yeah," Jaimie said, "and we're only going to do it about a hundred more times in the next week."

Tanker shook his head. "I don't think he finds any joy in his work." He watched the lights above the door until they flashed green. "Hit it, brother."

Jaimie pushed a button on the Goose and Nathan felt himself get heavier for a moment. He put a hand on the cargo door to brace himself. "What's that?"

Tanker shrugged. "The graviton pulse. We get a little bleed through. Uncle Archie thinks he can fix it in the next version. Look outside."

Nathan leaned toward the porthole. He couldn't see the monofilament line, of course. It was a little thicker than a few strands of hair and not particularly reflective. Then something became visible. Shards of metal and other junk floated through space toward an invisible line and started forming up. It trailed out straight behind the ship.

"How far out does the pulse extend?"

Tanker screwed up his face in concentration. "Uncle Archie says it goes out about ten klicks, so it's like a big bubble." He turned to Jaimie. "How much did we get?"

Jaimie checked a readout on the Goose's control panel and nodded approvingly. "Just over a metric ton."

"Good one," Tanker said. "We get paid by weight, so the more debris we remove the more we get paid."

"You know what the rate is?"

"Nah," Tanker said, "Uncle Archie handles all that."

"It's really only good for the small stuff, though, right?" Nathan said. "I mean, you wouldn't want something that weighed a ton flying through space at you."

Tanker laughed. "Nah, the whole thing is modulated so that we don't attract anything that weighs more than a few kilograms. You get some old Chinese rocket motor flying at you at orbital velocity and you can kiss your keister goodbye. You passed FTL flight school, didn't you?"

Nathan nodded.

"Okay, then you know that the gravitons set up the attraction but the mass of the objects is what's really important. Ten kilometers of monofilament has more mass than a nut or *some old pieces of metal. You point that modulator at a ship larger than us and you'd pull us right into it."*

"Yeah, I see what you mean," Nathan said.

"Next, we get rid of the junk." Tanker pointed at a monitor near the hatch. Nathan saw a sensor scan of space around them. "See, we just make sure there's no traffic around, then we tell the drone to dive for the ground. The whole mess just burns up in a few hours when it gets low enough."

"How come we don't salvage any of this stuff instead of letting it burn up?"

Tanker waved him off. "It's not worth the fuel to carry it back down planetside. No, just let it burn up. No one wants steel or aluminum that's been up here for a couple hundred years." The whole idea seemed clever and simple.

"Huh," Nathan said. "Archie thought that up?"

Jaimie nodded. "Yeah, but not until he'd spent a couple decades up here trolling for debris the old-fashioned way, by dragging mesh nets behind a tug. Can you imagine how boring that would be?"

Nathan nodded. He'd only been up here two months and the thought of doing this for twenty years made him want to take a walk out of an airlock without a pressure suit.

"I figure Uncle Archie will get his patent on the process and then retire," Tanker said. "Me and Jaimie will take over and we'll be set up for life."

"You know it, bro," Jaimie called from the Goose. "We'll be on easy street."

"If things work out Nathan, you could have a job to retire from flying this tug around, cleaning this crap up. There's so much of it out there you couldn't get it all in three lifetimes. How's that sound?"

Nathan thought it sounded dull but he smiled and nodded. "That's a sound offer, Tanker. I might just have to take you up on it." He smiled at Jaimie and walked out of the bay for the cockpit, sure in the knowledge that as soon as his contract expired he would never work for anyone but himself.

— «» —

When the van pulled up to Eldridge and Ari's worksite, Epsilon Eridani bathed the area in a light that seemed to have too much orange in it. Nathan got out carrying a sack full of breakfast take-out and set it on the large table under the canopy. Duncan followed and set down another. They started removing containers full of waffles, breakfast sandwiches and bacon.

Ari came out of the tent she shared with Eldridge and gave them the stink-eye. "What are you doing here?"

Nathan offered her a cup. "Want some coffee? It's much better than the stuff we had at the motel. Less roaches in it I think. Anyway, we thought we'd treat you to breakfast."

She sat down at the table and put her head down on her arms. "You're like those guests that don't know when the party is over."

Eldridge came out of the tent buckling a tool belt around his waist. "What's all this?"

Ari glanced up. "Look, honey, the repo men have brought us breakfast."

Nathan stood up and handed him a cup of coffee. "Dig in, Eldridge. We have a lot to talk about."

He sat down and eyed Nathan as he selected an egg and sausage sandwich loaded with peppers and onions. "Thanks for breakfast. So, what do you want to talk about?"

"Dodger crashed my ship."

"I remember. Is everyone okay?"

"They are, thanks to Marla," he pointed at the opposite side of the table and she waved a forkful of waffles. "However, it has put a crimp in our plans to leave. For that, we're going to need your help."

Eldridge stopped mid-bite. "What do you mean?"

"Well, my ship can't fly and we need to go. We'd like your help."

"I don't understand."

"I need three or four of your trucks. We're going to use them to haul my ship up to the *Corkscrew* and we'll stow her in an empty bay for the trip home."

"You must be joking," Ari said. "Not only are you going to repo our ship, which, by the way, shouldn't even be happening, but now you want to use our equipment to help?"

"That's right. We'll probably need some engineering assistance as well, to make the trucks do what we need."

Eldridge shook his head. "No way. Ari is right. If you want to repo my ship, do it on your own. I'm not helping."

Nathan put his fork down on his plate. "Listen, son, I wouldn't be here right now if not for you and your crew. We were doing just fine up there until your girl Scooter decided to kidnap us and drop us down here. Everything that's happened since has been because of that. So yeah, I expect you to do the decent thing and help get my ship off this rock and up into orbit."

Eldridge shook his head. "I'm sorry for what Scooter did but..."

Nathan held up a hand, interrupting him. "Look, I've been thinking. The *Corkscrew* can't hold that entire starliner no matter how many little pieces you chop it into. I figure you were going to make a few trips back to Earth anyway, right? You have to drop the salvage somewhere you'll get paid for it, and there's nowhere in the Epsilon Eridani system like that. Come on, tell me I'm wrong."

Eldridge sighed heavily. "That's true but the first trip isn't supposed to go until the ship is full and right now she's at seventy percent."

"Which leaves more than enough room to store my ship until you get back to Earth. See? It all works out."

Eldridge took a bite from his sandwich and chewed, considering the idea. "It would give me the opportunity to figure out what's going on with the payments to the bank."

"There you go."

"I still don't like it," Ari said, "but it makes sense. I could keep things moving while you're gone. We certainly have enough room to let the piles grow. We could just get caught up when you get back."

"Yeah," Eldridge said. "We can do that. What about Dodger?"

"What about him?"

"While we're gone I don't want him out here messing around and giving Ari a hard time. Daryl stopped by here this morning on his way out to his pile."

"What did he want?" Nathan said.

"You. We're supposed to call him if you show up so they can some get you. Then he reminded us about our deal with Dodger and how they can make this repossession problem go away. All we need to do is make one call."

Nathan became concerned. "Did you do that?"

"No," Eldridge said. "I'm not ratting anyone out to Dodger."

"Did he hurt you?" Nathan said to Ari.

She shook her head.

Nathan ran a hand through his hair. "I'm so angry at Dodger that I'm not sure I can think straight about him." He got up and walked a few steps away from the table.

Eldridge got up and followed him. "He's not right in the head, you know? He chews that crap to get high and then he does crazy shit, like what happened yesterday. Maybe we should just take him down so we don't have to worry about him anymore."

Nathan turned. "Chief Bell wants me to testify against him but it will take too long. By the time we get to court I'll be broke and out of business."

Eldridge walked over to Ari and put his hands on her shoulders. "If we pooled resources, maybe we could take him down."

"I'm not killing anyone," Nathan said. "That's not who we are."

"I'm not talking about killing anyone but couldn't we do something to get him arrested? We just need him locked up and away from us."

Ari stood up. "Babe, what are you thinking about? I thought you wanted to keep paying him off and keep the peace."

Eldridge took her hands in his. "I've been thinking about what you said, about what your dad would do if he were here."

She shook her head. "I didn't mean anything by that."

"No, you're right. We need to stand on our own because eventually he'll strip us down to nothing. As long as we have a credit to our name he'll find some way to take it."

"He can go to hell," Ari said. "I'm not doing anything for them."

"What about you?" Eldridge said to Nathan. "Are you saying you don't want a little pay back? He crashed your ship and almost killed your people."

Nathan took a deep breath. "You have to understand, Eldridge, that going up against him means that the gloves are off. He won't hesitate to kill all of us. If we do this, and right now it's only an 'if', we could just be buying more trouble. Bell said he's connected to the Syndicate so it's not just him. I've met these guys before and you don't want to tangle with them."

Eldridge nodded slowly, like he was considering Nathan's words. He looked at Ari and Nathan knew what the answer was going to be. "Maybe he shouldn't have messed with us."

"You're sure about this?"

Eldridge gripped Ari's hand and she nodded her approval with a look of pride on her face. "Yeah, we're sure."

Nathan turned to his crew. "What about you? Are you all on board with this?"

Duncan put and arm around Marla and a look passed between them. "Let's just be smart about it, okay?" Duncan said.

"I'm in," Richie said.

Nathan looked at Tricia and she smiled. "He tried to kill me. If we can do something about that, I'm game."

"Cole?"

He finished chewing the bite of sandwich in his mouth and swallowed before answering. "You talk too damn much, you know that? I told you last night that I'd back your play. So, what's the plan?"

Nathan considered his options and then grinned. "Gather around. I think I have an idea."

Chapter 20

Two hours later Nathan and Cole rooted around the storage lockers inside the *Blue Moon Bandit*. Cole thumbed the lock on one and it popped open. Nathan directed a flashlight into the metal storage bin. He saw three rifles, spare magazines and several cases of ammunition.

"Take all of it," Nathan said.

"Of course, but just so you know, I'm low on some of the special stuff like Rolling Betties and sticky bombs."

They loaded it all into a couple duffel bags. Nathan hefted them and walked them back to the top of the loading ramp. He turned back and yelled over his shoulder. "Don't forget the shaped charges we keep for busting clamps loose. We're going to need them."

"I didn't forget."

Nathan walked down the ramp into the late morning sunshine. The *Bandit* had been yanked free of the runway end by a crane at dawn. He would have preferred to be here when they did it but the spaceport wanted their runway back in operation. Now it sat crookedly on a landing pad because the tires on one set of landing gear had blown out. Three of Eldridge's trucks rested out in the scrub grass surrounding the landing pad. He heard a sound and shaded his eyes from the sun with one hand.

"How is it up there?"

Duncan and Eldridge stood on the uppermost hull. "I think we can do it," Duncan said as he gripped the maintenance ladder and started climbing down. He took each step carefully and without rushing.

"I'm still not sure," Eldridge said.

"Don't listen to him," Duncan said. "He's just worried we're going to bang up his trucks."

Eldridge gripped the sides of the ladder and slid down with an effortlessness you only have in your twenties.

"I'm not just worried about my trucks. I mean, yeah, I'm worried about them but what you're talking about is difficult. We have to synchronize three trucks together, lift this heap," he raised his hands, "sorry no offense, and then get it up into orbit. Then we have to maneuver it to the *Corkscrew* and dock it." He paused and shook his head. "It's one of those ideas that sounds good when you sketch it out but in reality, it's just really, really bad."

Duncan smiled at Nathan and shook his head. "Don't listen to him. We can do it."

"I don't know," Eldridge said. "It just seems kind of risky."

"Kid, there's risk in anything you do," Duncan said. "In our line of work, and in yours by the way, we constantly have to come up with original ideas and solutions. Sometimes there just isn't a manual to look at."

"There is a solution for this," Eldridge said. "You get a tug out here and lift this thing up using a vessel designed to move starships. It's not like this problem hasn't come up before."

Duncan waved a hand at him. "Stop worrying so much. 'Oh, Duncan, you'll break my equipment,'" he said, imitating Eldridge. "'Oh, Duncan, it's not meant to do that' Hell, kid, I don't even know if there is a tug on this planet and if there is, do you have any idea how expensive a tow into orbit would be, or how long it would take to get here? We need our ship in orbit *before* Dodger tries to finish us off. Nah, this is the better solution." He leaned over and slapped Eldridge on the back. "Trust me, at the end of the day you'll be glad you did this."

"You're crazy."

Duncan threw him a wink. "No, but I have great stories and it's because I have mad ideas like this. Now come on. Let's get these things set up. We're on a schedule."

Richie walked around the rear of the ship. Nathan smiled. "Hey, I notice you're taking the long way around. Why aren't you walking under the ship?"

The machinist mate answered him without any humor in his eyes. "I was on this thing when it came down and I know exactly how hard we hit. No way do I trust that landing gear until we've done a proper inspection."

"What did you do with the drogue chute?"

"Duncan and I disconnected it and stowed it in the number two hold. That's something else that will need to be inspected. I hope you have good insurance, boss."

Nathan grimaced. "Yeah, me too." He followed Richie to the side of the hull outside of the starboard engine. Richie mounted a maintenance scissor lift and rose into the air next to the ship. He pulled out a cordless impact wrench and started removing bolts from an access plate.

"Is that where we're hooking on with the trucks?" He said in a raised voice over the sound of the tool.

Richie leaned over the side of the lift. "Yeah, there are two hard points on this side and two on the other. We'll bolt the trucks on and lift it right up. I got the other side earlier so whenever Duncan and Eldridge are ready we can get this show on the road."

Nathan watched for half an hour as Duncan, Richie and Eldridge cleared the area of people and equipment. They all stood half a klick away from the landing pad. Nathan and Cole had nothing to do with this part of the operation and Nathan fidgeted with the binoculars hanging around his neck waiting for things to begin. He bit his lip to keep from asking the three of them what was happening. They all crowded around a rugged portable workstation Eldridge had set up. Finally he couldn't take anymore.

"Are we doing this?"

Duncan held up a hand. "Calm down. We're actually starting now."

Eldridge made an adjustment on the workstation and one of the trucks lifted off above the scrub brush and flew next to the *Blue Moon Bandit* faster than Nathan would have thought was safe. Before he could acknowledge that fact, the truck adjusted itself parallel to the hard points Richie had accessed. A second truck rose up and moved equally quickly to the damaged port side. Both trucks extended landing gear and settled in next to the *Bandit*.

The trucks adjusted their position relative to his ship and Nathan went back to biting his lip. He wanted to ask questions but he trusted Duncan so he kept his mouth shut and let them work. He couldn't contribute anything useful to the situation.

For several long minutes, he watched as Duncan made minute adjustments and the trucks completed their line-up. Duncan pointed to the monitor. "Come on and watch this."

He looked over Duncan's shoulder and the engineer said, "Go ahead, Eldridge."

Nathan watched as large polished cylinders with thick notches extended from the truck and inserted themselves into the hard points on the *Bandit*. The cylinders rotated and locked into place.

Duncan inspected the connection on the monitor. He smiled at Nathan. "That's one."

The view changed to the damaged port side. Luckily the engine was inboard from the side of the hull so the hard points could still be accessed.

Nathan pointed to them. "Are you sure this side will hold? It's pretty torn up."

"It should," Duncan said. "The damage all seemed contained to the engine and the engine compartment. The structure seems solid."

"Richie checked the struts supporting this side? He's our metal guy."

"Yeah, yeah, it's all good so stop worrying," Duncan said. He checked the monitor and saw the cylinders slide home. "And there we go. All right, let's lift this thing up."

Nathan shook his head. "Okay, we need to be really careful here."

Duncan put a hand on his shoulder. "I know, Nathan, that's why this part is automated."

"Really?"

"Don't worry; I have complete confidence that it will work."

"I programmed the sequence myself," Eldridge said.

Duncan nodded. "Yeah, so if anything goes wrong, it's on him."

Eldridge raised his eyebrows. "It will work as well as anything else I've ever tried and didn't adequately test."

"Do it," Duncan said.

Eldridge gave the workstation a command and the trucks on either side of the *Bandit* fired their main thrusters. They rose a few meters off the ground with Nathan's ship sandwiched between them. The landing gear on all three ships retracted and Nathan held his breath, waiting for the whole interconnected mess to fall to the ground. They held steady though, and moved as one unit toward the third truck sitting forward of the landing pad. With surprising grace the three vessels rose another few meters over the third truck and hovered above it. The computer made minute adjustments and the three vessels settled down, balancing on the third truck. Nathan let out a breath he hadn't even been aware of holding.

Duncan fist bumped Eldridge and Richie. Nathan saw all three men smiling at each other. "Good job," he said. "So we go up from here or what?"

The roar of thrusters from the linked ships answered him. Nathan watched as the most ungainly mess he'd ever seen rose up into the sky. The thrusters of all three trucks fired with a roar of noise and his ship rocketed toward space faster than he would have thought possible, born aloft by trash hauling trucks. A cloud of dirt and smoke washed over them.

Nathan stood shoulder to shoulder with Duncan at the workstation monitor watching the telemetry from the trucks. He pointed at the screen. "Watch your angle."

"It's good, calm down," Duncan said.

The engineer calmly scrolled through the data and Nathan felt like popping from the stress of watching his livelihood screaming through the clouds with no one at the controls. "The rate of climb is a little fast."

"It's good, Nathan. The trucks have plenty of lift. The angle is right where it's supposed to be."

Nathan backed away and chewed on his thumb. The flight computers ran the show. Even Duncan and Eldridge watched.

Just when he thought he couldn't take anymore, Duncan turned to him with a thumb's up. "We have orbital insertion. I told you it would work." The engineer slapped Eldridge on the back. "Still worried?"

Nathan thought so but the younger man nodded at Duncan and said, "It all worked."

"Of course it did. Now let's get it docked with your ship."

Nathan watched nervously as the automated systems pushed the mess up to the proper altitude and matched the speed and trajectory of the *Corkscrew*. More slowly than he would have thought possible the live feed from the recycling ship showed the two trucks bracketing the *Bandit* break free and drop off the screen. The last truck, with his ship perched on it, moved slowly toward the open cargo bay. Then it silently slipped inside and a couple 'bots moved to anchor it in place.

Duncan slapped Eldridge on the back again. "Good job, kid. You've got a real knack for making machines work together."

Nathan walked over to Eldridge. "He's right. You did a hell of a job."

"Thanks. That was the toughest thing I've ever programmed."

"Well, you did great," Nathan said. He helped them pack up the gear and they carried it over to where Cole lay on a couple of large duffel bags with his eyes closed.

Nathan nudged him. "You awake?"

"Yeah," he said. "How's the ship?"

"All tucked in for the ride home."

Cole stood up and dusted himself off. "Good. What are we doing now?"

Nathan picked up one of the duffels and they started toward the truck. Duncan and Eldridge followed them. "Now comes the hard part. We deal with Dodger."

Cole carried the other bag. "Good. Do we need anything else?"

Nathan nodded toward a pile of gear in the back of the truck. "I had Duncan and Richie pull off a few other items."

"Well, the bag you're holding has the rifles." He raised the other one and said, "I've got the charges."

"Good," Nathan said. "Let's go see about attaching them to something."

—— «» ——

"I said their ship is up here in one of our cargo bays," Charlie said through the crackle of static. "They towed it up here with a few of our trucks."

"When did they do that?"

"This morning, I think. Maybe a few hours ago. I've been kind of busy up here."

"Come on, man, you have to be timely with this stuff. You have to tell us when things happen."

"Sure, okay."

Morris nodded at Dodger in the office of the strip club and said, "You want this guy to do anything?"

Dodger shrugged. "What else can he do? We crashed the damn ship and didn't kill anyone. Hell, we locked them in that wreck out there and they're still running around."

"Maybe they're just going to leave."

"Maybe," Dodger said. He gestured toward the mobi. "Tell that dumbass to hang tight and let us know if they do anything else."

"I heard that," Charlie said. "We're on speaker."

"Sorry," Morris said. "Just give us a call if you see these repo guys or hear anything."

"Whatever." The call dropped and Morris put the mobi on his desk.

Morris suspected he didn't look his best but Dodger had the appearance of a corpse left in the sun too long. There had been a time when the boss seemed vain. He would spend hours in the gym lifting free weights and doing cardio. Now, he had lost enough weight that his clothes hung on him and his face had a haggard beard. Chewing Diamond K turned him into the kind of guy you'd find living under a bridge.

They hadn't heard anything about the repo guys yet today and he knew Dodger's paranoia would get the best of him.

Most of his men were still sleeping but a few patrolled the parking lot at Dodge Em's and watched over the apartment building where they made the Diamond K. Being awake for so long and their natural tendency to be lazy, left Morris wondering how effective any of them could be. Dodger's guys usually intimidated the local shopkeepers into paying protection credits or selling Diamond K to burn outs. They didn't do a lot of independent thinking.

"Are they still out at the wreck site?" Dodger asked. He toyed with crystals on his desk, arranging them in patterns and then chewing one every now and again. Morris didn't know how he hadn't overdosed yet.

"Daryl said he thinks so, but if they are they're laying low. He hasn't seen them since they beat the snot out of Turtle. The trouble is he's still out at his pile collecting our salvage and I haven't had any spare men to give him a hand. If they are out there and are willing to leave, I think we should let them."

Dodger stared at him for a minute. Morris didn't know if he was considering what he'd said or if he was just stoned. Then he snapped to and said, "What if they come back with Protective Services from Earth? They know who we are, where we are and where our production facility is."

"I don't know if they're as dangerous as you think," Morris said. He held up a hand to stop Dodger's objection. "Hold on, you're right about the apartment building. We should move out of that. If nothing else, they can tell Chief Bell and then we'll have him snooping around. As far as the club and us being here, who cares? This is where you're supposed to be. It's your business."

"Moving production to a new place only solves half the problem," Dodger said. "We still have to get the stuff off world. All Protective Services has to do is set up a quarantine and inspect the ships that come and go. They could do that with a few ships. No, I say we still deal with them tonight."

"You want us to do them right there or bring them somewhere?"

Dodger thought for a moment. "Take them to the warehouse across the street from the apartment building and call me. There's lots of room and no one around. Besides, I want to make sure you've got them all."

Because you're paranoid from chewing that shit, Morris thought. "Okay. I'll round up the guys and we'll get to work. It shouldn't take more than a few hours." He moved toward the door.

"Hey, Morris?"

He turned back. "Yeah?"

"They know I'm here." He had that crazy look in his eyes, the one that made Morris think he wasn't processing information properly. "Take some of the guys from the apartment building. I don't want them coming here while you're out and seeing we're light."

Morris nodded. "Okay, sure."

—— «» ——

Nathan and Cole moved toward Pile 4 and saw Daryl sitting tipped back in his usual chair with his feet up on a plastic storage bin. He had his hat pulled down low over his eyes and appeared to be sleeping as the 'bots pulled apart equipment and sorted the individual components.

Cole moved behind him and kicked the legs out from under the chair. Daryl jumped up to face them but Nathan grabbed the back of his shirt and swung him around, pushing him back down to his knees.

"What the hell?"

Nathan moved back and forth in front of him and Cole circled around back, keeping him off balance. "We've got some questions for you," Nathan said.

Daryl broke out a smug look. "I'm not saying anything to you. If you want to know something, go talk to Dodger."

"That won't work. I want to know about Dodger."

"Oh come on, what are you going to do? You want to hit Dodger because of your ship? Let me give you some advice, just go."

"How come you're not acting tough like you were this morning with Ari?" Nathan said. "Are the two of us too much for you?"

He held his hands up. "I was just delivering a message. I really don't care what you guys do. If you leave, Dodger can't touch you. He acts like a tough guy but that's just here in Bad Rock. You get off planet and most guys in the Syndicate don't even know who he is."

"They trust him enough to put him in charge of making Diamond K."

Daryl gave them a little laugh. "Dude, anyone could do that. Dodger got the job because he isn't good at anything else. Think about it; he sits out here where there's nothing and no one. All he has to do is make sure Chief Bell doesn't tweak to what's going on."

"Still, the Diamond K brings in quite a bit of revenue."

"Yeah, that's true but I don't know how much longer Dodger will be running the show. The Syndicate will probably take care of him for you."

Nathan didn't understand. "What do you mean?"

"He's using. All he does is sit in the back room of that strip club and chew K. How long do you think he can hold onto his position doing that?" He shook his head and fear crept into his eyes. "You want revenge, right? That's why you're here, hassling me?"

Nathan nodded and said, "Dodger really screwed up my business with his little stunt so yeah, there's going to be a little payback for that." Nathan hunkered down to one knee so he could look Daryl right in the eye. "You're going to help us out."

Daryl swallowed hard. "What do I get out of it?"

Nathan paused and raised an eyebrow at Cole, who seemed equally surprised. "You know, of all the things you could have said right then, I didn't expect that. What do you want?"

"Credits. Enough to get off world and go somewhere else."

"Well, you're out of luck because I don't have any."

Daryl licked his lips, thinking, and then he got a gleam in his eye. "Dodger's got plenty."

Nathan shrugged. "So? They're probably in a bank account somewhere. I don't have a hacker with me."

"There might be another way," he said, snapping his fingers. "He keeps credits on hand in his safe at the strip club. You could get it there."

Nathan waved him off. "Look, I'm not interested in breaking into his office but I can certainly make it easier for you to do. What we're going to do, well, it's going to make him angry. I imagine he'll be out of his office and busy. You should be able to get in and do whatever you want. How's that sound?"

"I don't know. I'm giving you some good information."

Cole leaned down close to the side of Daryl's head, causing him to jerk. "And I'm not beating on you with a pipe wrench. My friends were on that ship you guys crashed. Maybe you should just take the deal Nathan's offering you."

Daryl considered it and nodded his head. "All right, I can help you. Can I get off the ground?"

Nathan took a step back and righted the chair lying askew in the dirt. "Sit there, and give me your mobi. I don't want you calling anyone."

Daryl sat down and handed over his mobi. "Don't worry about it. There's no one left for me to call here."

"What about your buddy, Turtle?"

"I don't know," Daryl said, shaking his head. "If I score enough of Dodger's credits maybe I'll get him out of here."

Nathan sat down on the plastic storage bin and Cole kept circling behind the chair Daryl sat in. "So, tell me everything you know about Dodger, his club and that apartment building where he makes the Diamond K."

Chapter 21

Nathan sat at the table under the canopy with Tricia and Cole. They had guns spread out across it and Nathan helped as Cole broke each down, cleaned them, reassembled and loaded them. Tricia raised an eyebrow and nodded toward them.

"You sure you'll need all this? I thought the idea was not to shoot Dodger and his men?"

Nathan shrugged as he fitted together a pistol. "Well, that's the general idea but you always want to be prepared."

Cole slid a pistol to her. "You know how to use that?"

Tricia picked it up and pulled the slide to check the chamber. "Yeah, I know how to use it. Do you think I'll need to?"

"If things go bad, you need to be able to protect yourself," Nathan said. "It's just a precaution."

Tricia picked up the holster for the pistol and slid it in. Then she stood and fitted it into the waistband of her pants, adjusting it until it was comfortable. Nathan's mobi vibrated and an unfamiliar icon lit up. She pointed to it. "What's that?"

Nathan checked the device. "It's a remote control app for the gizmo Duncan and Eldridge installed in the back of the truck and for the thing Richie is hanging on the side of the truck." He turned to check on the kid's progress.

The machinist's mate stood on a ladder securing one end of a large digital display to the outside of the truck on the driver's side. A 'bot held up the other end. They had scavenged it from one of the casinos inside the *Athena Star*. He turned back to her.

"I really wish you would go up to the *Corkscrew* with Ari and the others. Is there any way I can convince you to do that?"

She shook her head. "No, you're going to need me to fix you up once you're done with this stunt." She smiled and her eyes narrowed. "Besides, I was on the ship when they tried to crash it. I want to see what happens to them."

Cole smiled. "Can we keep her? You know, if we ever fly again."

Nathan grunted. "Oh, we'll fly again. No way do we stay grounded because of some dope dealer at the edge of nowhere." He picked up another pistol and checked it. "Why do you think Dodger's left us alone? Shouldn't he have been out here by now trying to round us up?"

"He got the coolant," Cole said. "Maybe he'll leave us alone now. Besides, he may not know where we are. We've still got Daryl under wraps. It's most likely he's holed up somewhere getting high. He may even be waiting for us to go after him."

Nathan shook his head. "Or he's gathering his guys, getting ready to come for us. I don't see him just letting us leave."

Cole picked up the upper receiver of a rifle and slipped it into the lower receiver, reassembling the firearm. "If he comes early, we'll be ready but things will be messier than you want."

Nathan watched the empty road. According to Eldridge, Dodger had plenty of goons at his fingertips, enough to outnumber Nathan's group. "There's not much we can do if they roll up on us."

"How much more time do you think Duncan needs? It seems like he's been working on this all day."

"Well, he said about three hours an hour and a half ago so he should be done anytime."

Tricia frowned and glanced at the truck. "Doesn't that mean he still needs at least an hour or so?"

Nathan and Cole both snorted. "He always pads his time in case he's not as brilliant as he thinks. Come on, let's go see what's up."

They walked over to the truck and Nathan stopped by Richie, inspecting the sign. He nodded approvingly. "You know, it doesn't have to be perfect. It's only got a few hours left until it's a piece of scrap."

Richie gave it a pat. "I don't want you thinking I do sloppy work. Want to give it a try?"

Nathan took out his mobi and called up the app to control the sign. He typed in a message and watched the sign come to life. His message scrolled by in extravagantly bright digital letters, "Good Job, Richie."

They tested the sign with a few more commands then walked around the back of the truck to where Duncan and Eldridge sat on rolling stools admiring their work. Nathan smiled. "I take it you're all done?"

The two of them nodded. Duncan said, "Did you get the mobi app to work?"

"I think so." Nathan tapped the controls. The gizmo in the back of the truck rotated around in a circle. "Seems to be what we expected."

The two of them picked up their tools and moved to the tailgate. Nathan grabbed the toolboxes as Duncan and Eldridge jumped down.

"Are you really sure about this?" Duncan said.

Nathan put a hand on his shoulder. "They took my ship down and almost killed half the crew. Yeah, I'm sure."

"Okay then," Duncan said. "Let me show you how this works."

—— «》 ——

Morris sat on the steps of the apartment building and smoked a cigarette. No one on Earth smoked anymore but out here in the settlements you could still get real tobacco. The sun had dipped below the horizon a few minutes ago and the sky was a light shade of purple. The building faced an empty street. They'd chosen this location for production because this area of the city was pretty much abandoned.

He kept the guards out of sight in the lobby. Dodger had wanted them right out on the street where they could be seen because he wanted to intimidate people. Morris had talked him out of that. Why advertise?

He had to do that kind of thing often with Dodger. The guy could be clever but he didn't understand subtlety. If an operation called for quiet the boss preferred loud and brash. He finished the cig and flicked it out into the street.

The door behind him opened up and his nephew Cheech came out. "Uncle Morris? I've got the guys all ready."

"How many do we have?"

"Six volunteers. If we take all of them that leaves four guys to guard the place while we're gone. Is that all right?"

Morris sighed. "Not really. Dodger wants this taken care of and I'm not rolling out there unless I'm sure we've got enough guys to win. Our contacts back on Earth said these guys can be tough."

He blew out a deep breath and wondered again why he still worked for Dodger, still took direction from a junkie. Sure, he had done the hard work of getting this operation set up and had been fairly successful but those days appeared long gone. He could think of ten ways to improve the operation and Dodger wouldn't even understand them. He pulled his mobi from his pocket and dialed Dodger. The boss answered on the third beep.

"It's Morris. I need some more guys. I want to grab three or four from the club. You okay with that?"

Dodger rambled through an answer and asked Morris a question. "We're going right now." He shook his head and ended the call.

"How many did he give you?" Cheech said.

Morris held up two fingers. "We'll roll by the club and grab them first."

"Can I ask you a question?"

"Shoot."

"I know I haven't been around long but the boss is pretty screwed up, right? I mean it can't be normal to chew that much product and expect to make good decisions."

"No, it's not normal. You think we should do something? Is that what you're saying?"

Cheech shrugged. "I'm saying that if you wanted to make a move, me and a lot of the other guys would be behind you."

Morris stood up and eyeballed his nephew. "You guys talking about this behind Dodger's back?"

Cheech grinned, all white teeth paid for by military benefits. "We sure don't talk about it in front of him."

Morris nodded and put a hand on his shoulder. "Be careful. These guys are all tough when they're alone but there's a reason they work for a guy like Dodger. They all want to move up and that doesn't happen by fragging the boss. I'd be very careful about what I said and who I said it to."

"Yeah, don't worry. We're careful."

Blowing off his advice, just like that, thinking his uncle too old, too timid to make a move. "Get the guys and the equipment ready. You're in charge of that. Can you handle it?"

Cheech nodded. "I'll be ready."

Morris gave his shoulder a squeeze. "Good. I'll see you then."

—— «» ——

Nathan and Cole loaded their truck with the equipment they needed for the hit on the apartment building.

"What about Daryl?" Cole said.

Eldridge held out his mobi and showed him a video feed of the man tied to a chair in the cargo bay of the *Athena Star*. "He's been there all night with a 'bot and our man Fred watching him."

"Good. That should keep him from getting into trouble."

Nathan nudged Eldridge. "What time does your truck go up to the *Corkscrew*?"

Eldridge and Ari shared a look before he answered. "We're staying, Nathan. No one is going up to the ship."

"Well that's just stupid."

"The kid's right," Duncan said. "We talked about it earlier. The right thing is to stay here and support you in case things go badly."

Nathan shook his head. "So what's the plan? You sit here in these tents and hope everything goes all right?"

"It's my place," Eldridge said. "I'm not going to be run off. We'll hole up in the *Athena Star* if things go bad. If we can help, we will."

"No offense, but what can you do?"

"We can do what's necessary. Duncan says your plans never go the way you think they will so our knowledge of the wreck and the geography may come in handy."

"Duncan talks too much and," he said, throwing a look at the engineer, "my plans almost always work out." They all seemed to have their minds made up.

"Okay, I can tell I'm not going to win this fight so go make yourselves safe. Cole, Richie and I roll out in ten minutes."

He grabbed Duncan by the arm. "This is a bad idea. You know that, right?"

"Go do your thing and stop worrying about us. We've got it under control. Consider us Plan B."

Nathan nodded and they shook hands. "Take care of Tricia."

He turned to Cole and Richie. Both waited for him at the edge of the canopy.

"You guys ready?"

Cole checked the time on his mobi. "Let's get it done."

"Richie, you're always complaining about getting stuck on the ship and not seeing any action. I imagine this is going to make up for quite a bit of that."

The machinist had a huge grin on his face. "It's more fun than learning how to tear motors apart with Duncan, that's for sure."

"We'll see. Are the vehicles charged?"

He nodded. "The car and the truck are all ready to go."

"All right. You and Cole go first. I'll follow you."

"You're always worried about everyone else," Cole said to him. "How about you? Sure you want to go through with this? It's not too late to call Chief Bell and have him and his boys raid the place."

He shook his head. "Nah, he'll have a role to play soon enough. Let's go teach this guy a lesson. Give him a kick in the nuts and stomp on his cash flow."

Cole smiled and slapped him on the back. "Let's go do just that."

Chapter 22

Nathan stopped well short of the building, watching as Richie's float car took a right and dropped out of view as it went behind a row of warehouses. He powered down the lights and sat on the side of the road, double checking the automated tasks on his mobi while the others got into position.

He had to admit that, despite his earlier bravado to Cole about flying again, this could pretty much be their last hurrah. The damage to the ship looked extensive but until Duncan did a thorough examination he wouldn't know exactly how bad. There was insurance but there was also a deductible and right now there weren't enough credits in his account to cover it, even with what they would earn getting Eldridge's ship back.

His mobi buzzed with a text message from Cole displaying a single thumbs up emoji indicating he was ready.

A large float van pulled away from the alley beside the apartment building and swung in his direction. He leaned down behind the dashboard as it approached and went past. He sat up, checked the side mirror and saw it continue down the street. His mobi buzzed again and this time the message was from Richie. It said, "all set."

Nathan gripped the wheel and moved the truck down the street without any more hesitation. Whatever happened when they got home, whatever happened with the ship and the business, Dodger wasn't going to be earning anymore credits from making Diamond K in this building.

Nathan slowed the truck in front of the apartment building and crossed from the right lane to the left, pulling up as close as he could to the entrance doors to the lobby. No lights shone in the building or the buildings around it. He knew guards patrolled the building, though. Cole had scuffled with one and Daryl had confirmed how many worked inside. His mouth went dry as he imagined them inside now, staring at him, wondering about the truck sitting at the curb. He took a calming breath and slid over to the passenger side of the seat and opened the passenger side door.

He slipped down to the street and hurried across it to the warehouse, keeping the truck body between himself and the lobby. He made a quick right and scrambled for a narrow alley where he ducked behind a dumpster. From this vantage point he could see most of the lobby entrance but no one came out. If they had, Cole would have dissuaded them from his perch on top of the warehouse. Richie sat in the float car behind the apartment building, half a block away from the back entrance, keeping an eye on things.

He took another deep breath, winded from his short jog across the street. His heart beat hard as he pulled out his mobi. He placed a group voice call to Cole and Richie and spoke into the mic.

"Cole, get their attention."

Gunfire erupted from the roof above him, shattering the silence of the early morning as it echoed up and down the concrete buildings and sidewalks. The second floor windows of the apartment building blew out and sharp fragments rained down onto the sidewalk below. Nathan watched the door for a response.

—— ⟨⟩ ——

Vincent, one of the four guards left behind by Morris to guard the apartment building, sat with his feet up at a table in the apartment building lobby watching a movie on his mobi. If Morris saw him he would whine about him being lazy. Another guard, Hyde, slept in a chair.

Without warning, gunshots struck the building from the other side of the street and scared him half to death. He jumped up, noticed the truck outside and shouted.

"Hyde! Wake your ass up. Someone is shooting at us!"

More gunshots hit the steps outside. Chunks of concrete bounced off the lobby glass, leaving cracks. Vincent tipped the table over and ducked behind it until the shooting stopped. He heard a sound behind him and turned to see Hyde crawling on the floor and fumbling with his gun.

"Vincent, what's going on?"

"Someone is over on the warehouse shooting at us."

"What's with the truck?"

Vincent stole another look. "I don't know."

"It's blinking."

Vincent rose up a little, still crouching and saw a display on the truck blinking bright red squares.

"What the hell does that mean?"

They watched as the display changed, throwing up a message this time. Scotty, one of the guards from the back rushed into the lobby.

"Is someone shooting?"

Vincent nodded and pointed at the truck. A message started scrolling across the display. The three of them read it. Vincent did so out loud.

"This is a bomb. Get out. You have two minutes."

Hyde said, "Is this for real? Is that a truck bomb?"

The three of them stared at each other and then the truck. The counter kept dropping. Hyde spoke again. "What do we do?"

"Get everyone out the back," Vincent said.

"And stop production?" Hyde said. "Are you serious?"

Vincent bit his lip and nodded. "Yeah, do it."

"Dodger will kill us."

"Pretty sure the guys with the truck bomb who are shooting at us will do that too. Get everyone out the back. If we're wrong, it's just an unscheduled break, if we're right we'll be alive to get bitched at. Go, move now."

He glanced back over his shoulder as they went down the hallway. The time on the side of the truck read 1:29.

—— «‹›» ——

Nathan held up his mobi and spoke to Cole and Richie. "Any movement?"

"They cleared the lobby," Cole said. "There's no one in there."

"Richie?"

"Hold on, something's going on."

Nathan bit his lower lip and waited. They had to be relatively sure everyone was out of the building before proceeding to the next step. Cole said a lot of women worked in the lab and he didn't want to kill any of them. Then Richie spoke over the mobi.

"The back door is open. The guards are coming out and there are a lot of women with them. They're all running across the street."

"Let me know when it looks like everyone is out."

Nathan pulled up the app running the display board on the truck. The timer crossed ten seconds.

"Boss, it looks like everyone is out. The last guy to cross the street had a gun and no one seems to be behind him."

"Where are they?"

"Across the street, heading down the block away from me."

Nathan smiled. "I'm doing it. Richie, come get us."

He moved cautiously around the dumpster and snuck a look up and down the street. Nothing moved. It seemed like the residents of Bad Rock really did avoid the area.

Confident of their solitude, he pulled up another control on his mobi to activate the device in the truck. He tapped the screen and a lightning bolt appeared. The channel to Cole and Richie remained open.

"We're hot. It's going off in ten seconds."

He ducked behind the dumpster again, not bothering to run away. If anything went wrong, being the length of the alley away wouldn't help.

—— ‹‹ ›› ——

Vincent and Hyde ran down the block, waiting for an explosion. "It should have gone off by now," Vincent said. "It's past the deadline."

"What if there's no bomb? What if someone just wanted to get in and steal the product?"

Vincent stopped and turned back to the building. Most of a full shipment sat in the storage rooms, easy pickings now that the place was empty.

"They brought a truck," he said.

"Crap. Get Scotty. We have to go back."

He ran off, breathing hard, wondering how to explain this to Dodger.

— «» —

The device in the back of the truck rotated, sighting in on the apartment building. A stream of invisible particles reached out, locking onto the steel supports of the structure. It snagged a girder, dense and well anchored, that held up the second floor. The charge inside the capacitor reached maximum and a stream of gravitons raced from the Goose in the truck to the building, establishing a powerful attraction. For the briefest of moments the gravitic attraction of the building wildly overcame the gravitic attraction of the planet.

— «» —

Even though he expected it, Nathan jumped in amazement when the truck seemed to leap off the street and throw itself into the lobby of the apartment building. It happened so fast that it took him a moment to process what he'd actually seen. Noise from the devastation rolled over Nathan and he shook his head in amazement. If Captain Archie could see how he'd adapted his orbital cleaning process the mean old bastard just might give him a pat on the back.

A cloud of debris billowed out of the new hole and dust and debris settled on the sidewalk. He couldn't see much inside the building but he could hear plenty. Heavy metallic things dropped loudly, shattering the silence on the street. Cole's voice came over the mobi.

"Nathan, you okay?"

"Yeah, you?"

"Just fine. I don't see anyone moving in there. Are you going to hit it again?"

The truck had done what they wanted but Nathan wanted to be sure Dodger never earned another credit from the lab inside.

"Give me a second."

Nathan checked the controls for the Goose on his mobi. Sensors built into the device showed him the device remained active. However, it was now oriented at a ninety degree angle relative to the ground. The cage protecting it and anchoring it to the truck frame had worked as well as could be expected. Richie deserved a pat on the back for that. Nathan assumed the body of the truck had completely disintegrated. However, the Goose attached to the floor of the cargo area of the truck and through that to the heavy steel frame. All ten meters of that frame plus the anti-gravity drivetrain should still be intact and attached.

He adjusted the orientation and the Goose rotated so that the modulator pointed straight up toward the sky. The generator responded and started the charging process. As soon as the lightning bolt indicator popped up he spoke into the mobi.

"Here comes the second shot."

A terrific blast roared from the building and another cloud of debris exploded from the gaping entry hole. Nathan watched the display on his mobi and saw the Goose rush upwards through the interior of the building. He jumped back as windows blew out on floor after floor, as the remnants of the truck rocketed upward, attracted to trusses on some upper floor. The display snapped off as the Goose died.

"Nathan, we got flames in there."

It took him a moment but then he saw flames licking out of a second floor window accompanied by black smoke. He watched as it quickly spread, engulfing the entire front of the building. Nothing in the truck would cause a fire this intense but containers holding volatile chemicals in the Diamond K lab had probably ruptured. He held the mobi up.

"Cole, meet us around the back. It's time to get out of here."

Chapter 23

Richie stood on the throttle, tearing ass out of Bad Rock as fast as the float car would fly. Nathan put his hand on the kid's shoulder and said, "Slow it down. They're not chasing us."

The young machinist nodded with a wild grin on his face. "Yeah, but they'll be coming, right? That's what you said." The car swerved as Richie corrected their drifting course.

Cole leaned forward from the backseat. "Maybe you should drive. He seems a little rattled."

"He's fine. We've just kept him cooped up in the engines too long."

"That was the damnedest thing I've ever seen," Cole said. "I mean, you said it would work but you couldn't have done a better job with an actual bomb. I wonder why people don't use that more often."

Nathan turned to look at him with a puzzled look on his face. "How many people need to knock down a building?"

"I meant terrorists, you know? Criminals, those sorts of people. Not normal folks like us."

"If you knew how much a Goose costs you wouldn't ask that. Most people don't have access to a trashed faster than light starship, and those that do usually don't have the need to knock down a building."

"You think Dodger's coming for us?"

"Absolutely. Without that lab he's got no way to pull in the tall stacks of credits he's used to. That's going to piss him off. He'll be coming right at us, hard and fast."

"When do we call Bell to make the arrest?" Cole said.

"That's the tricky part," Nathan said. "We have to wait for Dodger to show up at the wreck site and then call Bell. If we call him too early it will look like we're expecting Dodger to come for us and I don't want to get arrested for that stunt with the building. I just need Dodger mad enough to do something stupid."

Cole grunted. "Well, I think we accomplished that."

— «» —

You look like hell, Morris thought as he looked at Dodger. They sat in his office in the rear of Dodge Em's trying to get their last two guys but the boss seemed to have second thoughts.

"We need to leave, boss, if we want to surprise them," Morris said, checking the time on his mobi.

Dodger nodded at him with those pathetic, red watery eyes. "I know, I just want to be sure we're covered here." He sniffled, wiping his nose on the back of his sleeve. "It's me they want, you know. That repo man is pissed about his, his you know."

"His ship."

Dodger pointed at him. "Right, that's it. You'll see. He'll hit us here, just wait."

Morris thought he could cap Dodger right now and no one would lift a finger. It might even be a mercy killing. There seemed to be nothing left of the fearsome thug who held sway over Bad Rock.

"Boss, that's why I'm going out to get them. We'll just hit them and be done with it."

Dodger nodded slowly, seemingly comprehending but acting in slow motion. "Yeah, okay, take the guys, get it done."

Morris's mobi chirped with a call from Vincent at the apartment building. Before answering he pointed at the two extra men they had come to pick up. "Get in the van outside. I'll be right there." He swiped the answer icon and held the mobi up to his ear. "What's up?"

He listened in horror as Vincent laid it down for him, babbling about a truck bomb and how the building had partially collapsed.

Dodger stared at him with new concentration in his eyes. "What's going on?"

Morris held up a finger, turning his head. Dodger jumped out from behind the desk so fast Morris barely had time to take a step back before the boss grabbed the mobi from him.

"I said, what's going on?"

He took a moment to gather his thoughts before answering. "Someone hit the apartment building after we left." He paused, the words hanging in the air between them. "The lab is gone." He pointed at the mobi in Dodger's hand. "Vincent says the whole building is gone."

"No!" Dodger fired the mobi across the room and it hit the far wall, shattering into several pieces. "Who did it?"

Morris shrugged. "Vincent said they used a truck bomb but he didn't see anyone. You know who did it. Who else would it be?"

"I told you!" Dodger said, suddenly animated. He stalked around behind his desk and started pulling drawers open. He rifled through them, dumping the contents on the floor as his hands searched. He smiled when they locked onto something and then he pulled out the biggest damn handgun Morris had ever seen. It was some absurd, chrome plated monstrosity that looked like it could shoot through a bus.

"Easy, Dodger. They're not getting away with anything. Just be careful."

Dodger slammed the gun down on his desk and Morris jumped. "How many guys did you leave over there?"

"Three or four."

"Well that doesn't appear to have been enough."

Morris got worried and his hand started moving behind his back. His fingers brushed the grip of the pistol tucked in his waistband. "This was not my fault. We are on our way to take care of those guys right now. More guys wouldn't have stopped a truck bomb anyway."

"You're on your way out there now?"

"That's right."

He picked up a bag of Diamond K and tipped the whole thing into his mouth. "Maybe you should have gone yesterday. If you had, we'd still be in business."

"It's just a lab, Dodger. We can build a new one."

"All the guys are in the van, ready to go? They're armed?"

Morris nodded and barely saw the chrome beast come up in Dodger's hand. He moved so fast that Morris only had time to take a single step back. The hand cannon pointing at his face didn't shake a bit. He held up his hands. "Hey wait..."

"No room on the crew for screw ups, Morris."

The last thing he saw was a muzzle flash.

— «» —

Richie pulled the float car past Eldridge and Ari's camp and continued on toward the Athena Star before he parked. Nathan got out and whistled the all clear signal. The small door to the cargo bay opened and Duncan poked his head out. "How did it go?" he said.

"Just like we planned," Nathan answered. "The lab is gone."

"The whole damn building is gone," Cole said. "You should have seen it."

"Yeah," Nathan said. "You and Richie did a good job. It worked just like we thought it would."

"Then they'll be coming?"

Nathan nodded. "They sure will. I think we have a little time to get ready, though. How are we looking inside?"

"I think we're as ready as we can be. How much time do you think we have?"

"It will take them a while to get their guys ready and then drive out here. Maybe an hour? Maybe a little more?"

"We've got about two minutes," Cole said.

Nathan turned and saw twin dust trails from a pair of vans. "Damn it. How did they get ready that fast?"

"Doesn't really matter, does it?" Cole said and hefted his rifle. "Let's get everyone inside."

Nathan caught Tricia's eye as he moved into the cargo bay. "I really wish you'd gone up to the ship."

She gave him a smirk and shook her head. "No way would I miss this."

"Where are you going to be?"

She pointed toward one of the rooms with the reactor coolant tanks. "We'll go in there and then up a few decks. Duncan showed Marla a secure compartment."

"Can you get a signal out from up there? We had trouble calling from in here earlier and we need to get the call out to Chief Bell."

She nodded. "Ari rigged up a signal booster."

"Then you should get going and make that call. We've really made these guys angry and it's time to get the law involved. I'm sorry, I thought we'd have more time."

She kissed him for the first time and he forgot about everything. Her lips were soft but firm and she took his breath away. His hands rose up and gripped her taut waist. She responded by leaning into him. Everything else sort of faded away.

Cole grabbed his arm. "Hey, are you ready? They're coming."

Nathan reluctantly let Tricia go and caught his breath. He told her, "Be safe, okay?"

She nodded and gave his hand one last squeeze before running off to Marla.

He watched her go and saw Daryl, tied to the chair in the corner where Fred watched him. "One second. I have to take care of something."

He jogged over to where the thug sat. He pulled out a folding knife and cut the ropes binding Daryl to the chair.

"Look, your boss is on his way out here. I'm cutting you loose, just like I said I would for you giving us that information."

"I remember," Daryl said as he rubbed his wrists.

"So you can either join him or go rob his place. The choice is up to you but I think I'd get the hell out of here. I don't see where you owe him anything and I can't promise he won't find out you told us about the guards and other details at the apartment building."

Daryl nodded in agreement. "Don't worry about me, I'm done with this."

"Then you better haul ass because Dodger is close."

"Absolutely." He stood up, stuck his hand out to Nathan and gave him a quick shake. "Good luck." Then he ran toward the open cargo bay door.

Nathan turned to his people. "Okay, let's do this."

Tricia, Marla, Ari and Fred moved off toward the compartment she had shown him. He stood still until he saw the pressure door close and the wheel spin, locking it. Satisfied he turned back to Cole, Duncan, Richie and Eldridge.

"Okay, they're going to call Bell and get him out here. In the meantime, we have to keep Dodger busy."

"Bell was supposed to be here already." Eldridge said.

Duncan hefted a duffle bag from the deck. "Remember the talk we had earlier about plans not working out sometimes and improvising? This is one of those moments."

"This sucks."

Nathan grimaced. "It usually does but look, you're with me and Cole and we're not going to let anything happen to you." He turned to his engineer. "Duncan and Richie, did you guys have a chance to get plan B in place?

Duncan nodded. "We sure did but that's kind of risky."

Nathan pointed at their pursuers. "Risky for them maybe." He turned back to Eldridge. "You know this wreck like the back of your hand, right?"

"Sure, but..."

Nathan clapped him on the shoulder. "Then we're in good shape. Now, what's the best way to get where we want to go?"

Eldridge pointed down a wide corridor. "That way. It leads up into the passenger areas. They're all dark and a mess. They'll have a hard time finding us."

"Then let's go. You lead the way. Cole, take up the rear and make sure Dodger and his men know which way we went."

Eldridge's head snapped around. "But why...?"

"We want them on us, not Ari and the others. These guys are killers. Come on."

They moved down the corridor away from the work lights and darkness closed in. The wide corridor allowed forklifts to pass, but Nathan still managed to trip over something and went down on one knee. "Damn it, do we have a light?"

Duncan turned one on and handed it to him. "You should get the eye upgrades like I did."

"Thanks," Nathan said, reminding himself that Duncan had implants that let him see in the dark. They came in handy working on engines in tight compartments.

"Eldridge, can you see in the dark? You're getting around pretty well."

"No, but I've been up and down this way searching for salvage."

They moved on again and came to a flight of stairs leading away from the corridor. "Are we going up?"

Eldridge pointed down into the darkness. "Yeah, this is a service deck for laundry and food service. If we go straight we'll come to a kitchen and believe me, you don't want to go there. The power has been off for months so everything has spoiled and it stinks so bad it's hard to breathe. There's a casino at the top of the stairs."

"Well, I'd say we're gambling today. Up it is."

Duncan reached into his bag and took out a chemical light stick. He snapped it, shook it and threw it up the stairs. It bathed the area in a greenish-yellow glow.

"This will let Cole know which way we went."

"Good thinking. Let's go."

They mounted the stairs to go up when an explosion of gunfire startled them.

— «» —

"There's no one in the main camp," Jonesy said. With Morris gone Dodger needed a new second in command and the hacker got a promotion. "No 'bots, no one at the piles and no one in the tents. We can't even find Daryl."

Dodger pointed at the *Athena Star.* "They're playing small games, that's all. They're in the wreck, thinking they're safe. Well, they're not. Get everyone together and let's get down there."

They mounted up in the two vans and drove toward the wreck. Dodger drove the van holding the guys from the apartment building. Cheech lay dead in a dumpster back at Dodge Em's. Morris's nephew would have been a pain about his uncle getting killed so Dodger had walked out into the parking lot and shot him while he stood next to the van. A bloodstain in the shape of a smashed cherry pie stained the van behind the driver's side door. That left him eighteen guys to take care of business.

Losing the lab was a real problem. The Syndicate would hold him responsible so he had to have someone to offer up in his place. Morris had been correct about one thing; the lab could be rebuilt, just not here in Bad Rock. By now Chief Bell and his deputies were probably climbing all over the building and they would find evidence of Diamond K production. Once that happened, they could forget about producing it here ever again. Protective Service agents from Earth might even get involved.

The vans pulled up short of the cargo bay and they quickly emptied out. Dodger watched as they milled around but he noticed none of them actually stepped up to enter the wreck. He grabbed the door and pulled it open.

"You," he said, pointing at Gary, one of his men from the club. "Get inside there and see what's going on."

A stunned expression crossed his face but executing two people this morning had the effect of stopping stupid questions. Gary gritted his teeth and stepped to the door. Dodger gave him a shove and he fell through. When nothing happened, Dodger followed him.

The cargo bay appeared empty. A pair of work lights illuminated the space and Dodger could see where they had collected the reactor coolant. He waved his hands in each direction to his men.

"Fan out and search the area. They're around here somewhere. Don't bunch up. It makes you a big target."

They walked around, checking behind equipment. Jonesy stopped at a hatch. "This one is locked, boss."

Dodger said, "The coolant tanks are in there. Break it open."

— «» —

Cole watched from the mouth of the darkened corridor as Dodger and his men entered the cargo bay. Nathan and the others had gone ahead but he had the task of drawing Dodger and his boys away from Marla and the others. They had numbers but as he watched them he realized they didn't seem to be much more than the run of the mill thugs they seemed to run into everywhere. They clumped together, didn't check the shadows or corners and seemed mostly concerned with making sure no one got the drop on them.

He adjusted his stance and crouched down further. One of Dodger's mooks swung by and glanced into the darkness but he stopped walking where the work light ended. Cole remained hidden in the shadow. The guy walked away.

From this vantage point he could see most of the bay. Dodger walked right through the center of the space and then disappeared from view before Cole could react. He heard the moron giving orders like some platoon sergeant in an action holovid. Then he saw one of them checking the hatch Marla and the others had gone through.

He heard Dodger tell the guy to get the hatch open. That absolutely couldn't be allowed to happen. He raised the rifle and sighted in on the nearest of the two work lights. A quick burst annihilated the light and darkened a large section of the cargo bay.

Dodger's men panicked. Cole hit the deck as bullets flew in every direction. No one had seen where his shots had come from, so he inched forward to the corner where the cargo bay met the corridor. Dodger shouted for everyone to stop and stepped out from behind one of his men. Cole aimed at him for a second but remembered that Nathan wanted as little bloodshed as possible. He changed his target to the second work light and squeezed his trigger again. It exploded and flew through the air, plunging the cargo bay into darkness.

This time they definitely saw where the shots came from. Rounds zipped all around him, ricocheting off the walls of the corridor. He laid flat on the deck with his rifle in front of him until they stopped. Dodger yelled again, trying to get everyone under control. They finally calmed down and the air grew silent.

"Keep your heads, damn it!" He heard Dodger yell. "Does anyone have a light?"

Cole slowly rose, careful not to make any noise. He smiled and pulled a ball-shaped object from his jacket pocket. He twisted the dial on top of it and thumbed the plunger before throwing it. A bright light exploded from the device when it landed. Dodger's men cried in pain from the intense flash. Then the secondary function kicked in. A high-pitched wail in the 115 decibel range issued from the device and deafened everyone in the bay. Cole covered his ears with his hands but he could still hear the device as it rolled around the area. The Rolling Betty would keep moving, screaming and flashing until someone found it and deactivated it or until it ran out of power.

Cole turned and hurried up the corridor to meet with Nathan.

— «» —

"What was that?" Eldridge said as the sound of the short battle carried up the stairs to them.

"Hopefully it's Cole keeping Dodger and his morons busy," Nathan said. They had moved up the stairs and stood in one of the *Athena Star's* casinos. The light from the glow stick carried almost the length of the room. It reflected off the tacky chrome and mirrors that littered the walls and floors. The gaming tables remained bolted to the deck but chips, chairs and drink tumblers littered the carpeted floor.

He walked over to a blackjack table and stepped behind it. "Let's wait for Cole here. It's a good vantage point for the stairs."

They all moved behind the table and he sighted in on the top of the stairs. He picked up some of the chips laying on the floor and thought about his money problems. "What about all the chips? Can you cash them in?"

Eldridge laughed. "I wish. They're all marked with the ship's insignia and have been retired by the cruise line. Ari and I joked that we'd be millionaires with a vacuum cleaner if we just swept up in here."

They heard someone on the stairs and Cole called out before he got to the top. "Don't shoot, it's me."

He came around the corner breathing hard and watching over his shoulder. Nathan waved him over and he leaned against the table.

"How did it go?"

"Dodger brought a ton of guys with him. I'd estimate more than a dozen."

"We heard shooting. You okay?"

Cole nodded and kept an eye on the stairway. "Yeah, they started messing with the door Marla and the others went through so I distracted them with my last Rolling Betty. I can't hear too well right now, between that thing and the gunshots."

"A dozen guys is a lot. If Marla and the others manage to get ahold of Bell and he comes out here he may not be able to handle them."

Cole edged closer to the top of the stairway, and peeked down it. "Nathan, I know you don't want anyone shot or harmed but if these guys catch up to us, we won't have a choice. You know that, right?"

He nodded. "I do but when this is all over I don't want to have to explain a bunch of dead bodies."

"We didn't have to explain the ones in Port Haven," Cole said.

Nathan recalled the two Syndicate hitmen who had snuck up on them while they escaped from the compound of the Children of the Apocalyptic Rainbow. One of them had managed to shoot Cole, and he had only survived because of an armored vest.

"I get what you're saying," he said. "We'll do what we have to. I'm certainly not asking anyone to get shot. Let's just stay ahead of them and let the plan work."

"Plan B kind of sucks."

"Well, it's the only one we have right now. Let's move a little further down the line."

— «» —

Marla saw Ari obsessively watching the door to the compartment where they hid. She took her hand.

"It's going to be okay," she said. "The guys will take care of Dodger. We have to make the call to Chief Bell."

Ari's eyes were wide. "Those were gunshots."

Marla stroked her arm. "I know, but Duncan and the others will take care of it. We planned for this, remember?"

Tricia came over and motioned her aside. "Nathan said things usually don't get this crazy."

Marla shrugged her shoulders. "This one has been off the charts, I'll admit." She put her ear to the door. "I don't hear anyone coming up. Maybe they lured them away. Now, how do we get to the signal booster?"

Ari pointed up. "Two more decks up but if we go out in the corridor and they manage to get into the coolant storage room, they'll hear us."

Fred stepped to the door and cracked it open, peering into the dark corridor. The coolant tank stretched up through several decks and the catwalk they climbed allowed access to them. He shined a light and shook his head. "I don't see anything, but I hear something. What is that?"

Marla smiled and pulled the door open the rest of the way. "That's one of Cole's toys. It should keep Dodger and his boys distracted and they won't hear a thing until they manage to shut it off. Let's get moving."

They filed out, Marla leading the way with Ari directing them, followed by Tricia with Fred bringing up the rear.

— ⟨⟩ —

Dodger lay stunned on the deck of the cargo bay. The light flashes blinded him and now the damn noise made him deaf. He closed his eyes and backed up instinctively. The cargo bay lay shrouded in darkness without the work lights that had been on when they entered. He stood up and felt around in the darkness.

He bumped into something behind him. His hands found a latch and he realized he had found the hatch they had entered through. He worked it, finally getting it open and letting faint moonlight in. He stumbled outside and fell to his knees as he tripped over the uneven edge of the hatch.

More men followed him, attracted by the pale glow visible in the hatchway. Eventually, all of them saw the opening and made their way out.

"What the hell was that?" Jonesy said after they got the hatch closed.

"Some kind of flash bang grenade," Dodger said. "I had a chance to buy some once. It's going to keep going off until someone kills it."

"We need some lights, too. Going in there without being able to see is suicide."

"Have a couple guys scrounge the camp. They've got to have lights around here somewhere."

Jonesy pointed toward Eldridge's maintenance rig parked near their vans. "I saw that when we pulled up. I'll bet it has what we need."

He walked over to it and pulled open the equipment lockers mounted on the bed. Sure enough, lights hung on hooks and he handed them to a couple guys. Then Dodger saw him smile.

"What is it?"

He held up a couple sets of hearing protectors. "These should work for whatever is rolling around in there."

He tossed a pair to Dodger and put a set on. They slipped back into the cargo bay with a couple other guys. Sure enough, the hearing protectors made the sound more bearable. Dodger tapped one of the guys and had him shine a light around. Something rolled into view and he raised his gun, taking a shot at it. Everyone joined him and a hail of bullets rained down on the device. It shattered into small pieces and the noise stopped.

Dodger pushed the protectors down so they hung around his neck. He slapped Jonesy on the back. "Good going. Now, which way do you think they went?"

"The guy shooting at us hid over there," he said, pointing to the darkened corridor.

"Okay, let's go that way." He stopped and nodded toward the coolant storage compartments. "One of the guys said those doors were locked right before the shooting started. Send a couple guys that way and have them checked out."

"You got it."

Chapter 24

Marla stopped on the metal stairs and listened. Something below them banged and the noise reverberated up the stairway. She turned and saw Tricia staring at her. They had all heard it.

In front of her, Ari leaned over the rail to catch a better look. As the beam from her light stretched down into the compartment holding the coolant tanks, someone shouted.

Tricia grabbed Marla. "We have to move. Someone is coming after us."

"I know." She turned to Ari on the stair above her. "How much farther?"

She pointed up the stairs. "One more flight and then it's the room at the end of the corridor. It will only take a minute."

"Then let's go."

They moved fast, with Fred bringing up the rear. The older man breathed heavily by the time they got to the compartment. Ari held the door open and waved at them.

They tumbled in and she closed the door, spinning the locking mechanism. "Okay, they aren't getting through that unless they have explosives."

Tricia took up a position beside the door and pulled out the gun Nathan and Cole had given her.

The running made Marla sweat and she pulled her dark hair into a pony tail with an elastic tie. She pulled out her mobi and the screen lit up. "How do I make the call?"

Ari breathed hard but pointed to a panel. "There's a cable in there connected to the signal booster. Just plug in and you'll get a signal."

Marla pulled open the panel. She saw a mass of tangled wires but nothing that would plug into her mobi. "I don't see it."

Ari gave her an annoyed look and shined her light into the panel. "It's right there..." She paused and put the light on the door. The markings read '5D'. "Oh damn it."

"What is it?" Marla said.

"We're in the wrong compartment. I lead us up one deck too many."

They all fell silent and looked at Marla.

"Well, crap."

—— «◊» ——

"Which way?" Nathan asked Eldridge. The young man pointed to the left.

"That way."

Duncan reached into his bag and brought out another glow stick. He cracked it, shook it and dropped it on the floor. "Do you really think Dodger will follow us?"

The engineer was sweaty and seemed anxious. "You worried about Marla?"

"You know I am."

"I think they'll be okay. We're leaving them a trail a blind man could follow and Cole got them good and angry at us. Besides this place is a maze. How would they even know where else to look?"

"I guess. I just want to get this over with."

"It won't be too much longer."

Eldridge led them down a corridor and Nathan had to keep a hand on the decorated walls to stay steady. The pitch of the ship threw off his equilibrium. He had to keep adjusting his footing so he didn't fall.

The corridor dumped them out into a lounge area. Large windows that could be used for sightseeing ran from the floor to the ceiling but corrugated shutters covered them. They had probably dropped into place during the re-entry to protect the passenger compartments. Upended couches and tables littered the area. It would have been a nice way to spend time on the cruise, watching the stars outside as the big starliner made its way through the darkness. The *Athena*

Star would never fly again, though, and maybe, neither would his beloved *Bandit*. He shook off the morose thought and got his head back in the game.

He let Duncan and Richie go past him and waited for Cole. It took a moment but eventually he rounded the corner into the lounge. "Are they coming?"

Cole stopped for a moment and pulled a water bottle from his belt. "They're back there for sure and coming fast. I can hear them so I'd say they're not much more than a couple minutes behind us. Can we move a little faster?"

"I don't know. The air in here is pretty stale and it's getting colder as we go deeper. Duncan is already tired."

"Duncan needs to lose a few pounds."

"Yeah, well, you tell him that." Nathan jerked a thumb back up the corridor leading into the lounge area. "Were you able to do anything to slow them down?"

Cole grinned. "I left them a present about halfway down the corridor, just to keep them interested in us. I didn't want it to seem too easy. We should get moving though, to keep ahead of them. Aren't we almost there?"

Nathan strained and found he could hear voices. Dodger and his goons weren't big on stealth. "I think so. Come on, let's catch up to the others. Stay close, okay?"

Cole nodded and they hurried out of the lounge.

— ❰❱ —

"There's light up ahead," Dodger said to Jonesy, pointing at the exit to the casino. "Do you think they went that way or are they trying to throw us off the trail?"

Jonesy shined his light around the casino, examining the layout. He saw four other ways in or out. "It's hard to tell. They could have chucked a glow stick that way and went another. How would we know?"

Dodger shrugged. "Damn it, this place is like a maze. Let's go this way and see if we catch any sign of them. Leave a couple guys here to make sure they don't double back on us."

Jonesy pointed to a couple guys and they leaned back against blackjack tables. He followed Dodger toward the exit with the light shining up ahead. It ended in a 'T' and so they looked left and right. Another light glowed further down to the left. A sign mounted on the wall had an arrow pointing to something called the Starlight Lounge in that direction.

"There better be one hell of a piece of cheese at the end of this," Dodger said. He led them toward the lounge. Halfway down the short hallway he heard something click and didn't even have enough time to shout a warning as something bounced up into the air, crossing the beam from his light. He managed to get an arm up to protect himself. The object exploded at shoulder height, covering him in a sticky mess. Stunned for a moment, he realized he had dropped his light. He wiped the mess away from his face.

The men around him shouted angrily and he bent for his light, glad that the device hadn't killed him. He shined his light on the men behind him and saw them coated with a thick brown gel that resembled syrup. He felt his skin tightening as it dried and tried to peel it off only to find he couldn't.

"What the hell is this stuff?" He shined a light on Jonesy, who worked his jaw open and closed, trying to loosen it.

"I think it's an entanglement grenade. I've only seen Protective Services use them. It's a non-lethal deterrent. I think it's safe to say they came this way."

"How do you get it off?"

"I don't know," Jonesy said, sounding exhausted. "I've got some on my hand and my fingers are stuck together. This stuff's like concrete when it gets hard."

Dodger picked at the sticky brown material covering his left arm. It dried quickly and when he pulled on it the skin below felt like it would tear.

"Let's get moving. These bastards are dead when I find them."

— «» —

Marla and Tricia took the lead as the group hurried out of the compartment toward the stairs. She was sure Duncan or Cole would have had a clever plan but all she could think to do was race like hell for the proper compartment on the lower deck. Ari and Fred followed them.

They reached the stairs and Marla dropped down them two at a time, careful not to fall but unwilling to go any slower than they had to. Tricia moved right behind her, gun drawn, medical pack swinging from one hip. After Ari discovered their mistake, Marla had been too busy cussing under her breath to react right away, but Tricia immediately picked up her weapon and peeked to check if their route was clear. She seemed to understand there was a time for action and complaining could always wait until later.

Marla glanced back at Ari in the dark. She definitely got the impression that Ari was in over her head but still managing to keep her focus. Marla could forgive her for getting the deck wrong. The *Athena Star* was like a dark, oppressive cave with the power off.

They reached the bottom of the stairs and swung back toward the compartment they needed. She shined her light in that direction and saw a large '4d' painted on the pressure door.

"Someone's up there!" She heard someone shout from below. "I see a light. They're right above us, come on."

Tricia grabbed Marla. "Go, I'll make sure the others make it."

Marla nodded and charged ahead. She got to the door and swung it wide. She shined her light around and the panel Ari had described stood open. Ari and Fred ran down the catwalk toward her.

Lights played off the walls as Dodger's men came up the metal stairs, making as much noise as a herd of cattle. Ari and Fred ran past her into the compartment and she shined her light back at Tricia.

"Come on, everyone is in!"

Tricia started moving backward toward her on the catwalk. Then the lights from below shined brighter on the walls. Dodger's boys closed in on them from the stairs, getting closer to their deck. Marla watched as the nurse brought her pistol up and let loose a volley of shots.

Sparks leapt from the walls where rounds impacted and the lights stopped moving. The sound from the gunshots echoed in the large metal compartment. Marla shook her head and Tricia almost ran her over. Once inside they slammed the door and spun the wheel.

"Did you hit anyone?"

Tricia gulped air and sat down against the door, shaking her head. "No, I don't think so. I just fired over their heads to slow them down." She held up the gun, dropped the spent magazine and pushed another home. "But if anyone comes through that door they're getting shot."

Marla nodded in agreement. "Okay. I've got a call to make."

—— «» ——

Nathan could hear Dodger and his men now without straining. They sounded angry. Eldridge had them in a service stairwell used for maintenance. He wanted to stop because they were getting tired from the long night of activity. Duncan gulped air through his mouth from all the running and giving him a break would have been a kindness but they'd left the access hatch open to lure Dodger in. He wondered how much farther they had to go. "Are we almost there, Eldridge?"

"This way," Eldridge said and swung open an access hatch on a landing. They piled through and found themselves in a tight maintenance corridor where two men standing side-by-side would be shoulder-to-shoulder. Everyone picked a spot and leaned against the walls.

"The compartment you want is just up ahead, on the left," Eldridge said. "Do we have enough time to get everything set up?"

"We will if we get moving," Nathan said. "Let's hustle."

They moved down the corridor and into the compartment Eldridge had pointed out. Nathan put a hand on the shoulders of Duncan and Richie. "It's on you guys, now. Can you get it done?"

The big man coughed up some phlegm and spit it into the back corner of the room. "No problem."

Nathan slapped them both on the shoulder, his rifle slung across his back. "Cole and I will make sure you get time." He turned to Eldridge. "When they're done, you call out and move them to safety, okay? Do it just like we talked about."

"What about you?"

"Oh, we'll be right behind you, don't worry. I've got no intention of being caught. Go get it done."

—— «» ——

Dodger put a hand up and stopped everyone at the top of the stairs just inside the hatchway. "Hold up, I think they're down there."

Jonesy and a couple others leaned over the railing. "I see lights, boss. Moving lights."

Dodger got a maniacal look on his face and dug out a plastic envelope from the front pocket of his jeans. He opened it and dumped a few crystals into his mouth. Jonesy's eyebrows arched up and Dodger clapped him on the shoulder.

"Don't worry about it; I just needed a little bump." He turned to the men behind him. "Okay, they're right down there. Let's get them."

They ran down the stairs, screaming and yelling, trying to frighten their prey.

Dodger entered the corridor first and he saw a hatch to a compartment farther down the corridor swing open. Teller stood there, rifle in hand and pointing right at them. He stopped, putting a hand up in the dim light for his men to stop advancing.

The Diamond K was hitting his blood now, giving him everything he needed to get the bastards who blew up his building. They would answer for it, right now.

Seeing Teller not five meters away, he grinned and said, "We've got you now. You're mine."

—— «» ——

"You think so?" Nathan said, standing in the shadows. "Look where you are. A corridor this tight? Numbers kind of work against you. Guess you never heard of King Leonidas and the Spartans, huh?"

Dodger shook his head. "Not really." He waved his arms around. "If you think the walls being tight is going to stop us from grabbing you and kicking your ass, you're mistaken. Jonesy," he said, "get them."

Jonesy hesitated a moment, unsure of what to do. "Boss, are you sure?"

"Now, Jonesy."

He moved forward this time with a couple men behind him. Nathan stepped back inside the compartment and Cole rolled out from the opposite side, looming over Jonesy with his rifle raised high. The slanted deck gave him a height advantage and he brought the butt of the gun down hard, square in his face. The thug dropped and rolled into the men behind him.

Nathan moved quickly, grabbing the man who managed to remain standing behind Jonesy. He pulled him into the darkness of the compartment and shoved him against the wall, repeatedly banging his head off the metal side until he cried out in pain. Then he hauled him back to the hatch and threw him toward Dodger, giving him a kick in the butt as he stumbled over Jonesy and the others.

"It's over Dodger. Just stop before someone really gets hurt."

"Don't you get it, Teller? That lab was worth millions and you burned it down." Dodger blinked rapidly in the dimness and Nathan thought he saw tears. "I had one job. All I had to do was protect it and you burned it down! I'm not going to answer for that unless I'm holding your head in my hand."

Dodger's arm rose up with a ridiculous, shiny chrome gun in his hand. He ducked back through the hatch and a deafening shot went wild. He felt the air move past as the round traveled down the darkened corridor.

"Shut the damn hatch," he yelled to Cole. "We need some cover."

Cole grabbed the door and pushed it shut. More gunshots came from Dodger, slamming into the door as it closed. Nathan felt something kick him hard and he fell back against the wall.

"We're good!" Duncan yelled from the compartment where he, Richie and Eldridge prepared their surprise. "Come on guys, let's go."

Nathan tried to raise his gun up in case Dodger and his men breached the hatch but he couldn't. His arm was numb from the shoulder down. He reached across his chest with his other hand and pain erupted from the effort. His shoulder and arm were wet so he pressed down hard to put pressure on the wound. Gritting his teeth he said, "Come on, let's go."

They hustled toward the door Duncan held open and stumbled through it. The wheel on the pressure door spun. Cole didn't have enough time to lock it.

"Are we ready?" Nathan said.

Duncan nodded and then saw his bleeding arm. "Oh my God! You're hit?"

Nathan nodded and saw blood seeping out from between his fingers. "Yeah, I don't think it's that bad but we'll have to deal with it later. Where's Eldridge?"

"He and Richie are down the hatch already. You're next."

"No, you."

Duncan grabbed him and pulled him to the open hatch in the floor. "I'm not arguing with you. Go and we'll be right behind you."

Nathan grimaced and dropped down through the hatch, just as he had a few days ago when they had used this same hatch to escape Dodger. The symmetry made him smile.

With his wounded arm he barely caught himself on the ladder that led to the ground outside. He hit the dirt and rolled out of the way. Duncan came next, sliding down the sides of the ladder with his boots and hands on the rails.

Cole stepped onto the ladder last and stopped to pull the hatch closed. Halfway down, he jumped off the ladder and landed on the hard-packed dirt under the hatch. He joined the group as they hustled away from the ship and out under the stars. "They'll be in that compartment any minute. We're out of time."

Nathan nodded and turned to Duncan. "Do it."

"Are you sure?" Duncan said. "This could still kill them. The overpressure alone will blow that door off its hinges."

"If they get any farther I'm sure they'll kill us."

Cole put a hand on Duncan's shoulder. "If you want, I'll do it, big guy."

Duncan shook his head in the glare of a flashlight. "No, they tried to kill my wife. I've got this." He took out his mobi, opened an app and with one last look of assurance from Nathan, he tapped the screen.

— «» —

Dodger watched as Jonesy and another man wrestled with the wheel on the pressure door. Teller and his people had escaped behind this stupid hatch and all they had to do was open it.

"What's taking so long?"

Jonesy leaned on a length of pipe trying to get the hatch open. Blood ran down onto his face from the gash Cole had given him across his forehead. "I don't know. I can barely see and my head feels like it's ready to fall off," he said, breathing heavily. "Maybe we can go around?"

Dodger threw his hands up, casting wild shadows on the walls across from the trouble lights. "And where would we go? This ship is enormous. They could be anywhere. Do you even know how to get out of here?"

Jonesy threw up his hands. "I think we doubled back toward the cargo bay but I'm not sure."

"That's just great. We're lost and you can't get this damn door open." Dodger stepped forward suddenly, getting right in Jonesy's face. "What good are you to me if all you can do is get us lost?"

"I didn't... are you serious? I never claimed to know my way around in here. You followed them in." He threw down the length of pipe he had been using for leverage on the wheel and it banged heavily against the crooked metal deck. "The air in here is awful, it's dark and no, I don't know where we are. We were just dumb enough to follow you."

Dodger grabbed him and Jonesy pushed back. The confined space of the maintenance tunnel didn't give them much room but the two men grappled with one another, each shoving the other against the tight walls. The Diamond K Dodger chewed along with the beating Jonesy had received from Cole took their toll. Dodger managed to get him down on the deck as his men scattered as best they could to give them room. He straddled Jonesy and pinned his shoulders.

"This is not my fault," Dodger screamed. "You told me you could control the 'bots and you let them get away when we had them. Now you've got us lost in this maze! I'm going to kill you."

"Get off me you maniac! I'm not going to make it easy." Jonesy got an arm free and grabbed his boss by the throat.

Dodger switched his grip from Jonesy's shoulders to his throat. He squeezed hard, determined to choke the life out of him. Then an explosion went off behind him, blowing the pressure door out of its frame. The corridor lit up with a bright yellow flash from the compartment they had been trying to get into. Pressurized air slammed into him and he was thrown into his men where they tumbled to the sloping deck. Then a wave of filth engulfed them, spilling into the corridor with such volume and force it pushed them up the slanted deck toward the aft cargo bay they had entered through.

Tumbling up the corridor, he banged into the walls and floor as waves of vile liquid rolled over him. He moved quickly, the pressure of the air and slime shoving him along in the darkness. Men collided with him, arms and legs flailing as they tried to grab something to stop their motion.

Then it ended and he lay on the deck. He tried to take a breath, to get his bearings in the darkness and a wave of God-awful tasting foulness flooded his mouth and nose. He rolled over onto his knees and grabbed the railing, spitting as he did so.

He pulled himself up, leaning against the wall for support but the corridor filled rapidly with a smelly, slippery mud-like substance that made the deck and walls slick. The already stale air became inundated with a stench so powerful he could barely breathe. His eyes stung.

Grabbing hold of the nearest man to him, he boosted himself again, determined to follow the angled deck to higher ground. The sludge rose waist high now but he could feel the deck beneath his feet. He moved slowly, crawling and stumbling over his men. His hands gripped the rail, holding on tight as waves of unimaginable nastiness passed by him, first from the rear and then from the front as it receded.

He realized he had been holding his breath and he finally let it out, involuntarily sucking in a deep lungful of the worst smelling air he had ever encountered. His stomach contracted and he vomited without being able to hold it back. He pulled himself forward, up the corridor toward higher ground against the pitch of the ship one step at a time, trying to escape. He stole a look behind him and caught glimpses of his men climbing over each other in the foulness, eager to find a way out. Lights flashed and waved around madly as they followed him, all of them desperate to escape.

— «» —

Nathan felt the starliner and the ground shake with the explosion as they ran away. The hatch they had escaped through made an ominous popping noise but when Nathan stole a look he couldn't see anything in the darkness. Then the smell hit.

"Oh, that's bad," Cole said.

Nathan smiled. "Well, thousands of liters of unprocessed waste is never going to smell good." He looked at Eldridge. "What do you think?"

The young man breathed hard from the excitement and the stress of running for their lives.

"I think it worked. We put the shaped charges right on the seam of the waste tank. Dodger and his boys ought to be swimming in sewage right now."

"Good. Let's get out of here."

They ran, eager to put distance between themselves and the mess engulfing Dodger's party. Nathan noticed the small, orange sun rising in the distance. After a few minutes, they came to the cargo bay. They stood there, exhausted and catching their breath in deep gulps. Even Cole showed signs of being winded.

He heard a cry from across the bay and saw Tricia, Marla and the others running toward them.

"Are you all right?" He said. "We tried to lead them away."

Tricia hugged him and he winced. "We're okay. A couple of them gave us a hard time and we had to fire at them. They took off running after that." Then she stepped away from him and saw the look of pain on his face and the blood on his hand. "You're shot? They shot you?"

"I think so. Good thing I brought a nurse, huh?"

"Let me have a look at that," she ordered, steering him out of the cargo bay.

A few meters away, Marla kissed Duncan, the couple standing in the weak light of morning sunlight shining through the door. Nathan smiled as he and Tricia walked past them.

They hurried outside, and Nathan couldn't remember the last time he had been so happy to see sunlight. He saw vehicles approaching from the access road. He turned back to Marla.

"Did you manage to get through to Chief Bell?"

"We did." She paused for a breath. "He's pretty upset. I think he's going to have some choice words for you."

"That's okay. We gave him a huge gift today."

Chapter 25

Nathan stood his ground against the onslaught of accusations and anger from Chief Don Bell while they stood outside the cargo bay of the *Athena Star*. Eldridge had the main doors open and Bell's voice echoed around the large area.

"…and another thing, some sonuvabitch threw a truck through a building over on the Southside and damn near burned it down. Do you know anything about that?"

"Um… no, not really," Nathan said, biting the inside of his cheek to keep from smiling. Tricia had his arm in a sling and it hurt whenever he moved it.

Bell paced around and his long black coat trailed him. "There was a lab in that building producing Diamond K. A lab we've been working very hard to find and then it gets served up to us by someone with the wherewithal to toss a truck from the street into a building. I can't think of a whole lot of people who could do that. How about you?"

Nathan shook his head. "I wouldn't even know how to begin doing something like that, Chief. It sounds damn complicated and we don't even have a truck."

The cop raised a finger and stuck it in his face. "If I find out you had anything to do with this, you could be facing a lot of jail time."

"I don't think you'll have to worry about that. We were out here minding our own business when Dodger and a couple truckloads of his guys showed up to threaten us. Speaking of whom, we should probably let them out. I don't think there's a lot of air in that maintenance tunnel."

The finger wagged at him again. "You better just watch your step, Teller. The last thing I need out here is a gang war over drugs."

"Absolutely."

They walked inside the cargo bay where a couple deputies stood by the hatch leading to the maintenance tunnel where they had left Dodger and his men. Eldridge had his hands on the wheel to open the hatch.

"What are you waiting for?" Chief Bell barked. "Get that thing open before I have to write reports describing how these chuckleheads drowned in a wave of crap."

Eldridge spun the wheel and pulled the door open. A wave of stink so deep and foul rolled out of the tunnel that everyone took a step back, except for Chief Bell. He strode up to the hatch and stood off to one side.

"This is Chief Don Bell of the Bad Rock police. You all come out of there without your guns. If I see a gun I'm shooting the man carrying it. You understand?" He waved a hand in the air. "My God, that's nasty. It smells just like the time the sewage plant had a pump fail during a rainstorm. The whole town smelled like this for a week."

"I'll see if I can get you a mask," Eldridge said and moved toward the cargo bay door.

Dodger stumbled into the light first. Nathan took a step back when he got a good look at the crime boss covered head to toe in grime and filth. "Teller! You did this! I'm going to kill you!"

Chief Bell nodded at the deputy he had stationed on the other side of the door. Just as Dodger took a step toward Nathan the officer stepped forward with a stun wand and shocked him. His body stiffened and he collapsed, screaming and twitching in a puddle of waste. Bell leaned toward the hatch.

"Anyone else want to give me a problem? If you do, I'll just lock up this hatch until you change your minds."

A chorus of voices begged him not to and the men came out one at a time. Another deputy directed them to an area of the cargo bay cordoned off with plastic sheeting. Nathan saw 'bots using hoses to rinse the men off before being offered jail uniforms.

He walked out into the sunlight and dropped down onto a dark green plastic shipping container. Tricia came over and sat beside him. He smiled at her. "How are you doing?"

She smiled back. "Pretty good, all things considered. This was a hell of a day."

"Yeah. Can I tell you something crazy?"

She nodded.

"Despite everything we've been through, I'm glad you came."

She squinted at him. "Yeah?"

"Yeah." He took her in. She looked lovely with the morning sun in her green eyes. "I know, this isn't what you signed on for and believe me, all of our jobs don't go like this. Every once in a while, though, they go sideways. Having people around who can keep their head is a good thing."

"Thank you."

"It also doesn't hurt that you can put us back together if we get hurt."

"Sure."

"And you're ridiculously easy on the eyes."

She blushed and shook her head. "You were doing really well right up to there, you know that?"

He shrugged. "I told you I'm terrible at talking to women."

She laughed and slipped her hand in his. "I don't really have anything else going on at the moment. Are you offering me a job?"

He shook his head and squeezed her hand. "Nope."

Tricia let go of his hand, her eyes serious.

"I heard you have a rule against dating your boss," said Nathan.

She turned back at him with a small smile. "I did say that."

"I mean, you can have a permanent job here, if that's what you want..."

"But?"

"But I was hoping you'd want something else instead."

She raised her eyebrows. "Oh? And what's that?"

He felt the heat in his cheeks rise. "You need me to say it?"

Tricia nodded, her smile widening.

"Well, *me*," Nathan said. "I was hoping that we..."

She laughed and pulled him into a tight hug. "Hey, wait a minute. Do you even have a ship?"

"Oh, yeah. Well I have insurance and Duncan. That guy can fix anything. The *Bandit* will fly again."

— «» —

The next morning, Nathan and his crew collected what little gear they had in Bad Rock and loaded it into Truck 12. He turned around and saw Cole grimacing at the shuttle. "I know you're not crazy about flying in one of these things but it's the only way up to the *Corkscrew*. Can you handle it?"

Cole sighed and held up his hands. "What else can I do? I want to go home and this is the way. Can we make the ride a little smoother?"

"Probably not," he said and walked out of the truck, back toward the encampment.

Eldridge and Ari stood under the canopy holding hands. He wandered in and nodded to them. "Are we ready to go?"

"I think so," Eldridge said. He turned back to Ari. "I still feel bad about leaving you here."

She shrugged and nodded toward the wreck. "It's all right. By the time you get back we'll have tons of salvage ready to truck up. Without Turtle and Daryl slowing us down, we'll get back on track."

"That's true but the mess from the waste tank is all over the inside of that thing."

"Well, that's for the 'bots to worry about," she said, wrinkling her nose. "It's not like I'm heading in with a mop. They'll decontaminate those sections. Just go back with Nathan and get this whole thing straightened out. We can still do this and get paid."

"I'm worried about leaving you alone."

"No need to worry. Fred is still here and you're leaving me Scooter, right? Besides, Chief Bell said he's going to have deputies stopping by. Dodger and his crew are all locked up and won't be getting out anytime soon."

"I guess."

"I don't mean to interrupt," Nathan said, "but I'd like to be in the air in five."

Eldridge gave him the stink eye. "Do you mind if we say goodbye?"

"I'll leave you to it," he said, smiling. "Wheels up in five, though, with or without you."

"It's my ship. I say when we leave."

Nathan responded over his shoulder as he walked away. "It's my ship now, at least until we get back to Earth. See you later, Ari."

The *Corkscrew* broke orbit an hour later carrying Nathan, his crew, his ship and Eldridge. Marla stayed on the command deck with Bobby, one of Eldridge's crew. Everyone else sat in the common room enjoying a rest.

"So what's the plan when we get back home?" Cole said. He sat at the end of the large table.

Duncan held a hand up so Nathan wouldn't answer and gestured to Eldridge. "This is your mess, kid. How are you going to fix it?"

Put on the spot, Eldridge leaned forward, putting his hands on the table. "The first thing I'm going to do is meet with Lewis and Molly and see how things got so screwed up. The guy doesn't have a hard job. All he has to do is invoice the customer and make payments to the bank and the employees. I'm sure it's just a misunderstanding. Then I'm going to check in with Bao and see just how bad the situation is. I need to know that, so I can formulate a solution."

"You should have a backup plan," Nathan said. "If you do all that and find out things are bad, you'll want to be prepared."

"I'm sure Bao will be understanding. After all, the bank has a lot riding on this."

"The bank seized your ship. That's the first step toward making themselves whole. They'll just sell it and leave you to go bankrupt." The mood in the room became somber but Nathan continued. "You're a nice guy Eldridge and you helped us out back in Bad Rock but there's not a lot I can do for you. My ship is sitting in your cargo hold wrecked and unable to fly. I've got money problems of my own. I just want you to prepare yourself to hear bad news."

Eldridge took the last swallow from his coffee. "We'll figure something out." He got up and walked over to the sink, dropping his mug in. "If you guys don't need me for anything else, I've got some things below decks to take care of."

They watched the young man walk away, shoulders slumped. Duncan turned back to Nathan. "That was good, what you said to him."

"I might have been too hard on him."

"No, he needed to hear it. He and Ari are smart but they're too trusting. He needed a little dose of reality."

— «» —

A couple hours later, Charlie found himself facing Eldridge down in the lower decks. "Anyway," the boss said, "now we're heading back to Earth to see what Lewis and Molly have been doing." They leaned against a bin full of junk. The two of them were in one of the reclamation bays watching bits and pieces of the *Athena Star* feed into the big units that mashed them into steel or aluminum cubes. This section was for the common metals. The more exotic materials were dealt with in other bays.

"That's quite a story," Charlie said. The recycler toed a piece of aluminum trim that looked like it once adorned a flight of stairs back onto the conveyor belt leading to a compactor. "It's hard to believe we could come out here to do something as simple as salvage a ship and end up involved with these organized crime guys."

Eldridge came off the bin and circled the area. "You were down in Bad Rock those first few days when we arrived. Did you ever have any contact with those guys?"

"Who? The Syndicate guys? No, I don't think so."

"No one came around and offered you anything for some information? The union guys, maybe or Turtle and Daryl?"

Charlie shook his head and said, "No, I wasn't down there long enough to really meet anyone. I just helped you guys set up the camp. Why? Did my name come up or something?"

Eldridge shook his head and kept circling the bay. He picked up a length of conduit and dropped it into the bin they had been leaning against. "No, nothing like that. I was just thinking, if I was Dodger, I would want some eyes up here keeping watch on things. You know, because they had the ground covered. Just makes sense."

Charlie stared him in the eyes for a long moment and then broke his gaze. "Yeah, I get what you're saying but no, I never spoke with anyone from Bad Rock. Like I said, I was busy."

Eldridge nodded but fixed Charlie in his gaze. "Right, that's what you said." The air between them took on weight as they stared at one another. "I just remember you complaining on the trip out here about being stuck on the ship and then when we got to Bad Rock you had an opportunity to stay planetside but you let Fred do it and came back up here."

"Are you accusing me of something?" Charlie felt himself heating up now, getting a little upset with the conversation.

Eldridge shook his head. "No, nothing like that Charlie. I just want to make sure I can trust everyone working for me. We're part of a team out here, all on our own. We have to have each other's back because no one else will. The temptation to take a couple credits for passing along information could be strong. I just want to make sure we're all clear on that."

Charlie swallowed hard and was silent for a moment before answering. "I understand what you're saying but you don't have to worry about me. I just want to do my job."

Eldridge gave him one more glance and then nodded, holding out his hand. Charlie took it and they shook. "Thanks, Charlie. I'm glad I can count on you." He looked around at the bins full of junk waiting for recycling. "Keep on this stuff. We're going to need some cash when we get home so this is all getting sold in bulk when we arrive."

"Will do."

Eldridge walked around a big metal container and exited the recycling bay.

Charlie took out the mobi Eldridge had issued him when they had started out on this job. He called up its history and saw the calls he had made to Turtle. He sighed. Eldridge would fire him if he knew about them and the money he'd accepted from Turtle.

He walked over to the conveyor leading into the compactor, just past the final sensor that checked for non-aluminum metals, and dropped his mobi onto it. He watched as it rode the conveyor into the open maw and mixed in with the other pieces to be compacted into cubes.

Chapter 26

They arrived at a space station complex in Earth orbit a few days later. Eldridge complained about the fuel that had been burned making the trip and Nathan smiled. He had exactly the right attitude he should have as the owner of a business. The young man and Duncan had spent much of the journey talking and it seemed to be having a good effect.

They docked the *Corkscrew* at Hightower One, an orbital station capable of handling large vessels. Eldridge made arrangements to unload the scrap and put some coin in his pocket.

From the command deck, Nathan saw several freighters having their cargo containers removed by enormous 'bots capable of gripping them and using thrusters to move them. The containers would be cross loaded to other freighters to move on to their final destinations or loaded onto shuttles for delivery to Earth bound destinations. It occurred to him that if he couldn't get the *Blue Moon Bandit* repaired he would probably end up with a job flying one of those immense space trucks. The thought gave him a chill up his spine and he resolved to do whatever he had to in order to keep the business running.

"I'd hate being stuck on one of those," Duncan said from over his shoulder. Nathan wondered if his engineer had developed the ability to read minds.

"Did you and Richie have a chance to complete the preliminary report on the *Bandit*?"

"Yeah, that's what I'm here for. I sent it to your contact link but I'll give you the quick and dirty version." They moved to the map table and sat down. "My estimate is about five-hundred and fifty-thousand credits and three months to get her flying again."

Nathan almost dropped the mug of coffee in his hand. "Really? That much?"

Duncan nodded and sighed. "Yeah, that much. Really. There's some structural damage we're going to have to deal with."

"I thought the runway arresting system prevented damage."

"It did. The friable concrete at the end of the runway saved us a ton of credits by bleeding off most of the kinetic energy from the crash landing. The cost is pretty much due to the initial impact in the sky and the damage done by that ridiculous rescue 'bot."

"Well, obviously the aft section will have to be rebuilt."

Duncan nodded. "Yes, but the real problem is that the port side engine is a total loss. It shredded itself as it came apart, taking out support braces and framework. The honeycomb structure that holds her together shredded like paper in dozens of places."

Nathan shook his head and breathed heavily. "That means taking that whole side of the ship apart, all the way down to the airframe."

"Yeah," Duncan said, "and that means breaking down the hull on that side. The good news is that once we do all the work and put it back together you'll have a mostly new ship. Everything that comes off will be scrapped and replaced with new metal and composite."

"I assume we have to do that?"

The engineer smiled. "You do if you want me, my wife or my friends to fly on her. There's no other way. I could never scan every piece and find all the micro stress fractures that may be hiding in there. Better to just lay in new parts and know it's done correctly."

Nathan stared out the window at the freighters again and contemplated a future where he scrapped his ship and just took a job. It was too terrible to think about. "Okay. I assume the work will be done at Saji Vy's ship yards down in Go City?"

"That's the plan. I factored the cost of a tow to the surface into my estimate. Why? Do you think he might cut us some slack on labor?"

"Couldn't hurt to ask." Nathan took out his mobi and reviewed the list of repairs and needed material that Duncan had sent him. "I assume you'll oversee the repairs?"

"I wouldn't have it any other way." Duncan paused for a moment and a strange look crossed his face. "Look, Nathan, I don't want to seem indelicate here but can you afford this? From what you said back on Bad Rock you're having financial troubles."

Nathan took a deep breath and thought about it before he answered. "I think so. I paid the insurance, so there's that. I just have to cover the deductible."

"Can you?"

Nathan smiled. "Yeah, no problem. I've got a little set aside and it should be enough. The deductible is ten percent of the estimate."

Duncan's eyes narrowed. "You have fifty-five thousand credits in an account somewhere?"

"I've got some credits and… some other assets I can turn into credits fairly quickly. You just concentrate on the repairs and let me worry about the cost, okay? Between the two of us we'll get her flying again."

Duncan regarded him for a moment with an unsure look on his face. "You know, Marla and I could always help you out."

Nathan shook his head. No way would he accept charity. Milky Way Repossessions belonged to him, totally and one-hundred percent. He didn't want to start selling shares and that was the only way he would accept credits from Duncan and Marla.

"Don't worry," he said by way of an answer. "I've got it under control."

—— «◊» ——

Eldridge opened the door to Crater Salvage's office in Go City. Molly should have greeted him with a smile and been surprised to see him. Lewis should have been at his desk taking care of the company's finances. Instead, both desks sat empty in the dark.

"Sonuvabitch."

"They should be here?" Duncan said from behind him.

"Yeah, they should be sitting right here," he said, pointing at the desks. He walked around Lewis's desk and sat down. The computer responded and logged him in when it recognized him. "Let's see what they've been up to."

It only took a half hour for Eldridge to pin down what had happened. Duncan moved around behind him, reviewing the display over his shoulder. The younger man pointed at the financial records. "They took everything. See this column?"

Duncan nodded.

"We were invoicing Great Star Lines right up until this month and they were paying on time, so we had plenty of credits coming in. Where did the money go?"

Duncan pointed at another set of records on the display. "Who are 'Lucky Cleaners'?" They got one hell of a big pay day last week."

Eldridge rubbed a hand across his head. "That's the janitorial service for the office."

Duncan raised an eyebrow. "Someone paid them several hundred thousand credits."

Eldridge slammed the desk with a closed fist and everything on it shook. "Lewis hired them."

"Hold on," Duncan said. He looked something up on his mobi. After a few minutes, he said, "I found them. It looks like the business license for Lucky Cleaners is in the name of Lewis Mairn."

"Damn it," Eldridge said as he pounded the desk again.

"You didn't know he owned the cleaners?"

"Of course not. He's the office manager so hiring the cleaners is the kind of stuff he did. I was busy retrofitting a starship and programming 'bots." He sat back, a dejected look on his face. "I can't do it all and Ari is just as busy as I am."

"Did he have a limit on what he could spend?"

"No, we're off planet and communications can be difficult so I didn't want to hamstring him." He rubbed his head. "I feel so stupid."

"Hey, don't beat yourself up. This is how you're going to learn, though."

Eldridge stood up and circled around the small office to the front door. "You know, you keep saying things like that and I have to tell you, these lessons are going to kill me. I've got someone I trusted here ripping me off and out at Bad Rock I had some hood shaking me down for protection money. This isn't worth it. Maybe Ari and I should just go back to work for her dad in his junk yard."

Duncan took a deep breath, trying to provide a calm influence to the young man. "Look, you're right. You've had some rough days, that's for sure, but you still have some things going for you."

Eldridge snorted. "Like what? I have a meeting with the bank later this afternoon and Bao is going to take my ship. With that gone I can't complete the *Athena Star* job. Where can I find the money to make the loan payments between now and then? I'm tapped out."

"That's all true but you still have the contract, right?"

"Sure, for all the good that does me."

Duncan smiled and sat down in a chair opposite of Eldridge. "Then that's the one card you have left to play. On the ride back from Bad Rock, Marla and I took the time to look at your operation and your people. We have a proposition we'd like to make you."

"What do you mean?"

"Well, you and Ari have done a good job getting Crater Salvage up and running and you have some pretty good ideas about how to solve tough problems". He leaned forward, a little more animated than he had been a moment ago. "You've automated the salvage process with 'bots and you're mobile with the *Corkscrew*. There are a lot of ships, equipment and facilities that need to be broken down all across occupied space. Humans have been going out to space for centuries now and we're a messy bunch. You can be the recycler that cleans a lot of that up."

Eldridge nodded slowly. "That's kind of what Ari and I have been thinking about. Expand the business by using the 'bots so we can work in almost any environment. So, what's your proposition?"

"You need to get current on the loan with Bao so he'll leave you alone and you don't have the credits. Even if Protective Services catches Lewis and Molly, you may never recover the credits they stole. When you get back to Bad Rock you'll still have to deal with the unions now that Dodger isn't paying off their leaders. Marla and I can help with all that. We'd like to buy in for a third of your business."

The young man's jaw fell open. "Really?"

Duncan nodded. "Yes, really. Like I said, we liked what we saw and we like you and Ari. We've been searching for a new investment and a new challenge. We can get you current on the loan with the bank and provide the payroll you'll need to hire a small workforce out on Bad Rock, at least until the credits start flowing again. It will cost a third of the business, though."

Eldridge let out a deeply held breath. "This is huge." The young man grew quiet for a moment. "The thing is, we kind of wanted this to be our thing. I'm not sure about bringing in more partners."

"That's entirely up to you," Duncan said and leaned back in his chair. "You need a mentor, though; somebody with experience who can see when someone is trying to take advantage of you. For example, you need a new business manager before you leave Earth. You are busy. How could you possibly invoice customers, pay loans and manage payroll while you're putting out fires in the field? Marla and I could take care of that for you."

"What about Milky Way Repo? Aren't you usually out with Nathan?"

"It will be a few months until the ship is repaired so I'll be grounded here. Marla and I can do both until you're done with the *Athena Star* and the *Blue Moon Bandit* is back in the air. After that we'll figure something out."

Eldridge nodded and his mobi dinged. "I have to leave for a meeting with Bao right now. Could you come with me and explain this to him?"

"Do we have a deal?"

"We do. It will be a tough sell to Ari but I'll square it with her." He stood up and stuck out his hand. "Welcome to Crater Salvage."

Duncan shook on it. "Glad to be aboard. Now let's call Protective Services and report Lewis and Molly."

— «» —

Nathan sat on his couch and reviewed his financial accounts with a feeling akin to horror. The invoice had been sent to Bao for payment on the *Corkscrew* job but he still looked to be way short of having the credits required to start repairing the *Bandit*.

He kicked back on the couch and put a foot up on the coffee table, grimacing at the bullet wound in his arm. The shortage of credits was substantial, at least forty-thousand, once he factored in living expenses for the three months they would be down. The only thing worse than the hovel he currently lived in would be sleeping in a doorway on the street.

Growing up, his mom had worked so hard and life had been so difficult. Getting into the military and learning how to fly was supposed to be his ticket to a good life. He couldn't imagine a scenario where he failed worse than this.

He got up and walked to his bedroom. In the bottom of the closet, right where he left it, sat the black duffel bag full of Diamond K from Bone Daddy's ship.

Carrying it back to the living room, he sat down and unzipped it. All the little plastic packets still lay inside. One-hundred twenty-thousand credits by Cole's estimation of the street price. That meant at least sixty-thousand if he got rid of it wholesale. Now that he thought about it, the value would probably be more without the supply from Bad Rock.

Did he want to be the kind of guy who sold drugs?

He could apply for a loan but a busted ship was the only asset he had to provide as collateral. It seemed improbable that anyone would give him a loan on a grounded starship.

With a heavy heart he decided to do the adult thing. He kicked the duffel bag under the coffee table and picked up his mobi. Swallowing his pride he tapped the contact info for Duncan.

Twenty minutes later he finished up the call angrier than he could ever remember. He held his voice steady, though, determined not to say anything that would end a long standing friendship.

"Duncan, I get it. Please don't worry about it."

"It's just that we've already met with Bao and assured him the funds will be coming through. My attorney is drawing up the partnership," Duncan said. "Nathan, I wish you would have just told me you needed the credits when we spoke earlier. Marla and I would have bought in, no question."

He bit his lower lip. "No, you're right. I should have been honest with you. I just thought I had one more rabbit in the hat, you know?" He saw pity on Duncan's face and anger welled up in him. "Hey, you know what? Don't sweat it."

"I wish we could do something but all our credits are tied up with Eldridge's operation now."

Nathan nodded vigorously, just wanting this conversation to end. "Hey, I'll talk to you tomorrow, okay? I have to go now."

"Yeah, sure. I'll see you."

"Okay." The screen went dark and Nathan sat back on the couch. The light faded outside and night began to fall. He zipped up the bag and shoved it back in the closet.

— «» —

Back when he had been considering the idea of selling his bag of dope Nathan figured that he knew at least three people who would help him. His first call had been to a guy named Scott that he had known in passing growing up back in the north. Scott had also found his way to Go City but rather than being a pilot he worked in one of Saji Vy's factories building engine components. He dealt on the side to supplement his income. Unfortunately the woman who answered his mobi had informed Nathan that Scott was doing a few years in prison for getting caught dealing at work.

Call two had been even worse. A woman named Charlene was first mate on an orbital tug. She sold to crew members on her tug and others in port to help them escape boredom, or at least she had until her tug collided with a freighter six months ago. Her mother had answered her mobi and bent Nathan's ear for almost an hour telling him the tragic story.

His last call went to a mechanic named Victor he knew from a firm that did starship repair work on the outskirts of Go City. They had crossed paths a few times when Nathan had repossessed ships out of the shipyard employing him. Victor had no problem accepting a few credits for information about which ships were sitting in the yard or letting Nathan and his crew in the yard to grab the occasional repo job. Once, he had offered to sell them something and though Nathan had refused, he filed that little nugget away for later use. Luckily Victor was both alive and not incarcerated so he agreed to meet with Nathan.

— «» —

Steel Eye Jack's was a dive bar within walking distance of his apartment so that's where they agreed to meet up. Nathan sat ensconced in a wraparound booth, nursing bourbon on the rocks and scoping out the crowd. Victor finally showed up after an hour.

He was a skeevy dude with long, thin hair and neck tattoos. Nathan didn't like to judge people based on their appearance but Victor seemed to go out of his way to ward people off with his appearance. Once you spoke to him though, he seemed nice enough. Nathan couldn't even fault him for taking the occasional bribe since it made his job easier. He spotted Nathan's raised hand and made his way over.

"Nice place," Victor said. "I hope this doesn't take too long. I don't want my car stolen."

"Yeah, this neighborhood sucks."

Victor fidgeted with his hands. "So, what's up? You need access to the yard again? If so, you should know the owner's got things locked up kind of tight with some new security measures. I mean, it's nothing I can't handle but getting in will cost you extra."

Nathan waved him off with one hand. "No, it's nothing like that. I need help with something else. Something not strictly legal."

"Yeah? Like what?"

"The last time we were out at your place, grabbing that private yacht, you offered to sell us something." Nathan put his hand on the table and slid an envelope of Diamond K toward Victor.

He glanced at it and quickly palmed it. "I remember. You turned me down."

"Right. Well, in my travels I've come across quite a bit of this and I need to unload it. Can you help?"

"How much?"

Nathan told him. Victor let out a low whistle.

"That's a lot. I mean, that is a whole lot. Where did you get it?"

"I got it. That's really all you need to know."

"It's real?"

"I gave you that sample so you could test it. I just need to move it quickly."

Victor sat back and rubbed his chin, considering the offer. "How much do you want?"

"Sixty thousand."

"Look, I don't have that much. You have to understand, I just deal a couple bags on the side to make ends meet. I'm not someone who can just lay out those kinds of credits."

Nathan nodded slowly. "I get that but I figure you probably know some people who can. I don't, so that's why I called you. I'm comfortable dealing with you."

Victor took a deep breath. "I do know some people but you have to realize the way this works. Everybody has to trust someone and everyone gets a cut. I can probably get you fifty thousand. Would that work?"

And just like that you earn ten thousand for yourself, Nathan thought. He considered it for a moment and realized he had no room to barter. "I guess that would work. I need the credits and I need them fast."

Victor chewed his lower lip for a moment and then leaned forward. "Meet me here in two days. Does that work for you?"

Nathan nodded. "It does. I'll see you in two days."

— «» —

He spent the next two days in his apartment, worried that Victor might talk to the wrong people and someone would try and steal the stash from his closet. He was stuck eating take-out and watching whatever he could find on the entertainment system. If this was an example of the glamorous life drug dealers lived the holovids had it all wrong.

Tricia had called to check on his arm and he had talked her out of visiting him by making up excuses about getting the *Bandit* put back together. He was afraid she would reconsider dating him if she saw the apartment but he was also concerned that he would spill the details about the deal with Victor. She was way too easy to talk to and he wasn't sure he could keep this from her if they were in the same room.

The appointed hour rolled around and he made his way back to Steel Eye Jack's. He thought about going armed but in the end he went without a gun. Carrying a bag of illicit drugs made him jittery enough. Getting caught holding a gun with them would just make things worse. Besides, if Victor or the people he represented wanted to rob him, he would be outgunned and outnumbered. He drew the line at shooting anyone over a deal gone bad.

He arrived early but when he walked into the dimly lit bar, Victor already sat in the red plastic booth. Nathan got a drink from the bar and walked over. He carried the duffel in his left hand to keep the weight off his bad arm. Tricia said it would be good as new in another week but he wanted to give it as much rest as possible. He dropped the bag and kicked it under the table as he slid into the opposite side of the booth.

"How's it going?" Victor said.

"All good on my end," Nathan said. "How about you?"

Victor nodded, his rangy hair falling in front of his eyes. "The sample you gave me tested positive so we're all good on that."

"Right. I figured as much."

Victor took a drink and eyed Nathan in a way he didn't like. "The folks backing me are a little concerned about where this came from."

"That's not important. Are we doing this or not?" Worry washed over Nathan. Not only was he alone but if a Protective Services officer walked in here and caught him with this much Diamond K., he could expect a decade of reform time in an orbital facility. It would be the kind of place where other, more powerful psychological drugs and therapy would be used to correct his mindset. A small chill ran through him.

Victor nodded. "Yeah we're doing it. We just want to be sure nothing funny is up. Diamond K is difficult to get right now. Apparently somebody hit a lab or something so when a guy who doesn't normally deal in it pops up with this much, well, questions get asked."

Nathan took a deep breath and felt his insides run cold as ice water at Victor mentioning the lab on Bad Rock. "I don't know anything about that. This stuff came from a ship I repossessed, okay? Now either give me my credits or I'm leaving. I don't have time for games."

"Did you know the bags are micro-encoded?"

"What?" The ice water in his veins froze into a solid ball in the pit of his stomach.

"The bags. They're encoded with data on where the product came from and when it was manufactured. See, I didn't know that either but when I showed your sample to my supplier it really got the attention of some people."

"The credits," Nathan said, "right now, or I walk."

Victor smiled. "I've always liked you Nathan. You've always been straight with me so imagine my surprise when a bunch of Syndicate guys showed up at my door and started asking me questions about where I got that bag?"

"Damn it."

"Yeah, I'm sorry, man. I didn't have any choice in the matter. I had to give you up."

Nathan's eyes roamed the bar. "Where are they?"

"They'll be here in two hours."

Nathan's attention snapped back to Victor. "What?"

"I told them the meet is two hours from now. Like I said, you were always straight with me and I've always appreciated the credits you've thrown my way. Besides, now you've got the big guy after you."

Nathan's eyes narrowed. "Who's that?"

Victor's face faltered a little. Fear crept into the edges. "Atomic Jack is looking for you. That Diamond K you're peddling came from a shipment impounded by Customs. A couple of his boys got shot up trying to retrieve it while he was out of town so naturally, when the bag you gave me was identified, the whole world fell down on me. I'm sorry but I'm not letting that psycho near me."

"I understand." Nathan's head whirled as his gaze fell to the drink in front of him. The last time he'd met up with

Jack the Syndicate had lost twenty-three million credits. That hadn't been his fault but he had been involved in a roundabout way. The lab in Bad Rock, though, that was all him and God alone knew how many credits that had cost them. Dodger and his guys on Bad Rock had surely given his name up by now.

He looked up from his drink to Victor. "Look, thanks for this but I have to go. I've seen Jack in action and I have no intention of letting him get his hands on me."

"Well, before you go, there is one more thing."

"What?"

"The Diamond K. I want it. I figure a two-hour head start is worth what's in that bag."

Nathan's jaw fell open. "Are you serious?"

"As a heart attack," Victor said and his hand came up with a pistol in it. He flashed it at Nathan and moved it under the table. "Just kick the bag over here and walk away. That's all you have to do."

"Yeah, that and run with no credits."

Victor shrugged with the confidence of someone who has finally landed a big score. "Sorry, man. At least you can run. I'm going to have to answer some questions about why you don't show up at the meeting."

Nathan considered his options and decided that he didn't even want the damned drugs anymore. They'd brought him nothing but trouble. Victor ripping him off actually relieved him of a burden. With as much contempt as he could muster he kicked the duffel bag across the floor. Then he stood up. "This isn't going to end well for either of us."

Victor nodded. "Probably worse for you than me. You better haul ass, man. The clock is ticking."

"Yeah. Good luck, Victor."

"You too."

Nathan walked out of the bar, convinced a car was going to pull up any second and grab him off the street. He wondered if Victor had run a scam on him, but the story had been good. The details about the lab being blown up were something no one would really know. He stopped, glancing back to the bar and then down the street but nothing appeared out of the ordinary.

Forty-five minutes later everything he could carry was strapped to the back of his float bike and he stood on the cracked sidewalk outside his apartment building. He wouldn't be coming back. If he wanted to keep breathing he had to stay ahead of Atomic Jack and the Syndicate.

That old fighter pilot's mantra ran through his head, *speed is life*. After one last look around he mounted the float bike, gunned the engine and sped into the night.

If you enjoyed this read

*Please leave a review on Amazon, Facebook, Good
Reads or Instagram.*

*It takes less than five minutes and it really does make
a difference.*

If you're not sure how to leave a review on Amazon:

1. *Go to amazon.com.*

2. *Type in Bad Rock Beat Down by Michael
Prelee and when you see it, click on it.*

3. *Scroll down to Customer Reviews. Nearby
you'll see a box labeled Write a Review.
Click it.*

4. *Now, if you've never written a review before
on Amazon, they might ask you to create a
name for yourself.*

5. *Reviews can be as simple as, "Loved the book!
Can't wait for the Next!" (Please don't give
the story away.)*

And that's it!

Brian Hades, publisher

About the Author

Michael Prelee is a graduate of Youngstown State University. He resides in Northeast Ohio with his family where he enjoys writing. His first novel, the sci-fi crime story "Milky Way Repo", was published in 2015 by EDGE Science Fiction and Fantasy. His novel, "Murder in the Heart of it All", a mystery set in Ohio, was published in 2017. You can keep up with him at:

www.michaelprelee.com.

Here's a look at Book one in The Milky Way Repo Series

Milky Way Repo

by Mike Prelee

Running a starship repo company isn't easy or cheap. It's just an endless string of fuel costs, ship maintenance, legal red tape, unhappy debt bailers, shady associates and uncooperative dock officials from one end of the galaxy to the other.

Nathan Teller owns and operates Milky Way Repossessions, a company that tracks down and repossesses starships. And although he's only managing to break even on his debt, he wouldn't trade it for anything. (His ex-wife holds that against him. No surprise there.)

When Nathan and his crew successfully steal a freighter from the clutches of a particularly tenacious and corrupt dock official, he earns the respect of their high profile employer. Opportunity seems a sure thing.

Nathan should be happy. But when that lucrative job op turns into a ransom delivery for a starship crew being held hostage by a cult, he suddenly finds himself pursued by a self-immolating loan shark hell bent on collecting a gambling debt.

How will it all turn out? You never know. Especially when Nathan and his Starship repo agents are up against a cult and the mob…

Praise for Milky Way Repo

The debut novel of Mike Prelee is a very entertaining Sci-Fi/Noir, with vivid, likable characters and a fast pace. He's got a great handle on plot and a knack for drawing you into the story. For fans of fast-paced space adventure with a smattering of crime drama mixed in, this should do the trick. I finished it in two sittings. High praise for sure. I would definitely read a sequel (or two).
— marc a. gayan

Milky Way Repo is a nice, light but exciting read. With just enough action and even a bit of romance and comedy, I definitely recommend this read to anyone who enjoys a good sci-fi/blue collar space opera.

I gave Milky Way Repo 5 stars because it provided me with a short, albeit adventurous, fun and light hearted escape for a few hours. It is well written, with well rounded characters and a wonderful storyline.

I have to say that Duncan was my absolute favorite character. Officially starting a Duncan fan club!
— Chaelsie Jenyk

For more on Milky Way Repo visit:
tinyurl.com/edge7003

———<>———

Need something new to read?

If you liked Bad Rock Beat Down, you should also
consider these other EDGE-Lite titles:

The Genius Asylum

by Arlene F. Marks

The truth is out there...

Earth Intelligence and Space Installation Security each
think Drew Townsend is working for them. They're wrong.

Sent undercover to set up a covert intelligence operation
on Earth's remotest space station, Drew Townsend finds
himself managing a crew of brilliant mavericks, making
friends with the most feared warriors in the galaxy, and
feeling more at home in the controlled insanity of Daisy Hub
than he ever did on Earth. Then he learns the truth about
his mission there, and it's time to choose. In the coming
interplanetary conflict, which side will Daisy Hub be on?'

Like the clues of a cryptic crossword, each book set in
the Sic Transit Terra universe contains a puzzle – perhaps a
riddle, perhaps a maze or an anagram – and in each case, the
answer to the smaller puzzle brings the reader and characters
one step closer to solving a much larger and more important
one. The Genius Asylum is '1 Across' – it initiates a multi-
book story arc that addresses one of the great mysteries of
life: Why are we humans the way that we are?

Praise for The Genius Asylum

"The Genius Asylum starts out on Earth as something that looks like a crime story, but it then quickly describes a world of interstellar travel and alien alliances. After the first act concludes, the story's complexity starts accelerating and doesn't slow down, and you'll find yourself drawn into the world, needing to know what comes next. It is an excellently written story that provides the framework for the series that is to come, and I'm looking forward to reading the rest of it."
— Chris Marks, reviewer

I thoroughly enjoyed this Sci-Fi Brainteaser. Very well written with incredible plot twists and turns. We've got a very intelligent double agent as the main character and an intriguing support cast. I was thankful for the planetary history at the beginning as it was helpful in understanding the different organizations mentioned throughout the novel. The Author has a witty way of expressing viewpoints, clearly has put a lot of thought into the storyline and created edge of your seat suspense and mystery! Admittedly, I was confused about the title of the book until about halfway through reading it but it makes perfect sense now. I highly recommend this absolutely unforgettable installment and can't wait for the next.
— Stephanie Herman

For more on The Genius Asylum visit:
tinyurl.com/edge6013

—— <> ——

Beltrunner

by Sean O'Brien

As an independent beltrunner mining asteroids in the frontier of space, Collier South is a dying breed. Scrounging and cutting corners to work cheap, Collier isn't a stranger to lean times and make-do repairs; in fact his onboard computer hasn't had outside maintenance in years and its beginning to show its personal quirks.

When Collier finds an asteroid that shows promise, he thinks he's bought himself some time. But his claim is stolen out from under him by his vindictive ex-lover and her shiny new corporate ship. Powerless against the omnipotent mining corporations, Collier has always been too stubborn to give-up without a fight. Broke and desperate, Collier has one last chance to land a strike. If he doesn't come back with ore, he'll end up destitute and trading his own biologicals for his next meal.

What he discovers in the farthest reaches of the belt has the power to change his life and the fate of the entire system forever. That is, if Collier and his onboard computer can keep his discovery out of corporate hands.

Praise for Beltrunner

This is a fast moving book that leaves you breathless with hair-raising action and unexpected twists. The world creation is well-developed and highly creative. The interactions between Collier and Sancho are particularly entertaining -

with Collier coming up with implusive dangerous plans and Sancho trying to talk him out of them. Highly recommended for action space lovers.
— Patricia Humphreys

Scavenging known space makes for a hard life, and surviving outside of the Corporations in the Belt makes it all the harder. It is not surprising that Collier and his unusual companion Sancho hit bottom, like many before them, until they make the discovery of their lives…or deaths, as it may turn out to be.

Beltrunner is a solidly enjoyable science fiction adventure, fast paced, and filled with the kind of characters that make you smile, break your heart, or just make you clench your jaw. I read it in one sitting and thoroughly enjoyed it. O'Brien builds a universe to get lost in that is as hard, gritty, and unforgiving as deep space itself. It is a well-written romp around space like many others, yet plenty of surprising elements give the story a depth and purpose all its own without the heavy strain of space melodrama. Read it because it is both light fun and thoughtful reading.
— A. Volmer

For more on Beltrunner visit:
tinyurl.com/edge6010

—— <> ——

Europa Journal

by Jack Castle

The history of humanity is about to change forever...

On 5 December 1945, five TBM Avenger bombers embarked on a training mission off the coast of Florida and mysteriously vanish without a trace in the Bermuda Triangle. A PBY search and rescue plane with thirteen crewmen aboard sets out to find the Avengers . . . and never returns.

In 2168, a mysterious five-sided pyramid is discovered on the ocean floor of Jupiter's icy moon, Europa.

Commander Mac O'Bryant and her team of astronauts are among the first to enter the pyramid's central chamber. They find the body of a missing World War II pilot, whose hands clutch a journal detailing what happened to him after he and his crew were abducted by aliens and taken to a place with no recognizable stars. As the pyramid walls begin to collapse around Mac and her team, their names mysteriously appear within its pages and they find themselves lost on an alien world.

Stranded with no way home, Mac decides to retrace the pilot's steps. She never expects to find the man alive. And if the man has yet to die, what does that mean for her and the rest of her crew?

Praise for Europa Journal

This book kept me guessing! It has an exciting start and keeps that same pace throughout the book. The building of

the character personalities keeps a depth to the storyline and makes the reader feel connected to each character. The background information given through Europa Journal gives a great balance between the history, future and everything in-between! I love the mix of fact and fiction to create the story and inspire imagination. I'm excited to see what Castle comes up with next!
— Dianna Temple

With an action-packed opening, page-turning twists,a well-built world, and characters worth caring about, Europa Journal is like a bulldog - it grabbed me and wouldn't let go! It seamlessly blends breathtaking imagination with the gritty reality of survival, and beautifully blurs what has been with what might be. I love Dr. Who and grew up with Star Trek, but this book has broken the sci-fi mold in a wonderful way!
— Stuntwoman, Elisa Brinton

From the opening space shuttle crash landing to the stunning finish, Europa Journal is a real page turner. Ancient astronauts, the Bermuda triangle, WW II pilots, space shuttle crews – what else could you ask for? Mr. Castle keeps the story at light speed, with plenty of twists and turns before the awesome climax!
— James Wahlman, Firefighter in Alaska

For more on Europa Journal visit:
tinyurl.com/edge6001

———<>———

For more EDGE titles and information about upcoming speculative fiction please visit us at:

www.edgewebsite.com

Don't forget to sign-up for our Special Offers